What people are sayir

American Fork

Spanning the mountain landscapes of the Great Basin and the coastal valleys of Chile, George Handley's first novel, *American Fork*, explores deep personal questions: how can solace be found in the aftermath of personal betrayal or catastrophic loss? Are family ties merely an artifact of shared ancestry, or can we claim — and if needs be, renounce — kinship on the basis of personal affinity or revulsion? Does a spiritual connection to the earth replace or augment religious conviction? Replete with detail, Handley's description of the ongoing debate between a believing young woman and a grizzled religious skeptic builds to a stunning but deeply moving conclusion. Following on the success of his environmental memoir *Home Waters*, Handley has here produced the most important ecological novel set in Utah since Edward Abbey's *The Monkey Wrench Gang*.

Paul Alan Cox, Goldman Environmental Prize Winner and TIME Hero of Medicine

This is a riveting story, beautifully written and skillfully told. It engages the reader in a fresh exploration of enduring themes of family and culture, nature and religion. It will change your perspective as it did mine.

Mary Evelyn Tucker, Yale Forum on Religion and Ecology

We know that novels are fictional, so we see them as unreal, and yet the very best twine inextricably with our lives to become part of our reality. George Handley's masterful *American Fork* unifies sadness and beauty, individuals and communities, humans and nature in profound and unforgettable ways. Alba and Mr. Harker's intersecting quests reveal (or remind) that everything is connected, everything significant, not only in the world of the

book, but in our world, which is the same.
Pat Madden, author of *Sublime Physick*

In this God-haunted story of a Job who has long since cursed God and the young Mormon artist who learns to reconstitute him, George Handley calls us forcefully to ponder where we as human beings begin and end. Where, in the glorious tangles of biology, ecology, genealogy, theology, mortal misery, and divine mystery can we be found, and who will, at last, do the finding? In this passionate environmental novel, Handley proposes a troubling, insightful, and deeply Mormon solution to the centuries-old question of theodicy: how could God possibly be good when our lives are, too often, broken by grief?
Samuel Morris Brown, author of *Through the Valley of Shadows: Living Wills, Intensive Care*, and *Making Medicine Human*

A leading voice in Mormon environmentalism—not an oxymoron—George Handley also speaks to the global ethics of stewardship. From his Utah home, he sees the world. Handley envisions a consilience of science, religion, and democracy—a gift of imagination in our current climate of danger.
Jared Farmer, author of *On Zion's Mount: Mormons, Indians, and the American Landscape*

George Handley's novel, *American Fork*, is a significant contribution to American letters. Handley is a familiar voice in Utah's environmental movement. His creative nonfiction work, Home Waters, which explores the history and meaning of the Provo River drainage, has already become a classic in Western ecological literature. This new novel will place Handley among that small group of Western writers who have beautifully mastered both fiction and creative non-fiction in ways that make his work in both unforgettable. Like his previous books, Handley immerses you in a sense of place, and draws a rich portrait of the land and its people. *American Fork* expands on that vision in this splendid novel, which ranges from Utah's Wasatch Front to the heart of Chile. From the opening scenes, we are pulled into the nuanced and captivating lives of the novel's memorable characters, Zach Harker and Alba. And as we come to understand their complexity, fragility, and weaknesses we see a mirror of the same in the landscapes they inhabit. Handley has a created a modern classic. This will be read for a long time, but there is no sense in delaying the pleasure and depth this book will bring. Read it now.

Steve Peck, author of *The Scholar of Moab* and *Gilda Trillum: Shepherdess of Rats*

American Fork

American Fork

George B. Handley

Winchester, UK
Washington, USA

First published by Roundfire Books, 2018
Roundfire Books is an imprint of John Hunt Publishing Ltd., Laurel House, Station Approach,
Alresford, Hants, SO24 9JH, UK
office1@jhpbooks.net
www.johnhuntpublishing.com
www.roundfire-books.com

For distributor details and how to order please visit the 'Ordering' section on our website.

Text copyright: George B. Handley 2017

ISBN: 978 1 78099 270 9
978 1 78099 540 3 (ebook)
Library of Congress Control Number: 2017937813

A CIP catalogue record for this book is available from the British Library.

Design: Stuart Davies

Printed and bound by CPI Group (UK) Ltd, Croydon, CR0 4YY, UK

We operate a distinctive and ethical publishing philosophy in
all areas of our business, from our global network of authors to
production and worldwide distribution.

For my parents, Ken and Kate

Other books by George B. Handley

Postslavery Literatures in the Americas: Family Portraits in Black and White (2000)

New World Poetics: Nature and the Adamic Imagination of Whitman, Neruda, and Walcott (2007)

Home Waters: A Year of Recompenses on the Provo River (2010)

Acknowledgments

I have benefited from the editorial eyes of many who read and provided feedback and encouragement at various stages of the writing, including Steve Peck, Dian Monson, Adam Miller, Paul Cox, Greta Hyland, Sally Smith, Jenny Webb, Marcus Smith, Oriana Reyes, Sam Brown, Kirsten Allen, Andrew Maxfield, Lizabeth Paravisini-Gebert, Jenny and Mike Pulsipher, Morgan Davis, and Amy and Eliza Handley.

I am grateful for the generous Eliza R. Snow Fellowship at Brigham Young University that gave me much needed funding to travel to Chile. My conversations with many there inspired and taught me more than I can account for but at the risk of neglecting some, very special thanks to Bernardo Reyes, Marycruz Jara Urrutia, Tito Urzúa, Maracena Aguiló, Julio Carrasco, Rodrigo Rojas, Leonardo Sanhueza, Jaime Quezada, and Antonio Skarmeta.

Chapter 1

The image returned. She remembered her father's hand reach down for hers. She could still see the raindrops that beaded on the back of his hand. How old could she have been? Three? Four? She could see the white foam of the violent ocean and hear its roar below the ridge they were on. Had she ever seen the ocean before? Likely not. Maybe it was the distance of time or maybe it was the pervasive light rain of that day, but it seemed in her mind's eye that the entire scene was suffused with a smoky blue-gray air as if the deep greens of the land were fading to black and white. The place felt lonely and haunted.

These many years later it was those shining drops that made her father's presence seem real somehow, tying his ephemeral ghost down to the earth. They grounded the memory, a fluid but physical anchor holding down the ethereal and elusive realm of the spirit.

It was also her earliest memory of the Spanish language. She remembered her father speaking of the *mar bravo*. At that young age, she already knew the dangers of *perros bravos*, so his words made her think of the sea as a pack of dogs, deeply baying and nipping at the heels of the land. Living landlocked and far away now, sequestered from that language, she had come to think of the sea as a place of oblivion and dispersion.

Her father's gift and her burden was that he wanted her to remember something she had never seen or could scarcely imagine and could now not fully recover. All she had were moments, not stories. Images, pieces of a broken body. How to assemble them and to make them cohere in her present life was the question that shadowed her. She would need more paint. She would need words too. And time. Lots of time.

The sound of a passing car, which was infrequent at this gray hour of early morning, snapped Alba out of her meditations.

Her focus returned to the task of running up Grandview Hill. Shorter and more frequent steps, she had learned, were the key. She observed her heart and legs and decided that she felt strong. Who else had risen at this hour? Not too many, she thought proudly to herself. At the top, she stopped and turned around to face the direction of the rising sun, which was still hiding behind the Wasatch Mountains. The dome of light above her head brightened with a diffused blush that made even her skin glow. Her heart thumped against her chest. She heard her breath. Her mind grew still, and for a moment she had the impression that she might be nothing more than light and air, that all things were one. The only forms that gave the light distinction were the uneven and low canopy of clouds that reflected brightening and broadening brushstrokes of salmon—or was it peach?—against deepening blues. Shocks of cadmium yellow shone within the core of the clouds. She tried to memorize the color patches for when she got back to her paints.

As the light increased in intensity, outlines and images sharpened. To the west, she could see the reflections of the dawn on the surface of the ancient lake lying utterly still. The ring of mountains behind the lake began to reveal itself. She imagined the morning light weaving through the windows of all the quiet houses, lighting opaque walls in remote, intimate rooms, stirring individuals. As the minutes passed, it seemed as if she had suspended her breath altogether. The light intensified, increasingly incandescent behind the eastern mountains in one last burst before all things lay as objects, separate and ordinary in the vague light of morning.

Witness beauty. Bear witness to it. That was all she understood. It fed some ancient hunger in her. Or maybe it only increased her hunger. There was the rub. The more she painted, the more she scaled her exile. Besides, her medium of light was a fickle friend. It brought the world into distinction, it brought attention to things and to moments, but it never stood still and it always abated and returned the world to the black night.

A glance at her watch and her meditations came up short again. She would subtract the time she had spent staring. Five or ten minutes maybe. She wasn't sure. Next time she would remember to stop her timer. She began the run back down into town to her husband and their apartment before the responsibilities of the day would own her. Sketches that were due tomorrow. Reading for her art theory class. Dropping John off at his summer internship later that afternoon. The phone calls to the sisters for visiting teaching reports. And her search for summer work. John would want her home in any case.

He wasn't so much worried about male predators, least of all at this hour, but he was wary of the constant threat of cars to joggers especially in the indistinct light of early morning. It flattered her that he worried for her safety. In the short time they had been married, he had proven steady and solicitous of her needs, even ones she didn't anticipate or recognize, giving her the luxury of security she hadn't realized she needed. But as she ran, she wondered if the luxury would blunt her desire for the freedom of movement and thought, if that is what happened to people content with stasis. Maybe the eyes tire of looking at something so protean as the earth, she thought, and people end up seeing its surface as a blur, like a sea of glass. Until the violence of collision awakens the soul to the facticity of things.

Alba was alert to the growing traffic as she descended into the streets of the city and approached the last turn to their rental, a small house painted light green. The branches of the Catalpa hung their fanning leaves and seedpods over the driveway and darkened the front walkway almost to pitch. She jumped up the steps to the screen door, the creak of which announced her arrival to her husband. He had drifted off on the couch with a novel opened on his chest—the one he was supposed to be caught up on for his senior seminar—but the sound startled him awake and he sat upright. The reading lamp was turned on, but by now the morning light was bright enough in the front room.

"Hey. How's the run?" John asked, rubbing his eyes. Alba stood above him in her black running tights and her bright fuchsia shirt. Her long black hair was held in a ponytail. Her dark eyes looked at him endearingly. John had told her often enough how much he loved her eyes, the dark eyebrows, and the brilliant light of her smile. He wore his favorite gray sweats and a BYU T-shirt. She liked the way his blond hair always looked disheveled and his eyes uncertain, like he was in a permanent state of just getting out of bed.

"Good. What a sunrise."

"Yeah?"

"Yeah. How's the reading coming?" she said with a teasing smile. She leaned over and brushed the loose strands of her black hair out of her face and kissed him slowly.

The salty smell of her sweat perked him up. Pulling away for a second and sitting himself up, he said, "Oh, I did all right. It's just . . . so many whales. More than I needed to know!"

"Whales?" She rubbed his hair.

"Yeah, pages and pages about whales."

"Hmm. Sounds awesome."

She touched his hand and left for the bedroom and began to undress. John craned his head around and watched as her lithe body entered the shower before realizing he had forgotten to get breakfast started for her. By the time she reentered the front room dressed for the day, with her wet black hair uncombed, the table was set with two plates that held omelets and smoothies.

"Wow! Thanks, sweetie. I'm starving." She sat down and attacked the meal with relish, just as John had hoped.

"Ready for class yet?" she said after a few minutes, looking up from her plate.

"Almost. If I hadn't nodded off. I've some time later to cram a few more chapters in." He glanced at the clock and then back at her. "I think you would like Melville. He has his moments."

"Summer reading, maybe. But I don't know. Whales?"

"Well, it's about everything, really. I mean, hard to explain. The depths of the sea. All those things no one sees. It's like nothing is lost on him, you know? Not even the whales are lost on him." She laughed.

"I guess not."

"Hey, I forgot to tell you last night that you got a phone call from a guy up in American Fork. During your class, I mean. Just your thing, you know? He's looking for a painter with botanical skills."

"Are you serious?"

"Serious. Sorry, I should've said something. It's just . . . I was so tired."

"So how . . ." she started to ask.

"It sounded like Professor Bailey recommended you. This guy, his name is Zach Harker. He wants wildflowers of the Wasatch Front, you know, painted. Watercolor, he insisted. You would like that, wouldn't you?"

"I'm definitely listening . . ."

"I didn't inquire about the pay, but he said something about a grant he has. He's hoping you'd be willing to hike, take notebooks with you, that sort of thing, as a kind of tryout, I guess. It was weird though. He said, like, three times that he's of the 'Humboldt school of thought.'" John made air quotes. Alba looked at him quizzically. "I didn't ask. Didn't want to sound stupid. Of course, I explained that you hate the outdoors and that you were in no kind of shape to be walking up hills." She laughed.

"Awesome. Did you get his number?"

"Yeah. It's by the phone." He pointed to the end table by the couch.

She got up to make the call. John cleared the dishes and headed into the kitchen.

A few minutes later, she joined him in the kitchen. John's

hands were sunk in soapy water, washing the dishes.

"Well?"

She leaned her back against the counter while he worked. "Sounds like a quirky guy, you know? But I told him I was definitely interested. The university gave him money to produce a book of wildflowers for the Wasatch Mountains. He has enough to hire a student artist, not a professional, he said. But he insisted he wouldn't hire anything but 'excellent talent.' And that this was going to be different than other books. Field observation, he kept saying, that's his thing. Plein air. I think that's what he means by Humboldt school. He went on about Humboldt as the first naturalist, he said, who understood life in 'ecological context'—not plants in isolation. So he says he wants images that convey *ecological context*. He said it, like, four times. He wants me to come to his house up in American Fork with some samples of my work and go for a short hike with him, and then I'm supposed to produce some samples of plants we find before he makes his final decision. Pretty sure I'm not the first person he's looked at. He was kind of condescending, said he didn't have high expectations."

"It'd be nice to know why he turned the others down."

"Yeah. That's just it. I'm in the dark on that."

"What's the pay?" John asked, as he handed her a dish to dry.

"Not sure. He said we could talk about it." She began drying the dishes as he handed them to her.

"Do you want to do this? It sounds right up your alley. You seem kinda unsure."

"Yeah. Of course. No, I want to. It's just that . . . I guess he just was kind of odd, you know? If I'm going to be spending lots of time with him, I want to feel comfortable, you know? He just sounded . . . old, and grumpy."

"Yeah. I got that feeling too. Blunt."

John went back to his reading. Before she turned to her sketches, Alba went online and read about the life of Alexander von Humboldt.

* * *

Driving along the east bench of the Wasatch Mountains, Alba looked at the Angel Moroni atop the white walls of the Mount Timpanogos temple. Homes spread in every direction. The length of the lake could be seen in the distance beneath the smaller mountains on the west side of the valley. A familiar suspicion arose in her as she watched the way the landscape around her shifted and turned with each bend in the road, a suspicion that she would never see the world from any other vantage point than from wherever she was. The world was fluid, and yet her perception of that movement was forever tethered to the fact of her own biology. And the paradox was that her body was itself in dynamic flux, only temporarily creating the illusion that it was a static, fixed, physical thing. As long as she was conscious, she would always be housed in the cranium and linked to swinging limbs, but always in love with the chaos of weather and its intimations of perpetual flux.

She drove with the windows down, preferring the rushing sounds of wind and the sensation of being anywhere and everywhere. She stuck her left hand out the window and let the wind push against her palm. She glanced back at the temple spires rising above the houses, and there she was again, anchored behind the wheel, driving exactly 37 miles an hour and buffeted by the limitations of time and space. And then the rebellious response: to cut the tethering line, close her eyes just for a moment, as she did often just before she began a painting, and imagine that her arms and legs could encircle the globe as she held the entire earth inside her.

She pulled off of the main road coming out of American Fork Canyon onto a sloping driveway that led down a gulley to a small faded white house in the shade surrounded by uncut grass and a dense grove of tall scrub oaks. After seeing so many new large homes and developments, it was a refreshing if unusual sight. A chocolate brown spaniel shot up from where he was napping on the front porch, ran to the car, and began yelping at her before she had even emerged. She rolled down her window and spoke to him to see if she could calm him down.

"Hey. Hey, good boy. I don't mean any harm." The dog's floppy ears drooped at his side as he bent his neck and barked. He didn't seem angry, but she wasn't sure. She couldn't quite bring herself to open the door and glanced nervously back at the house. At that, the door opened and a man came out yelling.

"Theo! Theo! Get your ass over here, you stupid beast! Damn it, Theo! Now!"

Theo started wagging his stump of a tail, but he kept barking as he backed off from the car. With her portfolio under her arm, Alba got out of the car and cautiously approached the door. Theo circled back to her, barking. He was too nervous and excited to let her pet him, but she could now see that all of his noise was just joy to see another human being. Zach Harker stood on the porch with his hands on his hips. He looked old enough to be her grandfather. His hair was a mixture of brown and gray, receding and thin at the top, and his beard, which was more incidental than intended, was short and mostly gray. He wore wrinkled tan hiking pants, well-worn hiking shoes, and a blank but dirty blue T-shirt. A dusty and rusted porch swing sat motionless to the left. She noticed the chipped paint on its sideboards.

"You brought some water and some food for hiking, didn't you?" His eyes darted, never settling on anything in particular. She had, but before she could answer, he reentered the house and then reemerged with a fanny pack in his left hand and two hiking poles under his right arm. She extended her hand for a shake.

"Nice to meet you, Mr. Harker."

"Oh, right." He turned his body awkwardly to extend his right hand so as to not drop his poles. It was a quick and awkward shake, his eyes looked at her briefly, and then he stepped off the porch.

"Follow me," he said.

She wasn't sure what to expect visiting a strange man at his house, but his age and curt demeanor reassured her. He hurried off and Theo gladly followed, shooting into the surrounding vegetation with glee. She dropped her portfolio by the swing, quickly put her sketchpad into her CamelBak, and cinched it up across her chest. Would he want watercolor too or just pencil? She quickly grabbed her brushes and paints and stuffed them in. He had already walked around to the north side of the house and entered a trail that emerged from the woods. Alba ran to catch up.

"I brought some of my work to look at, if you would like . . . at a later point," she said as she came up behind him.

"Oh, right. When we get back." He didn't turn around. Theo ran back and forth across the trail as they advanced. Alba found herself having to jog every so often to keep up. He stabbed his poles into the ground like a Nordic skier, pushing ahead with zealous purpose. Theo came back from time to time to check on her.

After a half-mile or so, her body found its rhythm and she could feel herself relax a little. She could see they weren't really in any kind of wilderness since houses appeared on both sides of what appeared to be just a slim corridor of green.

"Where are we headed?" she asked.

"Just a little jaunt up here to the Bonneville shoreline. Willow Canyon up here to the north we can find ourselves some good patches of toadflax, alfalfa, knapweed, just your basic invasive stuff. If we get high enough, we might see some Indian paintbrush or blue flax." They had begun to emerge from the gulley and were now in the foothills to the north of the canyon. "Take note here of the brush—two kinds—*ericameria nauseosus* or rubber rabbitbrush, and sage, *Artemisia tridentata*. Here, feel and smell the difference." He pulled at a rabbitbrush. "Feel that. You feel how rubbery it is?" Alba did as she was instructed and nodded. "And smell this." He pulled off some sage leaves and rubbed them in his hands. "That's how you can tell the difference between the two, and note the three leaves here. *Tridentata*. You've heard of the goddess, you know, Artemis. Mistress of the animals, she was. Anyway, also note the cheat grass—the bane of our existence!—and the gambol oak, called scrub oak around here." He was pointing in different directions and moving and speaking quickly, almost frantically. "But the names, the names, you know, they don't matter as much as the broader story here, which we will get to in time. The main point is that they are not separable from our story any more than they are separable from the sun. Look down the trail here. Notice the colors along the edges, the plants, all of them. Nothing here is without human influence, you see. Don't kid yourself. This isn't natural. I mean, it's not wild. Nothing is, you see. This is our story now, all of it. Seeds brought on our ancestors' clothing. It's as if we made it our own garden, except not intentionally and now . . . now, you see, the world needs our better thought, more conscious effort. What you need to remember is *biological synchronization*." He said the last words with emphasis.

"Synchronization?" she asked.

"Timing. Yeah, this is all about timing here. And timing is all about the sun, the cycles of the sun, the cycles of seasons and the plants in their deep evolutionary memory trying to match what the world is giving them, for better or for worse, moment to moment, day to day, year by year. When they emerge from the soil, when they pollinate, when they go to seed. They don't choose the cycles. They just absorb the insults of time. That's their job. No questions asked. That's also their wisdom, their brilliance, you see. Gotta have the eyes to see it. That's what I want. And of course, that sun, you know, would do us no good at all if it weren't for gases that trap the heat and warm this place, like a huge greenhouse, you see. And what we have going on here, well, it's a mess. The plants are struggling to keep up with rising temperatures. We may not like it, we may not see it, but we are the gardeners."

She had been south already a few times with John, walking in the narrows at Zion, camping in the San Rafael Swell, and she loved Rock Canyon and the mountains closer to Provo, but the grasp of new information, new knowledge, right in her own foothills, excited her. She wondered, though, if he had even noticed her yet.

"Here. You see the color purple lining the trail?" He pointed north along the bench. "You see the splotches of white here? It's no accident, you see, that a human trail would be shadowed by so much color. That purple. That's Iranian. Not kidding. Iranian. Can you believe that? Pretty, sure. But manmade or man-brought, in any case. Make no mistake. This isn't no wilderness, honey. Those bright green spears of high grass? Rye. That isn't native, I can tell you that. Why don't you give this a shot?" He stopped suddenly. Theo continued hunting in the brush, scaring magpies into the sky. Mr. Harker pointed at a lone white flower with pinkish stems and green leaves.

"A shot? I'm sorry?"

"Draw it, I mean."

"Oh." She dropped her pack and pulled out her sketchpad and pencil case. Choosing a pencil, she found a spot to sit on the hillside above the trail. Mr. Harker stood aside so he could watch, standing stiffly with his arms crossed. A few minutes passed in silence as she hurriedly sketched.

"Hmm." The gravelly voice didn't sound like approval. His rudeness just made her nervous at first, but as she worked to sketch the four folding and drooping pedals, it started to annoy her.

"No, no, no," he finally said. "Listen. Do you remember what

I said about Humboldt?"

He didn't wait for an answer.

"Where's the sense of context? Where's the sense that this is a plant in its *place*? And where is the sense that its place, as natural as it is, has already been man *made*? Or that you, *you* are looking at it. You see the upturned soil on the side of the trail, don't you? You see along the line of the trail, don't you? And this here, this is the plant as a creative response to all of that. Get it?"

His arms swung open and out, punctuating his soliloquy.

"You know, don't you, what a fatal mistake it was that we adopted that damn Linnaean system? What arrogance Linnaeus had! To think he could give everything its proper name, as if it all existed independent of us! Or independent of everything else? That the world in all its fantastical and bizarre and fluid—yes fluid!—movement from one form to another over eons of time, that he could take it all and stick a damn needle in it, name it, know it, and kill it! Yes, that's what he did. He killed the nature he claimed he loved. Okay, maybe unfair, but still." He spoke as if debating himself. "That's at least what we have done. As if God himself commanded this Swedish Adam to name the entirety of creation just so we humans in our puny hubris could imagine ourselves lords of our own dominion. Joke's on us, see, since we have barely even scratched the surface of naming life and yet we are killing it before we will ever know it. So this flower here, the desert evening primrose, we call *Oenothera caespitosa*. How does that Latin sound? Not exactly poetry, is it?" And then like a sudden key change, "Humboldt! Now there was a real man, a real poet!"

Alba listened to a long narrative about Humboldt's journey to the New World, his years hiking the most difficult terrain in the world, learning languages, all the while keeping painstaking notes and making careful sketches of what he saw. No camera, Mr. Harker insisted, no camera but his own eyes and what his hands could remember. Harker was strange and annoying, but she couldn't help feeling drawn to him and to what he could teach her. She absorbed every word.

His arms continued to swing as he spoke. "You know essentially nothing about life if you think of it as a bunch of discrete *things*. Everything, all life, is connected to everything else but always in particular, localized ways, you see. All of it is a creative response to what is given, to what *is*. Humboldt was the first to understand that a mountain's elevation creates microclimates, changing ecosystems with each drop in average temperature. You see, that's what I want to do. I want us to finally see this place in all its complexity. All its relations. Nothing exists by itself and nothing exists without context. And nothing, anymore—let's be clear about this—has existence or meaning without reference to the human story. We don't have to like it, of course. Lord knows I don't. It's just a fact. We rule the roost, you see. Mankind's the ultimate screenwriter. We will never stop destroying this planet until we begin to wrap our brains around that interconnectedness. I mean, it's like as soon as we start understanding how everything is connected, we already see that we have messed with the system. And good God! This place, we like to think, is all about individuals, see, or families, but never about the *community*! The whole of it, I mean. All of this; all of us. The air we share, the water we drink, the cell matter we exchange every day. Without Humboldt we wouldn't have ever come to understand our impact on the climate, but I don't suppose you know or care much about that."

Alba had heard about climate change. John's father certainly had strong opinions about it, mainly that it was false, a liberal lie perpetuated to increase government overreach, which was enough for her to want to argue with him. Not that she had any real understanding, but he always seemed to need an opponent but never had one. Everyone just nodded and agreed. And there was that time two students went at each other in class over it and the teacher just asked for peace. People acted like it was supposed to be part of your cosmology, something you either had faith in or didn't. But she had noticed that it was oddly the religious who framed their disbelief in terms of a kind of scientific rationalism, believing themselves the only ones tough-minded enough to see through the illusions. It all had left her in a state of confusion.

Mr. Harker was clearly not interested in knowing what she thought in any case. He didn't even pause for a response. He went on about Humboldt's thirty years writing up his findings back in Europe, determined, he said, to compose the greatest theory of the cosmos ever conceived. And who would update this story, Mr. Harker asked? Who could put it in the context of what we now understand about our irrevocable role in shaping the climate we live in? This would have to be our task, our responsibility, he said.

She looked down at her half-finished sketch. She could see how she missed the context. A broader frame would help.

"And do you think he worried himself for one minute about making sure his ideas matched the Bible? No, thank the good Lord, he was a man of the Enlightenment. He took botanical knowledge and rammed a hole right through the wall of superstition. He showed us the interconnectivity of all life! One time he found himself at the mouth of a cave, in Venezuela I think it was, and these Indians, they are all bent out of shape if they got too close to the entrance because strange sounds emerged from it, you see, sounds they imagined were the voices of the dead, speaking to them. Why is it always the voice of the dead we imagine? That's a good question. Anyway, Humboldt, you see, he understands that these are the sounds of a rare species of bat that is using its intelligence to communicate and see by echolocation." His discourse was on autopilot. "Only problem was he couldn't get any of those superstitious Indians to calm down long enough to go with him deep into the cave to show them. Supernatural nonsense. And don't think he didn't have his own obstacles back at home! Those Christians! Obsessions with papal authority, anxieties about modern science. You know, it's been Galileo over and over again."

"That's all really very interesting," she finally interrupted. "Really. But I can't draw and listen at the same time. And it doesn't help to have you glancing over my shoulder. It doesn't work that way."

Her comments snapped him out of his trance, and the realization seemed to embarrass and then irk him.

"Right. Right. I am sure this is all beyond your interests as an artist . . . at BYU."

She chose not to respond.

"But just be sure to see it in context. For crying out loud, I beg you—don't kill it!"

With this he walked north along the foothills at a leisurely pace, touching the blades of cheat grass on the hillside above the trail.

She turned to look more closely to see the flower's context. At first glance, it didn't seem to have much context at all, sitting as it did alone and apart from other plants. But she noticed that it had found what seemed the most precarious position on the upper edge of the trail in dry soil that looked overturned, open to the sky. Overturned by what? she wondered. Maybe the rains, and gravity pulling things down, and whoever it was who made this trail. Above the upturned soil, a line of cheat grass, already turning purplish brown in the sun, waited for its chance to colonize the soil below. She looked around at the atmosphere, the increasingly hazy warm air of early summer. She could see how the trail had created a steeper angle for the soil above it than the soil could handle. Rocks and small piles of dirt had rolled down onto the trail. No guarantee, then, she thought, that a trail remains a trail. It was a temporary truce, a precarious angle of repose. A truce long enough to allow this flower its moment of glory, lonely but proud. She noticed that there were a few other primroses farther up that were similarly balanced right next to the trail. So she started her sketch over again but with a broader frame and deeper perspective to catch the soil, the angle of the land, and the flower's fragile existence. Every so often, she glanced up and noticed that he was wandering slowly back toward her but that he wasn't coming close enough to make it look like a return. Only when she packed up her things and finally stood did he come back. As he approached, she handed him the sketchpad. He looked at it silently for a few minutes. She had a moment to observe him more closely. He had sinewy arms and legs. She noticed the coloring on his head through his thinning hair that extended to his neck and arms. It was more like a russet color, she thought, halfway between a burn and a tan. He was a sunbaked and aged version of the majority of the white people in this valley. His upper arms showed under his shirt, and she could see he was otherwise pale. He stared at the image for a few minutes in silence, grunted, then said, "I've got another one up here. Follow me."

Again, the pace was brisk. Alba thought that maybe talking to him would slow him down a little.

"So, primrose. Is that because it blooms in the spring. I mean it makes me think, you know, of *primavera*."

The perfect Spanish pronunciation caught his ear. He stopped and turned around.

"Alba." He said this not to address her but as a revelation. "You are Hispanic."

"Yes. Chilean."

"You don't look Hispanic. I thought maybe you were, I don't know, Middle Eastern."

"We Chileans confuse people. Would you prefer I look Hispanic?"

"Of course not. I just mean . . . oh, never mind. The point is, yes, the primrose is the springtime rose, the first rose, I guess. It blooms all summer, though, so it isn't the best name. Ever heard of the primrose path?"

"Something about how beauty deceives by hiding sin and danger and all that good stuff, isn't it?"

"That's the idea, anyway."

"Yeah, it was in a Shakespeare play I read for a class."

She watched as he fidgeted with his fanny pack, adjusted it, and then turned around and strode quickly up the trail. She followed as they moved quickly along the edge of the foothills, following the rise and fall of the mountainside until they reached a small ravine, at which point he turned east and headed straight up the mountain. Now the breathing got too difficult for conversation. She was determined to show him she could keep up. They didn't go too far up before he stopped and pointed to some Indian paintbrush mixed within a spot of sage brush and western blue flax.

"Obligate root parasites, these are, in this case of the sagebrush. A whole different world going on under the soil. And the Western blue flax, *Linum lewisii*, named after the explorer, right? Story to that, I tell you. Lewis suffered from depression. Anyway, the point is, it's a story and a neighborhood. Give that a try."

She put her pack down again and pulled out the sketchpad. She realized that this business of context necessitated a sacrifice: here, the precise detail of the flower's shape would need to be softened. She glanced up to see if he was watching. This time he stood at a distance.

"So pay attention. We are almost right between two ecosystems here, each with its own microclimate because as you look up the ravine, you can see the vegetation growing more dense and green." Now instead of a history lecture, it was straightforward ecology, like he had been starved for a student. "There is more shade, more water, and a more comfortable climate for plants to grow and the wildflowers that have evolved to flourish in such circumstances will find their way here, you see. But for how long, is the question, right? There is the shape of the land, the angle of the sun—but there is also the climate itself. Much warmer; soon enough even that niche there will be desert. For now, what lies below is an arid climate, the one you and I live in every day, the climate of the Great Basin. Far enough up and over these mountains, of course, we arrive fully onto the Colorado Plateau, a different beast altogether. The difference in rainfall here, just this high up in the foothills, compared to the valley floor would astonish you."

They were high enough up the ravine that they could see more of the immense size of Utah Lake as it spread out to the south of the valley. Alba could see the Jordan River heading off to the north.

"You called this a shoreline," she said.

He seemed even more animated now that she had posed what appeared to be a good question. "Well, that's just it. It is gone. Lake Bonneville filled this valley fifteen thousand years ago and it spread throughout a good portion of the Great Basin, including Salt Lake Valley, all the way up into Idaho, until it finally burst and flowed into what is now the Columbia River to the ocean." His hands pointed quickly as he spoke, marking the west then the north across the valley. "Utah Lake and Salt Lake are most of what remains. But this whole valley was submerged up to more or less where the trail is, about five hundred to a thousand feet above the valley floor. You and I live on an ancient lakebed, you see. The weight of the water was so great that when the lake drained, the surface of the valley floor surged upward after having been depressed for so long. Think about that."

An ancient and now invisible lake was context on a grand scale, she thought, time like she had never imagined. The gaps in her own brief moment seemed utterly insignificant in the bright span of earth's innumerable rotations. She had stayed up nights wrestling to understand her past, and here Mr. Harker, in one brief flood of words, was rearranging the very structure of time.

How could she convey the landscape's dark passage through time, its birthing pangs, morphology, tectonic shifts, and ever-changing weather all together in one line? She found her pencil hovering over the paper with ever more hesitation. How could one graceful curve bear record of this temporal weight? As she drew the small cluster of plants, the work suddenly felt monumental. What was a mere painting or portrait? What was a narrative of a life? Wouldn't a truthful context result in no context, since everything is, ultimately, part of everything else, nothing excluded or compared? The lie of her art was now suddenly exposed: the lie of the frame, of the idea of a moment. How to mark the passage of fifteen thousand years, let alone a million or two? How to trace what had caused plants to evolve, survive, adapt, and change all within the frame of deep time? We were so wrong about so much, she thought. So inadequate to this earth.

As she looked at the small blue flowers, she could feel things losing their objectivity and melding together in a flux of form. It was as if the paper below her pencil had suddenly opened before a great, fathomless chasm. All she could do was scratch and pull at the hem of creation. Context was a fiction, an illusion, aided by the artifice of climbing to a higher place or withdrawing to a distance and seeing from a different angle. Which was another way of admitting that all art was a self-portrait, even if the goal was anonymity. From here where they had climbed, the houses below revealed the slant of the valley floor that exposed the extent of the lake. It occurred to her that the great landscape painters had climbed mountains as a method for seeing otherwise, retraining the eyes and leaving them with the memory of having exiled oneself, even if only for a moment, from the flat geographical dimensions of human society. To look at the landscape, she thought, is to begin to see oneself, and once one sees oneself, one is displaced. You always have to imagine a higher vantage point to see oneself in a broader context. A way of seeing a way of seeing, she thought. The observer would always fall back into the scene no matter how impersonally removed. There was nothing to do but confess it, so she did, signing her sketch with her name, date, place, and time.

"What's that for?" he asked.

"Oh, nothing. I don't mean it as any grand gesture, but it occurs to me that this is a good way to keep track of where I am in relation to what I am painting, not only in time but space. I will never get it the same again. Even if I came back to this same spot, the light would be different, the weather. It's kind of like carving into the bark of a tree. 'I was here.' Only this seems less violent, don't you think?"

"Hmm." By now she realized that this was his strange habit, a way of evading direct communication, but it seemed to signal a whole host of possible meanings.

"Do you not like my sketch?" She thought she would go ahead and ask.

"Have you ever studied botany?"

"No. But I have always loved wildflowers."

"You don't seem to know much about them."

"I don't pretend to. But I am willing to be taught. And anyone who knows me knows I'm passionate about learning. I think I caught the context pretty well, don't you?"

His evasiveness was starting to make her nervous. She thought she better start advocating for herself in case her chances vanished suddenly.

"Hmm." No one spoke for a minute.

"I think we should head back," he finally said.

"Are you sure? I would be happy to sketch some more. I could show you what I can do with my watercolors. I saw some yellow flowers earlier that looked nice."

"Yellow toadflax. A pain in the ass. An invader. The Mormon of the weed family, driving out all diversity and native species. Look, honey, I am not here to spend my time painting pretty flowers. I am here to protect what little ecological health is left for these mountains, given this invasion, this invasion of white humanity here. Do you realize that we have caused more change and done more damage in the last one hundred and fifty years than this place has seen in the last fifteen thousand years? And who do you think did this? It sure as hell wasn't the Utes who had been here for hundreds of years, nor was it those who were here long before that, hundreds and thousands of years before. No sir. It was you Mormons, what with your obsession to make the damn desert blossom as a rose, to mechanize the world with your dams, your religious zeal for an economic Zion, not once even considering the possibility that the land didn't need your help, thank you very much. Religion and its intolerance for the substance of this world, this life, always assuming human life, human needs are more important than all the rest. The bottom line is that religion can't accept the equality of life. This world was so goddamn boring they had to make it into an amusement park. Your version of the Garden of Eden includes an ATM, sweetie."

Alba felt her heart race. "Please don't call me sweetie or honey."

"What?"

"My name is Alba. I'm not anyone's 'honey.'"

"Whatever."

She had had it. "No, not 'whatever,' either. That's rude and you should know that. And please stop swearing. I don't like it."

She started packing up. Despite the fascination of what she was learning, she decided that this was not going to work out.

"Hey. You don't have to get all huffy."

"I'm not *huffy*." She stood and looked him directly in the eyes. Later, she would remember the way he looked stunned and maybe a little frightened at that moment. "I just don't like the way you're talking to me, and I don't like the way you're talking about Mormons as some kind of weed or the way you assume we act in packs."

"It's the historical truth, girl. Don't just rely on my account."

She gathered her pack, stood up, and stared at him in the face.

"I am not a girl, either, Mr. Harker. This isn't 1950. It's 2001. I am twenty-four years old. And my mother sacrificed everything to get me to this country and to this school so I could get an education, and I am not going to spend my time sitting on hillsides listening to a stranger speak with condescension toward me or my religion. I'm not stupid. I can take criticism. And I'm more than happy to learn things I didn't know before. But I have better things to do with my time than working for someone who for all his appreciation for context and equality of life appears to know nothing about the very people among whom he lives while being more than happy to look down on them."

With that she started down the hill while he stood silently where she left him. She could feel her face flush with anger and her heart knocking against her ribs. She walked as fast as she could, and once she turned the corner away from his direct sight, she ran for a while to ensure no further dialogue with him would be necessary. As she got closer to the house, she looked back. He was nowhere to be seen, so she continued running again, even faster. The trail snaked smoothly through the trees. The dirt was soft with only an occasional root surfacing.

*　*　*

All the way home she was anxious to see John, but when she arrived at the house, he was gone. She found a note saying that he had gone on some errands, but there was no indication of what time he would be home. She dropped her pack and paced back and forth anxiously, unsure of what to do with herself. She sat down on the couch and stared blankly out the window at two birds dancing on the pear tree. She had always loved that tree, the way its leaves turned a deep green in the summer and the way it held its oval shape. She could look at the green and still find pleasure in anticipation of what it would become in the fall, aflame in bright red. Contemplating the tree calmed her, and she reached for her pack for the chance to sketch its reach toward the sky. But thoughts of the tree reminded her that she had left her portfolio on his porch. John will have to get it, she thought, or better yet, to avoid an argument, maybe she could retrieve it at night. Mr. Harker wouldn't have noticed, and maybe if he kept Theo inside the house, she could come and go without disturbing anything. Perhaps leaving them there might be better than the risk of having to talk to him again. She thought about each of the paintings that she would have to sacrifice. As she counted them in her mind, she was pretty sure she had only brought five, but she sadly knew there was one for sure she could not live without.

Her anxiety would not subside. She couldn't sketch and couldn't imagine concentrating long enough to read. When she started to shake, it took a moment to realize it was hunger, not nerves. She went into the kitchen to find something to eat.

John was barely in the door with a few bags of groceries before she began to tell him the entire story. All the composure she had shown in front of the old man was gone. She gesticulated, her voice was raised, and tears began to well up in her eyes. John listened quietly while he put away the groceries. It gave him something to do. He was not sure what she wanted from him. It wasn't that John didn't feel things, but he had learned at a young age that feelings, left unchecked, led to saying the wrong thing. Alba always seemed to know what she wanted to say.

"Will you call him?" she asked. "I just can't talk to him again."

"Uh, sure. I can just drive up there and pick it up. Get it over with."

So he went to the phone in the front room where he had written down the man's number and called. Alba retreated to the bedroom, but she still caught a few phrases. "She didn't like that." He said at one point. "I am afraid she is no longer interested." After a few more minutes, it sounded as if John was giving him directions to the house. She came out of the bedroom to try to signal to him that this was not a good idea, but it was too late. He was ignoring her signals as he wrapped up the conversation and hung up the phone.

"Is he coming *here*?" she asked incredulously. "John!"

"I'm sorry. I guess . . . I don't know. I tried, but he insisted. He was apologetic. Or sort of, anyway. Look, you don't have to be here if you don't want to. I will just meet him at the door and take the portfolio, and we'll be done."

"Why? I don't get it. Is it not clear that I'm distressed?"

"Yes, of course it's clear. Sorry. I'll take care of it, I promise."

"Whatever you do, don't give him a chance to lecture you about nature. He won't stop."

"I thought you liked that kind of thing."

"I love it. But he just couldn't resist mixing a few insults into his lectures. He assumed I didn't believe or care about things. He kept referring to 'you Mormons.' And although he never came out and said it, it was clear that as a woman, I wasn't intellectually up to snuff. You know, the swearing was annoying but mostly because I had the distinct impression that he was testing to see what my limits were. It was all pretty juvenile."

"Sounds like it. Man, I'm sorry. What a drag. You know he wants to hire you, don't you? He said so on the phone, but I told him you were no longer interested."

"I'm not. I'm really sorry. I know we need the money. I'll send out my resume again next week."

"You will find a job. I'm not worried about that. I'm just sad to think you will be working some office job or waitressing instead of painting in the mountains."

She was sad too. Deep down she wanted it badly. She lay slumped on the couch and watched as John moved around the

house straightening things—he was so kind— but for a brief
moment his steadiness seemed almost suspicious to her, as if
it hadn't yet been tested enough to be real. She had been happy
to marry into a conservative white Mormon pioneer family who
had lived in Utah since the nineteenth century with extended
family in every direction and with generations of family names
and family lore stuffed in manila folders and stored in boxes.
How many cousins of his had she met on campus? He offered
everything she didn't have, hers a broken fragment of a family
from Chile, just herself and her mother arriving in America with
a broken past, a father about whom she knew next to nothing
except a legacy of political trouble under Pinochet, and not a
genealogical tree in sight. She could scarcely coax a story from
her mother.

And so far, they had been happy, just as she imagined they
would be. It had not yet been a year, and while she didn't
doubt her decision, she was beginning to feel dismembered,
hungering for something that she feared she would never find.
Mormons talked about the Spirit of Elijah, that moment of
turning the hearts to the fathers which precedes an awakening
interest in genealogy, but all it did was leave her feeling hollow,
orphaned. Maybe art wasn't enough but the work of filling a
blank canvas at least provided some recompense. Besides, John
sometimes complained that growing up a Utah Mormon was
like living on one big family compound, forever limiting the
privilege of individuality. He seemed to handle it okay. Truth
is, he flourished. He always seemed to like all of his cousins.
And everyone else for that matter. That was just it. She hated
to think his love for her was just another version of a patient
charity he held for the entirety of the human race. Now that they
were married, she was surprised to find herself hungering for
something more particular, and mad maybe, something raging
in the chest that would have seized him up and made him hold
to her with fierce tenacity and possessiveness. *You and you alone!*

25

I want you! she wished he would say. In her better moments, she knew that this was unfair since she also loved the freedom she felt with him, the room he gave her to be on her own, to make her own decisions, to express herself in her art. He didn't get why she was so devoted to painting but he gave her the space to do it. That was no small thing. But sometimes the freedom just felt like solitude.

John occasionally glanced over at her, smiling. His sandy hair was still unkempt, his khaki pants and T-shirt threadbare and molded to his angular shape. He was just as informal as the day they met at a mutual friend's apartment on a Friday night for a class to watch *Wings of Desire*. Alba's roommate had invited her, and John, it turned out, was in the same class. Angels looking back longingly at the world they had recently departed. The movie moved her, as did his offer to walk her home that night. But already it was as if she had failed to learn the lesson of the angels because just a few months into the marriage, here she was, she thought, already feeling turned around as if she were taking leave of the life that she was just beginning to love as she should.

* * *

John paused in front of the window to watch the neighbor's sprinklers watering the sidewalk. Just then, the old car arrived in their driveway. Alba went out of the front room, but she left the door of the bedroom open to listen.

"Hello, Mr. Harker."

"Hello. Is Alba here?"

"Um. Yeah, but she is, ah, isn't available right now."

"Could I please speak to her?"

"Um, well, I think she is not available."

"Please. It is very important. I insist."

"Well, okay, just a second."

26

John closed the door without inviting him in and returned to the bedroom.

"I thought you were going to send him away? What are you doing?"

"I meant to . . . I don't know. Sorry. I can't just go back there and tell him you won't speak to him, can I?"

"Why not?"

"It isn't polite. Look, I wasn't expecting him to ask for you. I'm sorry. This is really awkward. Can't you please come out for just a second?"

She gave him a stern look, arose, and came to the door. She opened it to see Mr. Harker standing on their front step with her portfolio in his arm.

"You forgot this."

"Yes. I know. Thanks for bringing it back to me."

"Listen. I, uh, looked these over and I was wondering if you could tell me more about this image."

He nervously opened the portfolio and flipped through a few canvases before he pulled out a painting of a tree buried in a lake. He handed it to her and stood patiently waiting at the step. The tree was portrayed as if in an aquarium so that the roots were exposed under the water, groping with arm-like tentacles at the egg-shaped rocks bedded in the sedimentation. The branches extended out in a horizontal canopy with the outermost ones bending down to touch the water, like Michelangelo's God reaching for Adam. At the same point, the most tenacious underwater roots had begun to reach upward to the surface, as if they were seeking to close the oval sphere that the tree and its roots formed. Watercolor had seemed the right element for this thing she had tried to recover. But what was it? She could never quite name it. She had worked hard to achieve a feeling of ephemerality with the image, something akin to a dreamscape but without the ease of fantasy. She had pulled the image down from the ether of her mind where it had floated for years and had sought to make it something concrete, earthy. Now it felt more like a poem, a paean, or a haunting melody that might embody balance, or, she hoped, reconcile oppositions. It meant everything to her. She had tried once to explain it to John, but his face had just gone blank in embarrassed incomprehension.

"It's just a tree I imagined," she tried to explain. "I am not sure what I meant by it really. Just came on impulse, I guess."

Mr. Harker looked pleased. "It's terrific. Really terrific. I couldn't stop looking at it. I kept thinking that it transcends its botanical inaccuracies somehow with a kind of ecological integrity. That moves me. I can't explain it." His index finger loosely traced the image as she held it in her hands. It moved her to see his reverence. "I don't know if you know the tree, but this looks a lot like the Samaan tree, *Albizia saman*, in the tropics of Latin America. The cyclical connection implied here between earth and sky, liquid and solid, origin and destination." Like a lecturer in a museum, his hands motioned in circles around the image. "It's just terrific."

No one else had ever really noticed it before. More than praise, she had craved communication, connection. How odd that it would be with him.

"May I come in for just a minute?"

"Uh, yes. Sorry."

She opened the door and let him in. She glanced back to John with an expression of frustration and confusion.

"Have a seat." She pointed to the reading chair by the couch. He sat, awkwardly leaning forward, as if he might need to make a quick exit.

She sat down on the couch; John sat on the arm. There was a long silence. Mr. Harker looked out the window and scratched his knee. He hadn't changed his clothes from the hike. John decided to break the silence.

"So I understand you know quite a bit about ecology."

"Well, that does tend to happen when you spend a lifetime

studying something." He looked around the room aimlessly. And then more silence. Alba was beginning to feel sorry for him.

"Listen," she said. "I know I left in such a sudden way. It probably wasn't necessary, but I hope you can understand what was offensive about how you talked to me."

Mr. Harker looked at her with a kind of stunned amazement, the same look he had on his face when she brought him up short on the mountain, as if he wasn't sure why she would have been so indecent as to state the obvious. He hesitated.

"Yes . . . it was abrupt." He smoothed his shorts with the flat of both of his hands and looked around nervously. "Look. I, uh, I wanted to come here to tell you why, as I said to your husband, I had hoped I could hire you. I understand that you don't want to work for me. I guess I have chased off the others too, and I can't really explain that. I am just not good at this. But the important thing, and the reason I am here, is that I liked what I saw in the drawings you did and something about that painting really knocked me out. I don't suspect you realize just how good that piece is, but it shouldn't be sitting in some portfolio away from the eyes of admirers. I have been down to the Springville Museum many times. I have made it my passion to try to see what little artistic achievement we have been able to muster in this valley of ours, especially as it pertains to the land, you see." He seemed to be gathering courage. "And damned if I am going to let this chance pass me by to say that, well, whatever you decide to do with your life, Alba, if you were to ever to give up painting, even if you were to spend your years devoted to good things, raising a family and doing all that church service you folks like to do but failing to paint, why, I think that would be a real shame."

His presumption to be giving her unsolicited advice was surprising, but she was surprised too that she wasn't put off by it. At this he rose to go.

"Wait. Mr. Harker." She rose with him. "Thank you. That

means a lot." He turned to the door and seemed intent on leaving without even saying good-bye. He was halfway down the front steps when she called out to him.

"Mr. Harker." He stopped and turned around.

"If you think you can behave yourself, I would still be happy to work for you." She gave John a quick stare to fix him in his place, in case he thought this excused him.

It wasn't exactly a proper smile, but the expression on Mr. Harker's face as he got into the car looked like relief.

"That would be fine," he said. "Mighty fine."

Chapter 2

Dear S.,

Can you recall that time the three of us camped in American Fork Canyon, just by the river at Hanging Rock? Do you remember? I brought my four-piece fly rod, you know, the one I like to use on small streams? The spring water ran high, but I couldn't resist testing the waters. Your mom had stayed back at the campsite but you followed me and stood on the shore, perplexed by my obsession, while the fish struck sharply but always belatedly missing their target. I would have caught them all had they been fast enough to keep up with the swift current. I remember that the roar of the mountain water prevented us from hearing each other. You stood, moving your mouth, and I motioned with my arms that I couldn't hear you. Your index finger circled around your ear and I smiled and nodded. Yeah, I'm nuts.

I don't know why that memory comes to mind. It's only one of many. Seems like they come daily, but always in pieces.

It's a beautiful morning, I must say. Theo and I just got back from an early hike up behind Box Elder peak. Not many hikers go there, you know, least of all on a weekday. Theo ran hard, switching back and forth, doing his hunting. He's a good companion, for all the work he can be. He had to have a cyst removed not too long ago that had been ailing him for some time. It was strange to see him sedated because the fact is he is the very breath of life. Pure animal joy, that dog. If I don't get him outside, he just about goes crazy and he drives me crazy too. But once outside, it's a romp, an all-out leap into life. It's that linear elation he has, that leap. He was something to watch as he lost himself in the high bracken ferns. His brown head would pop up time to time from the green sea of fronds and his ears would flop, just to check back with me. I do my level best to learn his animal joy, but it takes discipline. I have to stay focused on the senses and really listen. Takes a lot to quiet this mind of mine, but today for a time I think I got close. At one point, I stood as still as I could and listened for the most distant sounds I could hear. The breezes quaked the aspen leaves above me, a meadowlark sang from up the slope, and Theo smelled his way through a rank bedding of matted grass—by the likes of it, elk was my guess. I made a sound or two of my own, just to make sure I was still alive. Sensation is the key, you see. Without it I don't have the foggiest idea who or what I am, and yet when I am really focused, sensation causes me to lose my sense of self altogether. That's the real blessing, and paradox. It lightens the burdens of life to be more fully aware, more alive. This was beneath that one stand of black aspens that burned a few years ago, you might remember. I wrote you about the fire. Could have been a lot worse, but thanks to the helicopters that grabbed water from Silver Lake, they were able to get it out in time. Of course, the mountain didn't mind, probably is better off now than it had been. Just ask the ferns. They seemed pretty thankful. And the Columbines, sticky geraniums, thimble berry, Indian Paintbrush, tapertip onion, Queen Anne's Lace, lupine, all those penstemon, they too have expressed their thanks. Utah is the penstemon capital of the world, for crying out loud. It's quite a sight. Death and rebirth, that whole saga in bright green and dark, dark black. I tell you, early summer on a mountain is something else. The whole place breathes and sighs and sings. It's a living mountain, to be sure. There is certainly pattern to all of it, just not much order, if you know what I mean. But that's life for you.

That's the golden question, isn't it? What *is* life for you? Your silence is cruel. Not intentional perhaps, but cruel nonetheless. At least my words are better than nothing. It gives me the illusion that you and I can still talk. Writing to you is how I hope.

I suppose your mother has given you a few reasons that you

should not trust me. No doubt she told you that I was unkind, impatient, and willfully distant. Maybe you even remember. Yeah, I get that a lot. And I won't deny it. I am not writing to disagree with her. I write because I think everyone deserves a story. And every story deserves an audience.

It was one thing for your mother to leave before I had a chance to apologize, to make up for my sins, but your silence is a kind of finality I just can't bring myself to accept. If I imagine you somewhere, however distant, experiencing who knows what joys and sorrows in what climes beyond the nine years I knew you — why, it keeps me alive to hope that you might have a future even if it has to be without me. Sure it hurts, but I guess I would rather sorrow and believe than to protect myself by forgetting. If I stopped writing, maybe I would eventually stop hurting, but then you would truly be gone. Isn't that something? It's like I am praying, except that I am praying to you. You know I wasn't much for God talk anyway. But can you see the paradox, can't you? I sit here many mornings writing to you, trying capture the intimacy we shared without words, and all I end up with are piles of my own words and your persistent silence. The closer I keep you, the farther away you are.

Gabriel announced to Zacharias that Elizabeth would bear a child in their old age. He was terrified and mute, but I want to insist on this point: here was a man who believed in angels — beings beyond physical knowledge — but what stunned him into his silence were the surprising and unpredictable gifts of biology. I, on the other hand, gladly dismiss what lies beyond this world but find myself enraged by the facts of our biology that I have spent a life passionately celebrating. I should state it clearly, in case it isn't already obvious to you, but I am a walking contradiction. Unlike old Walt Whitman, I find no solace in this.

I remember when I started out with botany I was definitely under the spell of that old dream to trace the handiwork of God. Anciently, of course, natural history was nothing but theology.

Everyone knew that. The Book of Nature as the corroborating story of God. But it eventually became obvious to me that even if such forensics were plausible, it was too late because we had messed it up. You see, we got our fingerprints all over the scene of the crime. We made natural history *our* story. The human story and the story of nature are no longer separate things. Maybe it was because I stopped being a religious man after you were gone, but I started to think that perhaps I could tell the story of our impact: I could trace our own handiwork and help wake us up from our obliviousness. Here we were, as dependent as ever on these mountains, as fragile as ever in our borrowed stardust bodies, but without even the slightest bit of awareness anymore of our own biology and what we are doing to the whole of it. It might sound cliché, but I've got an ominous sense about things, about the future. Reading the tea leaves, as it were, only they are the petals of my beloved wildflowers, and all I see is impending doom, a premature end to the most marvelous accident in the universe. That's why I decided that my magnum opus could be a book that would honor the beauty of the living mountain and catalogue its endurance under the hand of this civilization. A way, I thought, of documenting our sins. Hell, maybe even pointing toward the path of our repentance. We could start by knowing a thing or two about where it is we find ourselves on this planet. I am fed up with the way we look at nature as if we're peeking through a pane of glass at an aquarium or zoo. Always the illusion of standing apart from the world we watch. And that's just it. Our relationship to these mountains is too cold, like a photo calendar. The fact is you can never really *see* a mountain anyway. You have to experience it and your experience will always be just one small fragment of an infinite whole. I thought, I can do the writing but I needed an artist whose work would force the viewer to encounter themselves *in* the work. A way of showing our place in the world we observe as we observe it. I wanted a viewer to be able to feel the sun's heat and hear the buzzing insects.

But where was I going to get this artist? BYU's Redd Center had a grant, so I pitched the idea to them, and I was given enough money to hire an amateur. I tried a few applicants out but they were all hopelessly saccharine, bright-eyed and bushy-tailed Mormons who loved pretty flowers but missed all the rest. But one finally caught my attention. I almost chased her off too, but I was brought up short by a painting she mistakenly left on my porch. I don't know if you ever had the kind of experience this was for me, but maybe you can recall a time or two when you were transfixed by things you saw in the mountains, like that first time we backpacked up to Silver Lake and camped for the night. You couldn't have been more than six years old. When you saw the deep aqua color of the lake and watched as the distant waterfalls on the opposite side foamed silently in thin white lines down the towering granite talus beneath a cobalt sky, you were transfixed. Art does that to me. Not very often, mind you, because usually it bothers me precisely because of its false pretenses, its hideously proud subjectivity. Poor artists always seem to make the mistake of assuming that others already care what goes on inside of their puny minds, when in fact no one asked. But her painting left me feeling that she understood my project better than I did. It was metaphorical, expressive, but it was also something deeply attuned to the facts of the earth, you see, something ecological and emotional at the same time, I guess. We are too often given to romances about what nature should be, or about how nature reflects the drama of human existence, but we need to pay attention to particulars. We need to observe. Shut ourselves down. Not to pretend to perfect objectivity, in the end, but at least to construct dialogue with the world, you see, to build a bridge to the non-self, to the more-than-self. And it was that ambiguity, that feeling of being caught between self-referentiality and realism that caught me up. I couldn't stop looking at it.

I have to say that the talents she has brought to the project have come at a high price. Ever since her arrival last month, my solitary reveries are coming fewer and farther between, disrupting the illusion I had built up over the years that I was my own person and that I could retain the privacy of my own thoughts. I don't suspect anyone who knows me would guess what kind of conversations go on in my head or on paper. I have kept people at a distance. I prefer it that way, but after only two or three visits, she started coming into the house through the front door without notice. Last week, she treated herself to whatever she could find in the fridge like she was family. I never gave her this permission and frankly she never asked. I just started to notice that over the first weeks of her employment, she made herself more and more comfortable and I was so taken aback by her presumptions, I couldn't bring myself to tell her to bug off. So I have maintained my demeanor of cold indifference to her presence so as to communicate my disapproval, but either she doesn't care or is oblivious. She is an impulsive and enthusiastic personality, and she seems to enjoy showing off her youth and athleticism to me. I imagine that her husband, John, who is a bit of an introvert by comparison, must have to absorb waves and waves of emotions every day. It's a miracle he's still standing. He barely has the time or space to be interesting himself. I have compassion for him.

Just yesterday she complained about how dirty the bathroom was, cleaned it herself, and then shook her finger at me like I was some helpless old man. I discovered this morning that she seemed to have misplaced my razor that I like to leave on the edge of the sink for convenience. A man living alone all this time has a right to a certain claim on things remaining in their own idiosyncratic order and place. When I found it tucked away in the top drawer, I pulled it out and taped it down with masking tape. Perhaps that will let her know how I feel about misplaced things.

But listen to me, talking about misplaced razors. What I wanted to tell you is that this land contains more oddities than I had ever imagined and my mind is racing these days with questions about ecological complexity, about the paradoxes of interdependency, and even though this is a project of relatively modest ambition and God knows I am not writing it for those damn ivory tower specialists, I feel I might be on the verge of a truly new paradigm of understanding. And Alba is helping me. There is something about her artistic eye and the fact of her being foreign born that allows her to see beyond what the scientific eye can see. She is like my seeing-eye dog. I told her that once. I tried to anyway. It didn't come out right and she didn't take too kindly to the idea. I don't remember how it came out but it seems somewhere in the translation she thought I was calling her my bitch. I didn't even understand what that meant until she explained it to me. Every day it's a new adventure.

* * *

Another day. Another outing. Today we covered the northeastern slopes of Timpanogos. Alba couldn't make it, but no matter. I got in some good observations. I won't bore you with the details—they are in my notebooks—but it seems that the price of this winter's feeble snow is evident in the lower flows of spring water that seep through the ledges above Timpooneke trail. Especially in comparison to last year's snowfall. This has created some challenges for the flora. The monkey flower, by some miracle, always seems to find its little niche, sometimes in tiny clusters in the most unlikely and awkward places. The excitement of the morning was that Theo ran into a moose and about lost it. Poor thing was terrified. Thankfully, she spooked and ran past us as we moved ourselves into the scrub oak to get out of the way. I didn't care to go to the summit, but we did make it to the saddle where we were greeted by a small herd of mountain goats.

Theo recovered his bravery and tried to bark them away, but they stared us down without budging from the trail for a good five minutes. I couldn't shut Theo up. Their look is a haunting one, I tell you. I never quite get used to those creatures, what with their horns and long beards, like elderly men from another planet, and their eerie eyes. And so patient, silent, and wise. I did find the remains of what looked like one of their kin on the trail lower down. The lions are about, but I haven't seen any yet. There was plenty of lupine in bloom, especially once we got onto the main table below the saddle. It seemed a little early but then again so did the spring.

I'm somewhat ashamed about this, but I am not quite feeling the same satisfaction today as I usually do. Maybe it's just my usual struggle, I don't know. Or maybe my enervation is the spoils of a researcher who has grown so accustomed to discovery that surprise loses its luster. Fact blurs back again into fiction, and one comes to accept that what is most true is that truth can no longer be separated from desire. I confess that my passion for this earth is inseparable from my desire for you and your mother. By now, I realize that no matter how far I go or how hard I look to really see this world, I can't escape. It may be a world, but it's still my prison-house. This is hard to take, since I always believed my objectivity—my ability to detach and reflect—was the one advantage I felt I had over this community that is so given to self-reinforcing sentimentality and paranoid protectiveness and so caught up in the damn flow of things.

Perhaps you had hoped that I would be more gentle in my judgments by now, especially since I find myself staring at my own mortality. I am sorry if I disappoint you in this. It is just that there are those here who believe that the way you love something is to hold it tightly to your chest, protecting it from all harm and criticism. But that forces what you love to remain an object, impervious to the changes inflicted by time and happenstance, rather than letting it actually *become* anything. If this is your choice, however, you must remember that this will render you incapable of discerning between honest allies and insidious critics. You can circle the wagons so tightly around you that you might be the last one standing. Mormons may prevent the very things they desire to bring to pass (ah yes, I still remember those phrases): the flowering of this last dispensation of the fullness of times. What is full or timely about a timeless, static thing you endlessly thank God for the chance to caress?

I almost didn't find Alba. I had reached the end of my applicant list, as I said, so I made a call to the Art Department at Brigham Young University to see if there was someone else among their students I could recruit. It had been a long time since I had had any contact with the school, as you might imagine. While I was waiting for the secretary, who had introduced herself as Sandra Sorenson, to give me some names and numbers, I asked casually if she was related to Martin Sorenson. Lots of Sorensons around here, I know, but that's just it. They all must be related. "Oh," she said. "Were you a friend of his?"

"Well, yes, I guess we were friends. But it was many years ago now."

"He's my uncle. I am sorry to tell you this, but he died just last year. Colon cancer. He was eighty-seven."

Martin was my teacher and mentor and a great friend to me right at the time when I started seriously doubting my suitability for church life. I know it makes no sense. I mean, I had everything I had ever wanted: your mother, you, and an exciting life of the mind and in the outdoors. I do regret my depressions, my incapacity to love what I had. Especially considering what I have lost. That's what hurts the most. Martin was a good scientist, not terribly creative, but a good mind and more importantly a good heart. He was remarkable, really. He never flinched or seemed perturbed by my complaints about the irrationality of a belief in providence. He would listen to me explain how hard it was for me to reconcile the justice of God with suffering, how hard it was to understand the necessity of God in a universe as self-sufficient as this one, and sometimes if I got personal, about why despite my blessings, I found it so hard to believe in divine intervention or to just accept my gifts and be happy. My life sure never felt like it had any order to it—least of all the kind all the Mormons I knew seemed to enjoy—and maybe for a while there, being in love and finally, after so many years of trying, getting you, it felt like it might come into some shape and I could believe in providence. But then there were those moods, those dark clouds brooding over me, and my inner demons would erode my confidence in everything I thought I could touch and see as real. The blessedness of life would just run though my fingers like sand.

I told him of the miracles I heard about growing up and not a one of them ever witnessed by me. Far from it. Little tender mercies that seemed to happen to everyone but me, a sudden weather change (prayed for, of course), recovery from illness, a stroke of insight that resulted in a passed driver's exam, and then the kicker: Sister Biddulph. A woman who seemed to walk on water, all ablaze in grace and love, who lost her husband only for him to return to tell her that he would wait for her. And here I was, an orphan, see? Who was I to doubt her, but who was I to make any sense of such an event? And what was Martin's response? "Well, Zach, I don't know. I just don't know." But then I could never explain why I knew he felt I was wrong, or wrong-headed anyway. He used to say that one could be right about wrong facts, or wrong about right facts. That the mind needed the exercise of discipline but that it would remain a fickle and uncertain thing. Ritual was what gave life form, not ideas. His favorite? "Better to be good than to be right." I think he liked to sound esoteric and enigmatical. I sometimes suspected occasional puffery, but that man did give me pause.

So I was pained to imagine his death and to think that I never properly thanked him for the inspiration he was to me.

I admired him for the willingness to just listen. It kept me around. There's true Christianity in that, you know. You might think I have forgotten my doctrine, but I haven't. In fact, in some ways it burns more deeply into my soul than ever before. Lots of details have been lost to my understanding and much of the contemporary church makes little sense to me now, but I remember the meaning of charity is to bear all things, to mourn with those who mourn. That I remember.

I described what I was looking for, and the secretary gave me Alba's name. I didn't want some callow Mormon know-it-all who wasn't willing to take risks and I admit that I was suspicious that a woman could do the job. Go ahead and accuse me of sexism, but I am speaking of the problems in Mormon culture and not problems natural to the female sex. I don't know how you would have turned out, but the vast majority of these girls, I think, are marrying far too early, educating themselves far too little, and worrying themselves not a bit about anything other than the welfare of their own immediate circle of family and friends. The men aren't really any better—occupying themselves as they do with worries of work and financial stability but without a philosophical bone in their body. Except when they occasionally get into narrow doctrinal scrums with one another. I have heard such talk. It is as shallow as a kiddie pool, but they do enjoy the sensation of making a splash. Armies and armies of these types march out the doors of the Mission Training Center and out the doors of that university, all stable, loving men, without a hint of infidelity in them, but incapable of five minutes of interesting conversation. Fact is most of them don't know horseshit from honey butter. That's what I told her, the first week of her employment. I cleaned up my language a little but damned if I was going to walk around on eggshells.

"You need to get out a bit more." She stared back at me without irony. Her black hair was wrapped in a bandana behind her ears, poking out in unexpected directions. She brushed some of it from her face and placed it behind her ear. She shifted in the chair in front of me to adjust her bohemian yellow skirt.

"I beg your pardon?" I asked.

"I said, I think you need to get out a little more." She said this with greater care in enunciation and volume, as if my problem was bad hearing.

"Why do you say that?"

"Because I'm not sure who you are describing. I mean, if you're referring to the girls who grow up in small towns and marry out of high school, sure that still happens. But that has a lot more to do with their economic situation than their Mormon identity. And it might even happen from time to time here, but, setting aside the assumption that such things are a categorical mistake—and that's problematic to assume, if you ask me—if you're under the impression that that stereotype defines the majority of Mormon women my age, you're the one who is mistaken. Why are so many going to college? You should meet my classmates. Besides, when was the last time you spoke with a woman my age?" she asked with a bright smile. I stared back at her to see if she would flinch and the smile would collapse into open sarcasm and mockery.

It still didn't feel like an honest question, so I did not give an honest answer. "Just last week," I said.

"What? At the grocery store? Come on, all I'm saying is that I can handle this work and there are a lot more like me, so once you see the kind of work I can do, don't start thinking I'm an exception to some rule." I insisted that based on what I had seen, she was an exception, but she was adamant.

So you can see that she is not shy about arguing with me. I won't have her thinking that she is softening some hard-hearted bastard and that before long I will be begging for forgiveness and the chance to return to—what do you call it?—"full fellowship." This is one of the things that I find most maddening about Mormons. The way they love you, as if some grand and wonderful change is supposed to take place in your life just because you have met. I won't stand for such sanctimonious bullshit.

Sorry. Should I just say BS? Alba gets on me about my language. Fact is, I probably am related to the majority of people in this valley, and I don't hate them. I admire and envy them really, maybe not in the way your Mormon mind tells you I do, because it's not their beliefs I envy, it's their community, their connection to one another, and that way they have of finding themselves comfortable with people they hardly know. This is a beautiful thing. I remember that. And I remember that Mormons know how to weep with and for others. They have wept with me. You can feel some comfort in knowing that I have had my share of caretakers over the years, people who saw my losses and felt diminished by them. But I didn't ask for their sympathy and I didn't like the way it left me with the residue of obligation. My own burdens were enough for me and the thought that I had to go around for the rest of my life attending other people's funerals, weddings, and mission farewells, all of this was enough to drive me into the mountains for good. No, no thank you. A mountain and a book, that's all I need.

Do you remember the way you used to sit on the corner of a ridge and stare out over the valley, asking me where our house was, where your school was? There was something about the physical exertion it cost to get us there that released the tensions of the heart and we would talk. I am not much for small talk and I struggled when you were little. I couldn't think of what to say half the time. But on a mountain, we talked about everything and anything, and you so unafraid to ask questions, to make conjectures, and to experience the same joys with me. Your questions were beyond your age, even if they were simply posed. The mountains inspired this wisdom, I swear. You wondered about everything, and were always trying to understand who you were in relation to it all and what it all meant. What wisdom you must have now.

We would look down on the streets. So much noise, so much energy spent on human community, on defining and protecting social, political, and economic values, and yet hardly a moment's awareness of this vast expanse of deep time in which we wear out our brief days. Vanity of vanities. Despite the religious values that pervade every corner of this valley, we are as afraid of our mortality as the next person. What else explains this mad pursuit for the creature comforts that we acquire at rates that far outpace our aging? What else explains this obsession with the body, with beautification? And what, for that matter, better explains the ubiquitous denial of the damage we are doing to the planet? Mormonism has almost reached the peak of believing that heaven consists of reliable air conditioning, a great flat screen TV, and all the time in the world for popcorn. I remember your mother and I clearing out her parents' house after they passed away. There were new dresses in your grandmother's closet and unopened boxes of the latest gadgets in the garage. Which only means that most of us will never make full use of the things we own because there just isn't time. You would think that a fervent belief in eternal life would have resulted in something quite different: vows of poverty or droves of John the Baptists seeking sustenance from the wisdom of the wilderness on a diet of locusts.

This is our fundamental human failing, my dear. We humans don't like the life of the body, no matter how much we enjoy its pleasures, because it is always dying. We are like so many warm-blooded adolescents who still don't understand that life is short, pleasure will be stolen, and we are not the center of the universe. So I wonder what unity it was I felt with you and with the world? Was it biological? If not, then what made you and this place uniquely mine? Why, now, am I lost without you? And why do I only find familiarity in the face of a mountain but not in the faces of others?

* * *

We have had some productive outings this week, Alba and I. She is more freed up now that spring term has wound down, and because the season is ripe, I have wanted to get out as often as possible. Alba is now hired to work for me for twenty hours a week, not all of which would be spent at the house, of course, or even in the mountains since she needs time to do her own reading and painting, but I have tried to give her that time in the mountains as much as possible while the weather is so fair. It's still nippy at the higher altitudes and in the ravines. It keeps us alert. Alba arrived yesterday to discuss her findings, bringing me some texts that she had browsed or printouts from that blasted internet.

Anyway, she is now coming two or three times a week and always with questions and books and papers in her arm. Yesterday we must have talked for two hours. All about plant morphology, mainly. I had to dissect at least a dozen plants right there in the living room, just to help her learn her leaf blades from her petioles and her apical from her axillary buds and the reproductive parts. Once we were done talking things over, she made herself comfortable on the porch outside with her materials and painted for hours. As the late afternoon light began to dim, I went out to check on her. She was sound asleep. I roused her and tried to chastise her that she should be getting home. I really just wanted her gone, but I used the usual Mormon rhetoric about the importance of avoiding the appearance of evil. She looked at me in silence with a straight face for what seemed like several minutes and then burst into laughter. It was an awkward moment for which I could find no adequate response. But she did pack up and go home.

* * *

Sundays are always good for a long, solitary hike. I like to say that I attend the Wasatch First Ward. Theo and I just went straight up the ravine behind the house to find a perch and sit. From there at first I can see just a few cars belonging to those poor sots at their early morning meetings, and then by 9:00 am each chapel is completely encircled by vast pods of minivans, trucks, and the occasional Suburban. The streets are quiet, the air is still, the temperature about as perfect as it ever gets. This is my favorite time of year, no question.

I meant to say the other day that I don't pretend to know what you see and feel from your perspective now that you have gained the advantage of distance and time. But I do have to ask myself if these mountains and canyons haunt you, as they do me. I guess I like to imagine that it would signal some kind of forgiveness, and the world needs a lot more of that. Surely we can agree on that. I remember that fateful day when we thought we had been wronged in the Gulf of Tonkin. Something about being fired upon first, you see, only to later discover that we were the ones who began the battle. And yet we told ourselves we were fighting to protect something that apparently wasn't being attacked. I could feel the forces gathering, those that were demanding justice and reparation. In my experience, the word "justice" spoken by any mouth that is not the mouth of God always seems said through clenched teeth and with clenched hands and only portends violence. Forgiveness, not revenge, is the high moral principle, but I guess it is too naïve to expect a nation to behave like a man turning his cheek. I am not one to advocate pacifism in all circumstances but it does seem we ought to own up to the blood we surely have on our hands once we decided that we could right all wrongs. No doubt from your point of view, this is self-serving. Sinful men want mercy, of course, and the wronged want justice. All I mean to question is whether our feeble and violent methods will ever satisfy the demands for a fair world and if it isn't our intolerance and impatience with God's almighty slowness that makes the world so hellish. I mean if he is around up there, he sure as hell moves at a snail's pace, if you know what I mean. I don't know why he tolerates us. Or why we still tolerate him. To be honest, I certainly don't know why I am still breathing, still working each day, why he hasn't struck me dead with a falling rock by now, after so many years of hiking in these canyons alone. He has had his chances to take me, so the fact that I am alive at all I can only assume means that God's justice is beyond all reason.

It would be enough for me if you could at least remember American Fork Canyon. The way the edge of two mountains opened, split by the bracing white current of rushing waters that blur in their hurried pace to Utah Lake. After we perched above the valley, we wound our way up the canyon, Theo and I, and I have to tell you I don't know if I have ever seen it so beautiful. Okay, fall is great, but I prefer the fresh green of June. And what should I come upon as I walked along the river but two big horned sheep startled to see me on the other side. Theo was out of sight somewhere and missed the whole drama. They leapt with their auburn haunches into the scree above, sending a small rockslide in my direction. I was so startled myself that I came down on one knee and held my hand against my heart knocking against my ribs and the next thing I know I am crying.

My parents died years ago before you were born. I never told you all of it, I guess because you were so young and I didn't want to frighten you. My parents met relatively late in life, like your mother and I, in their thirties, which in those days was practically middle aged, and I was born as their only child. See a pattern? There was a miscarriage before I was born, I later learned, and this involved a name and a burial. I guess it was a little confusing to them whether or not he counted, you know, but they spent the money on a stone because they wanted him to have a place. His name was Joel. So then I came along, the veritable apple in their aging eyes. All in all, it was a decent start.

I don't know if you feel you had the same, but perhaps you can judge what value a happy childhood has when it is only short-lived. I have never known the exact circumstances, but Mom got addicted to opium not too long after I was born. Yeah, I know. Opium in Utah. But see there were opium dens in the early years of the twentieth century because of the Chinese labor that laid the railroad decades earlier, and I suppose it might have been an early Mormon attraction to alternative medicines or maybe she came into contact with opium even before Dad came into her life. I think I remember telling you about her adventure with her girlfriend traveling around the world. I certainly hope I told you because it seemed like something every woman, especially a Mormon woman, ought to do, before they get tied down with all that domesticity. But somewhere along the way she started a habit she could never break. Mom was a delight: sentimental, but always soporific and seemingly in a perpetual state of fading away. Until she did. I don't suppose I told you that I found her breathing unconscious on the sofa in our front room coming home from grade school. I do remember gently shaking her with no success. I sat on the corner chair and watched her lie there still for two hours, without moving, until Dad came home. She died two days later. I was seven.

I don't much blame Dad for how things went after that. He was studying soil engineering and this required that he travel frequently, enough that I was often bouncing from house to house and eventually from town to town. I left Price early enough that it is only a vague memory to me now. Maybe if he hadn't had to travel so much, he might have met someone new. We didn't have relatives in the area, so I was the perpetually adopted child. I wasn't really unhappy, just solitary. I suppose it was then that I learned the companionship of the mountains. It was a heart attack at age forty-eight, just after he had finished school, when I was eleven. Pushing a broken-down car, on assignment for the Bureau of Reclamation in the desolate region of the Uinta Basin.

We drove right past the place once on our way to a fishing trip on the Green River when you were eight, but I never told you.

I guess you could say that I was storm tossed by circumstances beyond my control before your mother came into my life. I had spent almost a decade working for the Forest Service, wandering the mountains alone, fighting fires, but generally avoiding contact with society. What it is exactly about love that makes you want to root yourself in a neighborhood of people and to work responsibly for a living, I will never understand. But in love I was. I followed her like a puppy, happy to be found, happy to have the prospect of a real life grounded in a community. I can see her outline walking ahead of me in that brisk way of hers, always charging up the trail with all four limbs in vigorous motion. I am not ungrateful that such memories still linger.

My point is that I have lived life without most of the dressings of American suburbia, outside of reasonable company, except for the few years we shared together, and you'd think that after so many years of solitude I would be content with silence. But the memories are not sticking, so I write. I still have photos, of course, and I do my share of blank and lonely staring, but it's when I close my eyes and try to picture you that I begin to panic. Why writing to you and telling you about my life would bring your face closer to me, I haven't the foggiest idea. Feel free to communicate any time you want, would you?

And yet I suppose I keep hiking because part of me thinks that it wouldn't be so bad to go the way of all the earth. *For all flesh is as grass, and all the glory of man as the flower of grass. The grass withereth and the flower thereof falleth away*. I think that was meant as an insult to our pride, but it could have been an invitation to a greater kingdom. Hiking alone around here requires a certain acceptance of mortality, since you never know if chance will finally take you with a rockslide, an avalanche, or the rare but not impossible bear or cougar attack. There are always those fifteen minutes or so in a hike when the hair on the back of my neck stands and I think, this could be it. And then I calm myself by telling myself that if it must be, it must be. This is it, I say. I think that I could do worse than to die torn and bleeding in the dirt. That sounds morbid, I know, but I really mean it. I have seen my share of dead deer, ripped and picked clean by packs of coyotes, and I think it wouldn't be so bad to have my cells dissipated into the detritus of the world. To be murdered by nature. Shat back into dust. I mean, when you think about it, who gets to escape such a fate in any case?

How is that for theology? I am sure you must think I am a coward. I am not one to believe that my agnosticism or atheism, or whatever it is, is a point of pride, that it is some kind of virtue to halt between opinions. I do admire those who have teetered and then finally made their leap. Truth be told, I envy them. It's the ones who never climb a fence high enough to even begin to teeter who mystify me. That's not an uncommon thing around here, as you know. So many will tell you that they have always known God to be real, always known that Christ was their Savior. I don't deny that some people are wired that way, but to use that as an invitation to belief is like telling the blind man that sight is like, well, not being blind.

I have to laugh at myself now because the only two metaphors about me that I could come up with paint me as a blind fence-sitter, just the sort of man I know people around here see me as. But I will tell you what I see and what my fiercest passions lay hold of, dear one. I see a world of incomprehensible beauty and complexity, one I never tire of observing. I see my home here in this valley and at the mouth of this beloved canyon, and I see I am not alone. I have the sun and stars as my guides. I wake to the earth's rotations. I have myriad companions—American dippers, the red-breasted nuthatch, rosy-finches, Steller's jays, not to mention the mountain goats and the deer. I don't know if it is fair to count the black bear or the mountain lion among my companions since they generally elude me, but I know they are there. They feel more present to me, in fact, than all the others, especially when I am high on the trails and away from all human contact. There are moose, of course, whom I have stumbled upon up among the basins and lush green areas below Timpanogos. And my beloved bighorn sheep.

If there is a God, he is somewhere in all of that wildness. I know that sounds like I am only restating an old idea. It's a bit more nuanced than that for me. I feel something divine in nature's absolute indifference to my presence, in the suspicion that I am nothing but a pair of lucky eyes to be spying in on such bizarre creatureliness. To find myself, even, in such a thing as this old bag of bones. I mean to say that if there is a God, he is not kind, he is not merciful, he may not even be lawful. We are still pretty much just beginning to understand what it is the world obeys, but I suppose if God is anywhere, he is in those laws. But that's just when things get interesting, you see, because for God to be in the diversity of life around me means that he is, as the great Haldane once said, guilty of "an inordinate fondness for beetles." Or for ants. Or for microbes. He certainly seems to like swallows. And bats. He really likes defecation and lots and lots of sex. Not to mention the unending violence. The point is, he doesn't seem terribly interested in *us*.

So I suppose if I find God, it is when I lose myself in this world, and that is not really so much a discovery of something or someone divine as it is a peaceful acceptance that I too am a dying body. This, I know, is a far cry from the idea of a personal, fatherly God up there. It's not that I don't like the idea. I barely experienced a biological father as it was. Besides, I am not averse to the idea that we are brothers and sisters, but biology already makes that clear enough. In fact, biology tells me my family is much larger than we think, or at least much more egalitarian. I reject the idea that this is some kind of large zoo we inhabit, some spheroid Ark carrying our pets, two by two, across the waters of the deep. At each turn this world proves resistant to every effort to tame it. It will not yield. So what motivates me, I suppose, is the chance to witness the evidence of its stubbornness and to embrace its defiant disorder. Lord help us when we can no longer feel the chaos of the wild pushing back against our passion for order and predictability.

Chapter 3

Alba couldn't escape the feeling that the earth seemed fragile to her, brittle, and maybe even suffering from a slight inadequacy. It had already been a tepid winter and a dry spring. Streams had long since lost their potency. Summer had advanced, as it always did, with the persistent monotony of dry, sunny, and hot days. The sear winds tossed the willows on the riverbanks and the cheat grass along the foothills, and the dimpled hearts of cottonwood leaves and the bladed leaves of mountain maples turned over and over again in the sunlight. The tall rye grass in the foothills had turned blond and the wildflowers at lower elevations had long gone to seed. Crackled stems, grayed leaves, and wilted bracken lay carelessly, wantonly about the mountainsides and forest floors, as the strange and fertile chemistry of the soil prepared to cannibalize the bodies of the dead. Reports of bear and lion sightings were on the rise, and their behavior seemed strange and unpredictable, as if they were no longer quite themselves.

And yet Alba knew too that the notion of fragility was absurd. Life was no pastoral affair; it was, as Mr. Harker was fond of quoting, "red in tooth and claw," fully functional, even if altered, due to its accommodations to chance, violence, and disturbance. If there was love in the world, the creation seemed unable or unwilling to give in completely to its force. Alba couldn't help herself. Maybe it was an incipient maternal urge in her, but she chose to care: she cared for the flowers, she cared for the mountain animals, and above all she wanted the balm of balance.

Every piece of trivia about this place fascinated her—the taste of horse mint or the name used to describe young, budding fern leaves ("fiddleheads!" she shouted joyfully to John as she arrived home one evening, "fiddleheads! Can you believe that name?").

But for every discovery that turned the world into something more familiar and more present, her mind circled back to her father and to Chile. John noticed that she had grown more pensive and withdrawn. She stared at her food in long silences or he found her sitting at the window gazing aimlessly. And she wondered out loud about Chile more than ever before, and he struggled to know what to say in response. Her homelessness had inspired him early in their relationship to want to surround her with the rituals and symbols of faith and national belonging his family offered.

He resented Mr. Harker. The way it sounded to John, Mr. Harker's world hummed like a machine and had no room for spirit. And all that bloody competition for life? How could that be a moral world? Where was the love, the hope in all of it, the cooperation? Where was the divine parentage of the human family? Why was this fascinating to Alba? Was she losing her faith? The more he listened to her reports about what she learned on the trails, the more removed he felt from the center of her excitement, just one year into marriage. She was still capable of raptures of affection for him, like she had been in the beginning, and part of him knew deep down they were genuine, but they were farther apart and were sometimes unexpected and almost irrational paroxysms that seemed to have no correspondence to their daily routines.

She called from Mr. Harker's. They were on their way from American Fork. Could they pick him up on the way to the Springville Museum? It was time to see the exhibit that had been announced in advance of the Olympics with considerable fanfare. They were Utah landscapes, the most comprehensive exhibit of its kind. John dreaded the thought of listening to more of Mr. Harker's long-winded opinions. The old man was never happy. Whatever this place offered, it was never enough. John had lived in Utah long enough to know the type. Always needing to announce to others just how confident he was in his embrace of the secular pleasures denied his fellow citizens. "Do you have any idea what a paradise it is to hike in Utah Valley on a Sunday, what with all of you poor sots in suits and ties on the pew?" he said once with a grin.

Things hadn't gone smoothly when Alba went to pick up Mr. Harker. She had arrived at the door and knocked repeatedly for a good five minutes before she heard some rustling in the house and finally Harker's footsteps coming to the door.

"Coming. Coming." She heard him grumble. When the gray door opened there was hardly any light in the house and Mr. Harker stood behind the dark screen door in his pajamas. His hair, always a little disheveled, was more so than usual.

"Did you forget I was coming?" asked Alba.

"No. No. I, uh . . . look: why don't you just have a seat there on the porch and I will be out shortly."

Alba sat on the old porch swing. The seat itself was discolored, in a faded and splotchy pink, as if painted for a child. The pillars of the veranda showed signs of warping, the paint long since eroded. One couldn't run one's hand along any surface of the railing without getting plenty of slivers. She imagined that maybe she and John could surprise Mr. Harker some day with a newly sanded and repainted porch. It certainly needed it. Surely his neighbors, mostly Mormon, knew of his existence, and surely they would have offered help. Even the tree cover the house enjoyed and its offbeat location in the gully below Timpanogos Highway couldn't evade their charity. Knowing Mr. Harker, he had probably rebuffed them enough to wear down their long-suffering.

She loved the feeling of the place, so unkempt, so comfortable with the oak trees, cottonwoods, and wild grass around it. He wasn't one for doing his own landscaping, but he loved his wildflowers. Seeds had no doubt been strewn about the yard a long time ago, because now the long and uncut grass was interspersed with Scarlet Gilia, red and purple penstemons, yellow buttercups, and he had never cleared any of the rabbitbrush. In back, there was his small garden. He was religious about it. Always gnawing on the peas or carrots, even with dirt still on his hands.

As she slowly swung on the chair, she could hear Mr. Harker talking inside on the phone. He sounded agitated, but she couldn't make out the words. But his voice started to grow in volume, until she could finally make out one phrase, "No. No! She was not! That is an insult to her!" She could hear that his voice was shaking with rage and then the phone slammed down. Never had he mentioned a woman in his life and she had never heard him speak with that kind of emotion. She could hear him muttering to himself and gathering his things and then suddenly he burst through the door and walked straight down the steps to the grass without waiting for her.

"Let's go," he said brusquely.

He sat in the passenger seat, waiting for her to get in the car, staring straight ahead.

As they pulled out, he was quiet.

"Everything okay?" Alba asked. No response.

"I love the feeling on your veranda. Do you sit out there much?"

"What for?"

"Just to enjoy your place. It feels wild and lonely. I love it."

"It's home."

"Seems like that swing was made for a child."

Mr. Harker reached into his backpack impulsively and began searching for something. He cursed. "Sorry. I mean, 'dang it to heck!'" he said in a mocking tone.

"Forgot something? I can turn around."

"No. No. Just, just . . . I'm fine. Keep going." He sat back in the seat and faced the road blankly. Alba didn't want to provoke him, so she just tried to strike up a neutral conversation.

"I am really excited to see this exhibit. I am hoping it will give me some inspiration. A couple of my teachers are in it, you know."

"God, I hate this traffic. And these homes! Like pimples! And this growing haze, can you see it? Our destroying angel waiting to strike."

Earlier that month he had ranted on about the curse of automobiles, about how they were connected to virtually all the essential flaws in our character as a nation—our willingness to trade death and degradation for speed and convenience, to the point of naturalizing the costs and consequences of the automobile as the normal conditions of life when, in fact, there was nothing accidental about air pollution, death, and maiming, not to mention the untold roadkill. And about the addiction to oil, the becoming a slave to the very source of energy that is now doing untellable damage to the climate. What was more problematic, he said, was the illusion of autonomy and separation from the world. A slow and sudden destroyer. And did Christians show any compunction in embodying those flaws? No sir, he said. What a joke: Americans still sometimes confuse Mormons with the Amish, as if Mormons might have the courage to disavow modern conveniences! Did she realize, he had asked, how our insatiable hunger for the automobile had caused everything to shift from agriculture to the family organization to our sense of place—all just to accommodate the fact that we no longer want to walk to the market but instead seek one-stop shopping as *the* goal of life? Paved roads appeared in even the most remote areas to make them accessible, blurring boundaries to the point that we have had to fight over the definition of wilderness. And what do they base that definition on? On whether automobiles and roads are allowed. Our love affair with the invention of the car and our dependence on fossil fuel, he insisted, had determined the majority of our foreign policies and politics over the past fifty years. And what had it done to our sense of community, he had asked, besides making it possible to live next to someone and only wave as we pull in and out of our driveways? We evaluate quality of life, he had said, based on how oblivious we can be to the well-being of our environment. As long as we can get everywhere we need or want to go, little else matters. The automobile made it possible for patriots to feel good about themselves because of their kindnesses toward their nuclear and extended families, as if that were the only community that mattered, and as long as everyone was happy and having a good time, then there was no need to worry about the rest of the world and its problems. The hardest kind of flaw to overcome, he had said, was a flaw justified by a virtue. Our virtue is democracy, which makes it almost impossible for us to recognize how we sometimes impose our democratic values on others in the most undemocratic of ways, never asking if our presence is really wanted. As long as they are protected and happy within their full-service automobiles on a long road trip to Lake Powell, others who complain about gas-guzzling, about environmental damage, about our obsession with pleasure and entertainment, can be seen as unpatriotic and anti-family.

He was in the same mood again today. She had to keep him from spiraling downward. Maybe a change of topic?

"One of my professors," she said, "has been trying to get us to see beyond representational depictions of the landscape. Says it is our obsession to see the world framed and beautiful, so that we can hold it intact on our walls, but no longer so that we can experience it, you know. It reminded me of what you have been saying about context."

"Well, I am not one for abstract gobbledygook, if that is what you are thinking. I mean, I want to see the location, the particular trees, the ecological truths of a place. I detest pretension, you know, the kind that seems to say, 'Look at me! I am being an artist!' I much prefer the anonymity of an honest look at the world. That is wonder enough." He was gearing up for a debate, but it seemed at least to lighten his mood.

"Well, I think her point was that it's foolish to believe that you can hide yourself, you know, from what and how you see. Even Monet," she said. "He saw the world filtered through a particular eye, a mind, a personality, and a history, and we might as well be honest about that. That's how I understood it."

"Well, it was one helluva an eye."

"That's funny. Some critic once said the same thing." Maybe agreement would reassure him.

"So what does she advocate that you paint? Your navel?"

She laughed. "Like I said, it was like what you've been saying. She said instead of trying to paint a thing, paint a relationship to that thing. Does that make sense? I thought, this is what I have been trying to do."

"Well, as long as you don't start painting these flowers as some form of autobiography! I mean, what is it with artists and writers these days, always assuming that their life stories are worth telling! Who asked them to share all those stories of domestic embarrassment? Who the hell cares about their brother or their grandpa and their favorite fishing trips? This is the age of self-indulgence. It happened to me, so it must be worth making others have to listen. That's about as far as they go in their thinking. They just dump it in your lap. It's not my fault if their life is boring as hell."

She wasn't sure how to respond. She turned off the highway to pick up John. Mr. Harker was silent. "Where does your intense love of nature come from anyway?" she asked.

There was a long pause. Mr. Harker rolled down his window and stuck his arm out. He looked out at the lake to the west. The sun was high, just past noon, and its reflections shimmered on the surface of the water. The Geneva Steel factory stood silently on the shoreline, and across the lake stood West Mountain with its gentle slopes. He finally spoke up. She leaned over to hear better. "I have never been asked that question before. Do you realize that? In all of my life, I am not sure I have ever been asked. I need to think about it."

"Did you ever have a family?" Maybe if she just came out and asked, it would seem natural.

"What's that?" He didn't raise the window but instead leaned out a bit more as if to create more air resistance. She repeated the question.

He acted as though he hadn't heard her at all. No answer was forthcoming. She was going to talk this over with John. His silences were almost childish, but she decided it best not to push.

After a few minutes of silence, he returned to his rant. "What is it about our predilection for billboards in this state? Can you make sense of it? Rather than looking at this incredible place face-to-face, we prefer to see images of the Thomas Kincaid gallery or to think about the next place we might make a purchase." She knew he was gearing up again, but maybe she could get it all out of him before John got in the car. John was not as fascinated by his diatribes as she was. In fact, he seemed increasingly irritated by the old man and distracted when she would come home to give her reports.

"This is one is my personal favorites." Maybe if she joined him, she thought. Alba pointed to a billboard that had a giant picture of a red-faced Indian, apparently a painting from the nineteenth century, with huge letters that said, "The Lure of the West."

"This is the special Smithsonian exhibit for the Olympics. It is spectacular. But I keep thinking how strange it is to advertise on a billboard for people like Bierstadt and Thomas Moran, while blocking the view of the mountains that inspired them."

"I don't know. Seems appropriate, doesn't it? The so-called 'New West' is just another billboard, Alba." His voice was calmer.

Once they got off the highway the Saturday traffic through town was slow as usual.

"But who knows, maybe this exhibit will surprise us," he said. "You see, it's not the big name artists that matter anyway. Those guys were all sponsored and passing through, looking on the West as a curiosity. What you want, what we still need, is the loving eye of someone, I don't know . . . it's not that they have to be native, because of course no one was. It's something else."

"Love, maybe?" Alba asked.

Mr. Harker looked at her quizzically.

"I mean, devotion, you know, a loving eye for what's now theirs. That's something, isn't it?" She glanced to see his reaction. He seemed pleased. She had calmed whatever storm had been brewing.

"It's everything. The 1860s. Imagine. Local artists removed from their arrival by just a few, slim years. You have barely built your own shelter and secured your survival in the wilderness, and you find the impulse to want to make art out of your new home? That *is* something. And it makes you wonder, who would want these paintings? Who could buy them and to what purpose?"

"I had never really thought of that before. They barely had houses then, right?"

"Houses, brick houses anyway, came with irrigation and the family farm. Slowly. Maybe at first the paintings served their true purpose of helping to open the eyes of the people to the beauty around them, to inspire a kind of reverence. But we killed that a long time ago. Nowadays, if you don't paint pretty landscapes that some rich guy can own in his big beautiful house—you know, the kind of house that ruins the very landscapes he wants commemorated on his wall—well then you might as well just get out of the way. You offer some criticism of society, even implicitly, in the painting and you are doomed, it seems to me. Just make it safe and comfortable and beautiful. And whatever you do, don't let your art be a mirror into the human soul, God forbid. Or a representation of what we are damaging. We wouldn't want people repenting, now would we!"

"I am not sure that the arts would have existed here at all if it weren't for Brigham Young. Theaters, temples, schools, all those.

He sent men to Europe to be trained, you know. Their conditions may have been primitive, but they were not primitive people."

"Fair enough, but I am not sure Brother Brigham wanted secular art. Landscape paintings for their own sake, you know, just plain devotion to physical beauty. He wanted something more spiritually devotional, that pointed the eye away from this world and toward the world to come, you know?"

"Oh, I disagree, Mr. Harker. He wanted the earth painted on the inside of the walls of temples. This earth, this beauty. The earth as a reminder of God's glory."

"All right, fair enough. But let's be honest: it would have been very difficult for the average Mormon immigrant to want to spend time to appreciate the earth. I mean, this place must have seemed so foreign, so hostile to their intentions. Who wants to stop and enjoy beauty when they are trying to survive, to overcome the threat that nature poses to their very existence? But we conquered, you know? And now look at us. The experience of such intense suffering was beat into us, you see, to the point now that we recreate with desperation and in considerable irritation whenever anyone tells us that we are doing the world harm. But we love this place, we say! Look at us loving it to death, we say! Deep down all we really want is nature to make us feel free from accountability. We certainly don't want it to remind us of our mortality or our mistakes. So play we must! Sure we can notice a little beauty now and then, but let's not get carried away and think that that we owe anything to that beauty!"

It was the first time she had ever heard him use the first person plural in reference to the Mormons. She wanted to point it out, but thought better of it. She had to admit to jealousy: even after all these years of living in Utah, her experience was the opposite. This was her community, her people, but she still referred to the pioneers in the third person. It wasn't her history, even if it was her heritage. A mission to Ohio and marriage to John had at first helped but lately it seemed there was a widening chasm between her and any kind of American home.

"Hmmm. I've never thought that landscape art was secular, but maybe that's just me."

"Maybe. Maybe not, but let's admit it: loving natural beauty doesn't come easily to the religious."

"I totally disagree."

"Then tell me why Christians the world over have persecuted pagans for being nature lovers, for hugging their damn trees, for loving nature more than people? Who decided a Sunday hike was a bad thing? The only reason recreation is secular is because they chose to make it that way. It's now a perversion of what was once a religious rite. Why make one day special anyway? Sin the rest of the week, I guess, and then get holy on Sunday."

"Well, I for one enjoy a good hike on a Sunday, just not the big ones I guess. I mean, I think we should be in church too, but why not have both? The Sabbath is a way to give the creation a rest. That was its purpose. I would've thought you liked that. All those Mormons and their cars. They stop working, stop driving. One day every week. They stay at home. That has to count for something."

"They sure as hell drive to church."

"Fair enough, but it isn't the same as driving to work, running errands. They should get a one-seventh carbon credit, don't you think?"

He looked at her and paused. "Maybe . . . maybe one-tenth of a credit. Don't forget all those leather belts and ties and dress shoes and all those damn minivans and SUVs. That has to be factored in. Just don't let your fourteen-year-olds sneak off into the woods—they might see God, after all!"

She laughed. When she remembered not to react defensively, she found genuine humor in his comments. He seemed to enjoy her laughter and it helped take the edge off whatever was bothering him. She had heard John's father complain that liberals worship the creation instead of the Creator, and some of her classmates had argued to her that environmentalists lack faith that in the end everything will work out and that the next life will be so much better than this one. She kept such thoughts to herself.

"In the end, what good is nature? That's the question. Because if it is just stuff, things to be used, bought and sold, and this is just some rental home we can trash and leave behind for the maid to clean up, what good is your religion? That's what I want to know. What good are *you*?"

She knew this would be another of his conversations that she would stew over for days. He was right about many things. Right, and wrong too. But she didn't feel smart enough to keep up. She couldn't draw a bead on him, in any case. He was slippery.

"So where do you stand? You don't seem too interested in finding God out there in the mountains, you know. Besides, since when is Mormonism just like any other Christian church? Weren't you just complaining the other day that no one seems to get us? I can barely look at the world and not feel a spiritual presence all around me." She muttered to herself: "Living souls."

"What's that?"

"Living souls. That's what we believe trees are. All of it. Trees, birds. The world is full of God's glory. That's what I think, anyway."

Mr. Harker raised his eyebrows.

"That's just it, Alba. Mormonism *is* different, but Mormons aren't acting any differently toward this earth than anyone else. So in the end, what good are those beliefs? I don't suppose you are like most Mormons, Alba. In fact, I think you are who you are and see the way you see despite being a Mormon, not because of it."

Alba bristled. "I'm sorry, but what do you really know about me? You don't even know where my Mormonism comes from." He had touched a nerve. She could feel her heart starting to race just a bit. She didn't want to respond to his bait, but his comment seemed to erase all the work she had put into being a Mormon, all the work of trying to become Christian. The very idea of being "naturally" one way or another had always offended her sensibilities. She disliked it when people made assumptions about Latinos or women being naturally spiritual or Mormons being naturally nice. Whatever goodness she had, it was work. And it was a choice. If there was one thing she initially loved about being a Mormon and about America, it was the idea that biology could not have final claim on her, that with enough faith and hard work, she could change her destiny, her very character. In America you were never bound by the past.

"No, I don't. But I do know that you weren't born here, and that your family history has to have a lot to do with you."

"And what do you know about my family?" Her voice was raised now and the warm feelings between them were gone. She gripped the steering wheel tighter and wondered if she was going to lose it.

"Nothing. The question is, what do you know?" He sensed weakness and was boring in.

"Look. Let's drop this subject, do you mind? I have spent far more effort than you can imagine seeking to understand and conform myself to the will of God. That's all you need to know about me. I take my religion very seriously and for you to call that into question is offensive."

"Okay. Okay. Cool it." He threw his hands into the air. "I didn't mean to upset you. I am just of the opinion that religious conviction isn't any different than other convictions: they stem from our history and our psychology. You can't pretend to worship God in some kind of vacuum."

"I worship him with blood, sweat, and tears." Her eyes grew glassy from the tears. She realized she probably sounded overly dramatic to him, no doubt evidence for him of her female hysteria or Mormon emotionalism. She stared straight ahead at the road with her eyes wide open waiting for the air to dry her eyes.

"You never told me why you worship nature, so why are you any better?"

"I think I know, Alba."

"Okay, so what is the big secret?"

"Did you know that that mountain there on the southwest shore marks a battle between the Mormons and the Utes that took place in 1849?" He pointed to the mountain. "It was a bloody mess. Piles of unburied bodies of Indians were left on the ice, in the middle of the winter."

"That's awful."

"Not all that shocking considering the time."

"What's your point?"

"My point? My point is that I can't look at that mountain without thinking of those losses. No one should. It's the same this whole place over. Nature's . . . it's a kind of commemoration. That's why."

When they arrived at the house, John was sitting on the curb. When he got in the back of the car, Alba turned and smiled, with a face that was enigmatical.

After a few minutes, Mr. Harker spoke up. "The greatest irony of this exhibit, you know, is that we flatter ourselves into believing that the whole world has come to see us, but we are really only generating new excuses to stare at ourselves. Have you seen all the pre-Olympics events up in Salt Lake? I am willing to bet that at least eighty percent of those who have attended were from the membership of the church from the area, coming to enjoy the fact that they were being observed by the world. Isn't that a trip. People watching themselves being watched, even before anyone else has bothered to show up, as if anyone cared!"

"Mr. Harker, don't go denying that you have been itching to see this exhibit," said John.

"John, itching is what I do when I encounter a patch of stinging nettle."

John looked into the rearview mirror to try to catch a glimpse of Alba's face. Alba stared silently at the road ahead.

Why Alba put up with this man was beyond John. He knew Alba had gone out of her way to get Mr. Harker out of the house for this trip, and this was the kind of thanks she got. John, on the other hand, wasn't much for museums and he struggled to understand Alba's art. It wasn't that he didn't like art or that he was unresponsive. He had chosen to major in philosophy because the rigorous logic of the classic philosophers would be the best help, he had been told, for law school. And more specifically because it was in his sophomore year, just a year after having returned from his mission in Ecuador when he came to the realization that he was Platonic, not Aristotelian. Learning about the ancient struggle between the great teacher and his most brilliant student helped him to understand why, if he preferred any kind of art, it was art that pointed directly and unambiguously to God and Christ as the source of all truth. He was suspicious of art that lingered too long on the ordinary or the ugly or that indulged in self-obsession only to then pretend to have reached for the heavens, but he knew enough, especially about his own wife, to understand how dated his views would seem to her, so he always tried to act interested, even if he didn't quite get it. He didn't feel altogether guiltless about his deception, because deep down he suspected that he was ignorant. Maybe it was Alba's sheer passion, the way she leapt into art without hesitation. No self-doubt, no circumspection. Hers was a genuine passion and a genuine set of convictions. Landscape art, bordering on the edge of abstraction, she said, was the greatest achievement of art. There was something, she said, about the way the world stops seeming to be out there but then starts to become an internal landscape of the mind. And in the end, she said, we are never sure which it is, as if the mind and the world had finally become one. She had taken a class on the early modern period and discovered a strong love for the artists and their work. John always wanted to nurture her interests, so after shopping around for a gift for her birthday, he found and bought her an edition of Kandinsky's early landscapes. She was ecstatic and pored over its pages for hours. It was habit now for her to consult it before embarking on a new work. The truth is, he found the book a bore and when he looked at one of her paintings and she looked to him for feedback, he was never quite sure what to say. She would describe the experience of painting, or she would compare the results of one work with another, but he would never quite see what it was that she was describing. It was like they were looking at two different things altogether even when they were standing together, shoulder to shoulder, looking between the same four borders of the frame. She would see an actual experience and he would see lines and colors struggling to coalesce from abstractions drawn from nature. He couldn't help but feel a vague urge to want to finish the work somehow, maybe to draw the lines tighter, to make the representations more real. It seemed to play too loose with the fundamental structures of the world. Batten down the hatches, he thought. Secure the anchor. Stop the drift, the uncertainty, the perpetual wandering of the brush. But he held back from saying anything. It was that fire in her that he wanted to keep burning even as he envied it.

When they were dating, she had tried to communicate to him the rules of composition. They were sitting on top of Squaw Peak above Rock Canyon after an afternoon hike and they could see for miles in every direction. She was explaining how composition works, how it selects and eliminates simultaneously. Touching both thumbs together and creating right angles with her index fingers, she made a portion of a square that she moved closer and farther away from her eye, and then made John do the same.

"Can you see how what fits into the frame changes so dramatically just with a few inches of distance from your eye? As you look down on the valley from here with no frame, other than the frame of your own two eyeballs, you can see more than you can represent." John did as he was instructed. "Now, turn forty-five degrees to the left and do the same thing."

John shifted his position on the rock and moved his hands back and forth in front of his right eye.

"You see, it is a different world altogether than the one we were just framing over there." She pointed back to where they had been looking to the north. "Now try it with objects close by. Here, frame this group of rocks here and see what happens." John obeyed. "It is agonizing, really, when you realize how much there is to see and how little you can fit into just one frame." Her voice was earnest with an underlying thrill of flirtation. "The trick is to represent in such a way that the world outside the frame . . . how do I explain it? It needs to open rather than close. You have to be capable of imagining what the painting chose not to represent." He kept moving his hands closer and then farther away as he looked around him. She smiled at him, apparently pleased with her pupil. She pulled his hands down from his face, flipped her hair behind her, and kissed him passionately. All he could see was the lobe of her ear and the soft flow of her black hair before he closed his eyes and the world outside fell away. He could withstand a thousand lectures on art for the chance to hold on just a little bit longer.

Maple Mountain stood to the east from State Street. The Russian olives hid the eyesore of the industrial park to their right, but they could not hide the pungent odor of smelter and of the rendering plant. From a slight hill, they could see the whole valley floor spread out before them, Mount Nebo marking the southwestern edge of the mountains that swung all the way around to the left, like a belt. The mountains' brown facades with their rough green patches of scrub oak and their striated texture were expressions of solidity and force. A portion of the mountains directly east had been on fire for a week, and they could see that the damage had run from where the houses began all the way up the mountain and into the canyons beyond the valley. Some kid had shot a firecracker or lit a cigarette in his boredom and the fire spread, lapping up the green and tan colors, leaving behind a black and brown remainder. After the blackened orange evenings with their surreal sunsets and the days of white skies, the air had finally cleared. The helicopters continued to fly overhead, carrying water.

They pulled up to the museum with rose-bush sculptures of cowboys that were laid out with care in the entry. Mr. Harker became quiet and serious as they entered the museum and immediately began looking at the earliest paintings at the beginning of the exhibit. John didn't last long in front of a few paintings before he found a bench to sit on and read. Alba and Mr. Harker meanwhile found themselves staring at each one for long periods of time. John looked up from his book to see Alba calling Mr. Harker over to examine one work in particular, an 1868 image of the Salt Lake Valley by George Martin Ottinger, an early Mormon artist who spent his life, after many travels, in the new Holy Land and consecrated his art to the building of the church in the West. The painting was full of rusted browns and faded blues and captured perfectly the dimness of Utah colors—what to many of the early settlers surely must have been an absence of green—and perhaps of beauty itself. So although Alba could detect all the signs of a classically designed landscape, including the unique vantage point of the valley behind Fort Douglas, with two figures observing from a bluff in front, below their own perspective as viewers with the painter, she loved that the painting refused to exaggerate a beauty that didn't exist. Ottinger somehow saw, in the valley's limited range of color, and in the almost humorously humble signs of civilization sprouting along the desert floor, a subject worthy of art in the nothingness around him. Of course, it was impossible to look at such an image without seeing in the mind's eye the absolute revolution that had transpired on that valley floor since those simple beginnings. All of the space in the painting, Alba commented, is now covered with homes, industry, and roads, all the way to the Salt Lake that stretches with its gentle ocean blue across the horizon cradled by the moonlike peaks of Antelope Island. Soon, soon enough would come the development of the avenues, the Federal Heights neighborhood, the capitol building, Temple Square, and the University campus that would occupy the scrub oak and sage in the very space from which he painted. The air, even on a good day, would never again expose such integrated color and light from the finely wrought clouds that Ottinger reflected in the rusts of the valley floor, with its drying grasses and dinosaur soil. So much death since his time—death and irrevocable change. Perhaps this really was a landscape of the imagination, she thought, or at least might as well be, since what it documents no longer resembles what the eye can see now. But at least then to have imagined the world this way, this was a gift. Or an adequate response. The world is lost long before one reaches for the pen or brush. It is always and already a world of one's own making. However intensely motivated by the urge to be present in the world, every work of art becomes a testament to exile. So then it becomes a matter of deciding what kind of world she wants. Now this image would become a part of what she would see whenever she looked at Salt Lake Valley, haunted by a landscape of the imagination. Perhaps too there is an even deeper landscape, graven upon one's mind from birth, memories of an earth never experienced but never forgotten.

Alba lost all sense of time in a museum. She would not remember to eat a meal if it weren't for a museum's fixed hours. She was transfixed by another painting, and this time John, perhaps a little jealously, approached her to see what had grabbed her attention. It was a scene of an aspen grove behind Timpanogos, painted by John Hafen in 1900. As he approached, she started to talk about the influence of the impressionists under whom he briefly studied to paint the murals of the Salt

Lake temple, with the looser brushstrokes, the splash of light against the silvered leaves, and the whited bark, catching the motion of air among the mountains.

"I simply adore this, don't you?" said Alba. "It seems so much more painterly than the others, more willing to love the least significant place. It is such an ordinary, almost spontaneous frame, too, the way it refuses to let you pull back and take it all in. You can only peek through the trees and catch glimpses of that magnificent mountain hovering in the background. It just seems so honest. And to think that this place has hardly changed in a century—I was just hiking there last week, and it seems the very same."

"What do you mean by 'painterly'?" asked John.

"As opposed to mimetic, right?" she looked at him. "It means the painter is less interested in realism and more interested in describing his relationship to what he sees. Plus, it means we can see the brushstrokes, like it wants us to notice that it is a work of art. I mean, it is no work of modern art, but compared to the other images, you can start to see an acceptance that what the painter sees is not what the world is exactly. It is a more interior landscape in that way. More poetic. Does that make sense?"

John recognized the idea. Aristotle had tried to topple his great teacher, Plato, by insisting on the value of imitation as a means to higher truth. But Plato was right to be suspicious of art, of all forms of imitation, because they too easily distracted us from the higher truths. This, for John, was also why he struggled to understand the place of art. Revealed truth. That should be enough.

"You don't have to convince me that imitation doesn't get us anywhere," John offered. "You know me. I like the ideal. But I don't see how this painting isn't imitative. I mean, it's a picture of aspens in the forest. We can all recognize that it's Utah, not just any place: it's the Timpanogos area. I mean, the whole point of this show is to celebrate Utah. Otherwise, it would be all abstract art, art about anywhere, any time. So how is that poetic? I guess I'm confused. I know you'll hate me for saying this, but sometimes I just wonder what it's for." There was a pause. Alba didn't flinch but remained focused on the painting. "Art, that is." John worried that maybe he had crossed a line but it felt good to confess the truth.

Alba's expression grew deeper in thought. She put her hands on her hips and started to stammer. But Mr. Harker, like the original snake, had been listening to the young couple deliberate in their garden and jumped in to set new terms for the argument.

"I think you miss the point, Alba. The point is that what we are looking at in this image is not, in fact, around anymore. It is dead and gone. It is a portrait of a world lost to development. You cannot forget about the development of Sundance and all those homes and try to pretend that nothing has changed. Let's face it, Alba, Sundance is an enormous difference from then until now. Don't get me wrong. Sundance is great, and things could be a lot worse up there. God knows they are worse almost everywhere else, but I have seen pictures of the area from when my parents attended BYU in the 1910s and the freshman class always used to take a hike up here. It was nothing but a family ranch; it was a glacier too. That's all but gone. I am telling you, it's not the same."

Alba didn't hesitate here. "Okay, fine. Not as raw as it was before the Mormons came. But the real question is, where does it end? This nostalgia?" Alba asked, with honest concern. "I mean *everyone's* past is the Eden to today's fallen world, right?"

"Right. Nostalgia is toxic," Mr. Harker said with sincere resignation.

John stared at Mr. Harker, trying to read his face. The man grew more mysterious to him every time they were together.

"So how do you live with that?" asked Alba.

"You don't. It's no way to live, Alba." Mr. Harker spoke earnestly. Alba looked at him closely.

"Okay, but still. How do you overcome it, then?"

"You don't. You stifle it; you bury it. You try to forget it. Repression as a way of life. That's it." The energy had gone from his voice.

"Well, that's just terrible. Is there really nothing left worth celebrating in your view? That can't be true. You want to do this book. What's that all about if not an effort to honor what we have?"

"Honor it before it is inevitably gone. On my darker days, I'm not sure what for. Maybe it's nostalgia for a future that will never arrive."

"You mean you have days that aren't so dark?" John asked. "I wonder what those are like." Alba gave John a disapproving glance. John shrugged his shoulders in response and mouthed, "What?" out of sight Harker's sight. Mr. Harker stuck his hands in his pockets and turned to look at more paintings. John slumped back to the bench.

"I was looking at this one earlier and I didn't get it. What does 'Halcyon Days' mean?" Alba asked as she approached Mr. Harker, who was examining a more primitive nineteenth-century painting.

"The good old days, the salad days, when things were peaceful. But did you know that the halcyon is actually a bird, the kingfisher?" Mr. Harker grew animated again. "A nesting kingfisher was believed to be an omen of calm and good weather in the depths of winter for the Greeks. It comes from the tales of Ovid when animals and humans were interchangeable. Turns out the daughter of the wind was married and her husband died at sea, so she threw herself into the ocean to drown, and instead of drowning, she was transformed into a bird whose flight across the waters was carried by her father's winds. To the Greeks, it was the most natural thing in the world to understand how intertwined we were with the climate. We could learn a lot from those old stories."

"Wow, that sounds amazing. I need to read Ovid! What did he write?"

"*Metamorphoses*. Tales of transformations. Great stuff. You know, it was over two thousand years ago that he wrote it, and in it he said his written words would make him immortal. Prophetic. Bold as hell. And we haven't come close to exhausting those myths."

"Too bad the painting seems so simplistic, though. With the exception of the brushwork on those leaves hanging over the pond, it feels naïve, don't you think? I mean, look at the reflection of the cabin in the water, with its sweet little trail of smoke coming out the chimney. No subtlety at all. The water is simply a mirror, all the images reflected with the same adorable exactness. It feels too cute, too cherished."

"I don't know. I guess I am getting soft in my old age. This just makes me sad. It's more profound than you think, despite its weaknesses."

At this, John rose again to make another go at it.

"What's profound about it?"

"It shows how the painter felt deep nostalgia for what we see here, how he had a sense that something was deeply right about simple living in a natural world that provided the necessary comforts and means of life. Given his conditions and his time, I think that is pretty remarkable."

"Well, maybe that is profound, Mr. Harker, but I'm with Alba. It seems profound despite the painting, doesn't it? I mean it was painted in what?" He leaned forward to read the plaque. "It was painted in 1885, almost a hundred and twenty years ago, and he is already nostalgic for the simple country life. That tells you something, doesn't it?"

"Tells you what?"

"It tells you that even though we look back on that time as the halcyon days, or whatever, as you call it, and yet he already felt that this golden age was already lost."

"What's your point?" Mr. Harker looked at him skeptically.

"My point? I would hate to spend my life in permanent regret. I mean, if this guy felt that way about something already gone, or going out, way back then, then maybe that says something about our own regrets, you know?"

Mr. Harker paused in thought and then said, "You know, my parents were born only ten years after this painting was done."

"No kidding? Wow!" John blushed as he realized the condescension of his astonishment.

Mr. Harker was unfazed. "Despite your youthful distaste for this work, it represents something truthful about all artists."

"What's that?"

"That artists all live with a painful awareness of transience and change. That what stands before you will shortly vanish, and your only consolation is that you might be able to arrest time artificially on your canvas. All art, then, is a lie. Or maybe it is some kind of elegy inspired by the law of death."

"I don't know. I think art means more than that," John answered. This surprised Alba. She looked at him with anticipation.

"What does it mean, then, boy genius?" Mr. Harker was amused by John's sincere effort.

"I don't know. I'll have to think about it."

The morning passed slowly as they moved from room to room. They repeated the ritual of standing, successively and by turns, in front of one painted image after another, as did many others, mainly older women who moved in small groups, in and out of the rooms. At one point a noisy group of elementary school children crowded around a large canvas of a snowy mountain peak, listening to their teacher talk about the upcoming Olympics.

Alba was excited because she knew some of the artists, a few of whom had taught her at BYU, but Mr. Harker lost steam. He sat for a while and then found his way outside to rest on a bench under a large cottonwood. It was hot out, but not too bad in the shade. The summer heat was not shy about coming early this year. He watched the cotton from the trees drift in the slow air and could see it gathered in clumps in the grass. He took deep breaths of the summer air, enjoying its precise dryness. He felt bad for his mood but he just couldn't understand for the life of him why Susan kept calling and asking for help as she did when Alba arrived. Maybe she was off the wagon again and that was why she said what she did about how his wife was prone to overreaction, that he shouldn't blame himself. How dare she? Maybe she had decided enough time had passed that she could try to endear herself to him again. When she was drunk, she was always a bit of a flirt. His wife's stepsister, her closest confidant, and this is what she has to say? Go to hell, he wished he had said. Go to hell. His wife's reaction was harsh but it was just. He never doubted it.

He looked back at the museum windows at the people pausing in front of the paintings. Being around all these saccharine people like John only worsened his mood. Alba was good for that boy. She would help balance him somehow. Funny how things seemed opposite of the pattern he used to see. As much as he posed as the prickly old man with Alba to toughen her up, he was a bit surprised by how much he had come to respect her judgment. Now he was beginning to worry that John was the one who needed help because he would never see what he had. She had that clean innocence of a Mormon, but she had a keen intellect and was patient in her thinking, certainly more patient than he was, he had to admit. They would make good parents, he supposed, but he feared that John would jump ahead in his chances at life and Alba would defer as so many do, and yet another fine female mind in Mormondom would slip into domestic oblivion.

He looked across the grass and could see the small clouds of sunlit midges reverberating above the turf. Bees hung around the roses to his left, while the wind cautiously brushed against the cottonwood leaves. There was scarcely any tree he loved more than the cottonwood. Not so much because it is the most beautiful. Certainly aspens and ponderosas, or the white pine, might be considered to be more beautiful, but it was the cottonwood that has always seemed to him to be the most indicative of Utah. Its riparian habit of congregating along the edges of severe streams, streams that survive in the dry heat despite all odds and grant green to an otherwise red and brown world. These, in his mind, were Utah's most stunning palette. The cottonwood's shimmer and the rugged grooves of its bark, twisting their way up and around the base of the tree like medieval armor—they moved him. The cottonwood offered unambiguous respite from the stress of forming human relationships, always had. A living soul, Alba had said. Guess I could do worse for companions, he thought.

Out they came from the museum, holding hands. John was gesticulating passionately and Alba listening attentively. She glanced in Mr. Harker's direction and gave a half wave as they turned toward him.

"Well, you missed a treat, Mr. Harker. There was some spectacular representational art in the contemporary section you would have liked." Alba was always inviting in her tone of voice: never chastising, never critical, only inviting. He felt a brief pang of guilt.

"The truth is my legs needed a little rest," he said to cover for himself. John was quiet. As they reached the car, John slipped into the backseat again. They pulled around the museum parking lot and turned onto the main street. As they drove north along the foothills, John leaned forward and finally spoke up.

"I was thinking about art, Mr. Harker." He paused for a moment. "I think— I think there are many ways to say we are sorry, you know, for what we do to the land, but art, art could be a kind of request for mercy. Does that make sense? A plea for forgiveness for who we are and what we do, even as we do it. That's what I think. Art as repentance." He repeated it like a mantra, the new flag of his disposition. His eyes were dead serious and gone was the usual chumminess. Mr. Harker looked out the window at the passing trees.

Chapter 4

Dear S.,

It is the necessary plea of any parent in this situation to say that it had nothing to do with you. I understand that saying so does not take away the costs, but it remains true. Where those costs go, how they add up, is sometimes despairing for me to consider and yet how they might get paid for is beyond my capacity to understand.

Every accident, science tells us, adds up to something. The world doesn't seem capable of losing anything. Nothing falls through; everything accumulates and adds to the shape of things. Every moment of consciousness is a culmination of necessity, even this moment here, these words, you reading them or just me imagining you reading them. In a sense, this means that there really is no such thing as pure accident or pure randomness, except that the paradox then is that we can't find the pattern. We can't go back and trace the laws of cause and effect closely enough to be sure of the genealogy of the present. What we do know, what we can understand, is that the world is present before us in all its complexity and it is there for the experience. Beyond that, we don't know a lick. You see, the world, the universe, is an incredibly efficient machine but its complexity is beyond our ability to predict. So even though the world operates according to law and even though every happening means something, comes from somewhere, we can never be sure where it is headed or what it means. It seems to be one of the great challenges of our time to understand the paradox that the more closely we examine anything in its fundamental structure, the less certain we are of what it is in fact that we are looking at or what the building blocks of physical reality are, and yet when we pull back and look at things cosmologically, it looks for all the world like something designed, something meant to be. Maybe you remember having an experience like that when we used to study the composition of the soil together. You loved the feel of the dirt between your fingers and you loved the minute forms of life everywhere. You could see that what was at a distance flat and maybe even green was anything but uniform in shape and color and it was certainly not solid. This is true too of mountains. Climb high enough and what for all the world appears to be the very epitome of solidity, of rock hard reality, is instead a pile of rubble, precariously balanced and moving ever so slowly and inevitably toward its destiny as sand. You see the paradox here, don't you? Our most common metaphors are drawn from misperceptions, or at least very shallow perceptions, of physical reality. The everlasting hills? I think not. Which only suggests that language is in need of a major overhaul, wouldn't you say? And when we look into the dark evolutionary past, it seems as if life could not possibly have intended to arrive at us, and yet it has, and everything—stones, butterflies, the magnificence of a red-tailed hawk, or the awkward bend of the cottonwoods at the edge of the river—everything contains the story of millions of years and millions of lives, all strangely coalescing briefly in the form of the present moment. The world is a complexity of stories and each strand, pulled apart from the rest for the sake of the telling, is an illusion of coherence and direction.

My problem is, I guess, that I haven't been able to gain perspective to look down on the tininess of my own life enough to see any pattern. I don't trust the illusions of perspective. I can't believe there is any vantage point sufficient for the pretension of telling the truth. Perspective is its own truth, I guess, as poor as it is. My eyeballs will only ever see from within the narrow confines of these sockets on this bobbly head of mine, sitting on these bony shoulders. So I stay immersed in the liquid flux of my own life's particulars, and I remain tiny, microscopically so, as if I were one of the particles of Heisenberg's uncertainty principle, moving at a certain speed and in a certain location but never able to determine both at the same time, never knowing exactly where I will be or when. And so my world, though no doubt insignificant by any serious measure of things—I mean, believe me, I get it! I am nothing—my world nevertheless seems immeasurably large and upon every choice, every accident I have ever been a part of, the very direction of the cosmos was turned. Choice has never felt insignificant, and even though some events flow by me each day in their daily rhythm—the sound of the morning traffic above the trees on the hill, the shape and sound of my faucet turning on every morning while I do my daily rituals—I never know when one small event, one small and seemingly insignificant linkage between such mundane choices as where I turn my car on a Thursday afternoon at 2:13 pm might rupture and transform the very shape of my world. You see, don't you, where this is taking me.

You are right. This is just a big buildup to a plea to let me off the hook, that my actions and my mistakes were all part of some complex process that we cannot understand and therefore shouldn't judge. But don't misunderstand me: even though this should be how you and I come to terms with things, I am caught reliving the mistakes over and over again, still believing that I could or that I should be able to change fate. I am, in fact, caught in the most absurd of all worlds, because despite my insistence that we would be better off as a culture if we could accept what the Preacher told us so long ago, that time and chance happen to all, I want to undo the concatenation of events that have ensued from accident and left me here alone without you both. I still read scripture, but mainly I find myself returning to Ecclesiastes and Job. I would gladly take the Preacher's advice and find pleasure in the momentary graces of being in the presence of those I love, of holding life, however temporary, in my arms, but obviously fate won't even allow me that much.

Your mom and I were an odd pairing, but odd in a good way. I found my proverbial harbor with her. Adrift and without family and wandering the mountains of Utah as a ranger, I was already thirty-four when I met her and her friends on the south side of Boulder Mountain. She was a few months shy of twenty-five. Mormon, formally educated, two well-matched parents who found each other after the death of her father's first wife, an older stepsister, and an incorrigibly sunny disposition. She and I were nothing short of miraculous, when you think about it.

Do you remember the place? We camped there a few times, the three of us, when you were no more than five or six. Not far from where I was born, you see, this was my native landscape. Fished there as a boy, so many years ago now, it hardly seems real. But that day, that day still seems real. Always will. It is a small wonder that Utah is not overrun by every last family on the earth searching for it. Boulder Mountain stands at some 10,000 feet of elevation looking over Torrey to the north, Capitol Reef to the east, and Escalante to the south. So the dramatic drop of elevation from that point means you are able to descend into hot and wild desert or ascend into lush alpine mountains dressed in aspen and pine, full of springs, lakes, and streams, all within a few miles. It feels like some roiling tectonic chaos of centuries has left the land a big and beautiful mess. You almost want to laugh at times at the strange formations of limestone that jut up from the earth, some like teeth, others like a wedding cake gone bad. Juniper are everywhere in the valley to the north of Boulder Mountain interspersed with bald spots of red earth and sheltered from the north by iron red cliffs. A place that really presses the point: we are strangers on a strange planet.

Your mom and her friends had come up the south side of the mountain with backpacks and were settled in on the shores of Divide Lake. I came upon them at dusk. They had a fire going and were making quite a lot of noise, their laughter echoing off the face of the granite on the north side of the lake. I tried not to startle them, but startle them I did. One of your mom's friends saw me coming through the trees as nothing but a moving shadow and screamed. The laughter turned to voices of serious concern, but I quickly spoke up.

"It's okay. I am a park ranger. How are you folks doing tonight?"

"Oh, my gosh. You scared me so much!"

"My apologies." I think they were still uncertain of my legitimacy as a ranger, so I came out into the light of the fire to at least show my clothing so they might be reassured.

"I am just making my rounds. The rainfall has been so little of late, we are almost to the point of banning open fires," I explained. "I just want to make sure you girls are being safe. I see your fire, for example, is a bit too close to the trees. I am going to have to ask you to keep that flame down."

Alba has gotten on me for calling her a "girl" so I have to explain that that is how everyone spoke back then. To be precise, this was 1964. I wasn't exactly a hippie, but I wasn't like the straight-laced boys of the time either. Vietnam was just about to heat up, you see. This was just weeks away from the whole Gulf of Tonkin ordeal that thrust us into the war. But I was already too old, too wicked for church, not to mention too stubborn for a settled life. I guess it is fair to say that I was a free soul, possessed by nothing and no one. I wasn't a rebel, but I was as open to life's opportunities as anyone else. I could have been pushed in just about any direction. Had a circus come to town, I might have fallen in love with the trapeze artist and spent my life on the road. I don't mean to sound flippant about your mom. All I mean to say is that I was so open to the world at that point that I would have been capable of finding any number of paths in life, except for the fact that I was utterly committed to the passive life. Didn't speak unless spoken to. Didn't act until I had no other choice, really. But there she was, at that moment and at that place. And there I was. She emerged from the darkness to toss some dirt onto the fire, to lessen its flame, and to shore up the circle of stones around it. And you will forgive me for the cliché but the flame in my heart pretty much rose proportionately to the flames she put out. I don't have to tell you that your mother was a looker, and even more so in her natural state in the woods, without a shower and all that. Her blond hair was pulled back, but strands fell across her face as she leaned over the fire, and against the blackening sky. It was something to behold, that face. I stuck around long enough to get a sense of the social dynamics and to notice that your mom was the leader of the group, the responsible one, and that she had a terrific laugh. I spent that night in my bag up above Divide Lake, alone, under the stars without much ability to close my eyes.

It was two or three days later that I saw them again, this time at the diner in Bicknell. I was on a break, eating a burger by myself, when she approached my table.

"Hey, aren't you the ranger we saw on Boulder Mountain?" She sat down across from me without my invitation. I wouldn't have had the courage to ask, but I was glad she did.

"Yes, I am. How was the rest of your trip?" She was showered now, and the afternoon sun coming through the window where I sat shone brightly in her hair. She had on a red plaid shirt that was clearly too big for her.

"It was terrific. We made it a loop up and over Divide Lake and descended back down to Highway 12. The only problem was that we didn't exactly close the loop and ended up having to walk a few miles on the highway back to our car! I think we expended a lot of energy, who knows how many bucks in gas, and five days of our time, and all I got was one small brookie for breakfast this morning. Pretty sad, huh?" She laughed as she spoke, as if we had known each other for some time. Who was I to pretend otherwise? I was on the shy side, and under normal circumstances I would never have managed such a conversation, but her smile, her brilliant blue eyes, and the way her hands danced on the table as she talked, put me at ease. Her friends were behind her at another table, and I could see them leaning over to take a look at us and giggling.

"Yeah, pretty sad. That's not exactly a cheap breakfast. I wouldn't quit your day job just yet."

"No kidding," she said.

"What is your day job?" I asked, hoping the conversation could get on to something more substantive before she vanished.

"Don't have one, actually. I am in school, at the Y. I bet I know what your day job is."

"I bet you do." There was an awkward pause. "But I bet you don't know what I want to be when I grow up."

"I bet I don't." She pulled her hair back over her ear in that way of hers when she is starting to get serious. "Tell me, aren't you grown up yet?"

I wasn't sure if we were still running with the same tone of humor or if she had suddenly given me my comeuppance for being a vagabond in my mid-thirties, maybe a peacenik, or worse, an experimenter. And she was from the Y after all. I grabbed a few fries and dipped them in ketchup to stall for time.

"I can't complain. But no, I'm not grown up yet. Don't have my B.A. for that matter, if that's what you are asking." My confidence must have drained straight from my face.

"I don't know. I kind of envy the excuse to wander in the mountains. That seems schooling enough, you know?" I looked up at her and grinned. Of course, I eventually learned that she meant this very seriously, even though she was the only reason I finished college and the only reason I began a graduate program in plant ecology. She drove me, you see, made me want to grow up—not because it was the responsible thing to do, but because she helped me to understand that fulfilling my dreams was the most logical way to express my own free spirit. I don't know why it is so hard for so many young people to understand this one thing: if you want to be free, discipline yourself to the dream of your choice. Perpetual wandering only gives you the illusion of freedom. Freedom isn't movement or the refusal to root oneself;

it is the capacity to will what life affords. I have never quite been able to put my finger on how it was your mother was able to clear my mind like that. Somehow she validated my vagabond ways while simultaneously helping me to channel that energy into something functional, even potentially allowing me to thrive in society, be somebody, make a difference.

I haven't done so well on this score in her absence. Anyone can see that. So maybe I am still not so grown up these days. I read the papers, I read in my field, and I read the great minds of our time, don't get me wrong. I think I would be comfortable in a room with the best of them, but the fact of the matter is I have never really managed to find a use for my own mind except as a companion. I rather like the companionship it provides, to be honest, but it is the coherence of thought and the coherence of my life that both seem lacking. I guess that is part of what motivated me to be writing to you, to gain some coherence, to make this mind of mine a sharable thing, to venture a tale. It's why I intend to write this book too. You will see.

Your mom was right. Something about the life of wandering the mountains alone teaches indispensable lessons about the art of solitude, something society could never teach. And after all my years of marriage, education, and work, I never came close to the level of self-understanding that was available to me away from it all. But there's the rub. What good does self-understanding serve in utter solitude? I have not hesitated to talk to the trees, the rock faces of cliffs, or to animals when the occasion calls for it, and of course to you, but the fact of the matter is, language is the vehicle of human understanding and understanding is the basis of human social relations. I mean, I could tell right then and there at a diner table covered with an unfinished burger and fries that I no longer wanted to wander alone, that I could spend the rest of my life in her presence and never lack for anything.

Sorry. I know that sounds hypocritical, given how things turned out. There were snakes in our garden and a restlessness in my soul that even she could not permanently cure, but I will never claim it was due to any insufficiency on her part that I found my wandering soul stirring up trouble later on. Whatever you may know and whatever you may think of your parents' marriage, please know this: your mother was all that I needed, and at the time, all the evidence my conscience needed that there was grace available to me in this free and forbearing universe. Yes, her love made sense of the idea of a loving God, which I readily admit is not the best reason to have believed. Just ask Job. Eventually all things come down and all coherence melts into dirt, sand, and milling air. Job had his convictions, convictions I never had. It can't be the worst thing in the world to have found hope, trust in grace, and the energy to do what life requires all because of the love of one woman. Why that should be considered a sin is beyond me.

At the time, and for many years after, her love made all things coalesce. I was pretty certain that it had not been accident but destiny that brought us together. All the loose strands of my life seemed to come together in our union and I could feel a kind of inner flourishing and synergy of my best instincts. We could talk about anything and everything and we could go our ways experiencing the world as separate beings and yet somehow in the sharing everything came back home, into one. The whole world seemed like nothing but possibility, potentiality. But that was then. It is obvious to me now that life is a series of dangerous forks in the road, each fraught with consequences that cannot be foreseen, controlled, or revoked once one has made one's choice. Because if it was accident that brought her to me, it was accident that took her away.

Maybe talking about accident sounds to you like I am refusing to accept responsibility for my actions, for the ways in which I allowed our union to falter, but I accept it fully. That is precisely why I insist it was accident and not destiny or any kind of providence that has written our story. The human mind is so foolish, so willing to embrace the positive consequences of accident as evidence of providence and yet so frightened by the prospect that all things—even our most terrible sufferings—must be just as boldly proclaimed as part of the necessary fabric of living. And I don't mean this in the saccharine Christian way of saying that all things work together for the good of those who love God. I mean, what if God is capable of terrible things? Or what if he is totally indifferent? Or worse, what if God is so personal, what if he punishes us with such accuracy, that his providence can only feel like cynical irony or sarcasm? How can we accept such "love"? I have given considerable thought to the contradictions of angry disbelief, which is really only a quarrel with God for being other than we would wish Him to be. Mature atheism would require a mere shrug of the shoulders at the oddness of this existence, and most of the time I am drawn to such shrugging, but then I am confronted with the problem of my sorrows at my losses. A mere shrug might be what God deserves but it would be an insult to your memory. But then who will stop all this aching, this banal and solitary crying? Does God make us care? If so, whence the cruelty? If not, what kind of God is He and what kind of obstinate sufferers are we to will this pain upon ourselves?

Ah, I have grown tired of my own questions. It is time for a walk. Alba will be coming soon and we will venture toward Silver Lake. The colors are close to changing, at least the maples. The aspen are just starting, some of the higher ones anyway. It should be a nice outing.

*　*　*

It was a lovely outing, in the end. It didn't start out so well again. But this time not for lack of trying, to be honest. I really wanted to be better behaved, but, you know, the events of this week have us all on edge. Alba said that she was sitting in the international studies center on campus that morning when the TV screen in the hallway began to show the images of the burning towers.

"Everyone just sat there, it seemed like for hours," she told me as she unpacked her brushes on the trail where we had stopped in front of a patch of Queen Anne's lace. John walked a ways up the trail to find a good place to read his philosophy. "The TV is usually on every day, broadcasting international news, and then suddenly there it was in that dark plume and then the collapse. People were audibly gasping and crying and for the next two days it was all anyone could talk about in my classes."

What was the content of that discussion, I wanted to know.

"It was mixed," she said. I sensed she was uncertain about how much to share with me since she knows I am not a big fan of that thick religious climate. I confess I could imagine a whole litany of silly reassurances from her professors. "Some people wanted to believe there was some divine purpose to it all, and some seemed downright ready to offer their theories. You know, punishment for our wickedness as a nation, and so on."

"I sure hope someone put a stop to such blather." I said. I can't abide easy and self-reassuring theology. "I hope someone pointed out who exactly had to die and suffer in that event, just so that their God could give them their reassurances. Let them read the names and the life stories of each one and then have them come back and give us their theory about how it all fits into perfect justice. This God they believe in, he is a pretty lousy surgical bomber, that's all I have to say. Way too much collateral damage to add up to any kind of satisfying justice. I mean, how many foreigners did they say died in those two towers, several hundred, dozens of countries, right? If this has some national significance, tell that to the German children of the German businessman who was in town for a few days. 'I am sorry, son. Your father had to die, so that I could send a message to my favorite nation,'" I said with a mocking tone. I noticed that the wild carrots had begun to decay in the harsh sun of late summer. It was important to observe the seasonal life of plants, you see, not just their state of most beautiful bloom, but their state of decay, the ways and times in which they go to seed and fall limp and brown after their moment of glory. That too has its value. She was happy to do it, but it occurred to me that our conversation was probably distracting. Timp could be seen to the south. All the mountains around us looked so strong, so serene. I felt for the girl. Somehow what we were doing there seemed utterly inadequate.

She stopped sketching and looked up. "Well, yeah, there was some of that nonsense, but I'm not stupid and neither are most people. I think they just wanted to talk about their shock and figure out ways to absorb what had happened."

"Well, yes, that's just it, isn't it? You see, we *won't* take the time we need." I felt pretty strongly about this point and wanted to make sure she understood. "Haven't you already noticed how we have handled this? So a nation suffers a tragedy of such proportion as this, and what can we think to do? We have a president who tells us to go shopping. And we have actresses pleading for money to help. This, the nation of Emily Dickinson, of Whitman, and no one bothers to recite some lines about lilacs blooming, about grass as the uncut hair of graves, nothing. What a waste. We just want to pretend that nothing is different, nothing is changed. I don't know about you, but it feels like everything is different. I just don't see the same America on the horizon."

She stopped painting and looked up at me. "All I know is that I find the whole thing frightening. I mean, what am I supposed to feel about the world I might be bringing a child into?"

"You aren't pregnant already, are you?"

"What do you mean by 'already'?"

"You haven't even been married a year, have you?"

"Just barely."

"Well, then, take your time."

"Why is it any of your business? Haven't you ever been taught that this is a topic that is off limits. It's bad enough when family intervenes but perfect strangers?"

She hadn't exactly behaved as a perfect stranger, but maybe I had gotten ahead of myself.

"My point is," she continued after a few moments of staring at the ground, "I want a family eventually. I'm just feeling more afraid. I mean, I don't want a world at war, where I can't be sure of my children's safety."

You of all people can appreciate just how hard it was for me to hear her say this. It didn't seem to be in her interest for me to let her down easy. "Girl, you have no idea," I said. "Let me tell you right now, there isn't any such place. Misfortune will find you. We all get our towers knocked down at some point."

She looked at me puzzled. Maybe I had said too much. I don't know.

"Well, that's probably true, I guess. I look at my mother and what she's been through. She didn't plan on losing a husband and raising her child in a different country. But this is where we came, this is where we found refuge. I don't want this to suddenly become a place of danger."

Danger was pretty hard to imagine on a day like today and in a place such as this, that's for sure. But I have my worries, worries about a slower kind of violence that is eroding even the strength of the hills. Even here.

"My mom always likes to say that there is something more important than fortune or fate. It's her mantra. But I confess that I don't think I know yet what it is, but I am learning to trust. But maybe that's all crazy religious babble to you."

I didn't know what to say. After a moment of silent painting, she added, "And for the last time can I ask you not to call me 'girl'?"

"Sorry. Old habit. It won't sound this way to your ears, but I mean it as a compliment."

"Thanks. But no thanks, *dude.*" She looked at me with a

straight face for a few seconds before a calm smile formed at the corner of her mouth.

"Point taken," I said.

We continued up to Silver Lake. Along the way the trail was dusty and dry. We just haven't seen the normal pattern of afternoon thunderstorms in the late summer. The ferns were sunburnt and weak, and the deflowered lupine had long since gone to seed. I could feel the impending death, which I suppose only made the beauty of the place that much more spectacular. As we reached the stands of aspen, I wondered if I had ever seen such a magical diffusion of yellow light. The air grew a bit nippy. I looked back at American Fork Canyon and Timpanogos in the distance, thinking that this elevation really has a tendency to clear the vision. The bright yellow leaves shone against the blue sky. I couldn't help recalling by contrast the stillness and grayness of the air in the valley we have seen lately. And suddenly I found myself tired of the monotony of sun and heat. What I wouldn't do for a good old-fashioned downpour. Haven't had one of those in quite some time.

I haven't been able to put my finger on it, but it does seem that this great tragedy has divided time, that we have now bifurcated from the nation we were or could have been and are becoming the nation we will be. I am not sure I like the feel of this new one. There have been moments of compassion, moments of deep feeling for those who died, for those who suffer on behalf of others—the firemen, for example—but there is too a growing specter of anger, of a nation hell-bent on balancing the scales of justice. When cinema first turned to color, there was no turning back and only many years later an appreciation and even nostalgia emerged for what came before. By contrast this feels like a moment imbued with immediate nostalgia, as if we must now admit that we have been living a dream, a dream of innocent prosperity, of oblivious disconnect from the ecology of the world, as if we were our own discrete national body, without context, impervious and impermeable and unanswerable to what we choose to ignore. Someone hates us, someone has hated us for a long time, enough to plan and enact a deed of such horrific and violent spectacle that all of us could only watch with shocked stupefaction at the collapse of two edifices of world commerce. Why would anyone do this thing? Why, indeed. But it isn't as if we haven't been known as the unwanted but pervasive presence across the planet for a long time, even hated in distant corners. We might not like it or think it fair, but it is nothing new. Despite the fact that to most of us, here on this soil, it feels like an invasion of the most unjust and unanticipated kind. This may be what we have lost, that American naiveté that operates like a wholly different landscape from the rest of the planet, an island of reclusive security far away from the turmoil and sufferings of people anxious and unsettled by the indifferent global forces set in motion right here in the centers of power. Probably the same reason we can't see the climate for the weather. Maybe it sounds like I want to blame us for what those men did. That would be above their dignity. All I mean is that the horrific crack of violence has shattered our illusions and we can never go back. And it gets me thinking again, ad nauseum you might say, about you and your mother, about what I lost, about what could have been, about what I have become seemingly against my will.

I will say this for my country. Just wandering the streets of this town, it feels like we see each other with a greater degree of warmth. I don't exactly have the reputation of being an active member of the community. I don't see my neighbors on Sundays, like they do each other, and while the rest of us find ourselves at gas stations on Sundays buying coffee or occasionally hiking or fishing in the mountains, I have generally made it a point to not join forces with the so-called Jack Mormons or the "inactives" or to forge alliances with others on the margins of the community. I find the inanity of majority cultures matched only by the inanity of minority cultures, what with their perpetual need to lick their wounds. The energy that this would require of me is something that I simply cannot afford. Just the thought of it exhausts me. But now I find myself seeing people in the streets, on the trails, coming out of the church parking lot, and there is a kind of compassion in the air and in the heart, a magnification of soul, an utterly free and energizing extension of mercy toward all because, you know, if it isn't extended to everyone, it isn't really mercy at all. It's just someone's idea of justice.

It's been a remarkable thing. This country can feel so fractious and bitter and that's when it's easy to feel it isn't so much a nation as it is a conglomerate of peoples, each with their own narratives that define their history and their claims to a unique belonging in this land. And Mormons have perhaps excelled like no other in telling a story of themselves as separate and apart even at the same time we make the boldest claim ever on this nation—the very same nation that expelled us—as the divinely appointed haven for the gathering of the family of God. Lately, America almost feels like it could move in that direction but only if it can get over its pain in the right way. I haven't much cared for the narrative of the last days, for that Christian longing for the end of all things, but the events of September 11 do feel ominous, I must say. I am not sure it is the end of times, but it is at least the end of one America I frankly am glad to leave behind, that land of fiction, of easy entertainment, easy suffering, easy prosperity, and fun violence. We have suddenly awakened from a deep sleep. People are real. Bodies die. Relationships are one-time affairs and human sociality can be torn suddenly and irrevocably, casting all experience into the dusty vaults of memory. Just like that, we became a nation in shared agony of what we lost, what we had to accept perhaps was never ours, and it is as if our arms remain extended to one another in recognition of our perpetual eluctability. Our tragedy is that we only seem to know each other in loss, in retrospective acknowledgement of the life we were not fully awake to until it was too late.

There's a lot of my own autobiography in these observations, a fact that you no doubt see with a certain irony. Yes, I am reaching out to you, too late. If all three of us were together again and reconciled, that would be nation enough for me. It's a fiction, of course, but a good one. At least it keeps at bay the voracious despair that overwhelms me in darker hours. Better to choose my illusions than to give in to fear.

Alba offers more information about her life than I do about mine, and she has started to notice the discrepancy. She is starting to pry a bit, and that is making me less comfortable around her. The last thing I want is pity. She is pretty free about her own past, and I confess I find it fascinating, but if she thinks it is going to be quid pro quo, she has another thing coming. You see, she lost her father in Chile, during the dictatorship of Pinochet. Her mother apparently never says much about him and has raised Alba to believe that her father was a source of shame and that it's best not to talk of him. Understandably this hasn't sat well with her, especially lately. Her questions about her father's story have increased, but I gather that the mother just won't budge. I tell her that it is her right to probe, that she shouldn't tolerate a wall of silence. Besides, he was probably quite heroic for doing what he did, fighting against a dictatorship that had squelched all hope of genuine democracy. That's not a bad legacy to have, I tell her. I have not met the mother, but perhaps she is like other successful immigrants, so taken by the American Dream that she can't see what it excludes. Alba seems different. She is shaken by the events this week, but she is not bitter at the terrorists nor at the nation. She seems less astonished by the fact that someone hates us than by the fact of our steeled determination to seek justice. I gather that she knows a thing or two about how quickly such ventures lead to unnecessary bloodshed.

I think that hike might have been a truce, finally. You see, we had had our share of run-ins on the trails over the summer. Never as bad as our first one, mind you. I had learned at least that much. One day we really got into it. I had taken her and John up to the top of Pfeifferhorn. You and I never made it all the way up there, but we came close anyway. We climbed up to the ridge overlooking Red Pine Lake. I don't think I liked the idea of guiding you over some of those boulders just at the last saddle before the peak. Too much empty space between the solidity of stone. You were an agile little hiker, but still. God, I must tell you, you can see forever from there, all the way south to West Mountain, Mount Nebo, Provo Peak, Timp, Box Elder Peak, Lone Peak to the west, and all that water. There are few views of Utah Lake that are more expansive.

But I digress. I had taken them up from Big Cottonwood Canyon. The wildflowers at the start of the trail to Red Pine Lake are exceptional and not to be missed in July. Deep and high and thick and oozing their pollenated aroma, especially the intoxicating horsemint, paintbrush, and sticky geraniums. We saw elephant heads, cowslip, corn lily (oh, I warned her about that one and the deformed lambs that are born to the mothers who ate from this lovely plant), buckwheat, columbine, fireweed, monkey flower in the creek beds, and, oh my Lord, my favorite, Parry's primrose, which we found up close to the very top nestled up against huge granite slabs. So many more. We took forever to get up the mountain what with all the sketching she had to do, and I was coming unglued with excitement at everything we could see. It got so bad, I even relented to having some photos taken for Alba to paint later. So while she stopped to sketch, I orated. Well, I guess my orations got a little much for poor old John. We had stopped right at the saddle before the final ascent to the peak where a backbone of boulders makes the trail all but disappear. We had been scrambling and swinging and leaping from one spot to the next and had opted to bypass a large series of boulders directly in front of us by climbing down on the northeast side. It was there that we found bunches of Parry's Primrose hiding in the shadows. Alba sat down and began to sketch and John and I found a place to relax in the sun.

I was sermonizing about the advances of secular humanism: equal rights for women, civil rights, environmental protection, and so on, and about how woefully inadequate Christianity, let alone Mormonism, has proven to be with regard to these advances. I admit that I am pretty desperate to get them to see how oblivious their religious life is to the concerns of our time. Sure, I meant to provoke. But I also meant well. I asked them if they could name any prominent Mormons who had been actively engaged in these causes. John made a go of it. He was sitting on a boulder while Alba painted, looking intently at the surface of the granite on which he sat. He ran his hand back and forth on the surface of the rough stone. He has a strange and unexpected kind of handsomeness. I am not sure how to describe it exactly. Maybe it is his crooked smile and slightly off-center teeth. And bright eyes. He is wiry and thin, and his sandy hair is never combed. I am not sure he is ever aware of it at all, so that does endear him to me, I guess, but he is too much the philosopher, which means he has an indefatigable capacity for calm reasoning. To my mind the boy needs to *feel* something. I am pretty convinced he has never really suffered a day in his life.

But the dialogue was fruitful, I think. It went something like this: After a moment, he blurts out, "Are the contributions of a religious community only to be measured in political terms, let alone politically correct terms? I mean, who decides these standards?"

"Who? Well, you ought to wake up, my friend. The twenty-first century decides. And you're either part of it or you're not."

"I think that's what bothers me about these issues. It's not that I am unsympathetic to the causes. I mean, who doesn't want equality and civil rights and environmental health?"

I couldn't abide this. "Wait a minute. *Who* doesn't want these things?" I had to interrupt. "Are you really that naïve? It seems to me that your church, among others, doesn't want them and, well, just look at who we have in office and tell me if *they* want these things?"

He continued as if unfazed by my interrogation. "It's just that I find them so, I don't know, divisive. Even the way you pose these questions seems to indicate a preference for division. You see them as questions of for or against. And only one right solution. Do you know the comedian, Steven Wright? He said, 'There are two kinds of people in the world. Those who divide the world into two kinds of people and those who don't.'" And then he laughed out loud at the brilliant philosophical irony of the joke. He took off his ball cap and rubbed his hands through his annoyingly thick blond hair.

"Do you see this ridge here?" I thought a parable might help. "These boulders. You see how defiant they are to the wind and the rain? The rain here will fall and every drop that lands will eventually find its way into completely different watersheds on either side of this mountain. And all of that will depend on the angle of each boulder. The boulders are the deciders. It's either one way or the other. There is no middle ground. They cut the world into two. You go one way or the other. I don't see how anything short of passionate commitment to a just world contributes to anything but injustice."

"Are you pretending that a passionate commitment to a just world has never led to injustice?" John responded. He seemed unusually passionate about the point. "Surely you aren't that unaware of this irony, right? I mean, one man's freedom fighter is another man's terrorist, as they say. Isn't there some risk in all that moralizing we do, that we will end up defending the wrong things and for the wrong reasons?

"Look, all I am asking for is the simple courage to call a spade a spade, that when injustice is happening, when evil reigns, we see it for what it is. The climate is going to hell and where are the Christians? No matter how stupid the war, the nation can always count on conservative Christians to enlist and demonize those who protest the bloodshed. Racism, sexism, discrimination— these are bad words, not bad deeds around here—they aren't even real to you. I mean, what does it take to get you Mormons off your duffs and into the streets?" Alba looked up from her painting. She had had enough.

"'You Mormons'? Really! Give it a break, please, Mr. Harker. It's like we are some big monolithic monster. We are individual people, you know."

I was too much on a roll. I wasn't going to be stopped. I said, "You would rather spend your time philosophizing about what is right than actually doing the hard work of making the world a better place."

John fought with his typical calm. "Isn't philosophy exactly what you're doing right now? You can't attack philosophy except on philosophical grounds!" He seemed rather proud of himself for noting my hypocrisy. "Seriously. I don't see you doing a lot of protesting or anything. And even if you did, is that really what matters most? You seem to lead a pretty quiet life. Nothing wrong with that. Fact is, I admire it. Look, I'm not going to defend our record on civil rights, but I will defend the right and the need to be, you know, *thoughtful*." He said this with special emphasis. He wasn't half bad to listen to sometimes. "Maybe I've been reading too much Nibley lately, but we've got too much zeal and not enough careful thinking right now. We could all stand to do a little more self-examination. Passion, sure, we have lots of that, and plenty of poor judgment. Besides, how are we all going to agree on what a just world is? All we have right now is a perpetual cultural war, you know."

"So you acknowledge that Mormons don't always do their own careful self-examination?"

"Of course I do. What do you think motivates me to study philosophy, as a Mormon? But man, give it a break! Why is it always about us Mormons with you? What's with your obsession that we have all the problems?"

I wanted to say that I didn't ask the Mormons to run this state, to represent me in D.C., to run everything in sight. I didn't ask the Mormon God to take away my family. And I sure as hell didn't ask the Mormons for advice about how to deal with my losses, advice that they gave me anyway.

"Mr. Harker, sorry to change the subject," interrupted Alba, "but why is this Parry's Primrose here in this unlikely place? It just seems incredible to me that at the base of this boulder, with hardly any soil to speak of, we could find this little garden of green and magenta, and so brilliant, here against the granite, and at such an elevation." She was genuinely stunned by the sight of the flower, and I couldn't help but admire her for having noticed its precarious position. Maybe this was one of her efforts at distraction to keep me from getting too heated up, but I appreciated the distraction. She will make a terrific parent of toddlers.

So of course, I trained my attention away from the debate. "Yes, it is its unlikeliness that makes it all the more remarkable, don't you think?" I said. "These primroses need the wet areas of streambeds usually, and they will typically bloom in the early spring, but they also grow in the high mountains in the summer in these spots where snowmelt may have left behind a particularly saturated spot of wet soil here just below this boulder that shielded the direct sunlight enough hours of the day to slow the melt in these dark crevices until relatively late in the summer, providing enough moisture and cool temperatures for them to take root. It's one of my personal favorites. Such remarkable and extravagant color, and such an unlikely location and time of year! Charles Parry, by the way, was one of the American West's greatest botanists."

Alba was thoughtful for a few minutes. I waited for a minute to see if she would speak, but she didn't. I was ready to move on and started climbing in the direction of the peak ahead of us to suggest that she had had enough time to sketch. When I noticed that she had begun to pack up, I headed up the steep ascent just below the peak. It was a long intense scramble over loose rock for another thirty minutes before I finally summited. I unburdened myself of the backpack, broke open a granola bar, and rested on a rock facing Utah Lake. I could see Alba and John below me moving steadily toward our destination.

To the south from there, you can see the entirety of the Wasatch Mountains heading down to Mount Nebo: Box Elder Peak, Timpanogos, Cascade Mountain, Provo Peak. Before me all was green at the top but brown and hazy in the hot summer light as your eyes move down the precipitous drops all around you to the valley floors. And that amazing and vastly underappreciated lake, like some sad forgotten orphan of still staggering beauty shining in the sun. What I love is how this peak feels like a swivel point, upon which one can sit and rotate and see different worlds. You can see to the west beyond Lone Peak the narrowed gap where the Jordan River flows into the Salt Lake Valley and the great tragedy of the Kennecott Copper Mine looming just to the northwest in the Oquirrh Mountains. You look to the north and can see Salt Lake Valley, the Great Salt Lake in the far distance, Mount Olympus, and of course all that you have just traversed to get here up from where Red Pine Lake begins. The Uintas hinted at in the almost bleached horizon line to the east.

When they arrived, I made sure they appreciated the rare pivotal perspective this spot affords. Alba spun slowly around taking it all in. She was perplexed.

"So I can see this peak from Salt Lake City *and* from Provo?"

"If you are west enough," I said.

"I feel stupid saying this, but I have always seen these peaks from both sides and assumed they were two different mountains. They look so different! But it is all one massive complex of peaks, I guess, with all these different points of view. This is just amazing!" She held her arms up high and continued to turn slowly. After a few more minutes of silence, she announced: "I don't think I know anymore what a mountain is. I mean, who could paint a mountain, when you really think about it? You could never represent just one. Picasso felt he could never paint a face for the same reasons. There are just too many angles, too many positions from which we see things. Too many faces. And too many mountains right here."

"Thirteen ways of seeing a blackbird," I said.

"Way too few," she said. She sat down with her back to me looking south toward Provo and West Mountain. John sat next to me. He was busy enjoying his peanut butter and jelly sandwich. Without turning around to look at me, she addressed me.

"Mr. Harker, tell me. Say it rains here. Say gravity pulls all the water down. Some drops go one way. Some go another. And some go into the groundwater. It all goes down, either way, and in the long run every drop will either evaporate to fall again or end up in the Great Salt Lake. It might up and leave for some other part of the world, but it is all one, in any case, at least in the long run, you know?"

"We don't have to say it. That is exactly what happens," I answered. "Water is really quite something when you think about it."

"Well, so say that this is what happens. This isn't really a ridge at all, then. It is more like, I don't know, like some kind of kaleidoscope, and all the uneven, jagged, and divided surface of the earth does is delay the inevitable reunion of everything that falls down. It all comes around and together eventually. It's like, I don't know, like division is just some kind of illusion, or at least some temporary thing that must be endured. Endured? Well, maybe. But maybe it is more than that. It is something we must learn to use to, you know, shape our lives. I mean, look, I can turn around and face to the north and then spin around again and face the south, and it's as if I'm looking at different worlds and I can't possibly capture all of it. I could never paint this, that's for sure, this sense of the world turning on perspective. But at least I start to understand that what I see is never enough, is one dimension, one side, one flat side of a big round and whole thing. This planet." She paused and stared at the ground for a minute. "And what we have in the meantime are pockets of beauty, like those flowers, just momentary flashes of hope, you know. In a broken world." At this she turned and looked at me with an earnestness I still can't shake. John had stopped eating and was listening intently. I looked down at my feet to gather myself.

She has given me pause, that's for sure, made me look in the mirror a time or two. I don't know what you think of all that. I promise I am not making this up, but I tell these stories because maybe they give you some idea of why it hurts that you aren't around to know this remarkable woman.

Chapter 5

All Alba knew was that her father had disappeared in 1982, when she was four years old and that her mother, Isabel, was no great fan of her father's politics. They had lived as a close mother and daughter, bound by a narrative of escape and rescue, not exile. Theirs was a journey to safety and security on American soil away from the influence of corrupt governments and corrupt men. Remarriage had certainly been an option on a number of occasions, but Isabel's feelings could never quite settle. There was always a trigger of suspicion, something that warned her away from men. She did have a soft spot for the church leaders she had known in Chile and in Utah, so much so that Alba sometimes teased her that she had bishop crushes. All of them in succession had been generous and mindful of her plight, assisting with church welfare funds whenever needed. Bishop Garland had gone so far as to personally find and paint and furnish their first apartment in West Valley. Isabel wanted nothing more for her daughter than to marry such a man, a man with a stable profession—Bishop Garland worked as a software engineer, Bishop Harden was a lawyer, and President Lawrence was a real estate developer—and utter fidelity to wife, family, and country. Her feelings about John's pursuit of Alba finally settled in a way that they never could for herself when she met John's parents. But just when she thought her work was done, one year into the marriage Alba's visits to West Valley for Sunday dinner were increasingly filled with questions about her father.

"Fue tirar piedras sobre el propio tejado," was her answer. It was a mess of his own making, she would insist, so there was no point in justifying him or dignifying him with more explanation. Besides, did Alba appreciate the chaos of those days? The long lines for food? The fear of collapse? Isabel recalled the tone of worry in her parents' voices in the early days of Allende's

election. Did Alba appreciate how much better she had it now in America, far away from such corruption and agitation? She didn't think of defensiveness about American ideals as a political position. Politics, to her mind, was anger and distrust. Although her own English was still heavily accented and she still loved her sopaipilla with pebre sauce and shopped for eel wherever she could find it, she had encouraged Alba's every step toward assimilation. But it seemed that after the collapse of the Twin Towers, Alba was losing faith in America and, Isabel feared, maybe in her church and marriage.

"I heard someone at church this morning blaming the attack on our own wickedness, for our acceptance of sexual immorality," Alba said one Sunday as she twirled her fork on her now empty cake plate. "I just don't get it. I mean, do they think these terrorists were agents for God? Jesus said it is necessary that evil happens but woe unto him by whom it comes, something like that. Sounds to me like evil is, you know, just evil—it's not some divine agency in disguise." Isabel kept busy clearing the table. John had heard this already. "Besides, what kind of dirty work is this that God tricks evil people into doing, anyway? Does God care so much about sexual morality that he would kill innocent people just to send the message? I had to point out to this good sister something Mr. Harker reminded me of, that hundreds of foreigners were killed in the towers. Maybe the terrorists intended to send a message to the nation, but why would we want to reward such evildoers by accepting their narrative? It was so much more. Not to mention the fact that it is repulsive to believe in a God who does his own kind of terror just to send a coded message to his chosen people. God is subtle, but I don't believe he is cruel."

John more or less agreed with Alba but he also knew that, like most things Alba said at dinners, this was not going to be easy to negotiate. The less he said, the better.

Isabel removed a stack of dishes from the table.

"*Mami*?"

"*Sí, hija.*"

"What do you think? I don't pretend to know what to make of it, but are we supposed to interpret it that way?"

"I have no idea, m'ija."

"But do you think we should go to war over this? You know they are talking about invading Afghanistan, don't you?"

Isabel stepped around the corner into the kitchen. John and Alba could hear the dishes being stacked.

"*Mami*?"

"*Sí, hija.*" She answered from the other room.

"What do you think?" Alba looked at John and rolled her eyes. With John's family, she was never shy about expressing her opinion. Unfortunately, his father wasn't either, but usually after a few anxious moments, it would end in a cool détente. Her frankness was one of the many things he admired about her, but it still made him nervous. Especially with her mother. With his father she would at least remain calm but conversations with her mother lately seemed to provoke the deepest emotions in Alba. Just a few sentences into the discussion and he already knew that she would be needing the drive home to sort through what she was feeling. It was his job to listen and to validate her emotions, but also to figure out a way to talk her through and out of her emotions. It was sometimes more than he could handle.

"How am I supposed to know? I don't like war. But, *tú sabes,* people who are willing to kill like that deserve to be eliminated. *Tengo confianza que el pais hará la cosa adecuada.*"

"*La cosa adecuada*? What's that supposed to mean?" Alba was getting irritated.

"The appropriate thing, the right thing. This country will do the right thing, Alba. Are you forgetting your Spanish?"

"No, I am not forgetting my Spanish. I just don't understand what you mean exactly. I mean, do you think killing is appropriate, *adequate*? Should we *eliminate* people? That sends chills down my spine. Doesn't that make you just like them? I mean, what about turning the other cheek?" Alba placed both hands on the table as she awaited her mother to return to the room.

"If that is what they choose to do, then I am fine with it too. As long as the killing stops." She came back in, wiping her hands on her apron and continued to clear the table.

"But what do *you* think, *mami*?"

Isabel stopped her work, pressed her hands against her apron. "*Ay*." She sighed heavily. "What difference does it make what I think? Do you think anyone cares what your Chilean mother thinks? What do you want from me, *hija*? Why so many questions?"

"Because it matters, *mami*. It matters to me. Why should I have categorical trust in the government to do the right thing? You and I of all people ought to understand the danger of such trust, *mami*. I mean, our family was broken and our lives changed because of abuse, abuse of power. How can you pretend that this doesn't matter? For you, it's like Pinochet never happened."

Isabel's demeanor changed. "We're not going to do this again, are we? Always the same. Why can't you leave it alone?" She turned to go back into the kitchen. Alba stood to follow her in there, but John put his hand gently on her back, hoping to signal that maybe she ought not to corner her mother in the kitchen. She sat back down. She looked at John quickly, as if to say, "I know what I am doing."

"I just don't understand what sense it makes to say that you trust a government to do what is right when you have no opinion of your own about what it should or should not do. That's a formula for abuse. And, I mean, such abuse cost me a father!" Alba was near tears. John rubbed her back. She took a deep breath, but the emotions were not subsiding.

Isabel reemerged. "*Mira, hija.* I told you. Be careful. This blaming is no good. That man can blame himself. Trust me. You don't need to blame Pinochet or anyone else."

"Oh *mami*. You always say that. Can't you understand how that makes me feel? I mean, you can read just like I can what people are saying about those years now. This class I am taking about human rights, *mami*, it would really open your eyes. I'm telling you, Pinochet deserved to be resisted. He was imprisoning and torturing thousands. What my father did was heroic, not shameful as you make it seem. Why are you so embarrassed by him? It's hard to feel grateful for those who stayed out of trouble. I admire those who had the integrity and courage to fight back."

"Integrity? Is that what you call it?" Isabel's face grew red. "I could tell you a thing or two about courage! Let me tell you something, Alba." She then spoke slowly and deliberately as if speaking to a child: "*You don't know what you are talking about. Okay? Me comprendes?* We are done here." Isabel left for the kitchen and closed the door behind her. Alba looked at John in desperation, but he just shrugged his shoulders.

"*Mami. Mami!* Come back!" Isabel didn't respond. Alba stood and spoke through the door. She didn't open it for fear of making her mother feel more threatened than she already did. "*Mami*, I am sorry. I didn't mean that you didn't have courage. I didn't mean that. You know I don't feel that way. I have never had anything but love for you, *mami*. But what am I supposed to feel for a father about whom I know virtually nothing? If I am wrong, tell me why. . . . Please." She could hear her mother crying in the kitchen. The door didn't open.

Growing up Alba had admired her mother's faith. It was her mother's ability to weather storms, to live with uncertainty, to provide a ballast against the background noise of life that had blessed Alba with a sense of home and belonging. Her mother was never moved by the headlines, by what stirred people up from one day to the next. She had her sights set on something much more important. When she gave a final farewell talk in church before she left for her mission, Alba even devoted the entirety of her remarks to these qualities in her mother, qualities that she suggested all should emulate. She felt she owed everything to her. Her mother had believed in her, built her up, comforted her, and led her to believe in herself with fierce determination.

As they drove home that evening, Alba asked John if she was wrong to be pursuing these questions.

"No," he said, "it's not wrong. But it is hurtful to her, obviously, so I think you need to be careful. She needs to know you respect her, that you are grateful for her."

"Of course I am. Why would she doubt that?" Alba asked.

"All I am saying is that you shouldn't assume she knows. I sense she is worried somehow that she is losing you. Maybe that is normal when your child gets married, especially your only child you have raised alone."

Alba thought in silence for a while as John drove. Maybe he was right. Why couldn't both things be true, that her mother had been enough, more than enough, but that she deserved to know more about her father and about what he had lived and died for? To have lived one's life against the grain and all for the sake of a national ideal was nothing to be ashamed of. That was cause for pride. We could use a little of that courage around here, she thought. Instead, we have too much patriotic acquiescence and too much criticism of other nations, other religions, other politics. She couldn't bring herself to say this to John, but she felt herself loosening from the anchors in her life, from her mother, from him, and from the story of American innocence. And it was her father's story, asking to be told, that drew her away.

"You and my mother are going to have to find the strength to make room for my father," she said out loud.

"Room? What do you mean?"

"If he is my father, he is the grandfather of our future children. You can't suppress his story too."

"Who said I was suppressing his story?"

"You aren't exactly encouraging me. Besides, what does the

Spirit of Elijah do if not stimulate a desire to see the names and faces and know the stories of those who went before? That's what's happening, John. I am not going crazy."

"I didn't say you were. I think you are overreacting, that's all." He glanced over at her, but she remained focused on the view outside of her window. He wanted to say something encouraging but was losing confidence he would say the right words.

Alba grew silent again. Maybe her mother's strategy of survival, a great strength in times of duress, was a weakness in times of peace. And maybe it was the Mormon paradox too: a people chased and persecuted by the government, a people who lost almost everything had to learn trust in authority in order to cobble together new families and a sense of belonging in the wilderness. They had not only managed to survive but also to create a caring and nurturing sense of family like no other. But now, it seemed, this cultivated conformity was just a form of trust that the nation could exploit for its own interests and a form of tribalism that abdicated responsibility for the collective whole. Why were so many so doubtful even just about the possibility of American complicity in injustices in the world? Her experience of her religion had been beautiful and personal, and had given her hope and strength, but she saw too how people's faith seemed to acquiesce to all manner of fear, especially lately. Which means it wasn't real faith after all. Why should her mother or John worry that something was wrong with her for wanting to know more? As she had learned more about Chilean history and about human rights abuses across the world, about human trafficking and the sex trade, her confidence in the benign appearance of the world fell away. She couldn't read about such problems without thinking that every one of these people who were treated as chattel was someone's daughter or son, someone's mother or someone's father. And always, there was her father's face, a face that she couldn't remember, and his name, a surrogate for all nameless and faceless victims. She had come to understand that all lives were connected. No life without context, as Mr. Harker would say.

*   *   *

It was only a few weeks later when once again the topic came up. This time Alba put John up to it, after some pushing. As a prospective son-in-law, John had not earned Isabel's immediate approval, but then again no one else had either. Isabel watched him like a hawk when no one else was watching, in the grocery store or at the mall or in movie theaters. She watched his eyes, she listened to his voice, looking for any indication that he had an accelerated heart rate around another attractive woman who might be in range. And there were plenty. But John's eyes never shifted, never looked over a woman's body, never followed or turned in the direction of beauty except Alba's. And unlike the other boys he didn't seem to crave that chance to be alone with Alba when they were dating. He seemed content sitting on the sofa, looking through old photo albums, listening to Isabel talk about cueca or Violeta Parra, or watching the news. She didn't know that men could be this way. They certainly weren't in Chile and all of the suitors she had resisted over the years always seemed to come looking for companionship much too soon after the death of their first wife, hungry for an escape from their solitude and sexless lives. As a single man John seemed content but engaged, and he proved his faithfulness by his patience with Alba's emotional ups and downs. Besides, he came from a strong extended family with deep roots in Mormon history that held annual reunions in the mountains every summer, who gathered from all quarters of the country just for the chance to spend another week with their distant cousins. And they were conservative, holding to the ideals of the America Isabel believed in.

So she was caught off guard when John brought the topic up again at a dinner a few weeks later.

"Isabel, do you think it would it be possible for me to go through the temple for Alba's father? This would be important in the future, especially for the time when we might have children."

"You *might* have children? You mean you might not?" she asked nervously.

"No, no. Of course, we plan on it, but I just mean, you know, for that time. We want to be able to tell the kids, you know, something about their, you know, their people."

Isabel looked very concerned.

"Of course, we are just thinking about his own endowment ceremony, not his sealing to you. Just to be absolutely clear."

"*Gracias*." Isabel put down her fork. "I need to think about this." Alba and John continued to eat in silence before Isabel finally spoke again.

"*Mira, mi corazon*," she said to John, avoiding Alba's eyes, "you need to know that I am very patient with the Lord. You should be too. It will sort out. The temple, it teaches me patience, you see? I mean, missionaries feel urgent. We should share the gospel now. That's true. But the temple is different, I don't know, a different tempo, maybe. Millennial time. Besides, what you are proposing is more complicated than you realize. Trust in the Lord, in his timing. Don't worry yourself about this. You and Alba have enough to worry about right now."

"Like what?" Alba interjected.

"Like when you *might* be starting your family, for one."

"*Mami*! That's our business, and besides, I want to finish my degree first."

"I understand. There is that. And John's schooling, let's not forget. But don't forget what it is all for."

"He's fine, *mami*. But help me understand. All my life you tell me that my goal is to go to the temple and now we propose that my father receive his endowments, and you say no? Is it that you don't think he is worthy? Did he kill someone or something?"

"Well, it's complicated."

"How is going to the temple for him complicated? I know his name. I am his daughter."

"You don't know what he did."

"That's why I ask, *mami*. Do *you* know what he did?"

"I know enough."

"Do I get to know at least that much? Why won't you tell me the truth?"

"*Mira*—he was involved with that group, those communists, *los Miristas*. I don't know what for. I never understood. He never explained, you see? And, you know, he was always out late, always keeping me from knowing what was going on, risking his life and endangering his family. And before long, he left the house for the last time."

This was more than Isabel had ever said before and Alba didn't want it to stop so she spoke gently. "Was this a relief to you?"

"Well, it didn't change much to be honest." John looked nervously back and forth at both of them. "I had already learned to be on my own with you."

"Oh, *mami*, *perdóname*. I don't mean to upset you. But, can I just ask, did you report him missing? Did you pursue any leads? What about his friends? Were they taken too? What if he was tortured?"

"It wasn't that simple. I did what I could. *Por favor*, let's talk about something else."

"But *mami*, please. It isn't enough for me anymore."

"It was not enough for me either. So why should it be different for you?" Alba wasn't sure what to say. She played again with her fork, drawing imaginary lines on her napkin. Isabel started to eat again. After a minute or so, Alba spoke.

"At least let me dream of bringing him some spiritual peace. You well know it doesn't matter how he lived. He has the same chance we all do to make good choices in this life *and* in the next. That's the whole point of our religion—to provide that chance for progress in this life and in the next. You always told me so. You wanted me sealed to John. I wanted it too. Because we both believe in the promises, in the generosity. Why would you want to halt his progress, condemn him because of our limited understanding of things? I feel like he is calling me to do this for him. I can forgive him. So should you."

"*No tiene nada que ver con el perdon, m'ija.*"

And with that she left the dining room and brought the conversation to an abrupt end, leaving Alba in an even greater state of perplexity.

Alba looked at John anxiously. "What am I supposed to do with this? She opens the door just slightly and then closes it again, just the same. It's always a dead end."

"Maybe with time, Alba. It is obviously going to take more time."

"Time? She calls this a rush? I am almost a quarter of a century old, John. I want to have a family. I want to know who I am."

"You do. You know the essentials. That's more than most people."

"What? You too? Do you or don't you think I deserve more information than she is giving me? Don't you think it is natural and normal to want to ask these questions? I want no part in this complicity . . . of silence."

"It's not a matter of what is normal, Alba. It's what your relationship with your mother can handle. Don't spoil the one relationship with the only parent you have for the sake of a relationship that you can never regain."

"What about what I can handle, John? I can't handle *this* anymore. Do you know what our lesson in Relief Society was about today? Family history. And you know, everyone was sharing stories about family histories they had taken, interviews with grandparents, anecdotes, journals, and Sister Whipple opens up a folded diagram of a family tree. She points to one spot on this matrix of dots and names and connecting lines and she says, "That's me, right here." And I kept thinking, *Where am I? Where is my place?* I am half a person. And the worst of it is, my own mother has locked the door to the other half."

At that Isabel reentered the dining room with dessert.

"Mami, I am all but decided that I am going to Chile. I am just going to find out for myself what no one will tell me. I want to know what happened to him, who he was, how he died."

"All but decided?" John interjected. He felt betrayed by this sudden announcement. "When were you planning on having this conversation with me?"

"Well, we're having it right now. I want to go, John. I have been thinking that this winter is a perfect time. Besides, I need to get to the bottom of this to complete my thesis. I have decided to make the project about family history and family trees in some way and I just feel that going there will inspire me to know what to paint exactly."

"This is way bigger than your thesis."

"No, my thesis is way bigger than, I don't know, a thesis. It's my life."

"Alba." Isabel was calm, which surprised Alba. "Alba, listen to me. This will only lead you to sadness. I understand you. I do. I just don't want to cause you more sadness. I already gave you too much. You have a wonderful life right here, with John, with us. Things have worked out so much better than I could have imagined all those years ago when my life was so broken and all I had was you—little, loving you. And now look what the Lord has given us. Look at his blessings, all around us. Just let it be enough."

Alba looked carefully into her mother's eyes. She saw nothing but love, as she always had, but sadness too and when she turned to John, she could see his love but also his fear. Right then their love didn't feel deep enough, like it was an ill-considered gift, something thrown together rashly in the hope of satisfying her but not conceived in careful consideration of her person. This discouragement coming from family felt like betrayal. Her mind was made up.

* * *

In the midst of a busy fall semester, Alba began consulting airline prices and lodging options as well as searching for information about how to identify the disappeared. She read of a vast vault of bones in Chile, a vault of the unidentified, the unknown, the lost. There was a surplus of demands for justice alongside a surplus of the unclaimed. Unimaginably brave women refused to forget their men; they carried pictures of their lost sons and husbands for years and proudly stood up against antagonism and apathy. She read about mass burials in the deserts of Atacama, burials by the ocean, places where criminals falsely imagined that untouched, remote nature would grant them impunity. Mr. Harker had told her about the desolate deserts of Utah and Nevada where men imagined that atomic explosions could take place without violence, only to discover that they had slowly and invisibly killed thousands. Evil seeks the desolate darkness, the remote corners of the earth where it can spread without notice. To combat it, men and women had to go into the darkness and shine a light, to prophesy to the dry bones, to allow the piles of stardust lying anonymously in the desert to reassemble into armies of the remembered. She would have to be one of those women, believing that her father's bones had an integrity—a self—that even the laws of ecology could not compromise. Stubborn belief and creative acts of commemoration as a way to answer the oblivion to which biology wants to condemn us. She imagined herself in the Santiago Temple watching while some elderly and gentle temple worker stood in for her father. It wouldn't matter who it was—any man's living old bones would do, because that was the beauty of it. An absence wouldn't have to signify a loss. Quite the opposite. The absence marked by an adopted presence promised reunion, restitution. All she needed was someone who out of love for the unknown dead would become Adam again and in faith and persistence in the face of mystery and opposition and death would walk out of the garden and into this beautiful, fallen world and wait on the Lord until his presence returned. She would witness this and she would know that her father whose story she would have gathered finally into her possession had received the gift of God's covenant and, like a prodigal, had come home to rejoin himself to his lost posterity and to the entire human family. In the temple was the great gathering: her life, her story just one brief but meaningful footnote in the archive of the unnumbered and vanished.

Her mind could not stop reconfiguring his face. She found herself sketching portraits of a visage that remained at large, inaccessible to her memory. But not to her art. She knew that at some point her young eyes had actually seen his face, so at least somewhere in the neurological networks of her brain lay the elements of composition. She prayed for the spiritual gift to bring the fragments together and worked for an answer. Sometimes he had a youthful countenance, a patchy, unshaven look, still not fully matured: hopeful, idealistic, unkempt hair, a kind of loose informality to his smile. His hair was always dark, like hers, somewhat long as was the style then, his shirt open slightly revealing a collarbone, a tilt to his shoulders, as if his intention were not to pose but to be gone. A man of strong instinct and passion. Did he wear glasses? She tried them on for him, cleaned his face, giving him a somewhat more intellectual, thoughtful appearance, the face of someone who well knew what he was doing, someone who read and debated late into the night concerning communal values, the prospects of a future without poverty, a future of universal flourishing, someone who undoubtedly and understandably had grown disappointed with his wife's political apathy and who was anguished but bold and clear-minded about the cost of ceding a fatherless life to his little girl for the sake of a world that he hoped his daughter would someday understand was still within reach if only enough people were willing to sacrifice for it. At times, she could almost convince herself that she could accept the sacrifice.

What, among her own traits, had she inherited from him, according to the hidden lines of influence—genes, atavistic powers, bloodlines—what was it that she had unknowingly inherited? Was he artistic? Was he spiritual in his own way? Was there something yet to emerge in her that would be a manifestation of him? Would she become an activist? Was he the one who inspired her to care for this earth, this life, this world here and now? Surely by now he could look down upon her with compassion and act in invisible ways on her behalf. This idea seized her one Sunday when a woman at church was giving a talk about the afterlife. The sister had been describing the extraordinary amount of death Joseph F. Smith, the orphaned nephew of Joseph Smith, had experienced. He first lost his father, Hyrum, who died in solidarity with his brother, the prophet Joseph, and then he lost his mother shortly afterward. He lost several children and his wife. And he then presided over the church in the midst of World War I and the influenza epidemic. And then, shaped by the experience of so much death, he finds himself reading in the book of Peter. Peter speaks of the mystery of Christ's work during the three days between his death and resurrection, and suddenly the prophet's eyes of understanding were opened and human understanding of death was suddenly and permanently transformed. Christ preaching among the dead. The dead awaiting and hungering for further understanding and getting it from the living and progressing beyond the short limitations of a mortal life always cut too short, always with insufficient understanding, a life subject to accident, subject to biology, to one's assigned time and place on the spinning earth. Each brief human moment here was a mere blip in the eternal expanse of time and human evolution toward higher purposes. So, of course, it would be him, she thought, a man so well acquainted with grief, who would understand that we can serve the dead and that they too serve us. "*We cannot forget them,*" the prophet had said, "*we do not cease to love them; we always hold them in our hearts, in memory; and thus we are associated and united to them by ties that we cannot break. If this is the case with us in our finite condition, surrounded by our mortal weaknesses, how much more certain it is to believe that those who have gone before can see us better than we can see them, that they know us better than we know them, we live in their presence, they see us, they are solicitous for our welfare, they love us now more than ever.*" And then, right then, shaking from head to toe, she knew. She knew who it was who stood behind and around her, bearing her up, protecting her, and who it would be who would guide her down in Chile, who it was whose hand she would hold again, who would guide her so many hundreds of miles away just so that she could finally turn around and see him as he is, as he was.

She hadn't bought the tickets yet and John hoped that maybe the plans would disintegrate, but he sought to downplay his anxiety since it seemed she was at some tipping point and he didn't want to push her away. He wanted to keep her close, to be the refuge she needed, but deep inside he panicked that he was losing her. She spent her evenings up late on the internet. He would try to wait up for her or try at least to wake up when she finally came to bed, but if he reached out to her in the dark, she was unresponsive. They were both frantically busy with school, so there was little time for informal one-on-one moments, let alone time for the kind of reflective talk that had been the backbone of their relationship. When they first met, it was all they could do to resist talking together about everything. They tried studying together but they always stopped to talk, to share ideas, to laugh. Alba was bright-eyed, happy, and passionate about everything and everyone. He couldn't get enough of her hunger for living. That was it: she loved life, she loved existence itself, and she saw miracles everywhere, cause for joy and cause for laughter. She was grateful for what was hers, but now all he could see in her eyes was a longing, a look into the distance, a focus beyond the present and beyond their place in this valley, a hungry need he could not satisfy. John could tell he was nowhere on that horizon that drew her away. It was as if she looked right through him. Knowing it was male vanity to feel hurt by this didn't make the pain go away. It didn't help that he was buried in research papers and barely had enough time to apply for law school. He knew they needed to talk about their prospects, about where to apply, but Alba seemed so focused on the past, it was too much to ask her to think about the future.

Not only had their meals with Isabel grown increasingly tense, but visits to his parents had also grown contentious. Alba and his father had never seen eye to eye on much, but at least they seemed to genuinely like each other at first. But when John's father learned of her plans, he sought to put out the fire by reminding her of her blessings as an American citizen, the difficult and costly American responsibility to keep the world safe from communist ideas and now from terrorism, and the creeping secularism of academia, even at Brigham Young University, that was leading to an increasingly misleading and distorted sense of history. "You don't have the whole story," he said. "You don't know what evils awaited Chile had communism survived."

One breakfast, in the rush of the morning, she announced her desire to leave the day after New Year's. Three weeks. She had contacted her aunt who lived in Santiago and she had offered her a bed in her apartment and promised, at least until she got there, to keep her decision hidden from her mother. There Alba intended to investigate her missing father, to talk with people she had been able to identify as involved in the recuperation of the dead. And she needed time and resources to travel if necessary to widen the search. She had saved up a little from working for Mr. Harker and had received permission to use some of her research funds for her thesis toward the trip. She had carefully gone over all of the projected costs and now it seemed doable.

"I thought you said we were at least a thousand dollars short. You know how I feel about credit card debt," he said.

"I am going to find a way to make it work."

"Sounds like you have it all planned." He didn't try to disguise his sarcasm.

"Yes, I do. I really think this is going to happen."

"I suppose it is. No one can tell you what to do."

"You sound like that is a bad thing. I thought you liked my independence. Why can't you be a little more excited about this?" She scrutinized his face. He didn't look up from the table.

"Independence is one thing. This feels different. I don't know. Were we going to talk about this at all? I mean, I understand why this matters to you. But still."

"Still what?"

"You could have consulted with me, that's all."

"What do you think I am doing now?"

"It sounds to me that you are telling me what you have decided."

"You don't think I should go?"

"No. I mean—look, what does it matter? You didn't want my opinion or you would have asked for it by now."

"I think I know your opinion, John. You have made it clear to me that this just doesn't matter to you."

"If it matters to you, then it matters to me. Isn't that good enough for you?"

"Why doesn't it matter to you, you know, all on its own? Why is this about supporting me in something you don't quite understand? Why can't you *understand* it? What would you do?"

"Look, it doesn't mean the same to me as it does to you, obviously."

"Obviously? I don't follow." He could sense her hurt and didn't want to exacerbate things.

"I am not going to pretend to understand what this is like for you. I don't have anything to compare it to, you know. I have always had my folks, always had my brothers and sisters."

"You could make an attempt. Just try to imagine not having any of that and not even having the feeling that the country you live in is your definitive home. You owe me at least some of your imagination."

"Well, I guess I'm not that imaginative. You've always had that gift, but not me."

"You got that right." She stood up and started to gather her things into her backpack for the day.

"Hey. That's not fair. Come here." He stood up and tried to reach her, but Alba kept gathering her things without looking up and without saying a word. "Alba," John helplessly offered. Throwing on her coat, she stepped out into the wintry air.

Chapter 6

Dear S.,

It's a strange thing to stand in the middle of a river, you know. You look upstream and you can see all the streams connecting into the main, but it's all moving together, like it was meant to be, like it is one connected thing, and then there you are standing in the middle of it, and you look down at your legs and the water splits, divides, forks away and around to accommodate you. So you start to realize that it was all an illusion that it held together as it did, that it isn't one thing but millions of molecules coincidentally pulled by gravity in the same direction. And then you look downstream and, well, the water has just adjusted itself and it is one again. It is all confluence. I don't know what makes me what I am. I don't know how to change the past and I have no idea what the future holds. And most of the time it all feels like every part of me has diverged from every other part. But at least I have the illusion of confluence when I write to you, like maybe it all comes together.

Your mother and I were happy when we married. And we were happy when we had you. You must know that. Especially happy. We weren't exactly as old as old Abraham and Sarah or my namesake Zacharias and Elizabeth, but we did have to wait a long time, you see, and after so many years of trying and so many tears shed by your mother, we had all but given up. I mean, we had a late start to begin with, right? What was I, thirty-four, when I first met your mother? Yes, and then two years or so of courting. And then, well, we were married for close to eight years before we had you. We had talked about adoption. I wanted it. I liked the idea, but it just wasn't financially feasible, given the costs of my schooling. So there we were, waiting, praying, and hoping. It is honestly the only prayer I think I ever believed was heard and answered. We were granted our one wish. One pure and perfect gift. Our little girl. I won't say I disbelieve the miracle now, but what's given, by definition, can be taken, right? So then what?

On the whole, your mom and I managed pretty well, but let's be honest, I didn't know the first thing about parenting. I am not trying to make excuses. Honestly. Just trying to say it like it was. I was ill equipped. Please don't misunderstand me. Our problems had everything to do with my own complicated journey and nothing to do with you. I own my responsibility. This is why I am bothering to write you. It's my way of tracing that responsibility, I guess, so that I can have a clearer idea of my responsibility and maybe too some of your understanding. I wish I knew for sure you were reading this. The truth is, I write in defiance of what I suspect to be true about the universe. So these words, you know, they just hang there, waiting.

What I want to say is that parenting is long and hard work. We humans are the slowest species to raise a young body into adulthood. I often notice the exhaustion on the young parents' faces around here and listen to the exasperation in their voices in the grocery store aisles and in the parks. Sure, there is happiness, but there is fatigue too, weariness from the strains and stresses of just managing a little willful body through the course of one ordinary day. And yet they do it over and over again around here, some of them with the reproductive capacity of rabbits. It's really amazing to me, even if incomprehensible. All of us come into the world so immensely helpless. As blurry or blank as our memories are as newborns and toddlers, I am convinced that we spend our lives aware of an utter dependency and a profound sense of hopelessness we learned early in life. And when we are met with love in such a state, as I believe I was, we understand instinctively that love is a gift, a kind of blessedness we could never have earned on our own.

And when I first held you in my arms, I couldn't help but love you, at least that is how it seemed to me. I didn't deserve any medal for such love. I simply couldn't resist it. You and I didn't have much of a relationship yet, other than staring into each other's eyes and working up smiles, so it wasn't as if I loved you because of your goodness. You were beautiful and fragile, which are almost synonyms to me, and in the glow of your beauty I felt nothing but astonishment and love for your very existence. I try not to resent others their children, their lives full of kin, but I would be lying if I said it doesn't hurt. I know this isn't altogether rational, but, you know, the way things seem now to be without pattern and broken in a pile at my feet, it makes me feel that perhaps all that love does is wound us. "Blessed are the poor in spirit," he said. Blessed and bloodied is what I think. I admit to my great shame that I have scarcely managed love for anyone ever since. Why bother, I wonder? It won't end well. And that's not because I am a pessimist. I am a realist. All things come down. All lives end. All, all is dust. Even these warm-blooded arms that once held you in gratitude.

Well, watching your mother being a mom was something else. She held you, rocked you, fed you. She carried you in a shoulder sling as she moved about the house and in the garden. She liked that idea, you know. She had heard that this was how Mayan mothers carry their children, so she wanted to try it. She took you wrapped against her breast on our hikes and nursed you in the open sun on a blanket in our front yard or high in the mountains. I mean this was a woman with a heart the size of a mountain who, while waiting for you to arrive, spent years wearing herself out in service of other people's daughters in our ward. She loved them like her own and they knew it. They frequented our house after you were born like so many doting aunts. She loved everyone and everything. God, she was a great big fiery ball of warmth for all God's children. She could have mothered an army. And then, finally, she had you. Can you imagine how ready she was by the time you came? Even she had lost hope when it finally happened, but then she shook off her pain like a deep slumber and launched into parenthood with relish.

Had I the talent, I would have painted the two of you on the grass. I wish I could have written poems about you, maybe composed some great music. I know that every time I hear great music or contemplate art of any kind, you two are all I think about. You shimmer there in my mind's eye like golden aspen leaves quaking in the wind and I am left with an exquisite sorrow. Of course, all that waiting and preparing put an enormous amount of pressure on her, and she was occasionally overcome from time to time by intense feelings of inadequacy and insufficiency. I've wondered about those old Biblical couples. Did they live in perpetual anxiety that something would go wrong, that they would prove unworthy of the gift? I wasn't much help. I mean, I knew I felt nothing but inadequacy and there she was doing her thing with such grace and beauty and perfection and she comes crying *to me* about her inadequacy? What was I supposed to say? All I wanted was to find a way to be more like her, but I felt stuck. I was more inclined in those days to believe in a benevolent deity, one who was more than willing to compensate for the failings of our best efforts, and I would remind her of this from time to time. I naively believed that all would work out in the end. I can see now that my optimism was fed by my own detachment. Your mom was all in, you see, all in. I tried to draw strength vicariously from her, telling myself her efforts were mine too, but as we moved forward, I could feel myself withdrawing, convincing myself of what I had always suspected, that I was out of my league.

Life was pretty simple before you were born. We had found our rhythm. We shared our labors. I didn't have to be the provider. Your mom worked at an office in town, making good use of her accounting degree. She made decent money, she liked it, and she was glad to work to support my graduate studies. We had plenty to talk about at the end of the day and plenty of joy too together in our moments alone or on the weekends in the mountains. I never thought that a pursuit of knowledge and the love of my wife and daughter would be in tension, but when you finally came, it felt like the mountains and my books were competitors with family life. Maybe I kind of wanted it that way on some unconscious level. I don't know. And I don't know why. I sometimes wonder if things only fall apart because we don't want to hold them together. I mean, I took botany seriously, like it was part of my religion. It wasn't just the study of plants. It was the study of everything. How can I explain this? Goethe, the great German poet, perhaps accomplished his greatest work in the field of botany. I can't speak for his family life, of course. Maybe he was as flawed as anyone else, maybe he too couldn't hold it all together, but he saw botany as a key to the universe, a key to understanding the nature of reality. He was terrified of passing through life only to discover that he had failed to penetrate the true nature of things around him. He knew that we are incredibly subjective, willful, even narcissistic creatures, but like a good romantic, he didn't see our willfulness as at odds with truth. Unlike your garden-variety romantic, however, he worked to nurture the imagination with careful empirical observation. He was an avid hiker, a lover of mountains and mountain flowers, so why not observe as much as he could about plants? He started to appreciate the many forms and functions of leaves, of seeds, of the metamorphosis of life, and he theorized about the deeper structure of all life, something that any of us can grasp if we but observe long and hard enough. And his great achievement was a kind of thought that was simultaneously spiritual, scientific, and poetic. Imagine that. Find me a mind like his today. Or like Humboldt's. They don't exist. They were friends, by the way. Can you imagine their conversations? Goethe unlocking the secrets of plant forms and Humboldt the secrets of climate. So without such minds, we cannot even imagine, let alone accept, the facts on the ground—that the climate is changing and life forms are dying. Goethe felt that science was a kind of spiritual seeing that combines empirical observation and insight and thus reveals the true nature of things. And what Goethe found was a kind of archetypal plant structure in which all plant life participates and that tells us something key about the very work of creation ongoing in the world every moment all around us. He understood that the intensity of this inner impulse in plants led to forms far more various than would be dictated by the need for simple survival. Think about it. What you have then is a world of forms that ultimately surpasses anything we might merely call mechanical or instrumental. We have a world of intrinsic value, a world full of autonomous forms that need no one and nothing to establish their value. They are valuable simply because they exist. Like any newborn child, you see. Like you.

So you see, I wasn't just learning plant names, understanding how to identify species. I was learning how to exist. I was learning what it meant to be alive. I had my religious sensibilities to thank too. Everything I learned felt spiritual. Nothing was merely temporal or secular. It was all of a piece and I drank deeply, I tell you. I was ecstatic. I didn't think that religion and science were irreconcilable, and I didn't think the life of the mind and the domestic life should somehow be at odds, but I eventually got my rude awakening. You see, on the one hand, science in those days still held to its own kind of faith in its capacity to know everything. Lord knows there is no shortage of scientists who still believe this. And because it was telling a story far different from what it set out all those centuries ago to tell, science was suspect. It certainly wasn't unanimously embraced in those days in the church. I am not sure how different it is today. I don't really know anymore. I couldn't even begin to explain to my fellow Mormons what wonderful thoughts and insights about deep time and evolution rolled across my mind. I was met with blank stares or disapproving reminders that the world and humanity were only six thousand years old. Even some of my fellow students seemed unenthused by the task of making holistic sense of it all. They seemed content just to get information that would get them an income. Can't blame them, really, what with all those mouths to feed, but I do blame universities for knowing better than to cave in to the pressure to produce workers rather than citizens. But I digress.

What I want to say is that I regret that from the very beginning I wasn't more intimately involved in nurturing and caring for that little body of yours. Here I was devoting my time to my passion for holistic understanding of the world and it was only opening up a divide between my domestic and academic worlds, between theory and practice, between the life of the mind and the life of the body. And that is, in essence, what a family is: a communion of bodies, a way of organizing ourselves in covenants around the use and reproduction of bodies. I have never had an argument with the domestic theology of Mormonism. I don't mean to suggest that I was particularly neglectful as a father, but, you know, when you cried, when you stirred in your sleep, when you needed to be held, I assumed it was largely your mother's work, and maybe it is just now in my solitude that I look back on this with so much useless regret. I do remember one long night, after a series of long nights with you. You had been sick and were probably teething too and your mother was so exhausted that she could barely move from the bed when you stirred. I insisted that she stay in bed and that I would give it a try to take care of you. And you and I wandered back and forth in the front room of our little apartment in the dark. I tried holding you close to my chest but your little body wriggled and writhed. You would not be consoled or distracted. I had my own pressures at the time, with my exams coming up, and I desperately wanted your mother to catch her sleep. I suppose in my mind I wanted this for selfless reasons. She was struggling, you see, to be that person she had been. She was simply too tired to be full of love for life and for everyone and I took it personally, probably because I was so dependent on her passion. She was getting increasingly distant and detached and seemed lifeless to me, and I wanted that warmth back, that person who could look me in the eyes, believe in me, and restore all things to their proper place. I was so damn weak. So maybe it was resentment for what you were doing to us, but I shouted at you, helpless thing that you were. I held you out in front of me and shouted. I wanted to shake you, but I didn't, thank God. Of course, this did nothing at all to provide your mother with the rest that she needed. She came out of her room and took you from my arms and left me morally defeated. I was never really able to regain her trust to care for you in the night after that.

I don't know why such a memory sticks around like that, but it does. I wish it would go away. It's stupid, really. There were many happy hours we spent together, many more than the dark ones to be sure. As you grew older there were moments when my confidence grew too, but I nevertheless could see the seeds of my undoing in those late hours of the night. Maybe my enemy was nothing more than self-doubt, a faltering of confidence that I could step up and be the kind of father I knew your beauty and fragility deserved. It was deflating to think that the best I could do would be to imitate my father, a man who was present but perpetually and hopelessly distant and cool. As impenetrable and unfeeling as a stone, that man. Old Bonner was more comfortable in his solitude with a newspaper in his hand than with a child, or a baseball mitt. The bottom line is that he didn't much care for people. Around him you learned to be disappointed in people, not surprised, and you certainly never caught him in open admiration of anyone. Made sense, given his hard life of mining in eastern Utah. I mean, he was punished, I tell you, having to live and work there. His father was no better. His harshest judgments were for politicians of any kind, public servants, clergy, academics. You name it. You stuck your neck out there in public service and he was more than willing to cut it off. Of course, I think he was right most of the time, and I always sympathized with his underdog status, but over time I began to realize that a human being, in my father's view, was a pitiful sack of bones, capable of only the most inadequate efforts to get things right. Bottom line, he was an ornery son of a bitch. For him, there was no point in overpraising a child, or praising him at all. Praise was like congratulating him just for existing, as if our individuality were some prize we had earned, since that only contributed to our sense of entitlement. To my father, humanity was cursed with a tragic combination of inability and overconfidence. We were better off admitting this to ourselves, and even though he never said it out loud, it seemed we were better off not existing. If he had been religious, he would have been a self-flagellating sackcloth-and-ashes monk, no doubt about it. This world was something you just had to learn to suffer through. The worst of it was that he never offered his children any reasons why.

Which is perhaps what made your mother so appealing to me and what, at least initially, made Mormonism so appealing too. Despite the fact of my baptism, I really knew nothing at all, to be honest. So I was more than happy to embrace a philosophy that directly opposed his pessimism and his cynicism. We were gods in embryo, children of a living God, brothers and sisters all, and this life was a unique and eternally significant chance to learn love, in this body, on this earth, here and now. We had answers, direction, and life—every single one of us had both pattern and purpose. We were made for joy. All things in fact were made for joy—the plants, the animals, all of it. And what we made of life here would translate into future spiritual realms. It was Christianity on steroids. It was a program designed to revolutionize society. I devoured Joseph Smith in those days, and I still consider him one of the great minds in American history, even if he was deluded. What hope the gospel offered me! I felt completely and totally renewed when I began to live a spiritual life. Sure, I was baptized way back when I was eight. I don't have the foggiest remembrance of that day. I have no idea who performed it. And I tell you I don't think I ever set foot in a church again. It was some arrangement with the bishop who was putting pressure on my parents to be right with the Lord and to get me dunked. But the conversion came much later and then the eventual unconversion, I guess. Around the time I started dating your mother, I began to open the scriptures for the first time. I still had them from my baptism. The bishop had given them to me. And I tried a few prayers on my own. I confess it was transforming. I did it because I wanted to, not because your mother was urging it on me. There was just something about finding myself in love with her, believing in a purpose, a destination, being called into life, and when I read and prayed, I felt a real intoxication, I tell you. To believe that you are born again, starting over, that nothing—not biology, culture, psychology, history, or sin—nothing could confine or define you, that is something. Every word was precious; it tasted sweet to me. You might be pleased to know that I still read the scriptures. They are beautiful to me, but I don't feel the same aura about the words and I don't read them for the same reasons, I guess. The poetry of belief has never left me, just the feeling. It's like listening to music you know so well it has ceased to move you deeply but you also can't exactly live without it. It accompanies you, you know. Because the truth is that I wasn't able to retain that feeling for very long. Precisely because I sincerely felt changed, it was shocking to me to discover that it wasn't exactly true that all that baggage was gone. As I aged into parenting, it was agonizing to have to face the fact that I felt no better than what circumstance and genes had long before dictated. I mean that's the strange thing about marriage and aging. You start this new life, and mine was made new not only because of your mother but because of my conversion, and then you find yourself in a set of circumstances for which you have no training at all and you fall back on instinct at each challenge only to discover that your instincts are all learned or programmed by your history and that you are nothing more than a sum of your parents, a sum of your past. And what's worse, your instincts are all wrong. I could see that I would be a no better father, and as I look back on it now, it was as if, like Oedipus, the harder I tried to avoid my fate, the more I fulfilled it. It is hard to have faith in God when you can't have faith in your ability to honor God enough to change, when you don't know where your demons come from, how to defeat them, or why, like changelings, they persist beyond the most earnest efforts to grow up.

My studies were going well. I was being groomed to replace Professor Hamblin at BYU. He had been there for ages. I took my first graduate seminar from him. He was a large, heavy man with an indefatigable curiosity about everything, and he was jovial too. Not sure why, but he liked me, despite my rather somber personality, and I liked him well enough. And he told me one day in his office that he had given it a lot of thought and had decided that I was the one he wanted to replace him. That was the way it was back then. I had always had this intense passion for learning but had never been able to imagine myself as a scholar of any kind, and then suddenly in my professors' eyes I was a budding scholar with promise, someone on whom they increasingly came to rely for help with their research. I was getting my name on some of their papers. I was growing increasingly interested in the field of ethnobotany, paleoethnobotany in particular. I wanted to know what purpose plants held for the ancient inhabitants of this valley but also elsewhere in Utah. We didn't know much about climate change back then, of course, but I suspected that there was a kind of dance among plant life, climate, and human culture that I needed to understand better. I was gone on long research trips with teams of researchers, leaving you and mom behind for long stretches. I did miss you, but I must confess the freedom of research was intoxicating. I could forget about my inadequacies for a while, you see, and return to my true love of the wilderness. That is where I was meant to be, and it little mattered to me if that wilderness was the desert, the high country of the Colorado Plateau, or the alpine forests of the Uintas. I wanted it all. Your mother was always interested in the research and she was supportive, but I could also sense that it was sapping her energy to spend so much time alone. Or maybe that isn't the right way to put it. I could sense, little by little, that she was learning to live without me, and maybe even so well that I began to wonder if I was even needed around the house. I don't mean to imply that she was mean or pushed me away, but you two were such a miraculous partnership and I could scarcely look upon you without feeling a tad jealous that I didn't seem to be an essential part of your intimacy. Maybe I just started to doubt that the new life I had adopted was real or really mine. I guess I had begun to think of the wilderness and my house as two separate spheres, each making incompatible demands on me for my time and attention and focus. This is perhaps my own thorn in the flesh I am describing, my constant sense of never really wanting to believe in the reality of things once they are placed right in my hands. I prefer the search, the yearning, the perpetual deferral. As much as it hurts to admit it, I probably deserve your absence. It suits me, even if that doesn't make it right.

There is a great irony in all of this now. You see, I spend my time thinking of you and your mother in the wilderness. That is where my memories of you are the most vivid and where I feel most whole again. It is where I think that maybe I am not alone. And when I am not in the mountains, I am in my house, a place that provides a constant reminder of your absence and of my failures. In my solitude, I spend my time reading and researching botany. I make some money here and there doing ad hoc work for the Forest Service. I get a research gig once in a while. I fight fires. I don't need much, so I get by, and have time enough for my own thoughts. Not such a bad life, really. Here I have a window onto the great wide world.

You always came with us whenever I was in town and could find time to explore the mountains with your mother. Hiking was our first love, so it was only natural that you would begin hiking as soon as you could walk. There was nothing quite like seeing the world through your beautiful eyes. I remember once hiking alone at dusk with you on my neck. I held your little ankles at my chest. You wouldn't have been much more than eighteen months old, only barely starting to make language, and as we walked, a great horned owl swooped silently just over our heads as it moved from one tree to another. It was only a hush, really, a slight movement of wind that caught my ear before I saw its heft in the shadows. You saw it and pointed at its dark shadow as it passed and managed to say, "bird!" I remember too hiking with you down by Capitol Reef. I knew about a location that had the remains of an Anasazi settlement. We came into an area with a cliff overhang and ruins of a wall against the stone, and I found a small matted ball of fiber from an agave plant on the ground. I explained to you that this had been in the mouth of a man over a thousand years before, that he chewed the plant like we chew gum, and that here it was, lying on the ground all these many years later, leaving us a clue about his life, just a trace of how he lived, loved, worked, and carved out his existence in this dry climate. You cupped your hands and I dropped the matted ball into your hands. You rolled it around for a moment and then let it fall back onto the dusty soil. You scooped up the red soil into your hands and let it fall back down again and said, "I love the desert, Daddy." You were only three, maybe four, but I was struck at your capacity, even at that age, for astonishment. In time, it was apparent that you loved all kinds of places: you were eager to experience the world with your little animal body, tasting whatever you found on the ground, touching whatever came into reach, throwing, tossing, measuring the world. I learned a great deal about my own relationship to the mountains from watching you. Your small body was such a miracle to me, and I loved scooping you up into my arms, hugging you, holding you on my shoulders or back, holding your hand as we walked, or letting you sleep in my lap when you were finally overcome. I can feel your little spine in my memory, your soft arms, and your tangled and wild hair. Not having seen the adult version of you, it is impossible to know what would have become of you.

* * *

My body is aging. The seasons come and go, and every day I see more evidence of our impact on this place. The pine beetle is slowly making its way across the state as the winters grow warmer and end sooner. This is killing the pines, you see, in droves. The fire season starts earlier and stays longer, and each year we anxiously measure the decreasing snowpack. Even when it is sufficient, no one can say how long we can sustain this population growth and the increasing demand for water. Not to mention our endangered air quality. Mormons gave up smoking but we sure seem slow to give up our cars. It is hard to watch with indifference. The future weighs heavily on me. I suppose if my father were around, he would say that humanity deserves this, so why bother worrying. I am not immune to such thinking. But somehow the vague thought of what it used to mean to work for your future still keeps me going, even though I no longer have any idea what the future means to you.

But consider what we are up against. I mean, I notice the smaller things: the stress on plants and animals we cause, the way we slowly morph everything around us. I like to say that I study slow violence, the kind no one notices until it is too late, but most of these larger symptoms are not hard to notice. It's not ignorance we have to fight. It is active and persistent denial, as if we could pretend that all of these symptoms had nothing at all to do with fossil fuels. Science gets thrown under the bus, you see, and you can believe whatever you want about the world. We no longer have to answer to an empirical, factual account of anything. There are no serious alternative studies providing any evidence to the contrary, only spin on what the science suggests, but no matter. You just tell stories about extremist scientists collaborating in their labs to bilk the government out of billions of dollars of research funds by selling us an alarmism that will guarantee their luxurious lifestyle and threaten our freedoms for years to come. The worst of it is that this crackpot conspiracy theory is governed by a theological narrative about the end of times, as if it is our moral duty to bring this world to a rapid and definitive conclusion. Exactly how is this supposed to be an inspiring theology? It's divinely sanctioned suicide, that's what it is. It's eat, drink, and be merry, for tomorrow we will resurrect. Seems to have nothing to do at all anymore with joy, at least not meaningful and lasting joy. Adam fell that men might be and men are that they might recreate. This is nihilistic at its core and deeply hateful of the poor, our children, and of our very earthly existence. Imagine. The world's miraculous capacity to regulate the climate, the delicate interplay between deep ocean currents, the cycles of weather, the balance of atmospheric temperatures, all in play in such a way that for the past 10,000 years has made civilization and human development possible. And then just when we discover that our behavior over roughly the last 150 years has disrupted that balance and is warming the planet and putting future generations at risk, all we can manage is a shrug of the shoulders. It must be necessary, we say. We can't help what is beyond our control, we say. Or it simply isn't happening at all, we say. Somehow we have convinced ourselves that we live in a universe that is not only indifferent but also invulnerable to our choices. So I ask: how exactly is this a defensible form of morality? We have become the weather makers, the new dominant force in the earthly system, and everything, from polar ice caps to our beloved wildflowers, is in a fragile state of rapid and unprecedented change. And all we can muster is a passive acceptance, or worse a forceful denial that uses God as its defense. It would be one thing to claim that the devil made us do it. Around here it sounds as if God did.

And so whom am I working for now, if not for you? What is it I hope to protect and why? Maybe it is just an elaborate form of anger management, but deep down I think that if I can get this book published, it will awaken enough people to beauty, to fragility, and to a sense of responsibility, that maybe their children will someday thank them and maybe even forgive them. In God's absence and in my better moments, maybe now I labor for children not my own.

* * *

I am fortunate to have Alba working for me. We have made good progress. Just this week, she and John came up to the house to sort through some of her paintings. We had been focusing on the results of the summer and trying to figure out which were our best options. John had gone to some length to organize the paintings according to color and petals, and he was rather proud of himself as he helped Alba spread the paintings out on to the floor.

"No, no, no," I said. "We have something very different in mind." I started pulling out as many alpine plants as I could find from the various piles and throwing them together.

I guess I was a little abrupt, because John was exasperated. "*We* do? Does that include Alba and me? Just wondering. I mean, it's not like this didn't take us some time to do." His hands were on his hips. Alba sat silently on the ground.

"Look, this is all wrong. I mean, sure, every wildflower book you can find uses this kind of cataloguing, but it's all wrong. Wrong. It's the whole point of the project! The last thing we need is yet another dry and rational encyclopedia of flowers ripped out of context. No life without context." I could see John and Alba look at each other with a grin.

"Okay, go ahead and show us." He stepped back and put both of his hands out, as if to usher me in.

"Look, no need to get pouty, John. I have been at this for years. It's only understandable that you would get this wrong." He thought I didn't notice him roll his eyes at Alba who just smiled back. I didn't care. He needed a good lecture, and I was ready to give it. It's terrible really, but I couldn't help myself. They were a captive audience.

"We need another model," I announced proudly. "We need a new cosmology. Let me see if I can help you understand this. Flowers have distinct qualities and yes they belong in families, but they belong as much to families as they do to context. Descent is only one part of the story. The genetic code of all living things is a map that reproduces likeness so it is only natural to assume that we can best understand life forms in terms of descent, in terms of family trees, but you see that doesn't quite get at it. Only a shallow understanding of time would lead us to see the most obvious markers of that likeness as predominantly significant. We pretend as if the genetic code of life, its intrinsic quality, if you will, is all there is, but that ignores extrinsic qualities, qualities that have to do with relationships, with context, with interdependency. Because, you see, the sum total of what makes a plant is derived from the complex interplay of intrinsic *and* extrinsic forces." I was on a roll and I was not really caring any longer if they were even listening. It was the sweetness of my own logic I enjoyed.

"So when we imagine that two different flowers with yellow petals should be grouped together in some book for handy referencing, all we do is reinforce the mistaken idea that we humans can categorize the world and not have to see it in context and in relationship. These books, as well intended as they might be, simply divorce us from life, letting us imagine living things as static. I want to tell the story of relationships, you see. A relational botany. This book is far more than a guide to wildflowers, it's going to be the Bible of the wild to bring about the great reconciliation!"

At this, John started laughing. "What's so funny?" I shot back. I wanted to bring down the full weight of my wrath on the twerp, but Alba's presence kept me in check.

"Well, I don't know, Mr. Harker, but that seems a little ambitious, don't you think? The 'great reconciliation'? Really? It's just a book of wildflowers."

"Just a book . . . just a book. Yes, well maybe you are right, it's just a book. But I didn't hire Alba to produce 'just a book.' It's going to be a work of art, the whole thing." I turned back to the paintings and continued my organizing. There were many fine paintings, and Alba had done a brilliant job of capturing the feel and personality of an individual plant and the quality of soil and context too. I could feel the weather in them.

"This one is pretty good," I said, holding up the painting of Parry's Primrose nestled in the granite.

"Glad you like it," Alba said. "I remember how much you liked the flower."

"Well, you can see it here in context, right? That's what we are after. You caught that strange spot beneath the boulder. What an unlikely place to be! I love it."

"I've got a question for you, Mr. Harker." John was not ready to back down. "I see your point, but I am just wondering, doesn't the book risk just being a mishmash of images? I mean, how are people going to find a plant that they want to find?"

"There are other books for that sort of thing. This book isn't about finding and naming plants. It's about creating relationships between the reader and this place. It's about a different way of seeing. Our mistake all along has been this penchant for naming, which is really born out of a kind of conquest mentality. We name things in order to fix them on a map, hold them in place."

"But at what point does emphasizing environment just, I don't know, sort of erase all distinctions? I am no scientist, but surely color, petals, genetic codes—these things matter. It's not as if a seed of a columbine that I take from the mountains and plant in my window box in New York City is going to come up a daisy. A columbine doesn't forget that it is a columbine and it won't survive if it isn't treated like one." John wasn't stupid. I knew that much.

"I can bear witness to that, that's for sure," interjected Alba. "I was born Chilean and transplanted here, and for the longest time I thought that my environment was all that mattered, that I was American just like anyone else. But lately I am beginning to doubt it. As American as I dress and speak and sometimes feel, something in me holds me back, pulls me back, and won't let me be changed by this environment."

"Well, let's not get too romantic about this. We are talking about plants, not people. Chileans aren't a different species, in any case. Or are you?"

"Very funny." Alba smiled sarcastically.

"Well, it's a serious point. If you feel Chilean, it's not because you are genetically wired to feel that way. It's because of experience, memory, and environment from your childhood. You see, it only reinforces my point. And maybe a few visits like ones you've no doubt had only reinforces those feelings of difference."

"I have never been back to Chile. Left when I was four. That's it. Crazy. It's like I spent decades there, the way it pulls at me."

"Why have you never gone back?" I asked.

"Well, that's a complicated story." She glanced at John. "Lately it feels as if I should go back to explore my roots." John's body language grew tense.

"Of course. Why not?"

"My mother, you know. She just doesn't say anything good

about it. Doesn't want me to know. And the more she protests, the more I want it. It feels biological to me. I mean, sure, there were memories but the fact is I don't remember much at all, so whatever I learned in context is just so deeply inside of me now, I don't see the difference."

"There's nothing intrinsically Chilean about you, no genetic code telling you to like certain foods or music."

"It's a lot deeper than food and music, Mr. Harker."

"My point is, there is no such thing as Chileanness that comes down biologically from your ancestors."

"That's easy for you to say. Maybe you are so thoroughly surrounded by likeness, you can't see your own roots. I think that is the way it is around here. What is this valley, eighty percent Mormon? With the vast majority coming from Scandinavian and British people? It's pretty easy to argue that the rest of us should just give up on our obsessions with our past because your past, I don't know, it just comes out in the wash. I mean, I used to believe that. We act as if the past had no relevance to who we are. I just don't buy it anymore."

I expected John to seem pleased that someone else was willing to argue with me, but he looked perplexed by Alba's argument.

"Well, of course the past matters but only as context. I am not arguing you should give up your interest in it. Quite the contrary. That's my point. Had I been born in Chile, things would feel a lot different for me, even if I might still look like everyone else around here. I would want to go back too and I would not hesitate to go."

This seemed very reassuring to Alba. She looked at John and said, "See?"

"Look, your children will certainly feel more American than you do, and their children even more, until no memory of Chile remains or until the family transplants itself again. That's what environment does. Anyway, the fact that you are caught between two environments is a merely temporary fact in the long chain of your family line."

"That's exactly what I am afraid of," Alba insisted.

"What is?"

"Forgetting Chile, erasing the past. Making my father even more irrelevant to his posterity, making the fact of my being born there as insignificant as, I don't know, having been born on a Tuesday. My story matters, just like everyone else's and I shouldn't be expected to suppress it or pretend that it doesn't matter. That kind of thinking makes me crazy. I don't really care what it is that makes me feel this way. The bottom line is that I feel this way. It's who I am!" Her hands gesticulated whenever she got serious, which was often.

I was concerned that we had strayed off topic. "Look, for the sake of clarity, let's not confuse categories here. We are talking about flowers and evolution through deep time, not culture and the shallow category we call 'identity.' I know identity is all the rage these days, that we love to, you know, 'find' ourselves, find our voice, and everyone gets a trophy and all that horseshit, but in an evolutionary sense, it is all nonsense."

"Nonsense? You consider it nonsense to concern myself with who I am? With where I came from?" She was hopping mad again.

"I am only trying to say that your personal circumstances don't have anything to do with what we're talking about. Small-scale shifts of an individual plant, or even of a person, in space or in time tell us so little. We have to pull back out from the moment and look at the bigger picture. What a life form carries inside itself as it unfolds into the world is just as important as the world into which it unfolds. Atmosphere, climatic conditions, ecological interdependencies and collaborations, predators and risks—these all shape and morph that code over time to make for new possibilities, even speciation. Suddenly you face the possibility of new life emerging precisely out of that interplay, you see? Environment and how species respond to it, in other words, is part of the creative process of life, not just genes. So these flowers, you see, each one is a miracle, a testament to the creativity of life and no two forms are exactly alike! That's the marvel of it all. Life never gets monotonous, at least not to those who have the eyes to see. But you have to pay attention! That's what I have been saying. We aren't paying attention. So we need to organize all of this according to season, elevation, and microclimate. That way they are visible in greater context with their neighbors and, you know, more relatable."

Alba and John were suddenly both silent. Alba was emotional, staring at the floor full of her paintings. I hate that, I really do. Not sure how to stop it though. She has a lot going on. Maybe I had managed to offend them both, which is not new for me, I guess. I am never quite sure how it happens, but it does. I appealed to my better angels.

"I don't know the first thing about being Chilean, so guilty as charged, but not because of my philosophy. Just because I am ignorant. What does it mean to you to be Chilean?" Her shoulders relaxed almost as soon as I asked and so too did her voice.

"That's just it. I don't know. And I guess that's why it feels so deeply rooted in me, like it's part of my genes. My mother took me to this country when I was four years old after my father was killed. And that's about all I know, if you can believe it. So it's hard to be convinced that somehow it's the environment that has stayed with me, rather than something inside of me when I remember virtually nothing about the place. But it's like the facts of the case have defined me, even without my knowing anything about it. How does that work? I mean, it's not creativity on my part. There's nothing to respond to, except what comes up from inside of me. The truth is, for me, it's not biological or cultural. It's something else altogether. I keep telling John, I feel the spirit of Elijah. I feel called to know his story."

"You know your father was killed?" I asked.

She nodded. "He was disappeared during the Pinochet dictatorship. I don't know much else. I have no contact with his family, and my mom doesn't like talking about him at all. And as I have gotten older, I find myself thinking about him nonstop. John and I have been talking about finding a way for me to go back to find out more." She gave John a glance when she said this. He now leaned against the sofa with his arms folded. I could sense my opportunity.

"What's stopping you from going?"

"What is stopping me, John?" she asked, with pain in her voice.

"Well, money, for one. Look, I am not stopping her, but I just don't understand what good could come of it. Her mother doesn't either."

"It must be an expensive flight down there. What is the cost?"

"It's like $1200 or so," John quickly answered. "To say nothing of food and lodging and what it costs to move up and down such a long country."

"Hmmm. Well, I think you should go. I think John and your mother should encourage it. It's only natural."

"Natural? Isn't that ironic." John was stinging. "All this time you want us to believe that identity is a ruse, that context is what matters, and suddenly Alba tells you that she wants to go back to find her roots, that it's not just biological, but that it's spiritual, something you don't even believe in, and you say it is 'only natural.' I think you should just stay out of this. I don't see how this is any of your business."

I think I could feel in the back of my mind that I had relished a little bit the chance to drive a wedge between them, and maybe that was because of my need to make sure I had room to deepen my connection to Alba. Maybe that was unnecessary. Maybe there was on some level a kind of competition for Alba that was just my own immaturity. And maybe others would think something creepy about this, but you understand, don't you?

You know my pain; you know my loneliness. You know my need to feel redemption, to get another chance, you know, to be the kind of father I failed to be. And here I was already getting it wrong before it had even really taken root. But the girl should go to Chile, for crying out loud. That much is obvious.

We had talked enough and feelings were raw. So I crouched down and continued the work of rearranging the paintings according to my criteria while they watched. I occasionally made some explanations to help them understand my logic, but I didn't try to press any further. John was pretty eager to have the morning over and done, but he was stuck. Alba was quiet but she watched what I was doing closely, and as the flowers began to find their neighborhood, so to speak, she was struck by the juxtaposition of colors and textures, as was I.

"Why not paint them in neighborhoods? Why bother painting them as individual plants at all?" she suddenly asked. And just like that it suddenly seemed obvious what we would be doing next. I sat back for a moment on the ground and wrapped my arms around my knees, looking at the paintings and then looking back at Alba.

"Well, now I know what to pay you to do next spring and summer. This is exactly what we need. We can intersperse the individual portraits with portraits of plant neighborhoods to introduce each chapter. That is a brilliant idea!" Alba's melancholy had worn off. It never seems to last too long, and she genuinely seems to love this project, so that made me happy. The sulky guy in the corner was another matter.

As we put away the paintings, now in their new order, I asked if I could have them for a while, to pull out and consult to inspire me while I wrote. Alba agreed. John was already in the car before I had a chance to put things away, but Alba lingered. I saw my chance.

"Hold on just a minute, will you?" Alba waited while I went in to my bedroom. When I came out I handed her a check written out to her.

"Listen. I know that you might feel uncomfortable accepting this, and if you end up deciding you shouldn't or that you can't make the trip, I will understand. Just rip it up. But you can plainly see, as can everyone else in this valley, that I don't have any family to worry about, and I can see that you need to go to Chile, so please just do me the favor of making much better use of this money than what it was doing just sitting in my account, okay?"

There was a long pause and I could see tears welling up in her eyes. She took the check and pressed my hand. John honked. She laughed at her tears and quickly wiped them before she turned and headed out. Before she shut the front door behind her, she turned back and mouthed an emphatic "thank you."

Chapter 7

In the predawn, it was cold and dark and, as was often the case in the early morning hours of winter, the blanket of inversion pressed down low against the valley floor. It was close to two weeks since it last snowed and the air had grown thicker with smog. Alba would be glad to miss this. She was struggling to get through the winters as she grew older. She noticed it at first when she started college and at the time it was hard to distinguish what she was feeling from the stresses and strains of student life, but as the years passed she realized that by the time March rolled around, she was near emotional exhaustion. Chile was the allure of a reversible world, a profound upturning of everything she knew: what it meant to live as an American, to speak English, to have only known life with a mother, to be married as a certain kind of woman, and what it meant to be Mormon. And right now it promised the fullness of summer. For months now, she had been groping in the dark for the passageway to find what alternatives were available to her. She knew that John felt all of this as a kind of reprimand, a rejection of all that he had offered her life. He drove to the airport in silence. Despite his reservations, he had gone to great lengths to facilitate the trip, not to mention the money he agreed they could spend.

"Do you remember that poem by Robert Frost, 'The Road Less Traveled'?" she asked suddenly to break the silence.

"Sure."

"I remember discussing it in my American lit survey class when I was a sophomore. And all these kids were so confident about what they thought it meant, you know, that great tribute to making the bold and uncommon choice. What was particularly exasperating was that the professor seemed to encourage that line of thinking. But have you really read that poem?"

"Well, I read it once, maybe in high school. Not sure, but I think I remember the basic point. Right? He takes the road less traveled and that has made the difference. Something like that, right?"

Alba sat up and stared at the dark highway. The fog grew thicker as they approached the airport. "Well, that's my point. What difference does it make? The poem never really answers the question. He simply states that it makes all the difference to choose between alternatives, but there is really no way of knowing that taking one road or the other was the right one. All he says is that it makes a difference to choose. And there you have it. You're still stuck with the uncertainty of your choices." They both sat silently for a moment. "I wish I spoke up more in class. That's what I wish."

John seemed to catch the drift. He chose his words carefully. He wanted to get it right. "You are making a bold decision right now." He paused. Alba was silent. "I know you . . . you don't necessarily know if it's the right thing to do or not, right? I mean, I get that. But I admire it. I admire it . . . because, you know, you are being *you*. You always are. I wouldn't have it any other way. If we could afford it, you know I would go with you, but maybe it's best you go alone anyway."

His words touched her. She looked at him as he drove. Her fears rose to the surface.

"What if it's all a waste? What if I find nothing? Or worse, what if I find something I don't want to know?"

"We can weather the storm, whatever comes. I will be here to welcome you back with open arms, Alba. You know that, right?"

He put his arm on her leg and gave it a gentle squeeze. She rubbed the top of his hand with hers and squeezed him back. She fought back the tears. She felt stupid: stupid for having made such an urgent demand of him, for the intensity of her emotions over the past couple of months, and for the immense expense of money, especially after her hard-earned salary working for Mr. Harker. The thought that this was a terrible waste and a gesture of indifference toward John seized her. She leaned against the window away from him and stared into the dark.

John pulled to the curb and dutifully emptied the trunk of their old Honda Civic and placed her luggage on the curb. After a silent embrace, he kissed her carefully and then, without a word, returned to the car and drove away. Inside the airport, she found a phone and called their house and left a message, even though she knew he wouldn't get it until he got home from school later in the day. She didn't know what to say exactly, but she felt something was necessary. "I'll be thinking of you," she said. "And thanks, John—thank you for what you said."

The airport was bustling in its last-minute preparations for the Olympics. They had been expanding portions of the airport for a few years, and it was starting to look and feel like a real hub of an important city. This clearly was the ambition all along. She remembered watching the news as a child and seeing the elation on the faces of the Salt Lake Olympic committee when the news broke that Salt Lake had been chosen. And as the Olympics had approached and all the preparations were in full steam over the past months—the expanding of the highways, the construction of venues, including expansion of key ski areas, even a hockey rink in Provo, and the development of downtown Salt Lake—she and everyone else in the state had grown skeptical about the value of the deal. What was so wrong with being remote, provincial, an undiscovered country of hidden beauty? And there were so many anxieties about the security at the Olympics in the wake of 9/11. Would they be able to prevent an attack? Would someone aim their anger at the LDS church headquarters? Would the events heal the nation of its fears or reinforce them? And the scandals that had erupted, news of bribes offered to officials of the Olympic committee, offered by two Mormon men who had had the trust of the public to do this the right way. They were intent on defending themselves, claiming their innocence. The mayor and the Salt Lake committee had hired some big gun, some Mormon man who had made his name in the consulting business, someone the papers described as the knight in shining armor who would save the integrity of the Olympics.

The mutual mourning the nation had undergone in the wake of the attack on the Twin Towers had morphed into an anxiety: an anxiety about losing the authentic America and a fear of strangers, of people who dressed differently, spoke differently, believed differently, people who not only didn't admire the American way of life but who might target it as the enemy. Alba knew that her dark eyes and dark hair marked her. The problem was that she didn't feel she had a story to even explain her difference. And all along circling around in her mind were those verses every Mormon knows by heart, repeated to Joseph Smith by an angel in a vision, that the hearts of the children must be turned to the fathers and the fathers to the children or else the earth will be cursed. But now in the wake of the collapsed towers it seemed that being American and following the Spirit of Elijah were mutually exclusive choices. Sure, honor your ancestors, just not to the point where it makes your differences too pronounced. It's a lot easier if your story fits. She had heard and loved the pioneer stories since she was young, but all the telling and retelling of these stories of the great crossing across the Atlantic, and the crossing to Utah, the yearly parade and celebration of the Mormon arrival to the "right place" had begun to feel too linear, too white. Her mother's family's trek was a jagged line—once Sephardic Jews in Spain, Catholics by way of Chile, and now Mormons replanted in American soil. And who knows what labyrinthine paths her father's line followed? And if you wanted to go back to your past? Were you like Lot's wife, ungrateful for the chance to escape? Her roots had been papered over by the acts of governments and men. It was a conundrum to know how to imagine and honor crooked lines, how to restore things to a workable coherence. She knew at least that she wanted all of it. She wanted no part in willed erasure, in indifference to whatever part of her might be an atavism of the past. She had genetically absorbed the features of her ancestors but it was another thing entirely to recognize and give a history to each of those features.

A Hispanic family sat near her at the gate. She wondered, as she always did, about their legal status. Legalization had all but become impossible for many immigrants in Utah since 9/11, and people she had known and come to love in her wards and people she saw in the markets, on the trails, fishing down by the lake, people from every walk of life and from virtually every Latin American nation right here in the shadows of the Wasatch Mountains were losing their hope for the privileges of security she had been given. She had been lucky, of course. With the aid of several former missionaries who knew her mother, they were able to travel to Utah and make a persuasive argument for political asylum. Now Utah was preparing to welcome the world, even as the borders of the country grew tighter and citizens grew increasingly anxious about so many strangers in their midst. It was as if strangers were suddenly multiplying before national eyes, as if no one had noticed them until now. Alba wondered if maybe she had become, or had always been, one of those strangers, not a fellow citizen with the saints as she had been made to feel so early in her life.

* * *

"Ay, ¡aqui estás!" Her aunt, Marycruz, held her arms outstretched and kissed her on both cheeks, as she deplaned. *"¡Que hermosa eres! Aún más que yo me imaginaba!"* She held Alba out in front of her to take her in. She had the same frizzy hair of Alba's mother, dark too like her own. With alabaster skin, she was well dressed in a flowing burnt orange skirt, a white blouse and a delicate navy blue scarf wrapped around her neck. She was the younger sister, the only family contact Alba had in Chile. When

her grandparents died a few years back, Alba's mother could only afford to fly herself back and only for her mother's funeral. Alba knew that her mother had great admiration for her sister, although she had often lamented the fact that Marycruz had not had good luck with men. "Not as bad as mine, of course," she often corrected herself. Marycruz was petite, just a little over five feet tall, Alba guessed. Her many bracelets tinkled as her arms reached out repeatedly to touch Alba's face as if to reassure herself that Alba had really come. Her warmth was comforting. She had never taken an interest in her sister's religion, but she had written to Alba a few times when Alba served her mission in Ohio. Alba encouraged her at the time to look into the church, but Marycruz never acknowledged the suggestion. Until Alba had written about a possible trip, they hadn't communicated since her wedding to John.

As they waited for her luggage, she watched those around her and admired the intimate familiarity they shared with their language, their accent, their expressions. It occurred to her that this intimacy was what she shared with people in Utah even without recognizing it, the way the mouth forms familiarly around sounds, idioms.

As they exited the airport, Alba immediately felt the pleasant shock of full summer sunlight and heat. She could sense her skin's response to the warmth as if a part of her were coming out of hibernation. Despite the long night of travel, adrenaline had kept her entirely alert and awake. Marycruz asked about her sister, about John, and even about Alba's art. Since the wedding, Alba had spoken Spanish less often and she noticed the difference. Her vocabulary felt weak and Marycruz spoke rapidly, causing her to have to respond from time to time with a "*¿Cómo?*" Or when that got too embarrassing, she just pretended to understand the full extent of what her aunt was saying. She was interested in the landscape around her. The air was thick with pollution. She could just make out a ring of mountains around the city, and where they drove was dry and almost desolate, reminding her of her home on the edge of the Great Basin. As they got closer to the city, the traffic slowed and the streets narrowed. Marycruz lived just a short distance from La Moneda, the presidential palace about which Alba had heard so much. It was the site of the coup in 1973, and was bombed by the military only moments before Salvador Allende ended his own life rather than surrender.

"Eso fue un día espantoso, te lo digo," Marycruz volunteered just as they passed in front of the palace. People streamed up and down both sides of Avenida Bernardo O'Higgins. The sun beat down on the streets in full summer splendor. "There is part of the campus of the University of Chile. I was a student there at the time of the *golpe*, you know. Terrible day. The day this nation fractured, broke into pieces. We have never forgotten the role your country played in changing our history. We are still trying to piece things together, but we are making progress at least." The streets were now all one-way streets and they were circling around her apartment complex. The sidewalks were paved with tiles, open circles or squares around the maple, sycamore, and occasional acacia trees that lined the streets. Construction projects blocked portions of the streets, around which pedestrians walked—businessmen and women, students, young families, the elderly. Alba noticed how many walked with cigarettes in hand. There was a kind of ethnic homogeneity to the people, but Alba couldn't quite put her finger on what it was they had in common. Certainly a lot of dark hair, like hers.

As they drew closer to the apartment building, Marycruz was eager to teach Alba as much as she could. She spoke with brightness and energy. "The bombing happened pretty early in the morning, but did you know that Allende spoke to the nation on the radio before he died? They say it was a spontaneous speech, but it was remarkably coherent and moving. I was at home. A friend called to tell me to put on the radio, so I caught most of it. Many of us memorized it over the years. I still remember the last line: *mi sacrificio no será en vano, tengo la certeza de que por lo menos será una lección moral que castigará la felonía, la cobardía, y la traición*. I remember being desperate to call your mom to tell her to listen too, but she was commuting to work, so she didn't learn about the events until later in the morning. Your mom met your dad several months later, I think it was. We had our differences over that day, your mom and I, but we got along okay. She has never been too dogmatic, you know, but always gentle and willing to listen. That's what I respect about her. She was the same way about religion, thank goodness. That too could have been the end of things for us. To be honest, I was the dogmatic one. I have improved." She smiled at Alba. "Well, at least a little bit. It didn't sit right with me that she wouldn't take a stronger stance against the government. She and I both knew the government was a disaster. She was never a defender, you know, just cautious, worried. That's what I remember."

"That's not the impression I got growing up."

"What do you mean? What impression did you have?" she asked as they pulled to a stop in the parking lot.

"That she thought the revolution was dangerous, foolhardy even. She always said my father created his own mess."

"Well, we will talk about that." She patted Alba on the leg. "That's what you are here for, right?"

She stopped and rolled down the window to greet a friend, an elderly woman, who was walking on the street. She introduced her niece to her and the woman reached across the driver's seat to touch her hand.

"*¡Qué gusto conocerte!*" she said warmly.

"*Gracias, mucho gusto.*" That was almost natural, she thought in self-congratulations. Marycruz drove on and resumed her discourse.

"For some reason, I was desperate for her to validate my anger and I think maybe because she was afraid that the anger had no chance of resulting in anything good, she always tried to cool me down. At the time, it only made it worse." At this, she laughed at herself. "*Ay*, I could have strangled her sometimes. And this was right on the heels of her baptism, you know, so that didn't sit well either. I was pretty much becoming a Marxist atheist and here she was, believing in speaking angels and golden plates! Imagine that! Our problems were nothing compared to what many families experienced, especially afterward, but at the time they felt pretty monumental. I am embarrassed about that now. We caused our parents a lot of stress, I think. Before they passed away, they were finally at peace with things, but still. In the end, even before she met your father and before he was disappeared, she was aware of how profoundly undemocratic things were and she was pretty sympathetic to our cause."

"Your cause? You mean you were involved in the resistance?"

"Well, we called it a revolution, but yes. Many of us were."

"What did you do, exactly?"

"My job was to read the newspapers, especially international ones, in order to gather information about how our story was being told and what kinds of pressure were being brought to bear on the government, because of course none of that news would ever appear in our local papers."

"But back then you didn't have the internet. Where would you get these papers?"

"Oh, in the libraries. I was a journalism student, so that was my excuse. But when I took notes, I had to hide them inside of folders that I carried around and delivered to others. I would have been in big trouble coming out of the library with a pile of notes on what the rest of the world was saying about Pinochet. We had a slit that would open inside the folders for papers that could be hidden. I held my normal school notes in the main pocket. It was quite something."

"I had no idea you were involved. My mom just doesn't say much about those days. Growing up, that was normal, I guess. I mean, I didn't really know any better, but then, you know, as I started to learn more about Chile, especially when I took a class in college about human rights, her silence began to bother me. I started to accuse her of being a defender of Pinochet, of blaming my father for his own death. She said it was more complicated than that, but she always refused to talk about it beyond that. It got insufferable. All those walls. All that silence."

"Ah, well, you have been having a real Chilean experience then! We Chileans know all about silence and walls, and all for the sake of getting along."

They pulled into a driveway that led to a gate. Marycruz punched the code and the gate opened to a basement parking lot. "*Tía*, I can't thank you enough for welcoming me here. This means more than I am ever going to be able to express."

"*El placer es mío, mi amor.*" They parked the car and began unloading the luggage from the trunk. "Here, let me take that. *Ven.*"

She started to pull her bag on its wheels toward the elevator. Alba followed with her backpack.

"You travel light!"

"I don't travel. That's just it. And I don't have much, anyway." They went up in the elevator.

"I live on the 11th floor. It's got a nice view, you will see."

It was a small but stylish apartment, with wooden sculptures from other countries and trinkets either hanging on the wall or nestled in a corner. A large bookshelf stood in the main room. Heavy curtains gave the place a dark and cozy feeling. She stood by the main window in the dining room, looking out on the city. She could scarcely make out the mountains in the distance because of the smog, but she could see a vast expanse of buildings, some taller than others, and narrow streets, a mixture of apartment complexes, businesses, government buildings, and the university. Santiago made Salt Lake look like a small town. Marycruz sat behind her and continued speaking.

"Tomorrow we can go to the *Vicaria de la solidaridad*. It's very close by. Originally the work of priests, you see, men of the cloth who were not afraid to play Jeremiah. They have been compiling the names of the disappeared and helping to bring the perpetrators to justice. It's not a perfect system, and I will tell you that for many of us bringing back the memories has been excruciatingly slow, but we are getting somewhere at least. *No hay justicia sin memoria, ¿sabes?* And justice delayed is hardly justice at all, of course, but you take what you can get. It is the honest effort that is important above all. It means a great deal to have a society commit publicly to clean the cobwebs off the past. It's risky, of course, because if you don't succeed—if this turns out to be just an empty gesture—it's almost as offensive to the human spirit as burying the truth in the first place. So we are precariously balanced, you see. I call it the *Precaria es la solidaridad*. Yes, I made that up!" She laughed. Alba turned and sat down with her at the dining table. She listened intently.

"You see, the effort could easily collapse and all will have been for nothing. It took all this time just to get the bastard back into the country. You know the story, right? They'd been carting him around in a wheelchair in England, you know, claiming that he was suffering from dementia and physical ailments that prevented a trial. Well, he lands here, just two years ago, mind you, and steps out of the wheelchair and greets and hugs those who came to give him a warm military welcome. Imagine that. And he arrives with millions he stole from us. But then, you know, he is suddenly too ill again, too demented, to stand trial. I can tell you one thing: demented is what he is—always was. And we are still waiting to put the very father of our criminal past to trial. It's not over. Nothing ever is, I suppose, but it hangs over us, divides us still, and refuses full resolution. There are still lots of strong feelings of support for the man, and for that time: people fail to remember or to acknowledge the crimes. But they can't be buried forever.

She pointed to the couch. "Lie down if you want. Let me get you some food. You must be exhausted."

Alba moved to the couch and lay her head back for a moment and took a deep breath. Marycruz went into the kitchen around the corner to begin preparing some avocado and bread and tomatoes and onions. Alba could see and hear her from where she sat.

"So he is still alive, right? And still free?"

"That's the sum of it," Marycruz replied as she opened the refrigerator. "We are having to accept the possibility that he will never be convicted or never even brought to trial. I mean, there are those who have devoted their entire lives since those days to bringing people to justice, to keeping the names and faces of the disappeared in our memory, but the reality, Alba, is that a great many never find resolution. They never find their loved ones and the perpetrators walk free. And yet their searching continues. It defines them. I have a friend who lost her son in the north in Calama. She moved there and spends every day—every day, I am not exaggerating!— walking the floor of the desert with a stick, moving it back and forth over the surface like this." She stepped back into the dining room and moved her arm from side to side in front of her, like a blind woman guiding herself.

She spoke with special intensity, almost on the verge of tears.

"And what for? So that she might find remains of her son, who has never been found. She is convinced that he was buried there. I don't doubt it. We have had reports in the news over the last few years of mass burials just discovered. You would think that it's a treasure that she is seeking, but of course it's only resolution, some kind of physical remnant of a life stolen from her: the flesh of her flesh. All she wants is a bone, a shoe, anything to be able to say that against all lies, here, here lies my son, here he died, here his name was wiped off the annals of history, and here I return him to his proper corner of memory."

She moved back into the kitchen again but kept talking.

"I understand that feeling, *tía*—that's what brings me here," Alba said.

"I don't doubt it, *mi corazón*," Marycruz said with tenderness from the kitchen. "The heroism of these women is larger than life, and if it weren't for them, for their persistence, we would scarcely know or believe any of it at all. But their heroism has a cost: the search defines them totally and completely. Don't get me wrong. I don't blame them, but I pity them, even as I envy and admire them. That's the complication, you see. You want justice, you believe in justice, but the pursuit of justice in the face of the insanity of the regime that defined you turns you into an obsessed hysterical woman in the eyes of the world. And you *are* hysterical, you *are* obsessed, and it is no way to live, but who would want the alternative? So, for most of us, we hover in this state of in between, fearing the perpetual madness of the search and wanting closure so badly that we risk accepting a false offering or a hasty compromise on a faulty deal."

Until that moment, Alba had not even considered that her search might bring her into contact with the name or the face of the perpetrator of her half-orphanhood, the murderer of her father. It was hard enough to imagine her father's face or his story. And now another name, another face. "Maybe this sounds shallow, Marycruz, but I came with more selfish interests. I just want to know who my father was, and who I am. It's hard enough not knowing who he was, how he died, what he lived for. I am glad others work for justice, I really am. And no doubt I'll benefit from their work. But I feel too young, too new to all of this, to pretend to know what justice would look like."

"*Ay*, who really knows what it looks like? I have given it a lot of thought and all I can say is that I think I know how it ought to feel. That's all I know. If you don't feel filled with anger like so many of us do, then count it a blessing. It's best not to borrow trouble. It's a heavy cross to bear, anger is. I wouldn't wish that upon you. But be warned. The more you learn, the angrier you can get, if you're not careful. And it will devour you, rot you from the inside. My feeling is, I want to help, but I don't want to hurt you. That's been my fear since you let me know of your intentions to come. And I know this is what worries your mom."

"You have been in touch with her?" Alba sounded worried.

"Of course, *mi amor*. I did as you asked and kept it quiet, but she contacted me, you know, once she found out you were coming. We had a good long talk."

"What about?" Alba tried to disguise her irritation that they might have colluded behind her back.

"*Mira*. I told her that this was probably inevitable. Obviously, she hoped it wasn't. She just doesn't want you to get hurt. That is a weakness in her, but you have to understand it is a weakness that this whole society suffers from. I tried to explain what is happening here, that democracy has led to a slow but necessary reopening of the past. *Teme las tentaciones del pasado.*"

"What does that mean?" Alba fidgeted on the couch. There was just a hint of anger in her voice.

"People here worry that if we get too serious about unearthing the sins of the Pinochet dictatorship, we will ruin our chances for a civil society, that we will go back to fighting the same battles as before, continually living in a divided world of competing and irreconcilable worldviews. It's too easy to idealize the victims and demonize the perpetrators, when what separates them might not be as much as we hope. And as much as I hate to admit it, there is something to that. The difference between the torturers and the victims isn't always as great as we might believe. It is stunning what monsters the dictatorship made of otherwise relatively normal people."

"Yes, but surely you can't create a healthy society based on, you know, lies, or on repressing the truth! And what kind of family relationship is it you have when you act as if certain things didn't happen or weren't true?" She could hear her voice growing louder. "I came to know the truth. I mean, he's gone.

He was never a part of my life. I can't change that. And I can't explain why it matters to me now, or what difference it is going to make, but I just can't tolerate the mystery anymore. I want you to understand." She could feel her face growing flush. The sight of the pillow on the couch made her feel suddenly consumed with fatigue.

"I am with you, Alba. I told your mother. Don't misunderstand me. You are absolutely right. It's just not easy to find the balance, you know, because the truth hurts and we have to work through that. I don't want to hurt you and I don't want to upset your mother either. It's hard to know how to avoid both, but I am with you, on the side of complete honesty. I don't mean to sound like I am accusing your mother of dishonesty. I think she has just tried to protect you and perhaps protect herself from too many layers of sadness. Are you angry with her?"

Alba shifted somewhat uncomfortably on the sofa.

"Angry? No. No, I am not angry," she said pensively. "Well, maybe a little, I guess. Don't get me wrong. I love her, but I've been disillusioned and I'm wrestling with what that means. In some ways, it's almost worse, I think. I mean, all those years *mami* treated this like a great shame, as if my father wasn't worth the time to speak his name, and for most of my childhood, I respected that, believed it, even. And I adored *mami*, I admired her courage, her faith, her journey. I still do. I was never allowed to forget the privilege of living in a free country, of having the gospel in my life, and I observed daily the strength it took *mami* to bring me and raise me there, all by herself. The decision to come here was very hard for both of us because of what I knew it would say to her. It would feel like to her that I was rejecting all that she had done for me. But you can't hide the past from your children and expect them to grow up without a hunger for where they have come from, who they are. I have a right to that understanding, just like everyone else, and it's bad enough that violence and brutality have lost me a father. Why should a mother add another layer of obstruction on a daughter's journey to discover who she is? That's just not right. I'm strong enough to handle the truth. I don't want to be treated like a child." She looked intently at Marycruz.

Marycruz set down plates on the table and then approached Alba on the sofa, sitting down next to her. She placed her hand on Alba's knee.

"I believe you. You will find you're not alone. Tomorrow we can go and see some people who are working on reconciliation, and they will be helpful. You can't imagine how many lives were disrupted, lives just like yours. The political, especially when it is so brutal, always becomes very personal. This is a great time for our country, because many are simply not going to be stopped in doing the great work of learning the truth of the past, to get the facts out in the open. Too much evil has been done in darkness, too much suffering borne alone, and it is time now for a genuine reconciliation, genuine solidarity. That is how many of us feel and it is finally becoming a possibility. So you have come at a good time. You are part of something much larger than you realize." She paused. Alba stood with her back to her, staring out at the streets below.

"I can see you are very tired. Let's eat something, shall we? And then you can rest."

Alba slept soundly that night, the kind of deep sleep that feels like a little death, without dreams, without reason, without awareness of place or time. When she awoke in the morning, it took a few minutes to orient herself. Her body was a strange place of inhabitation, and her conscious mind a source of wonder. She could feel the cool air of morning on her naked arm and she could hear the rush of traffic outside the window. She watched the bright sun shine across the room, and instinctively she recognized it as the light of a summer morning, rather than the fainter, slanted light of a northern winter. When she heard the clink of dishes in the kitchen, and Marycruz's voice indistinctly on the phone, her memory was restored in a flash.

That morning Marycruz and Alba walked through the central part of town, just off O'Higgins, where they found the *Vicaria de la solidaridad*. As before, the streets were packed with pedestrians. She saw the *Moneda,* the presidential palace, and the guards that stood watch on the street corners. When they arrived at the fifth floor of a building nearby, they were met by a man in his forties, Tito Ordenes, a gentle and kind man with a warm, round face. He held his hair in a ponytail and his beard showed just the beginnings of gray. He wore a Harley Davidson shirt, a money pouch around his waist, well-worn gray pants, and sandals. He invited them into his office and asked how he could help.

Alba spoke first. "I have returned to Chile from the United States. I am looking for my father's story. He was disappeared here in Santiago in 1982 when I was four years old. I have never been told much else."

Tito gave her a reassuring smile. "Well, our first task is to look through the registry of names that have been reported to see what information we might have about him. What was his complete name and birthdate?

"Luís Alberto Sepulveda Torreon."

Tito quickly scratched down the name and then leaned behind him where he ran his finger over several red paperback volumes. They were ordered according to year. He pulled out 1982 and moved his index finger down the opening pages over a list of names.

"Hmm. I don't see the name here. There were not many disappearances reported in 1982 in Santiago. Look, here you can see the numbers.

"Two? How is that complete?" said Alba.

"Well, that is only disappearances. We have a different registry for those whom we know were executed. We can check that in a moment. And of course, there were thousands who were detained and tortured. Those are the numbers we expect will increase as soon as we can get people to allow themselves to talk about it." He read silently for a moment. "So his name doesn't appear here either. Are you sure it was 1982?" He leaned back and pulled out the volumes for 1981 and 1983 just to be sure. "It doesn't hurt to look."

Alba looked at Marycruz, who spoke: "It was definitely the twenty-third of September, 1982."

"Okay. Okay." He quickly scanned the other volumes with similar results. "Not there. Let me check the registry of executions." Tito swung his chair around and looked through another volume. Alba and Marycruz waited while he leafed through the pages. "Not here."

Alba knew she couldn't expect answers on day one, but she still felt panicky. "I'm sorry but are you sure? I mean, are you sure these are all the names of those who were disappeared and executed? Surely there are cases that were not documented—I mean, what happens if the family never reported him missing, you know, when it first happened? I doubt the government has published their own truthful accounts, right?" Alba's voice started to sound desperate and emotional. Tito heard the pain.

"Well, that is the work we are in right now. There was an official history of the military actions published after the collapse of the dictatorship, in 1991, called the *Informe Retting*. Because of cases like this, many believe that we have not gotten all of the truth. That report was published in an atmosphere thick with impatience for a quick resolution. Democracy was still fragile— it felt that way, anyway, and people were willing to take what confessions they could get from the military as long as it didn't disrupt the stability of our new democracy. But it wasn't nor will it be enough. At least that's my conviction, but we won't get more information for many years yet. Of course, our work here is to keep looking, so with your assistance, I can fill out a new report of the missing and I will start doing research on it. I promise. And in the meantime, let's be sure to get your information so that we know whom to contact when and if we get more information."

He opened a file drawer below him and pulled out a form that he began to fill out—the form of a newly reported missing person.

"Date of birth?"

"The 17th of March, 1952," Alba replied.

"Place of birth?"

"We don't know."

"Names of the parents?" Alba looked confused. "His parents." Alba looked at Marycruz.

"We don't know," said Marycruz.

"Do you mind my asking why not?" Tito was direct but nonthreatening in his demeanor. Alba and Marycruz looked at each other. Marycruz began to explain.

"He was my brother-in-law, and I never met or knew his parents, and neither did my sister. The problem is that he wasn't much of a father. He wasn't around much, and then he disappeared."

"And his parents rejected him because he became a Mormon a few years earlier here in Santiago, so my mother never had contact with them," Alba added. Tito nodded and made notes. He then peered up from his papers at the two women.

"What did he do for a living?"

Marycruz answered: "He worked as an auto mechanic at a place near Cerro Santa Lucia. I think it was called Serviauto, or something like that. It isn't there anymore."

"How do you know he was disappeared? I am not asking because I am doubtful but because it is helpful to get as much information as we can."

"My sister, his wife, was living here in the city. He was involved in the revolution, but he wasn't around the house much." Marycruz stumbled a bit. "It's a complicated story."

"I have yet to hear a story that isn't." At this he smiled, which put Alba a little bit at ease. "The more information I have, the better chance I have of finding out what happened."

"Understood." Marycruz looked at Alba, and placed her hand on her knee again.

"Was your mother also involved in the revolution?"

"No," Alba answered.

"Are you sure?"

"Yes, I am sure." She looked at Marycruz for confirmation and Marycruz nodded.

"My sister was not political. She was just trying to raise her baby."

"That's unusual, you know, that a husband is involved in the revolution but the wife is not. That was considered too dangerous by many. Did he not have any friends? Do you know with whom he might have been working?"

"That's just it," Marycruz interrupted. "He didn't work well with others." She pulled her chair closer to the desk and put her elbows on the table. "Look. My brother-in-law was not a good father, and I don't just mean that he was working too hard on the revolution to be around at home. I mean that he was dishonest about who he was and what he was doing."

At this Marycruz had the full attention of the other two. So she continued.

"He wasn't working well with others at the time. He was . . . well, how do I say it? There was the problem of compromising the integrity and secrecy of the cells. He had a tendency to drift from one group to another, apparently. You know what I mean, right?"

Tito nodded, but he could see that Alba was confused. Tito explained that during those years cells had to work independently of one another to minimize the chance that if someone was captured and tortured, they would reveal the names and full scope of the revolution. So it was by design that people often worked in ignorance of all of the others who might be collaborating.

"Do you know why he was doing this?" Tito asked.

"Well, I have some idea, yes." She looked at Alba with a reassuring smile. "This is news to Alba here, and I am sorry, *mi amor*, but, you see, he developed a reputation for being involved with several women in the revolution. Sexually, I mean. And that was strictly against policy. And when one of the women was disappeared, along with a few other men in the other cells with whom he had had contact, well, it was clear he was endangering everyone. He wasn't much of a father, as I said, and this came as no surprise to my sister. She suspected as much."

"What was the response to those disappearances?" Tito asked.

"What do you mean?" Marycruz asked.

"I mean, well, was he let go? Did he try to run off?"

"There was some blowup among those he worked with, and then things completely unraveled. You see, two men showed up at my sister's apartment and asked her what her name was. At first she worried that they were undercover policemen, but they told her that they worked with her husband and that he had lied about being married. They had assumed he was single, you see. They could see Alba there in the apartment as well, and they could sense the seriousness of his deception. They said that people had been disappeared as a result of his carelessness. They told my sister that the situation was now beyond repair, that they were going to cut off all ties with him."

"And then what?" he asked.

"Luís came home later and Isabel confronted him with what she knew. He went out again that same night, saying that he was going on a special assignment that would make things right with everyone. That was the last she ever saw him."

"Ah. And I assume," said Tito, "that she at least tried to confirm that he wasn't found dead somewhere."

"Of course. We went to the morgue, to the hospitals, and we gave his name to the police, just in case, but nothing ever came up. But you know, she was afraid for her own life and maybe from both sides, you see?"

"And you say that was September twenty-third?"

"Yes." Tito requested a moment to write down the information she had given him on the form. Marycruz looked over at Alba and Alba gave her a firm-lipped smile. She liked and trusted Marycruz. Frank. Direct. And self-possessed. Like her mother, but unlike her too. More . . . what was it . . . world-wise, maybe. Someone who had not been afraid to dirty her own hands in the work of the world. She had a kind of dignity that was unmistakable, admirable, living alone and directing her own life as a journalist. Alba was glad to claim Marycruz as hers.

Tito suggested that perhaps the next day, if she had time, he could take her to *Villa Grimaldi,* a prison and torture site that was now a memorial and general cemetery. Perhaps, he suggested, she might benefit from hearing more stories about that time, something to give her a broader context to understand what this all meant. In the meantime, he said, he would investigate the name and date further and see what he could come up with. They agreed and Marycruz and Alba left to locate some lunch.

* * *

Sitting across from Marycruz in a café that spilled out into the street in the full summer sun, it seemed unreal to Alba that winter was becoming a distant memory, that the air could feel so heavy with summer, that the light was filtered through the sycamore leaves that hung above their heads along the backstreets of the city, and that she was only wearing a skirt and a short-sleeve blouse. Alba explained to Marycruz that this wasn't the first time that she had considered the possibility that her father was a womanizer. Her mother's silence had left plenty of room for this possibility, but Alba had already made up her mind that although she couldn't condone it, she could forgive it. Devoted to a cause, sacrificing one's time and risking one's life for a nation that could only become a reality with courage, that was something honorable. For all its dark nights of despair, the flame of the nation had survived thanks to the thousands of brave men and women who fought and resisted on higher moral ground than their enemies. He deserved at least the interest in rescuing his story, warts and all. He certainly didn't deserve the apathy that her mother wanted from her.

"Do you remember your father at all?" Marycruz asked, between sips of her tea.

"Nothing at all, except one image that has been with me for years, for some reason. I remember holding his hand, somewhere high on a hill above the sea and I remember it had rained that day because our hands were wet. That's all I got, *tía*."

"Well, that's something, I guess, but honestly you would have more memories if he had been a better father."

"I'd have a father if it weren't for the government."

"True enough. I don't excuse them, and I don't think your mom means to either. But imagine yourself newly married, right, and imagine that John, almost as soon as you are married, starts to leave the house for days at a time, imagine that he doesn't say exactly where he is going, and imagine that even though you want to believe that he is taken away by a great and important duty, you begin to find evidence that he is mixing business with pleasure, that when he does come home, he comes home smelling of other women, that he speaks of his activism cryptically and with an inflated vocabulary, but you know that underneath it all, he is using his clandestinity as an opportunity to be unfaithful to you. And then, you learn you are pregnant and you must bear this child and raise her essentially alone from the beginning. I only mean to say that he wasn't the political hero you might have hoped he was."

"John would never do such a thing."

"You say that, but your mom carried hope and trust into her

marriage, just like you did. He had joined the church, remember, just before their wedding. She was so happy!"

"John would never do such a thing."

"We don't need to argue this point."

"No, we don't, but I just want you to know that John would never *ever* do such a thing." Alba spoke with vehemence.

"I believe you, Alba. My point is to ask you to imagine being in your mother's shoes."

"But how do you know my father wasn't going to make things better, as you said he wanted to do? I can accept that he was a flawed man, but he didn't deserve to die. He deserved a chance to make things right, just like the rest of us. Are you saying he deserved what happened?"

"Of course not. I am saying that I'm convinced his heart was not in it for the political cause but because he had wandering eyes. I will be honest: I never liked him nor did I trust him. It was a conflict for us as sisters. Your mom thought it was mainly about our religious differences. I wanted to like him, I really did, but he never felt right to me. What I want to say, Alba, is that I don't believe your father ever really loved your mother. I mean, maybe he loved her in theory, at the beginning, but love is a commitment. We all know that. Early on, he knew how to be romantic, very much so, but then it was like once he had her to come home to, a switch turned off in him and he could be so unkind to her and cruelly distant. He would be mean, and then he would try to make up for it again. It was a terrible up-and-down experience for your mother, since she wanted so desperately to believe in the man who said he loved her, who said he wanted to make things right with her, who acted as though he wanted to rise to the occasion of being a good father and husband. But it was also clear that he was running from something deep inside him, something that he maybe once hoped your church and your mom would heal but which only made him angrier and more desperate than before when he realized nothing had changed.

By the end, the most he could muster was to bring her what little money she needed to get by, sometimes delivered through a friend. I always thought it odd that he barely spoke of his own family and never really let anyone into his life. It was like he couldn't integrate all the parts of himself. Maybe your mom just liked the idea of marrying someone who joined the church with her. I know she was attracted to him, and I think maybe when he announced that his family had cut him off, you know, because of the baptism, I think it made your mother want to fill that void for him. She felt such pity for him, for this wound inside him. But, by the time your mother got pregnant with you, he was already half gone. I'll admit that I was not all that heartbroken about it. I secretly wished the marriage would just end. Back then, the Catholics, who controlled all talk on such matters, had no tolerance for divorce, zero. I don't imagine your church was much different."

"It isn't a categorical thing. It's not encouraged, but it is allowed."

"Well, it should be. You can talk about loosening morals all you want, but until you have a situation that won't trap poor women like your mother in a domestic prison-house, I am not all that sympathetic to talk of preserving traditional values. It's just wrong, Alba, to do that to women and children. And it's always the men who get to make the rules. My God, do you think women would have thought up a zero-tolerance policy on divorce? Do you? He, why he could do whatever he wanted, but she was boxed in. And he could come home when he wanted, have sex when he wanted, risk transmitting sexual diseases, which thankfully did not happen to your mother, and impregnate her whether or not she was ready, and meanwhile all of society was looking at her and saying, 'Just hang on a little longer, exercise more forgiveness and patience. You can work it out.' I figured you make a mistake early enough in life and you should be allowed a do-over. Of course, once you came into the picture, that complicated things, but biology doesn't mean anything without love, without commitment, without all the stuff you Christians say so much about. I certainly wasn't going to fill my poor sister with nonsense about trying to make it work. I was going to make sure that she had a way out. This whole damn society was just one big prison and even more so for us women, so after he left, your mom was frightened for your safety and helping my sister get out of the country seemed like part of the same work. Previously, I had just tried to talk her out of the marriage and she was resistant, but once she understood the kind of risk he had exposed her to, we looked into an exit from the country. And to your mom's credit, she started by writing a letter to her elder, as she always called him, "*mi elder*." What was his name?"

"Elder Paul Hensen. He's still close to us. He always looks out for us."

"So now you know. Your exit to the States didn't happen overnight but it was in the interest of your safety, see? You became refugees. I certainly didn't wish what happened to him, but, something you need to understand is that in all of that struggle, people were still just people, capable of the same mistakes as always, fraught with the same weaknesses. I mean, I want to say that the revolution brought out something in people, a kind of purity of integrity that was really beautiful to observe when it happened, but, you know, others, well, it was, how shall I put it? A kind of background noise is all. They still sought their chances to get something they wanted selfishly for themselves to get ahead. There were plenty of those who worked hard for the dictatorship who did so with a sense of high purpose. They believed in what they were doing. They had convinced themselves it was right. It was profoundly wrong, but that, at least, has some logic. It's all the people in between, the people who can't ever quite assume a role in history and in society, who confuse me the most. I know that might seem like a contradiction, especially considering the high price he paid. The point is, not all fathers are paternal, not all victims are martyrs."

Alba poked at her piece of cake with her fork. Couples walked by, businessmen and women, all on their lunch break perhaps, enjoying the sunshine. There was a faint brown pall in the air. Alba blinked her eyes to ease the sting.

"You don't think he just fell in love with someone else while he was spending so many hours away from *mami*? I mean, there very well could have been lots of occasions for relationships like that to develop."

"No. There were too many. Look, he was already strictly forbidden to be involved as a married man, unless his wife was also involved. I kept telling your mom to ask him about this, because it just didn't square. The only time I had a chance to confront him about it, he claimed others knew but gave him special permission. He wasn't falling in love with anyone, Alba. He just knew too many people and couldn't seem to sit still. He had a reputation for always asking about women who worked in other areas, always seeming to be more interested in sex than in politics. He was smooth. And there you and your mother were, alone in your apartment, increasingly vulnerable to losing the only source of income you had. And you know, normally I would have admired him, but knowing that it was his insatiable thirst for sex that was endangering you and compromising the integrity of political conviction, well I just couldn't respect that, no matter how much I believed in what we were all trying to accomplish."

Marycruz slid her chair a little closer and spoke a bit more earnestly. "If you don't understand anything, just stop me. I can tell you something else I didn't say to Tito. That night when the two men came to her apartment, your mom told me that what most shocked her was Luís's reaction to the news. He went ashen. I mean, here she is, frightened by the appearance of two strangers in her apartment talking about her husband as if he were some other man, some other person altogether, and when she tells him, he doesn't say a word of apology or recognition that he has been unfaithful, let alone that he had endangered your lives. She tells him that the men confirmed that he was having affairs and putting the lives of many others at risk, that he would no longer be able to work for the revolution, that he was *persona non grata*, and that as far as she was concerned, he could no longer continue to be your father and her husband. Just like that in one night, he lost his friends, his family, and his cause." Alba listened intently. "You see, she made up her mind right there that she was leaving. She wrote to her elder and told him that her husband was heavily involved in the revolution and that she feared for her life and could he please begin proceedings for an invitation to come to Utah. But my point is that what struck us both later when we rehearsed that night's events over and over was that he was worried sick about losing the trust of his peers but said nothing about losing hers. He asked for detailed descriptions of the two men, asked if they threatened violence against him, if they were carrying arms, or if they asked when he might return. Your mom told him no, but it was obvious that he was afraid for himself. 'If they come again, tell them I will prove my loyalty. Tonight I intend to make things right.' Those were his words, his last words. And with that he was gone."

"For good?"

"Yes, for good. We never saw him again. I mean, he didn't even stay more than five minutes and he was out the door. He didn't say anything more to your mom. That was it. And in case it matters, he didn't say good-bye to his only child on this earth."

Alba sat silently for a few minutes. It was a lot to take in. But then she asked what to her seemed the obvious question.

"Did it occur to mom, to you, to anyone, that he might have intended to go kill himself? You said yourself that that night he lost everything he had. Could that have been what he meant by making things right?"

"Alba, *querida* Alba." Marycruz reached across to Alba and brushed her hair. "At your mother's insistence, we searched every hospital in the city to see if by any chance his body had turned up. This was standard procedure for a disappearance, of course, but we did it with precisely that question on our minds. But your mom was pretty sure that he meant to do some heroic thing and that he knew he was risking being disappeared in so doing. This may have had a touch of suicidal desire in it, no doubt. He certainly had nothing to lose at that point, but, you know, suicides are a lot harder to hide than sequestered, tortured, and disappeared men and women when you have total control of the police force. In fact, it was not uncommon for someone to be executed in a way that was made to look like a suicide, so even if we had found what looked like a suicide, we would still be living with doubt, you see? Besides, what your mom noticed was that he was more afraid than despondent, afraid that his co-conspirators would take revenge on him. And he certainly wasn't penitent in the slightest. I always found that a curious thing."

"And what of that? Could *they* have killed *him*? How do you know they didn't kill him for revenge, or for protection? Obviously he seemed to have considered that possibility."

"Honestly, I don't know. But I don't believe it. Again, no body ever turned up. And the government was always more than happy to blame deaths like that on violent terrorists. He would have been a great catch for the government. Besides, disappearances among his cohorts continued after he was gone, and I always imagined they squeezed every last name out of him until they did away with him."

"You won't like this question, but I have to ask. Wasn't the disappearance of a husband who had willfully neglected and endangered his wife and child a story that worked better than a widow of a suicide? I mean, wouldn't mom's chances of getting to the U.S. have been improved by such a story? Didn't you both want this to be true?"

Marycruz leaned back in her seat. She paused a moment and then said, "You are tough, Alba. I respect your questions. But you need to respect my honesty. It's one thing to want to know what really happened and another thing to pitch a story to government officials. Those are separate matters. We never got the full story but not for lack of trying. We didn't invent the danger she was in. It was right and good of your country to take her."

After another silent pause, Marycruz spoke again. "I will say also that we treated it like a disappearance and yet we came up completely empty-handed. Sometimes family members might get lucky and find some information about where they might have temporarily been detained before they were later killed, or someone gets out of prison and says that they saw so-and-so in the same prison being carted off to who knows which detention center. We had nothing, but I suppose this was not surprising considering how disconnected he had become. I think others felt as I did, that maybe he had this coming. But he really vanished. That's the price of the kind of violence the government was engaged in, you know. They ran so scared and were so unsatisfied with seeking to capture and kill the revolution's most visible leaders that anything and everyone who moved in the wrong way was under suspicion. They could no longer tell the difference between a genuine enemy and a tree blowing in the wind. We kept thinking that the disappearances would stop, but they didn't. Sure, they had slowed down after the first few years, but in fact, things were just heating up again as the economy was really hitting rock bottom and people were getting more and more publicly agitated."

"And yet now, we have no record of him at all." A heavy exhaustion fell upon her. The sun felt burdensome, as if it were sapping her of the very energy it had just given her. "Look, I am really tired again. Do you think I could catch a nap back at your place?"

"Of course. Of course."

*   *   *

Alba felt torn between two worlds, as if she would have to choose to either betray her mother or her father. Mr. Harker had complained to her about the increasing polarization of politics in the States, but here it seemed that this was polarization on a different order. How can you choose between being sympathetic with torturers and sympathetic with violent communists? She had to admit to herself that she knew relatively little about communism, other than the fact that it was defiantly atheist, that its communitarian aims had failed, and that it was supposed to have disappeared when the Berlin Wall fell in 1989, the same year Pinochet stepped down from power. Maybe the binary divisions of that old world hadn't gone away. Maybe they had only retreated from sight temporarily and were busy multiplying in the darkness. The anxiety of 9/11 was how to choose to live, what to live for, what to die for, if we could no longer confidently identify our enemies. How will our enemies not become whoever we wanted or needed them to be?

She wanted to honor both parents. But her mother's silence, which she interpreted as sympathy for the Pinochet dictatorship, tempted her to sympathize with extreme leftist politics and this was anathema where she lived. She knew that in John's family if you really wanted to insult someone, you called them a socialist or a communist, or maybe an environmentalist. They were all the same. They opposed all that you held sacrosanct: the free market, free enterprise, small government, minimal regulation, Christian social values, and America the pure, the great, the one last hope for humanity. If problems were supposed to be taken care of by the market, you didn't have to agonize about how to stop endemic poverty or protect the environment because people and nature were never "exploited." Ever since she had begun to work with Mr. Harker, it had started to bother her that the cherished values of John's family, of many people she knew, never spoke of the real consequences of anyone's greed. Sure, they could admit that greed was a sin, but when it came down to it, it was never imagined to harm anyone or anything. It was just bad for the soul, but it was still spoken of as necessary. Besides, whatever damage we did to the world would either be absorbed by nature or taken care of later by God. And even though, for many people, you could blame the American government for just about everything wrong with the country, it was always seen as innocent, incapable even, of any sin of aggression or intervention internationally. It was hard to imagine that she would ever see a comparable conversation in the U.S. like the one taking place in Chile about national sins and collective responsibility. She wondered if the country would have the will to resist the rise of evil in the presidency especially if it invoked the name of God to justify its violence?

Even before she left for Chile, John's father was adamant that she had, as he put it, drunk too much of the "academic Kool-Aid" when she brought up the CIA involvement in the coup of 1973 that brought Pinochet to power. Here, the U.S. involvement was common knowledge, but at home it still sounded like crazy talk. "That's the fantasy of professors with too much time on their hands and too much money to be earned for publishing anti-patriotic drivel," John's father had said. She had admired his success in business as an owner of tire franchises all over the state. He was honest and decent to his employees, and he commanded the respect of others. He was gregarious and affectionate, but he had a penchant for needing to be at the center of discussion, to have the final authoritative word. He had tried hard to treat Alba like a daughter, and she couldn't help feeling that his kindness was meant to subordinate her, and she suspected that their political differences would complicate things even more.

The next day Tito arrived in his car at Marycruz's apartment to take Alba to visit *Villa Grimaldi* and the general cemetery in Santiago.

"This isn't the happiest form of tourism, but I think it would be essential for you to make these visits," he said, after she had climbed into his car. "How do you like Santiago so far?"

"Well, I love the summer weather, I will say that. I really haven't seen much yet. I really appreciate you taking this time. It is very kind of you."

"Oh, you are very welcome. I love to show people this country, both the ugly and the beautiful, you know. I own a touring company, so I go on the road a fair amount with people. So any questions you have, I can try to answer them." They pulled onto the busy streets of the city as he negotiated his way.

"It's strange. So much is different, but I can't get over how similar this city feels to where I am from. I mean, it's certainly a lot larger as a city, but these mountains surrounding the city, the dry air, even the pollution, they feel similar."

"Yes, I can see that. I saw some images of your city just recently on the television, in preparation for the Winter Olympics, right? I can see the similarity. But here, you know, our mountains are hardly visible because of the pollution. You can see how magnificent they are here, as we get closer. The Olympics start soon there, don't they?"

"Two more weeks or so, I think."

"Cheer for our Chilean skiers, okay?"

"Of course!"

As they found their way farther to the east side of the city, the streets were narrower and the traffic a little lighter, until finally they were headed straight to the mountains and the area started to feel more suburban than urban.

"This used to be all fields. It was pretty remote and quiet out here, which is what made it an ideal place for this detention center here. It's called *Villa Grimaldi*. It's up here on the right. That gate there, that's where they brought prisoners into the site." They pulled into the parking lot in front and walked in. It was an open space more or less surrounded by a high brick wall on all sides, with various remnants of buildings, mostly at ground level so that one could walk in and among the various spaces where torture took place.

"So the gate over there is where the prisoners were brought in, but the question is on what conditions did prisoners ever leave. This was a torture center, intended to get information out of the detainees by force. Prisoners would stay here sometimes for many months. And many left by helicopter."

Alba looked at him quizzically.

"Prisoners began to associate the sound of a helicopter with death because when they heard the helicopter, they knew they were coming to take away some of the prisoners never to be seen again. The helicopter would remove those who were no longer useful or no longer cooperative, and they would dump their bodies directly into the ocean, which is only about 100 kilometers away. They would strap their bodies to rails, you know for train tracks, so that they would sink to the bottom. It's hard to look at the ocean here in Chile and not think about what it is hiding from our view."

Alba was silent. The place was strangely beautiful. They walked slowly among trees and flowers planted among the remains of walls.

"Listen. There are many of us, many of us who can't get access to the stories of our parents, you know. You need to know you aren't alone."

"Many of us? Were your parents disappeared? Is that how you got into this work?"

"My parents were tortured. And they eventually died due to symptoms of the torture years later. But no, they were not disappeared, at least not in the strictly physical sense."

"I am so sorry," said Alba.

"No need to be sorry. Like I said, we are not alone. Something is coming from all this suffering."

"Why were they imprisoned, your parents?"

"Why was anyone? Isn't that the question of the century? My father was a government functionary. He had retired to a small community outside of the city in Pichidegua. He was democratically elected in 1972 as a regional delegate tasked with implementing the measures of Allende's government. I met him, you know. Salvador Allende. He wouldn't be called Señor Presidente. He was Compañero Presidente. Very warm man. Down to earth. But my father couldn't bring himself to do all that he was expected to do. He was reluctant to force the appropriation of lands to the state. He tried to work with people to see if he couldn't achieve effectively the same results with more modest reforms, just so you have a sense of how moderate he was. On the morning of the eleventh of September, I was on my way to school. I was fourteen, and when I got there, practically no one was there, and someone told me to return home immediately. So I did. And when I got to my house, President Allende was giving his radio address to the nation. I heard it live. Unforgettable. You know the words? *Tengo fe en Chile y su destino. Superarán otros hombres este momento gris y amargo, donde la traición, pretende imponerse. Sigan ustedes, sabiendo, que mucho más temprano que tarde, de nuevo, abrirán las grandes alamedas por donde pase el hombre libre, para construir una sociedad mejor.* He was not going to give those men the pleasure of killing him, so after the speech he shot himself."

"I don't know what to say. I have read about him, read about those days, but it is all pretty new to me to be honest. I was not raised on these stories."

"No, I don't imagine that you were. Not many were, to be honest. But I was a child of a government functionary, so it was our daily bread to be thinking about the cause of equality. Of course, my father knew right away what was coming. Within very short order the police arrived. Here I was, all of fourteen years old, the oldest of six children, and they beat our parents in front us. One of them hit me in the face and struck me with his baton twice in the ribs, right here." He pointed to his side. "They took my parents to jail. I mean these were good people, as good as any parents you might have known, kind and loving and good to their children, contributors to their community. Mom had worked at the Center for Mothers in town. She was loved by all who knew her. Imagine your own mother being taken and beaten like that. We were allowed to bring them things once a week, but I didn't see them for almost four months. The torture was on and off during that entire time. They never spoke to me about any of the details regarding exactly what they went through, except that years later my mother mentioned being hung upside down for two hours from her ankles. And that has to be just what she could tolerate saying. Years later, my father developed excruciating pain in the right side of his head. When we took him to the doctor, the doctor asked if he had ever been electrocuted. At first he denied it, but then he finally admitted that he had been laid on the *parrilla*."

"The *parrilla*?"

"It was a metal slab on which victims were laid and then electrocuted."

Tears started flowing from Alba's eyes. "What for?"

"The absurdity of it was that they were convinced that Allende's government was hiding arms from the Soviets or from the Chinese, and they arrested as many of the government officials as they could and demanded to know where the weapons were hidden. And they tortured us kids psychologically. They kept telling me that my parents would die on such and such a day, the day would pass, and they would tell me I was lucky, that I had a second chance, and then they would announce again that they would die soon. It appears they meant to kill them eventually, but somehow my father managed to get a letter out of jail to his sister, meant for a man who was a conservative and a high-ranking official who had known my father to be a good and honest man, who could attest that his actions were honorable during the previous years. And it worked, just in time. You know, I didn't believe it when they told us to show up at the jail. I remember they released several others that day, and as they came walking out of the jail a man came up to me, skinny, so skinny, nothing but skin and bones, bruised face, and no hair. And he said, with a broad smile, 'Do you not know your own father?' He told us a joke. That's the way he was, always telling jokes. I didn't believe it at first but he held me and said he loved me and I finally accepted that it was him. The most emotional thing for me was seeing him come out looking the way he did and shining with his inner dignity still intact. It is the most painful and most beautiful thing I think I have ever seen. Mom was quiet, I remember, but she almost couldn't let go of us for days. The thing is, you think that is the end, but it was just the beginning of a living hell. You see, every time someone came to the door, every sudden noise, everything put us into a panic. This was the grip that the dictatorship had on the entire country. It was more difficult for my parents than it was for us children. It took my parents a couple of years to be able to function semi-normally. Me, I think it was the darkest time of my life. It's hard to describe, but that kind of violence and evil, it forces a decision upon you. It has generated a lot of hate, oceans of hatred, you see, unstoppable distrust, paranoia without bounds. I got to the point when I realized what was happening to me. And I said to myself, 'This is it. This is the end. I will be filled with anger for the rest of my life and I will die a *guerrillero*.' I felt assigned by fate, by forces far beyond my control. And I lost plenty of friends that way, I tell you."

"What was it that led you down a different path? I mean, look at you now."

"*El matrimonio y tener hijos. Tener hijos es algo sagrado.* I kept thinking, I can't give hatred to my wife and children. I can't pass on that legacy. I needed something else. I wasn't sure what it was for a long, long time, but I eventually understood it was what I had always known: God's love and the command to forgive."

Alba stared at a grove of birch trees in ordered lines.

"That's where the torture cells were. Those trees mark the tight spaces where prisoners were kept in total darkness," explained Tito.

"*Para que nunca más en Chile.* That's what this is all about. You know, I can look at my fellow countrymen, and it is easy to let the thought of those criminals wandering free make you crazy. It's easy to imagine that anything and everything remotely conservative, religious, or related to armed force—even a good policeman!—that they are all signs of decay and slipping back into dictatorship. Everyone is afraid of dictatorship and for good reason, but somehow you have to find a way to see gray when everything seems black and white and to trust when trust has failed you in the past. And I am not going to pretend that it has been easy. I have many conservative friends, and they have their feelings about the dictatorship, about how it brought much needed order to a disordered reality. They remember the food lines, the shortages during Allende, but they don't know what I saw. One night my father and I were walking home late in the evening and we saw a truck full of milk and coffee dumping the entirety of its load into the river. This was the kind of thing that was done to create the shortages and the desperation that laid the foundation for the coup, an act that was supported by the majority of the country. I mean, here the Junta announces on national television within hours of the coup that they pose no threat of vengeance to liberals and to Allende supporters in the country, that they assume this responsibility out of altruistic motives to restore order, these the same men who swore loyalty to Allende only days before. I can understand that without witnessing the lived reality of people taken prisoners, tortured, or disappeared, it was all too easy to take fiats like that as truth. But you know the time has come to no longer see differences as the enemy. You can't build a civilization on hatred. You can and should build it on differences, because differences do not make people enemies. We have our differences, but we must learn to live together. It's hard to be a victim, but the villains have their own hell, either now or later to look forward to. A great number have committed suicide. So this commission, this work, is about a clearer idea of justice, but it is not by a long shot a perfect method nor will it ever be complete. You and I, we are going to have to learn to live and make meaning from spaces of oblivion, from interrupted and disconnected human lives. So I need to tell you: be careful. This thirst for the truth, it needs and deserves a response, and you have my commitment that we will work as hard as we can for results, but if you aren't careful, even if it gets what it wants, it won't be satisfied, and it may ultimately have to face the utterly silent indifference of the world to its demands. *Tenemos todos una deuda pendiente. Hay que reconocerla."*

After a moment of silence, Alba asked, "*¿Cuantos hijos tienes?"*

"Three. Well, if you include our four adopted children, a total of seven. That's another long story, but a few years ago we took in three siblings, one of whom was pregnant. The mother was completely poor and unable to take care of them. And the father, no one knows where he is. He abandoned them early. We have made them our own as much as we have been able." His eyes shone brightly.

* * *

The next day Alba received a phone call from Tito. He had made an important discovery and wanted her to come down to the office to talk. She rushed to get out of the apartment and down to his office, this time by herself. She felt a tad more comfortable walking the streets and negotiating the bus system on her own. It made her feel like she just might be able to blend in. Even her Spanish started to sound more Chilean after only a few days.

"What do you have for me?" she asked anxiously when she arrived at his office.

"Well, I am not sure what it means, but I contacted some of the regional offices outside of the city where they are also gathering stories, and it seems the staff down in Temuco just recently got some information about two brothers. Here, have a seat."

Alba had been standing with her hands on the desk in anticipation of a revelation.

"I don't see your father's name on a report down from there, but I might have a connection. Do you know anything about his history?"

"Nothing. Nothing at all. All I know is that his family cut him off when he decided to become a Mormon and that he married my mother here in Santiago. My mother never said where his family was from, so I am in the dark."

"Does it sound possible that he was from Temuco?"

"Where's that?"

"In the south. Araucanía. Land of volcanoes and glacial lakes and forests."

"It could be anywhere, to be honest. I have no idea. Why, what have you found?"

"Well, it appears there were two brothers who were captured by the military a few days after the coup."

"But what does this have to do with my father?"

"Well, they have the same last names, Sepulveda Torreón. Didn't you say that he was born in 1952?"

"Yes, that's right. He was eight years older than my mother. That I know. She was still eighteen when they married in 1978."

"Well, we have the ages of these brothers, both in their early twenties, so that makes some sense. He could have been a younger brother. In any case, it's not much, but it might fit. If you have the time to make a trip there to meet with my colleague, Berta, and search in the area for the family of that name, you might find something out. I'm afraid it's the best I can do for now."

Alba knew immediately that this was the next step.

"Thank you, Tito. Thank you! This is great. I'm going."

Tito gave her Berta's contact information and told her he would let her know to expect her the next day. It would be a long all-night bus ride from Santiago. Alba stood to leave but turned to ask, "Were those brothers disappeared? You never said."

"They were both dropped in the ocean."

Chapter 8

Dear S.,

She has been gone for just a few days and no word. I have found myself pacing the house, asking myself if I was wrong to encourage the trip. She signed me up for an email account just to be able to send me updates and I run down to the library to check every few hours it seems. They have never seen so much of me, I can tell you that. I worry that it won't go well, that she will learn nothing, or worse, that she will learn some dark truth.

She changed her mind about the money initially. She called me that same night to talk it over.

"I can't accept this from you," she announced. "Look, it is really very kind of you. I think it is the kindest thing anyone has ever done for me, but it is a lot of money, and, well, I just don't think I can accept it."

"I told you. I have no use for it. And I think you owe this to yourself, to your children. Think of that. All this silence imposed on you against your will only leads to greater misunderstandings as the years go by. It's your life, your story. You have a right to know. And damned if those government bureaucrats who made a living burying the truth from people like you are going to have the last say. I think you will regret not trying."

"I am sure you have some use. Don't you have any family members who could use it?"

I improvised.

"Well, sure I have family, I mean, yeah, who doesn't? But they don't need it. Trust me. I would have been giving them money for some time now if they did." It wasn't exactly a lie, but not exactly the truth either. Sure, there is Susan, even though technically she is only your mother's stepsister. You never met her. She calls about every six months to ask for money. Always claiming she is sober this time. Always needing just a little help.

I did for a while, you know, until it became obvious I was just an enabler. One minute she flirts with me and the next she accuses me of being a hard ass, that her sister was a fool to marry me, that she never understood what a crooked man I am, and so on. It's not fun, but I won't stand for her abuses, I tell you. Plus, how could I tell Alba about her without having to unravel the whole story? I couldn't stand that look of pity in her eyes if I did. I had enough of pity already.

She didn't buy it.

"What kind of family? Have you ever been married, Mr. Harker? I have always wondered."

"You and all of my neighbors. Look, let's not lose our focus here. We are talking about your trip to Chile. I know you need more money than I could give you, but I will get a little more in a few more weeks and I can add slowly to my contribution. If you have a credit card, maybe you can get yourself around in Chile on that and we can work on paying that off as soon as possible."

"I am calling you to tell you that I can't take your generous offer, and you are offering me more? No. I can't do that. John wouldn't like it anyway. He is a very frugal man. And I like and respect that about him, so no, I am not going to go into debt for this. There is a chance for funding from BYU, but I won't know for a couple of weeks. I have this idea about my final thesis project, about trees and roots and family history and, well, it's not very well formed yet, but if I can put something together, they just might see the benefit of me going."

"They will if they have any sense at all. But you know you can't count on that. Let's agree to this: you hold on to the check for the time being, knowing that you are able to use it when and if you need it. I am not taking it back, unless you get fully funded."

She paused for a moment. "This is really very kind of you, Mr. Harker. It feels uncomfortable."

"Deal with it. I am not changing my mind."

"Okay. I will let you know. Thank you. Thank you." She paused again. "Listen, I want to say something else. I need to ask for your discretion. I am not saying much about this to my mother and as little as possible, for now, to John."

Well, a few weeks later she let me know that she had obtained some modest funding from the university. It was still not going to be enough to cover the trip, however. It was hard for her to accept my help, but she was tantalizingly close to realizing her dream. As the final preparations got under way, I guess she told John she was going for sure. To his credit, he didn't stand in the way. Probably hurt his ego a little bit, but I will say, for all of his less-than-admirable qualities, he isn't a bad egg. The problem was that Alba got cold feet. She was near tears just days before she left, wondering if this was worth all the effort, what it would amount to.

I could certainly understand the hesitation. This trip meant no more guessing or imagining. And whatever she learned might shatter a part of herself that had taken root from the seeds of a lie, or a fantasy. I get that. Believe me. I was both envious and terrified at her prospects. It would be like me being able to find out for sure if you actually read these letters. Light reflected in a closed space bounces back and shows us the dimensions of an immediate surrounding reality, but light, you know, light shining out into the immensity of space, like a flashlight aimed at the night stars, tells us only of our hope to see but nothing at all about what is out there. Or not there. How many times I have lain in my bag under the stars at night, alone in the wilderness, and felt so utterly small and insignificant and so unable to grasp what it means to be alive. Four walls and a solid roof just don't last. We all have to stare into the uncertainties of the night sky or the distant plain at some point. Orphans. Widows. Widowers. The parent facing a child's grave. (Is there even a word for that?) I am pretty good at the staring, but if my experience is any indication you can never really stop the longing. I mean, I would have thought I would be more at peace by now. I imagine walls, I construct roofs of the mind, like these pages, to keep my thoughts, my dreams, my inner conversations with myself from flying wildly off into space. I need gravity, solidity, anchors of what is, but they are so easily taken, and when they are, one just goes back to the task of rebuilding and reframing houses of the mind. I am ashamed to admit that I can't tolerate the cosmos. I pity those who never learn to contemplate the night sky, who never know any other reality than the roof over their heads, but then I envy them too, envy a security that is palpable and, for reasons that escape me, resistant to doubt.

John is still around. I know he is down in Provo and I have used this as my excuse to leave him be. But Alba made me promise that I would reach out to him, that I would work harder to be better friends with him, but every time I contemplate contacting him, I go cold. Maybe he is hurting a little now that she is gone and knowing that I encouraged the trip. It's not all my doing, I would remind him.

* * *

I haven't been in the mountains for the past few weeks. Before she left, I got pretty sick with a flu. Honestly, I don't think I had had a flu for more than twenty years, and suddenly I was bedridden staring at the walls of my own room. I had a few moments of delirium, my temperature got high enough, and I found myself talking to the silence, talking to you and your mother. Theo would look up at me with his sad eyes, wondering what in the hell was wrong with his old friend. He was anxious at first, not sure what to make of the fact that we weren't going out for our daily constitutional. He is as antsy as I am and can't stand being stuck in the house. He pined and moped around for the first few days, coming up to the bed and nudging me with his wet nose, urging me to get off my sorry ass. I tried to explain it to him, but he just got sadder. Now he just lies at the door of the bedroom with his head on his front paws. He doesn't even get excited anymore when I get up because he knows it won't be anything more than a trip to the bathroom or for some water or food.

"Believe me, Theo. I feel your pain," I told him. My snowshoes lay on the front porch all that time, my snow pants in a pile in the corner of the room with all of my other clothes. There isn't anything quite like a walk in the mountains under the moon in the middle of the winter. We did it a few times, you might remember, usually up above Tibble Fork. You can't believe anything could be so beautiful as Pfeiferhorn under the bright disk of reflected light and the feel of the bitter cold air freezing the snot in your nostrils and momentarily burning the lungs on its way down. Theo and I, we are animals, that's for sure. I prefer the activity of the body, moving through the beauty around me, to any and all kinds of thought. Ironic, I know. I mean, listen to me, thinking on paper for days on end. These thoughts, my anchors, not to what is perhaps, but to what could have been, what should be. To the impossible possible. I don't know. Why can't I bring myself to write your mother? Have you asked yourself that? I know I have.

Well, in my fevers, like sometimes happens during a sleepless night, my mind couldn't follow the flowing stream of dreams but would instead revisit over and over again that fateful night I lost you both. I had become estranged and easily angered at your mother. Had been for some time, you see. We were getting along fine, at least on the surface of things, but I think if the truth must be told (and let's admit it, it must, it is long overdue), things had taken a turn for the worse in the last year or so, but especially in the past few months. I was gone on a number of longer research trips over the previous summer especially and I was enraptured by my studies. I was enraptured too by other things. I don't know. I think I had become a little fatigued by the Mormon way of life, the strong sense of duty, the demand it makes on you for an uncompromised heart. There is no middle ground there, and I could feel myself slipping. I would have been content sitting on the back pew, watching others, listening to their struggles and triumphs and drawing inspiration from their talks and lessons. I just didn't want to have to talk or have a responsibility at church. It seemed that every time I opened my mouth, I would alienate others. I couldn't manage to speak the language of the community. I wanted to talk about what I was learning about the mysteries of deep time. I wanted to talk about the wonder of a creation that didn't make it obvious where God was in the universe even though it seemed, at the time anyway, that there was little reason to doubt his existence. I mean, I felt God. I sensed he was there. I had ever since I began dating your mother. She had that way of hers, you know, of just making the idea of God so welcoming, so natural, so damn appealing. And when she offered me her love, I could feel what must have been what everyone told me I was supposed to feel. Some kind of exalting, transcending love and joy, something that made me feel connected to all things. That was the spiritual experience I thrived on. But what constrained me, what caused me guilt, was the sense that this church, this way of life, was robbing me of some inner freedom, some core of who I was. I mean, look, I know this sounds silly, but you put me in a button-down shirt, let alone in a tie, and I feel like I am being hung from the rafters in my own noose. And my God, I could never really give up on the coffee. Coffee in the mountains in the early morning dawn. That is something. And why, I would wonder, would God forbid such a thing that he apparently placed here on this planet with its miraculous properties to make the heart beat faster with anticipation and possibility? Do you realize how much great thinking has come of that stuff? I am serious. Granted, I am not going to pretend that there is anything noble about my petty bristling over these matters. And nothing noble about addiction, I get that. Maybe it didn't really matter, but there were daily, weekly reminders that I didn't use proper language, proper clothes, proper mannerisms. I hate shaking hands. I hate smiling when I don't feel like smiling. I am what I am, and I felt my bishop at the time, Bishop Garry, why, he just wanted to reform me. He wasn't content that I was there, that I was loving you and loving your mom, that I was what I was. He wanted me to become a high priest. He kept suggesting to me that I hadn't yet realized my potential in the gospel, that I could do more than just warm a pew every Sunday. He tried me out for a while with the Boy Scouts, which made sense, I get that. But those kids just about drove me batty. All they wanted to do was fart, joke about it, and fart again. And no matter how hard I tried to communicate to them the wonder of this world, the ever precarious and magnificent interconnection of all life, I just got blank stares and, worse, gentle corrections from Brother Jensen who always seemed to feel that I was one card shy of a full deck, more than a few billion years off in my estimation of the earth's age, and, well, just too secular, too scientific, too interested in this life and not enough in the life to come. I think the bishop assigned us together so that he would keep track of me. The man's condescension toward me was palpable. Help them to see who they *really* are, he would say. Well, call me stupid, but whatever else they might be, they are a radically unique organization of carbon, taken from this earth—dust, don't the scriptures say?— and ultimately taken from the stars, and they are exchanging cell matter every moment of their brief lives with the world around them. Made and makers, we are, and utterly dependent upon the miracle of life that gives us daily breath. I didn't initially think of this as a kind of grace, but when I found religion, God was breathing all around me, and all the world alit with his fire. Life itself was sufficient evidence of God's love. Brother Jensen's theology seemed to me to make of this world some kind of dime-store wind-up toy. He wanted to emphasize the world to come, the glory, the beauty. He used to quote Joseph Smith to me and the boys, about how the telestial kingdom, the lowest of the three kingdoms that he said awaited us, was so beautiful and wonderful that had we a chance to catch a glimpse of it, we would commit suicide just to get there. Well, Joseph Smith said a lot of brilliant things, but that wasn't one of them. How anyone can find themselves atop a Utah peak in the fullness of summer, how anyone can stand in the mountain stream and watch the caddis flying upstream in the clouds, lit up by the dying summer sun, or how anyone can look at a Doug Fir draped in fresh snow on a sunny winter morning and claim that we have fallen from some paradise is full of horseshit and hasn't even bothered to open their eyes to the world, and by God, if you believe *He* is the creator of it all, how can you call such indifference *religious* or even remotely spiritual? Even if it were true that the worst version of the next life surpasses this, it is meaningless to say so because it demeans the beauty we are still trying to develop adequate capacity to see.

Brother Jensen was a good man. I know that. I know what he did for me after I lost you. It wasn't just the meals, the visits. He fed our pets when I was too sad to leave my bed for a piss. That was something. I know the kindness he is capable of. But someone ought to make sure he steers clear of theology. It's like handing a chain saw to a prepubescent boy and asking him to carve a bear sculpture out of a tree trunk. He is more likely to saw off his own limb and make a bloody mess of himself. And that is what we have been willing to let people do: cut and hack and leave in shambles a theology that might have stood a chance to pass muster with the world. I mean, no one in Christianity as far as I can tell has come any closer than Smith to a Christian theology that allows for evolution, for chance, for chaos, for the free play of a physical universe that has made the infinitesimally remote possibility of our life a reality. But our trouble is, we want to make so much sense out of things. We want a rational religion, a rational theology, made after the image of the self-made man. Good consequences that come from good actions. Every blessing a reward for compliance to some law. If that were true, then we would simply have to redefine "blessings" so radically that they would end up looking no different than plain old life. Is it a blessing to be healed? Is it a blessing to get sick? Is birth a blessing? What of death, accident, trauma? Seems to me that Jesus tried to get us off such logic when he healed the blind man. No sins of his, no sins of his parents, but that the works of God might be made manifest in him, that's what he said. But then I still have to wonder, are God's works not possible, not manifest, in the life of a blind man who *never* sees? I guess if I have faith anymore, I sometimes imagine that maybe I still belong to God even if I can't tolerate him anymore. Maybe he gets that. Maybe he gets tired of himself too, from time to time. Tired of all the contradictions.

Over the years I have gathered stories of absurdities. Not out of some kind of morbid obsession but because I have wondered what sense to make of such a world. You can tell me all of the miracle stories you want, and all you are doing is selectively choosing to tell stories that conform to your idea of a miracle. The last-minute decision to put on a seat belt before an accident that could have otherwise killed you. Great. Well, what about the kid who was decapitated while he was driving innocently with his friends because someone threw a brick at the car? True story. The impression a mother followed to check on her toddler, just as he had escaped the house and wandered toward the street full of traffic. Well, what about the child who slipped and fell down the stairs in her own home while carrying a rod for blinds her mother had asked her to bring downstairs and the rod went through her throat and killed her? True story. The family that prayed their soldier son home to safety. But what of the four veterans, apparently saved during wartime, who are killed by a train that collided with a parade float that they were on in a parade in their honor? I am not making this stuff up. I am just asking for a theology that is at least adequate to the reality I encounter in this world, the one I can read about in the papers, the one that happens on the ground without all the dressing up we do to reality. The problem with fiction isn't that it is implausible. It is simply never as strange and awful and beautiful and rare as this life always is, moment to moment.

Which is perhaps why Job and Ecclesiastes are my bread and butter. I don't mind a little of the Book of Moses either, a gem of Smith's. I mean, let's admit a few things: the race is not to the swift nor the battle to the strong but time and chance happen to them all. Stop saying otherwise. Stop giving yourselves credit for things that you can't possibly claim were the earned consequence of righteous living. Righteous living might matter, but certainly not because it determines outcomes. Just ask Job. It gives integrity, something I would have done well to remember before I lost you, since my obedience had begun to erode. But maybe that's just it. I wasn't Job. My losses feel too much like obvious punishment, and that's perhaps the most enraging thing of all, not because I can't look at my own sins, but because that's all I can see these days and surely, surely whatever mistakes I made in my life were not so bad that you and your mother deserved what happened. I don't mind being punished. But why punish the innocent just to make a stupid point to the sinner? I wish I could look back and claim that I had been a man of perfect integrity, but I wasn't. I lost you and all my innocence was shattered. All I could see in the mirror were my sins. My anger at your mother for things that are just too stupid and banal to bother recalling. And my immature impatience with you as you grew. I wanted and expected you to be my peer from the very start, and you know, remarkably, you were so much of the time. We could talk about animals, plants, and the stars, and you absorbed it all. I remember telling you about the stunning ability of some plants to produce sperm that swim. You were eight and you grasped the utter wonder of it. That is no little thing. And on more occasions than I can number, you showed exceptional aesthetic appreciation. Do you remember that one night we backpacked together, just the two of us, up Rock Canyon, and you refused to go to sleep because you were waiting for the appearance of the full moon when it would rise above the mountains that surrounded us? I could barely stay awake myself. Adrift into early dreaming, I came to when you shook me. "Daddy, Daddy!" you said, "Look! Look at the moon!" It shone through the netting of our tent which we had pitched without the fly. I thought to myself at that moment that I could die and be happy, seeing you so full of joy at such a simple thing. But when I think back on the times when you were just being a young and impulsive little girl, when you understood so little about the world, and how your behavior was nothing more than a minor inconvenience and I treated it like some kind of violation of the laws of all that is right and proper in the world and would snap at you, yell at you, or just plain walk away from you, well, this is more than I can bear. You admired me so, and this hurt you. What an abuse of the privilege it was to be your father.

And then, there is your mother. The one person in all the world who truly understood me and truly loved me despite all that she could see, the one person who become mother, father, lover, friend to my immature and poorly formed soul and had me believing in what I could become. She gave me hope and security. And my thanks for it was to allow my chafing at the church to affect our relationship. I could talk to her about how I felt, but maybe it was precisely the way that she accepted me so fully, so completely, that I couldn't tolerate. I guess it meant that I had to stick it out. If she could take it, so should I, it seemed. But when I was alone in the mountains or away in the mountains with other researchers, there came over me a feeling of solitude so profound and familiar, I hardly seemed or wanted to be connected to anyone anymore. I could sit on a rock and listen to the crickets, the wind through the trees and the soft murmur of mountain water and slowly all my vocational cares, all the attentions the world demanded of me would pass before me. I could feel them slipping out of my grasp. At first it felt like a kind of dying, or betrayal of responsibility not to remain preoccupied by life, but I found a way to drift there, carried along quietly by time, cradled in the world of vegetable and animal and mineral, and I would forget entirely who I was. I felt some guilt about my craving for this feeling, but over time I found that this was how I could truly embrace my existence in the purest sense. The universe felt free and forbearing, utterly without law, at least any moral law, and meaning was what we created for ourselves. I could just never quite figure out how to then create that meaning when it seemed it was already scripted for me. So I found myself increasingly in a state of perpetual hesitation.

During that fateful summer, I spent almost every weekend on extended research trips with a group at the University of Utah. We were collaborating on a project that brought together entomologists and botanists, trying to understand the effects of snowpack and water levels on the biodiversity of the riparian communities that moved down the quick slide to the Salt Lake. We were in the Uintas, and well, you can imagine that I enjoyed this immensely. And I am not going to pretend I didn't enjoy the break from church, the chance to drink my coffee openly and freely in the morning hours with a group that felt far less judgmental and overbearing. And, well, at this point I've got nothing to hide, so I might as well admit that I made a friend. Her name was Millie. She was younger than I was, by almost a decade. It wasn't like I was unhappy with your mother. At least I hadn't yet imagined so, not to the extent that I started to anyway. I only found her appealing, refreshing, and delightful. She was from out of state, not LDS, and passionate about nature. Again, it wasn't as if she offered something supplemental to my life that

I was missing in my relationship to your mother, but she was there with me in those moments of intoxicating freedom and intellectual stimulation in the wild. We found ourselves talking more and more frequently, exchanging stories and perspectives about what we were studying. She was early in her MS degree there at the U, and I an aging PhD student with wanderlust still in my veins. I guess as we deepened our friendship, which was innocent enough at the start, I started to imagine an alternative life with her, one freed of the constraints of Mormon life, one that would bring me back to the freedom I had relished so much before I met your mother. Despite the joy I felt at converting to this life of religion, when I found myself contemplating the rest of my life, I wondered if it was all there is. I am not proud of this. I don't tell you this out of anything but a profound shame and perhaps with the hope of some forgiveness. I have nothing to hide. I want understanding but I don't need justification. Those feelings for her are very far from my heart now, as I hope you can appreciate. I look back on it with a sense of strange wonder, as if looking in upon the life of a stranger.

So Millie and I would sometimes get paired up (she being an entomologist and me the botanist). We were expected to explore various bends in the streams where we could identify concentrations of plants and insects that could provide evidence of the impact of water levels. I was looking specifically at monkshoods, the prevalence of which was in question at such high altitudes, and which in a season of heavier snowfall as we had had the previous winter, we expected would be flourishing. It wasn't, and we didn't know why exactly. Millie was looking at the stoneflies mainly. So we would wander and stop at stream banks and observe the darting brook trout spooked by our sudden appearance. We passed a good six weeks like this, and I found myself so comfortable with her it seemed like the most natural thing in the world that she would touch my shoulder when she wanted to say something with particular emphasis or when she touched my hand to point something out to me.

Looking back on it now, I obviously should have asked to be transferred to another team. At first it seemed unlikely to develop into what it did, and by the time it had developed, I couldn't quite bring myself to walk away. There was no way this could end well. I didn't consider it at all at first and then when I did, I didn't believe it could be true, but she was falling for me. That had never really happened to me before, you see, with the exception of your mother. That's the oddness of it all. Only two women that I can think of ever had a thing for me, ever took initiatives that other women never did, and frankly it was only women like that who ever had a chance with me anyway. When I was younger, I could spend months interested in someone, but my interest barely made a difference in how I treated them or acted around them. I would just freeze in fear inside and wait for something to happen, and since nothing ever did, I remained alone for a long, long time. I don't mean to make excuses, but for what it's worth, I did not mean for anything to happen and I never made a move to get things going. I know, I know. I sinned in my heart in any case, so what difference does it make, right? And it doesn't bring the two of you back either way, so I might as well own it all.

Sure, I remember electricity running through me when she touched me. I remember thinking we could somehow be together in the mountains forever, forever studying, forever sharing our amazement of life, and where you or your mother fit into that, well, I never gave a thought to it. All I could think was that I could love her, be with her, and we would hold on to a happiness with a fierce determination to never let it go and never allow anyone in: no community, no extended family, no neighbors but the trees and the elk. We could run from sightings of our fellow humans, and we could enter society when and if we chose, but only because we wanted to. I wanted to write her poems. I wanted to hear her call my name, over and over again.

I let myself go, inside. I was freely and fully in love, inside. But I held it down, like a murderer suffocating his screaming victim with a pillow, hoping it would die.

One weekend, we got caught in a storm. Millie and I were a little too high on a ridge for our own good and we were seeking shelter. I know it sounds like a cliché, but the weather drove us under some rocks by a cliff. She huddled up next to me as she was shivering from the cold and I began to rub her back to warm her up. We were a good mile or so from the camp, and, well, I could see we could act in that moment with impunity. She told me how she felt for me. I listened. I stopped rubbing her back. And I thought silently for a good while. I think she was terrified by my silence. And like a chess player, I contemplated my next move, where it would lead from there, and what my options were. I knew what I wanted in that moment, but I also knew what I was incapable of doing, and I could see the utter stupidity of the whole thing that I had allowed to develop. You see, I enjoyed being on the edge like that. I enjoyed the warmth of the flirtation, the pleasure of contemplating what could be, and I was drunk on the adrenaline it gave me to make her smile each day. But that's all I really wanted. I wanted to keep her in a state of expectation. I knew it would be crushing to lose that interest just as it would to submit to it.

After a good long while, the rain began to dissipate, and there came that perfume of saturated pine bark and soil and plant matter. Oh, how I love that smell. I stood, but as I rose, I grabbed her hand and squeezed it. It was all I could manage. We left the crevice and walked back to the camp in silence. At one point, she reached out and held my hand, and well, I didn't let go, at least not for a few moments. When I let go, I told her that I thought I had done her a disservice, that I would request a different partner and that she was a beautiful and wonderful soul, that someone far more deserving and appropriate would find her before too long, and that I wanted nothing but her happiness. It's weird. As I said those words, I listened to myself and laughed, knowing full well that I was trying to convince myself of their honesty. She grabbed my shoulder and pulled me toward her and kissed my cheek.

"You are a good man, Zach, a good man," she said.

I guess you could consider that a moral success, in some ways. I mean, I well know it could have been much worse, and at first I felt pretty good about myself. We were back at the camp and I enjoyed the feeling of liberation it had given me to know that I could pass on such a thing, but as I looked at her that night, across the fire we surrounded together with the group, I wanted her more than ever and found myself in a state of panic. I barely slept that night, and in the morning, before the sun had arisen, I got out of my tent and went for a walk. I attempted a prayer, you know, a kind of plea for help and forgiveness. I begged God to take this desire from my heart, to help me make things right again with your mother, to be more appreciative of the blessing you two were in my life, and to recognize how much he had given me, how content I should be with who I was, what I lived for, and for the plot of life fate had scripted for me. As I sat on a flat stone away from everyone and while the sky lightened by the minute, I saw a herd of deer wandering through some sagebrush and at their sight, tears came hard, like the rain of the evening before, to the point that my gut hurt. They heard me and all stopped feeding for a moment and looked at me in that wondering and dumb way of theirs, turned to the side. It was a wet and stunning morning that was coming on, and I felt better after praying, like maybe I could move forward. But I knew then and there that I had to tell your mother everything, everything that I had felt and allowed to develop. I could reassure her that nothing had happened, but I wouldn't lie either about the sins of my heart. I wanted to recommit to her, to reassure her of my utter fidelity that she could count on for the rest of her life and for the kind of father I would be from then on, more attentive, more appreciative of your youth and fragility.

I thought I could do it right away, but I was so happy to be back in the home with the two of you, I couldn't help feeling ebullient. And in my joy, it seemed so irrational at that point to say anything. How would your mother have made any sense of it? I should have been coming home with my tail between my legs, you see, sulky and sorrowful, and all I could feel was the incredible blessing it was to be married to her, to have you as my daughter, to be given this one small chance at real happiness in our little corner of this planet. God never seemed so real to me, so palpable, so proximate as he did then. He was in every breath, every breakfast, the end of every day. I prayed more fervently than ever before with you and your mother. And I read the scriptures with a kind of hunger that left me savoring every phrase, every contemplation. And insights rolled through my mind in waves. Not that I had anything I could have put into words, but the world in all of its myriad forms of beauty and strangeness, the chaos at the heart of the universe that had made so much life possible, and the reality of God's love—it all made perfect sense to me, or perhaps it is more proper to say that I intuitively grasped it, trusted it, and loved it. That seemed more important than understanding it. My mind felt a greater capacity for learning than ever before. It was a crucial time for my studies, and I dove into them with relish. I was really moving forward, and your mother could sense my joy. So it started to seem like an unwise idea to say anything at all. After all, my heart was never in a surer place. It was a month or so later when I was summoned to Salt Lake for a follow-up meeting with the team of researchers I had worked with on that trip, and it was the first time I would see Millie again. I was not at all worried about it. I knew where my heart was and what I wanted, but damned if I didn't feel the most sudden seizure of my heart when I saw her. I was mad as hell at myself but I was also blinded. I was stumbling, barely thinking, like I was drunk. We were at a restaurant, all of us, and she and I had found ourselves next to each other. As I wrote that, I realized that is dishonest. We sought each other, moved toward each other to greet one another as everyone was arriving, and I think we didn't want to lose sight of each other as the evening played itself out. So we stayed together and talked as if no one else was there. My heart raced, my body felt entirely weak, and I lost my sense of who I was, what I wanted. I don't say any of this out of an excuse, just so you understand what it felt like to have it happen the way it did. We were talking about everything, about our research, about anything surprising we had seen in the mountains, and we spoke as if we both wanted to be poets. Finally, she stopped the conversation up short, looked me in the eye and told me in all sincerity that it was good to see me, that she had missed me, that she hoped we could find a way to see each other more often. And then the selfishness of wanting to sustain this feeling in her even or especially if I knew I couldn't requite it, well, damn it, it possessed me again. I thought of no one or nothing. I was all feeling. I reached under the table and rested my hand on her thigh and gently squeezed her. Her hand found mine in a split second and we held hands for a few minutes under the table. We both looked aimlessly around the table and smiled at others and pretended to engage in conversation. And then it hit me. I hadn't reformed one ounce. It was worse because there I was, wanting her more than ever before.

I hate to offend your sensibilities, but I can't hide anything any longer. I can't afford to. Besides I have no one to hide things from in any case. Oh, how I wish I did. My heart was far gone. That was the most disconcerting of all, especially given what I felt for your mother and what I had been saying to her most recently. I well knew what Jesus said about feelings in the heart, and no person on earth can deny the truth of what he said. We all know it. So this is what it feels like to fall for someone else, this is what people do when they ruin a marriage, I kept thinking to myself. Is this how it is going to end? Will I lose everything? How could it possibly be worth it? I was frozen, unable to turn away and unable to move forward. I didn't know what more to say to her and I knew what I didn't want to do as much as I knew that I wouldn't be able to not do it if I didn't stop things. When I thought of the evening ending, of being alone with her to say good-bye, I froze up inside. I knew I would forever be standing here, torn at a crossroads, and wrong for my indecision, condemned for wanting more than one life. I got lost in the thought that there might even be some virtue in this indecision, that the more virtuous man is a less decisive man, someone who sees the world for all its complexity and can't stomach the violence of a cold morality. I had always envied those types of Mormon men who just didn't seem capable of the same weaknesses, who lived their lives with a kind of arrow-like purpose and direction, men like John. I can see it in him. He has a kind of perfect fortitude. It's not so much an unwavering commitment, although no doubt he understands himself as a committed man, but it has more to do with how he has been formed, what kind of a heart has evolved inside of him, and that, I suppose, is the real genius of Mormonism: its capacity to engineer the kind of hearts that won't waver. It's not so good with hearts like mine that never seem capable of reform. But it can produce firm minds, firm minds and unwavering hearts if it can get a hold of you early enough and with enough love. But, you know, and I feel this toward John, in my more arrogant moments I see such men with pity, as if they are half-formed, as if their heart and mind and passions were stunted like so many Chinese women's feet, kept within strict and unbending bounds from early on so that they were never wild. I wanted you to be wild. Sure, I liked that you had a spiritual sensitivity, that you felt God. You talked about him comfortably, as if he were a casual friend, and I loved that. Honestly, I don't know that I was all that good at teaching you much at all, but I did think that if I were to inculcate God in you, he would be the fire behind your passion for life, not its wet blanket. Your mother was better, but hell, we made a decent team. I think what shocked me so much about myself is that I hadn't ever considered myself an unfaithful type. I was a pretty simple man, and I had spent enough time alone for a good portion of my life, that I kind of relished a monk-like existence. I have certainly proved my mettle there, haven't I! You must laugh at me now or feel pity, I don't know which, but I wander around this house in all intimacy, barely remembering to clothe myself, and I haven't a clue how I would talk to a woman should I meet one interested in me. I walk around in this old lean body of mine and I mean everything is old and lean, if you catch my meaning. I have no fire in the belly anymore.

Millie called once, you know, a year or so after you were gone. She had heard about my woes and felt some pity on me, and had asked around about me until she found my whereabouts, but I was starting to learn the effectiveness of cold brutality, you see, and I told her that she had no right calling me to offer comfort, that she was nothing to me, utterly nothing. My words exactly. You see, before that night at the restaurant I thought I finally understood what repentance was all about and what the so-called "mighty change of heart" meant. It had felt like a new heart inside of me, but it had not apparently made the difference. Since that time, I learned that the difference is more easily made by simply becoming an angry and bitter man. I had decided to live like such an asshole that no one would ever want to come close again.

And it wasn't virtue that night either that saved me. It was cowardice because as I sat there and ran over the facts in my mind, I realized that the only thing that I had failed to do was to tell your mother. *Tell her and it will all be all right,* I thought to myself. She will understand. She will mother me and help to bring me back from the brink. She will make the rightness of my path seem more clear to me. I knew that telling her would hurt, but I felt that if I didn't say anything to her, then I would only sink deeper into this attraction and temptation. I excused myself from dinner and left early, avoiding any further conversation with Millie. And when I came home that evening, you were doing your nighttime reading in bed. She had been cleaning up and was reading on the couch with her apron still on. So I told her everything.

Oh, your mother was a beautiful woman. I could have told her that a few times. Might have done me some good. I just wasn't much for those kind of words, or even for the small daily shows of affection. I am sure that seems odd to you now, what with my verbosity. But I am different now, at least different on paper. I think it sometimes hurt her that I couldn't manage that much. She had asked on more than one occasion. She was gentle about it. "Just hearing you speak kind words to me makes all the difference in the world," she would say. I told her once, on her twenty-sixth birthday, that she was as pretty as a sunset. Not great poetry, mind you, but she practically swooned and would mention it from time to time, as if she wanted to encourage the right behavior from me, rather than to be full of complaint. Well, I never knew how to be delicate. I just told her what I had felt for Millie, and I guess I mentioned that Millie was beautiful. I wasn't trying to offer excuses but just to lay it out there. But the more I spoke, the more withdrawn she became. I didn't blame her of course, but it was very disconcerting to see her retreat from me as I tried to reach out. I guess I expected that all of her unconditional acceptance that had always been there for me would continue, but this was different. She was hurting and felt betrayed. I had never seen her like that or heard such anger in her voice and nothing I could say could convince her that she should feel anything different. She was beautiful even in her sadness. I remember her sandy hair, placed up in a bun that was loose and falling out. She was wiping tears quickly from her face, as if she resented that she was shedding them at all. She had on one of my old flannel shirts that she liked to wear in the evenings when she was doing projects in the house. She was helping with a group quilting project the Relief Society had organized, something to send to homeless shelters. I remember because the sewing machine was out on the kitchen table. These are conversations one wishes you could have over again, because if I could, I would say something very different, something about how there are two kinds of pain in life, pain that we cause and pain that we experience as just part of living, and sometimes it matters to make the distinction and sometimes they are one and the same. Maybe forgiveness feels a little bit like the latter only after you have accepted responsibility for what you have caused. I don't know. I have tried to find that peace, but I can't. I guess I don't want it anyway. To accept that peace means I have to accept the terms of my loss, which I just can't do. It means having to accept absurdity, a plot so stupid and simplistic and yet so utterly vile.

Time and chance happen to us all. And without either, we have no life on earth. And yet life feels destined or designed to be what it is. I used to make sense of this paradox, but I can't any longer. All I can understand is fate and fate is like a chain around my neck, holding me down and linking each and every event of my life to a sequence of cause and effect, and the curse is that I am not allowed to undo these links, unbind time and event and circumstance so that I might face a different future than the one that stares me in the face every day without you. Every morning the sun rises, every night it sinks below the western mountains and I am still here, you are both still gone, and I am just one day older, still cursed to spend my time without you.

I know plenty of people in the world have suffered far more insults than I have and I should be able to accept what time and chance did to me and to you and somehow move on, but then I can't make sense of what it means to have loved you. It means love is nothing but a kind of suffering. Attachment to anything or to anyone only brings on the suffering of loss. So if I am going to care at all about the world and about the people in it, it means

I have to tolerate the stupidity and waste not only of our human errors but also of God's "purposes." I have to suffer God in order to love him, suffer your loss in order to say that I loved you. Well, hell, that just makes no sense to me. All I know is that after all these years I can't stop loving you, missing you, wanting and needing you both back in my life. That is the only thing that seems real to me, that and my mountains, of course. Those are real.

Chapter 9

The bus barreled through the night with merciless speed, at least that's what it felt like to Alba. She scarcely slept, in part because she was not accustomed to a *semi-cama*, the chair-bed hybrid that allowed her to lean backward but not far enough for a full recline. But her less-than-comfortable accommodations were not what kept Alba awake: her mind was fully occupied, imagining potential outcomes. It was like she had to write ten different novels of the same story just to begin to cover all the possibilities. When the path to the past is unknown, then it is multiple. Rather, it is no path at all, but instead a fan spreading itself in every direction except the future. One must venture a few steps in each direction, imagining scenarios and plausibilities, to tease out and perhaps with some luck narrow down the realm of possibilities. If the future was the real mystery, why did the past feel so infinite? Despite the appearance of an infinite past fanning out before her, she had to continually remind herself there was only one man who was her father and that he had lived only one life and made only one set of choices. There were not three or four or ten or twenty options available. There was only one. But as she contemplated her own singularity rolling through the dark of night toward southern Chile, were there a single dot to track her movement, were she capable of believing she was one, she would deny it because no single caption, no summary of who she was, of what she was doing, what awaited her, and what she was feeling could possibly convey the universe that was her heart and her consciousness. This had always been the great mystery of life for her. It didn't matter that she carried a specific name, bore genes, spoke words, moved in distinct spaces: life was experienced as eternity and infinity, always and forever. She could not be confined. And if this was her conviction, surely whatever it was that her father did, whoever he was, whatever his end, he deserved the same concession she demanded for herself that her story would never be finished. That seemed the least she owed her father and that all the disappeared deserved. It would be the most banal and superficial and unfair of conclusions to decide that death is a sentence, that it brings anything or anyone to a close. After talking with Marycruz, now she imagined him wanting to be more valiant than he was, falling for women when he should have been focused on the more important objectives. Maybe some of the women were not altogether innocent in this. Maybe he had a weakness. Maybe the trauma of losing his brothers had infected his reason. In her darker and more cynical moments, she blamed her mother for his behavior, just a little, because she knew her to be an officious and formal person, something that a young man from the south, who perhaps grew up performing manual labor on a farm, might have found difficult in the end. And given her political indifference, how might he have felt not being able to share this central core of who he was with her? She knew that it wasn't fair to blame anything on her mother, but as Marycruz had said, not all victims are martyrs. Even Marycruz would have to admit that this has to cut both ways. Her mother can't have been an angel. She was young, she might have felt confused, desperate, maybe even panicked. Of course, if he was a louse, then there must have been some story to that too. And the question of his conversion was puzzling too. Of course, she wanted to believe it had been genuine, but she well knew from her own experience that sometimes people joined for other reasons. But it disturbed her even more if indeed it had been genuine. Why would he have thrown it all away and so quickly? His actions suggested that perhaps something didn't stick. And what of his mental health? Surely little was known about mental illness and available medications. Was he unfit to make his own decisions?

She could barely get past all of these scenarios to begin to imagine his torture and execution. Tito had told her more about the tortures and she had talked to a number of people at the Vicaria who shared their stories with her. These stories left her numb. She found the stories so awful that she struggled to believe them. She knew this wasn't fair, but it all still seemed so implausible. Upside down rape, with tools. Psychological torture of a parent over the fate of a child in the next cell. Abuse of pregnant women. Something about the secrecy of evil allows it to spread its black wings in unabashed wantonness. And this was the way of it with evil. It left victims with the burden of believability, which was more often than not denied, and they were left to carry it into the world with broken tongues, shattered memories, fractured selves scarcely able to know what to feel, whom to trust, what to believe. Some of those tortured stayed for months at the camps, to the point that they almost became friends with the torturers, knowing their moodiness, their gait, their accents. If her father had had contact with so many cells, surely he would have been a valuable resource: if captured, someone who would benefit the government for remaining alive. Did his body give out? Did they get all they needed from him and then did the helicopter come and carry him away where he was dropped to the bottom of the sea? Did fish eat his body, bit by bit and is he now found somewhere in the sand, in the shells, in the life of seaweed, in the bodies of living fish? This violence and this ending in utter oblivion so far surpassed any wrong he could have done in his life that all she could feel was a profound pity for the man. She imagined him long since relieved of his suffering and now, perhaps freed of the prison that his body had become, he had been able to accept what had happened. And she wondered, not for the first time, if his spirit guided her now.

Surely not all of those who were disappeared could be accounted for: in his case, his family's rejection of him at conversion explained why they would not have known his whereabouts or cared. And despite Marycruz's reassurances,

Alba didn't feel confident that her mother's efforts to find him would have been enough, especially given the state of their relationship, not to mention her politics. From the way her mother talked, political radicalism and infidelity went hand in hand. Unfaithfulness was what you could expect from someone who would actively undermine and subordinate in the darkness. Alba was raised to agree with her mother, but that was before she understood how important it was to assess the true nature of the conflict. Surely under many circumstances, stubborn rebellion or even surreptitious deceit was a virtue not a vice. Knowing that so many were captured and tortured and killed and knowing what courage it took to fight for democracy and for transparency and justice, she wondered if she could forgive the silent and acquiescent majority who pretended that these sorts of things just didn't happen. People like her mother.

The sun shone at a steep angle from the east, having just topped the cordillera of the Andes. The mountains could barely be made out because of the intense white light that beamed almost horizontally across the wheat fields and through the trees. To the west a blanket of clouds hung low, hugging the coast that was well beyond sight from the highway but which felt near enough, if only for the temporary impression that the land sloped down to the ocean. What a strange sensation to be in a country that was part of such a massive continent and yet, by fate of geography, was more like an island, sealed off by the ocean and by a mountain range that would not cease until one arrived at the very end of the earth. Two or three hours in either direction and one confronted the edges of what it was to be Chile. The land morphed with each passing mile, now flat and open, now hilled and variegated. Bald spots of open land appeared everywhere, cleared by human hands since the turn of the last century, but where the trees were abundant, it wasn't because they were wild. They were cultivated, straight rows of trees, farmed for industrial uses. This was the land of the Mapuche, the proud and resistant people who had managed to defeat the earlier Spanish colonizers and kept them from going farther south along this narrow corridor for close to three hundred years. It was also the land of booming development, of growth and industry, of westernization. Just as it had in her own home in the American West, the frontier had been vanquished by the arrival of the train, the automobile, and by big money.

When she arrived and took a taxi into town, she could see that Temuco was a bustling city spread out without many high-rises but with a high density of people, people walking to work, people carrying children, students carrying books, *micros* filled with people carrying them to their next destination, *colectivos* racing the streets in search of the next passengers. Alba could detect a slight shift in the population: people had more angular faces and somewhat darker complexions, but they engaged in the same business as everywhere else where urbanization had taken hold. Construction projects were under way on almost every corner, road improvements, sewer lines, lines of honking black taxis. People of all ages filled the sidewalks—young mothers pushing strollers, elderly men and women shopping or strolling or sitting on park benches in the central plaza, students, men, and women on the way to work. Only once did she catch sight of what looked like an American or maybe European couple, with unshowered ragged looks, carrying heavy backpacks. She fit in reasonably well, so she felt confident in asking for directions to the Center for the Investigation and Promotion of Human Rights.

She found it, a few blocks from the main plaza. She buzzed the door and was let in, finding her way down a narrow hallway until she passed an open office door. A young woman sat behind a desk.

"I am looking for Berta. Is she available?"

"Yes, yes, of course." The woman stood up and indicated that she should follow her down the hall. They entered another office, this time one occupied by a much older woman who looked to be in her sixties. The young woman pointed to a seat in front of her desk and then left. The woman introduced herself as Berta.

"Welcome. Tito told me you would be coming," Berta said. She had serious dark eyes, a face worn down by years of sobering work, but it was comforting to Alba to know she had found the right place and, she felt, the right person. "What can I do for you?"

"I have come from the United States. I have been in Santiago already for the past week, and I came up empty there. I am looking for my father who was disappeared in 1982. His name doesn't appear in any of the registries we looked at, but Tito did find two brothers with the same last name who were captured and killed here in Temuco in 1973. Since I have no family tree or anything, I can't know for sure if they are related, but I thought I should come and perhaps find out more. I really know nothing at all."

"That's fine. That's often where we have to start. What are the names of the brothers, then?"

"Roberto José and Manuel Carlos Sepulveda Torreon. My father's name was Luís Alberto. The brothers were disappeared in late September 1973. My father, some time in September of 1982."

"Hmmm. I think I remember reading the case of the brothers. Let me take a look here." Berta pulled out a large loose-leaf notebook that had copies of reports, presumably the same ones available in Santiago but here each had additional information stapled or paper clipped to the pages as it became available. Some cases had no new details, but some appeared to be growing in substance. After several minutes of silence while Berta calmly read through her files, she spoke.

"Yes, this is a case where more information has been gathered than what you might have seen in Santiago. Their father and mother helped several years ago now to piece together a few more details. The names of the brothers appeared in the original

Retting Report of 1991, but some time after that, probably after the parents were able to read the report, they wrote more information. Shall I read it to you?"

"Yes, please." Alba's breath shortened.

"*The brothers Roberto Jose Sepulveda Torreon and Manuel Carlos Sepulveda Torreon, age 25 and 22 respectively, were detained for the first time on the 14th of September 1973 after reporting themselves voluntarily, together with one other brother, Luís Alberto, at the police station in Temuco. Hours earlier police officer Rolando Cepeda, accompanied by three other police officers, had personally visited the home of the three men with the purpose of arresting them. Upon not finding them in the home, the officer gave notice that they should present themselves at the police station. They were held in prison for a few hours but were then allowed to go free with the obligation to return and sign every morning and night at the police station. Before being allowed to leave, their hair was cut short.*"

She looked briefly at Alba and then continued: "*On the 21st of September, one week later, they returned to sign in on schedule, but this time they were detained, except that Luís Alberto was given his freedom. This same day, the two detained brothers were taken away by car to the Comisaria de Cunco, several kilometers away. There they saw the arrival of three other newly detained men from Temuco, all of whom had been arrested that same day. This was where they were both last seen alive. One of the surviving victims, Julio Humberto Arenas, stated in his judicial declaration that he spoke with the two brothers there. He and his cell mates were ordered to lie face down on the ground while the two brothers and the three others taken that day were led out of the cell where he heard one of the police order them 'to get into the vehicle.' The two brothers were never seen again. It is believed they were transferred to Santiago and that they may have been buried at sea some time between October and November of 1973.*" There is more here, but it is detail about the efforts the family made to find their sons. I can make you a copy. What is new is the information about their brother. We were not aware of his arrest until they wrote this to us." The paper she held was typed on blue office paper.

Berta waited for Alba to speak. She was numb. Her father had not been pronounced dead, not yet anyway, but he had been pronounced, which made his disappearance seem that much more unnatural and unfair.

After more silence, Berta finally spoke. "I suppose it has occurred to you to try to contact the parents."

"The parents? I, uh, this is the problem. I . . ."

"Your grandparents. The parents of Luís Alberto."

"Oh, right, right. Yes. I mean, is that possible? I didn't know their names and Tito couldn't find anyone with their last name in the directory in Temuco. Do you have any information about them?"

"Well, I have this letter they sent that we attached here after someone dictated the information." She turned the pages and found an envelope stapled to the letter. It had a return address. "Here it is: 8 de octubre 1452, Puerto Saavedra. Do you know where that is?"

"No, is it close?"

"Two hours by *micro*. It passes near by the plaza, down on Lagos and Bello. Just take the one for 'Puerto Saavedra.' You can't go wrong. It's a tiny town and everyone will know where they are." Berta made copies for Alba and gave her a number to call in case any questions or problems arose. "It would be most helpful," she said as they concluded, "if you remain in touch and inform me of any developments."

"Thank you so much."

She took the *micro* as directed and sat in the very back of the bus where the only open seat remained next to an older woman who looked indigenous, wearing a well-worn and faded red blouse with a blue skirt. She carried a large watermelon in her lap. Although she had learned to be especially extroverted as a missionary, she was by nature quiet in such situations and, especially under these circumstances, she just didn't feel like talking. On her left sat a young boy, maybe six or seven years old, and his mother. He was a little harder to avoid. She could feel his face looking up at her while she sat staring at the road ahead. Finally, he got up the courage to stir her out of her reverie. Something wasn't right and he needed to know.

"Where are you from?" he asked.

"From the United States." She realized as soon as she said it that she could have said Chile. He sensed she was different—her clothes, no doubt, or the way she wore her hair in a ponytail perhaps—and she might as well help him out.

"Where is that? Very far?"

"Yes. It is very far. To the north."

"Concepcion? Rancagua?"

"No. Much farther away. I had to come by airplane to get here."

"Brazil?"

"No, even farther." She smiled at him. He was sweet, with dark and unafraid eyes. He was holding a soccer ball in his lap.

"Which team?" he asked.

"Oh, where I live we don't have a team yet. Can you imagine? We are supposed to get one soon." She wondered if he knew anything about basketball, or football, but she didn't ask. "What is your name?" By this time, the mother was fully engaged in listening in to make sure he spoke politely.

"Felipe."

"She speaks English, Felipe. Ask her to teach you something in English." Alba practiced saying "hello" and "what is your name" with him. He copied her well.

"Do you speak Mapudungun?" he asked.

"No. Do you? Teach me something."

Felipe seemed excited by this but didn't know where to begin. Alba pointed to the river Cautin that ran hurriedly next to the road. Felipe looked as his mother.

221

"There are lots of words for river. But *maya* will work."

"*Maya*," said Felipe. Alba repeated.

How do I say hello?

"*Mari mari*," he said.

And on they went. It was a welcome distraction. She taught him to thumb wrestle. He told her a riddle, but she didn't understand it, and this made him giggle hard. Felipe grew tired from the windy road and the distance and found his mother's lap for a nap. Alba herself drifted off.

A loud bang awoke her. The *micro* had blown a tire. The driver managed to pull over and everyone spilled out onto the side of the road in search of some shade. It wasn't overly hot. It was cooler than Temuco, in fact, mainly thanks to a stiff breeze. The clouds above were high and thin and they moved quickly. Beside the road was a larger river that did not appear to be moving at all. Alba guessed they couldn't be too far from the ocean. She moved down to the bank. The hills on the other side looked sad and overworked, as if no one had been able to make up their mind how they would be used. There were patches of planted trees, which were getting easy to recognize for their unnaturally straight lines and even height. That can't be good for biodiversity, she thought. Mr. Harker had made a point of that many times. Difference and diversity, he had said many times, they are what drives life. They were the context without which life was impossible. But closer to the river there were many wilder looking trees, large willows drooping their branches to the water's edge, and some tree that was flowering in a very faint yellow color. What caught her eye was the way the trees along the shore were mimicked with almost perfect symmetry and clarity by the still and opaque water below. She dug into her backpack to find her sketchbook. It was the first time she had even thought of sketching during the entire trip. This hadn't been a conscious choice. It had simply not occurred to her until this moment of stillness. Felipe came down to her to watch. She explained to him what it was she was trying to capture. After so many classes in the fundamentals of drawing and painting, it was easy to grow impatient with the kind of still attention the world demands, and especially here, in this foreign place. But she had learned that it was vital to pay attention to the morphology of plants, to their leaves, the inner structure of their branches, their habitat. Mr. Harker would be disappointed if she rushed into her whimsies, as he liked to call them.

Before long the trip continued, and it wasn't more than twenty minutes before they turned away from the river, which now flowed in what appeared to be a widened delta. Cattle could be seen making their way through some of the tall grasses. Birds she didn't recognize floated above in the strong winds coming from the sea. As they drew near enough to the coast, they were suddenly enveloped in fog. Large cypress trees bent into the wind. The temperature had dropped considerably. As the road turned south onto the Main Street of Puerto Saavedra, houses and small shops lined the street. When they were more recently painted, they shone in bright yellows, greens, and reds. Otherwise, they were deeply faded, the paint flaking off in large pieces. People were gathered mostly by the stores that sold *provisiones*, but there were shops too for visitors to the beach, offering empanadas, *mote con huesillos*, or *pollo asado*. Stray dogs of all sizes wandered back and forth across the street. Dogs here never seemed interested in barking; it seemed like they were just too tired. To the west, she could see a hint of the sea. It wasn't that it was far away. It appeared to be just a few blocks away, but visibility was still bad and she couldn't be sure. The bus stopped right in the middle of the town halfway to the end of the Main Street. As she stepped off the bus, she could just make out some thinning of the fog above her head and the emergence of some blue sky. Everyone had told her how much it rained in this part of the country. She just hadn't seen any of it yet. She wrapped her arms around herself as she stood on the street to get oriented. She had no idea which direction to go in, but for some reason asking a stranger seemed too hard at the moment. Just then Felipe approached to say good-bye.

"*Pewkayal chaltumay*," he said with a smile. Alba repeated what she heard.

His mother was standing a few feet away waiting for him. She smiled at Alba.

"Listen, do you live here? Do you know where the eighth of October is? That's the name of a street, as far as I can tell."

"*Si, Si*. What's the address?

"1455."

"You're looking for Gardenio?

"Yes, actually, I am. Do you know him?"

"Sure. He is two minutes away. Just two more blocks down, turn left on Prat and Eighth of October is two more blocks, running parallel to our street here. His house is two houses farther down to the south, on the right. Bright green. You can't miss it."

As she walked, Alba's heart began pounding again, but she was beginning to learn that it didn't necessarily mean anything portentous. She braced herself for more disappointment. She could see her feet moving forward but was certain that no mind of hers had given the orders.

When she got to the house, it was quiet. A stray rooster bobbed its way around the front step. A sickly looking skinny black dog with wolf-like ears watched disinterestedly from across the street. She approached the door and knocked.

"*Voy!*" she heard someone say from inside. After a minute, an old man who appeared to be in his eighties stood at the door. Later she would tell John that it was like looking at a man who had worn the same clothes all of his life, not so much because they were not recently cleaned, which they were not, but because their folds and creases seemed to anticipate every angle of his bony frame. He wore a white shirt, but it was worn enough in his elbows and on his back that his copper skin showed through. His brown pants were similarly conformed to his legs and were held up by what looked like a makeshift belt, as if he had recently lost weight and had had to punch a few extra holes in the leather. He had a white mustache and white hair, with just a faintly receded hairline, and a weatherworn and sun-beaten face with deep age lines that nevertheless looked hardy and vibrant for his age. His green eyes darted at first, as if he was distracted with something or someone in the house and preferred not to be disturbed, but as Alba stood wordlessly in front of him, he found focus on her eyes, the shape of her cheekbones, the slope of her shoulders.

"I am sorry to bother you, but are you Gardenio?"

"Yes, I am."

"I don't even know if you will know who I am, but, um, I have come a long way."

Before she could understand what was happening, he stepped forward and wrapped his arms around her and said with reverent intensity, "Alba. Alba. Am I right? Yes, you must be! Tell me that I am wrong! Tell me!" At this he stepped back, with both hands on her shoulders to get a better look at her.

"Yes, I am," she smiled. He embraced her again, this time hard. "How did you know?" she asked incredulously.

"Alba. Alba." He repeated. At last he loosened his embrace and led her into the house. It was lit by daylight from the windows, all of which were open. The sea breeze caused the peach-colored curtains to breath in and out. A worn couch was pushed under one of the windows. He invited her to take a seat.

"I was afraid you wouldn't know who I was," Alba answered. "I am Luís's daughter, your granddaughter."

"I know who you are."

"I have come to learn more about the disappearances of your sons," she said.

"Alba, of course you have come. Of course! And of course, it is you! I suppose it is about time for that, isn't it? Yes. Yes, it is." He was nervous and excited, which only added to Alba's nervousness. "I am only so sorry to tell you that your grandmother passed away last year. How she would have loved to see this day! What can I get you? *Jugo? Te?*"

"Juice would be lovely. Thanks." They sat and talked for a good hour, dictated entirely by his many questions about her mother and how they left for the States, about their life in Utah, and about her marriage to John. She expected that perhaps he would be off put by any discussion of her religion, given his reaction to Luis's conversion, but he was curious and even admiring of the details she shared about their life, including the story of her mission and their temple wedding. He was a lively old man, affectionate, with a kind smile that flashed across his lined face every time he learned a new detail about her life. Speaking to him was comfortable and natural, so much so that she lost all feeling for time. The hour flew by. His curiosity was flattering, and she almost lost track of her purpose as she relished the chance to share her life with a man who was her grandfather.

"We haven't even talked about you yet. And I came to learn about your sons."

"I would love to show you a space I have created, you know, in their honor."

"In their honor?"

"My sons. In honor of my sons."

"Oh, yes, that would be lovely. I would love to see it. Is it in the back?"

"No, we have to drive a way. Would that be okay?"

"Of course."

Gardenio stood up and walked out the front door where an old dented white Ford truck was parked on the patch of sandy dirt by the road. Alba wasn't sure if she was supposed to follow, but when he didn't immediately return, she sheepishly followed him out into the direct sun and breeze. She could hear the steady rustling of the ocean in the distance. Everywhere it seemed salt was in the air. Much of the fog had already cleared. He was already in the car, so she climbed in.

"How long are you here?" he asked as he turned down the main street.

"Well, I am here in Chile until next week, five more days. But I am not intending to impose on you for all that time."

"Do I look like I have a lot going on? As I said, *mi mujer, tu abuela*, died last year, so you can imagine my days are pretty long and uneventful, especially at my age. A lot to think about, maybe too much, but time? That I have in abundance. *Esta es la tierra de los Mapuches, sabes? Tu abuela siempre andaba convencida de que tenía sangre Mapuche, quien sabe de dónde, pero nunca la creí. Es una clase de fantasía entre los Chilenos que viven por aquí, pues así les hace sentir un poco más, que sé yo, acomodados en esta tierra salvaje. Pero no importa. Es una gente de la cual se debe sentir orgulloso de todos modos. Nuestro país tiene sus tragedias pero tenemos nuestro orgullo también.* Haven't you seen some of this in America, where you live in the West? *Así es aquí.* And things are far from settled. Issues with land ownership, rights, survival of cultural traditions, and the like."

She liked how he called Chile "our" country. It hadn't felt that way, but maybe, she was beginning to imagine, maybe it could.

He seemed to feel the responsibility to communicate context for everything about the place and he spoke like a wise sage. Alba didn't dare disrupt him.

"You know, the Chileans couldn't get into this territory for many years. The Mapuche had the help of the land. With a *cordillera* to the east and the sea to the west, this narrow corridor of land was easier to defend. Papa was born just east of here, in Carahue, in the 1890s, just after his parents settled. The area was covered in forest, in those days. Lumber was the fuel, fishing the industry. He used to say that the smell of freshly sawn wood was stronger than the smell of the sea. The railroad had only recently arrived. Sometimes I get sad, looking around at what's become of the place, but I like what little remains of the rawness. You know, after I lost my sons, I thought about pulling up roots and moving to Santiago, but one trip up there was enough to convince me it wasn't for me."

"Was that before or after we left?"

"Much before. I think I made the trip in '77, maybe '78. But even back then Santiago was already getting pretty polluted, and I couldn't stand so many people."

"I was born there in 1978." She didn't know how to bring up the subject of his rejection of the family directly, but she thought that maybe this would lead him into his own explanation.

"Oh, I figured that out later. It's awful what time we lost, Alba."

"Well, we have today, don't we?" She smiled at him, trying to reassure him that she didn't harbor bad feelings. He didn't seem like the kind of man who would hold a grudge. He had been so warm.

"I am glad to know you feel that way."

He turned down a dirt road that headed down toward the river. Several cows and a bull stood still in the middle of the road, looking at the truck as it approached. Gardenio slowed and honked and kept talking.

"You know, the situation was terrible, people were still disappearing. We spent years pursuing justice in the courts, but I am sorry to say that we have not yet been successful in finding out the names of the perpetrators. They still walk the streets today, somewhere. I am not reconciled to this, but I suppose God's justice must be counted on at some point. There is at least that. Some say that we should leave all of it in God's hands, that we can't play judge, that we should let it go, that that is the true meaning of forgiveness. I have never wanted vengeance, but I do want justice, Alba. Besides, look how well that attitude has served us. And who do you think it serves? The weak will never find protection without law and law will never have force unless there is punishment, consequences, you understand? Of course, human justice isn't perfect but, you know, if we don't at least pretend to believe in it, the law has no teeth, it is just meaningless words sleeping on a page. With the law asleep, evil awakes voracious in the night, that's what. You wake in the morning, in the bright light of day, the light of civilization, and it is already too late. Every citizen awakes strapped to their own bed by the tentacles of terror. Civilization takes careful cultivation, spade work it is, turning the soils of history and culture, and pulling out, one weed, one stone at a time, all that stands in the way of the growth of democracy." He motioned with his hands, as if he had tools, as he spoke. "Only in this way can justice become a reality. Impunity is the fantasy of power, and justice is our only hope against the abuse of power. The tentacles of terror reach everywhere, I tell you, finding every form, every location, every expression it can to fill all the empty spaces on the map with its blank ink. And as we have learned here in Chile, while justice must go through the courts, it does not live in the courts. Justice lives in the heart."

He pounded his chest. "Justice is what we imagine life can and should become, and it is what we are willing to work hard enough to achieve. Nothing more and nothing less. When there is no vision, as the Bible says, the people perish. *El que sigue la justicia y la lealtad halla vida, justicia, y honor. El sabio escala la ciudad de los poderosos y derriba la fortaleza en que confiaban, como dice el profeta.* So we must have vision, and where do we suppose this vision comes from? From the visionaries who help the rest of us to see what is possible. That's why they are the first to go in any system of fascism, the first to be purged from the very womb of society, ripped out like viscera from the belly. Books are burned, writers are killed or exiled, artists are held under suspicion. Why is that? Only because they have the capacity to imagine life otherwise. It's not because they are all communists.

No. It's political enough just to be able to look at the bald-faced lies of propaganda and know that life, that reality, might be otherwise. The embarrassing truth of naked power is that all power wants and all it ever gets is the illusion of structure, the bare bones, but not the bleeding heart, not the fleshy organs of life, just a hollow shell. And you would think that for that reason shameless and illegitimate power would be the easiest thing to detect and reject, but somehow it not only persists but grows. It doesn't need compliance from everyone, of course: just enough to tip the scales so that the majority can fall into their stupor of acquiescence. And from where does this compliance come? From the weak-hearted, from the fearful, from the children of fate who do not respond to the cultivations of courage taught to them in their youth. Instead, they cower in the face of what is asked of them. They run, they hide, and they deny the very footsteps they leave behind them, as if they could choose without consequences. They are utterly crushed by the weight of their own liberty and choose instead to make fate their father, choosing to believe that the world was inherited, not created, that all choices are necessary and that no one need answer to anyone else. And the great irony, then, is that these children of fate turn against their own blood and prove the freedom of human will: that nothing is determined in advance, not by biology, not by environment or upbringing, that we humans are as free as the birds, as unpredictable as the wind, as varied as the surface of the ocean."

Alba was stunned by his spontaneous poetry, his gift for wisdom, she thought, that a lifetime of losses had taught him. She relished every word, fearful she would forget it all. After a moment, he spoke again.

"I have always believed that there is no use in being ashamed that we are what we are, free and unpredictable, cast upon the open sea with no rudder. Might as well create order, direction, pattern, and beauty whenever and wherever possible."

"Like an artist?"

"Exactly. As an artist. That is what we are. We Chileans just can't find our paintbrushes yet. Most of us, anyway. Still hoping that the work is already done, that it is all written in some sacred document somewhere that gives its blessing on all that is. *Te digo, no basta con ceder a las cosas. Hay que crearlas.*"

He stopped the car just above a small outcropping that overlooked a small tributary that flowed from the hills to the south into the delta.

"*Ven.*"

He stepped out and she followed him down the hill. At the bottom, close to the edge of the water were two saplings, each with a circle of recently turned, loamy soil. Behind some rocks a few feet away, Gardenio lifted a bucket, dipped it into the water and watered the trees.

"They are Temu trees. They don't really need me to water them, but I just like to help them along. They love the water; their red bark and roots hunt for the water's edge. They can handle floods. That's why I picked them. And you came just in time to see the white blossoms—they won't last too long. It's what people are calling *ecomemoria*—it's like a restoration of the land, an enrichment of the soil, the air, the riparian system, while using one tree to stand in the stead of each life that Pinochet sought to erase with his violent rapaciousness."

Alba was confused. "But there are only two."

"Yes. Of course, there should be thousands. I am not the only one. Many others are doing it too for their *desaparecidos* all across the country. It's a small forest, when you think about it."

"No, I mean you lost three sons. There should be three trees."

Gardenio looked at Alba. There was a long pause.

"Lost is one word for it, I guess." He took a close look at Alba's face. "What did your mother tell you about your father?"

"That he was disappeared. In 1982. That's just it. She never really said much more than that. It was a sore topic between us, especially as I got older. She just wouldn't say much at all, and I finally took it into my hands to find out the truth on my own. That's why I have come alone. I couldn't find his records in Santiago, but I thought maybe you could help me."

Gardenio paced in front of the trees for a good while. He wiped his shirt with his hands and then began to speak very slowly.

"Alba. When you said you wanted to know more about my sons who were disappeared, I thought you meant these two. These are my sons who were disappeared. Your father was not disappeared."

"What do you mean? Was he executed?"

"As far as I know, your father is still alive."

"As far as you know? Wait . . . what does . . . why, why are you saying it like that? Isn't he your son?" Alba was losing breath quickly. She reached for something to hold on to, but found nothing. She reached down, felt a large rock, and sat.

"Yes, he is my son, but I am afraid it is a very different story than you have been led to believe."

"What is going on . . ." Alba held her head in her hands and began to cry uncontrollably. Gardenio approached and stood silently by her for a few minutes while she cried. Finally, he reached out and stroked her hair wordlessly until she calmed.

"I'm sorry," she managed to say. "You have no idea how confused I am."

"I might have some idea. This hasn't been easy for any of us."

"No, of course. Of course. Please tell me you have more to say."

"*Claro. Ven.*" He reached out his hands to help her up and bring her back to the car. "I want to show you something else and then I will tell you more."

They returned to the main road and continued on toward the ocean in silence until they arrived back in Puerto Saavedra. Alba stared out the window. She was glad for Gardenio's temporary silence. She rolled down the window for fresh air. The clean breeze felt good against the skin. Santiago weighed heavily on you, like a blanket, but here the wide-open spaces, the green hills, the mountains in the distance, and the feel of moisture and salt in the air were alleviating. She felt comfortable with Gardenio. He reminded her of Mr. Harker, only much nicer and warm and noticeably more frail. He had rare wisdom, ecological in a sense too. He carried a wound, and carried it alone. Maybe Mr. Harker carried a wound too, something he too had borne alone and that had given him insight. Gardenio's smile could not disguise his sunken and tired eyes, and there was something too in his composure that spoke of years of weathering the intense circumstances of a life almost entirely crushed by history. He's like Job, she thought. He's lost everything and through no fault of his own. Anyone could see that he was a dignified and good man who had lived a life of integrity.

She didn't know why he was waiting to speak, but she respected the silence. No doubt this was his natural state. After all, whom did he have to talk to? And where did all those words come from, all that wisdom, except from deep within? What more would he have for her? All in good time, she thought. I am here, I am here, she repeated in her mind, as if she hadn't yet believed it. She began to pray, and as she did, she realized she hadn't prayed in weeks. She had been driven by overwhelming instinct for some time, almost as if she had grown afraid to consult with God. *Please, Lord, bring me peace. Please comfort me. Please. Help me to know why I am here. Help me to know who I am. Be with me now, please, Lord, and be with my mami, my John. Hold us together, hold me together. Where are your children? Where are they all?* She thought about the horrible way the police got rid of the dead, strapping them to metal rails and then lifting them in helicopters over the ocean and dropping them into the depths to disappear forever from human sight, but not from God. No one, no life, no hair on the head was lost to Him. He was the great law of completion, the gathering of all human memory, of all human suffering and striving and anguish and silent prayers and unspoken thoughts, needs, and desires. Surely no thought in Gardenio's head was without audience. Surely she could not be his only witness. She would listen to him and absorb it all as best as she could. Children of fate. That she would remember. His passionate condemnation of passivity and of evil.

But what of the things she would soon forget? What of his inflections, his expressions, the intricacies of his thoughts could she hope to preserve? The cadence of his Spanish. His turns of phrase. She looked at his hands on the steering wheel and told herself not to forget them, as she had done all those years ago with her father's hand. How, without writing everything down, inflecting them again through her own imagination and words, would they be remembered? She could do that, she thought. She could paint but she would write too. God heard his words, every syllable of his fell into a great net, somewhere, somehow, and all would be restored as it once was, but she should hold on to as much as she could in the meantime. His words carried forward an ancient thought that was not his alone but was stored up against the erosion of memory, against violence, and against time. It was impossible not to imagine, as she had so strongly felt while talking to some of the survivors at the Vicaria, that remembrances of the disappeared are the very stuff of godly love. Every step taken to commemorate, to honor experience, to remark upon the miracle of each individual life—from person to leaf—witnessed life. It didn't seem to matter what one's politics were, what one's failings were as a person, for surely all the dead were as incomplete as anyone else, but the fact of disappearing from life, of having been loved, and of inspiring a striving to be remembered in those they left behind, this was the invisible line between heaven and earth and our very substance as spiritual beings. Tito had shared a letter from a prisoner to her family that stayed with her: *El Senor está vivo en el hombre. La vida es nuestra.*

Qué sentido tiene la vida de un hombre si no es de morir para vivir y dar vida, dar realmente vida. El Senor está con nosotros. Yes. Yes. Yes. The Lord is alive in humankind, she wanted to shout.

Without a prompt, Gardenio began to speak again before they stopped. "*En el principio no tenía ninguna razón por la cual creer que tu padre era diferente, que no era como sus hermanos.* Sure, he was more quiet, you know, the last of the three, and he lacked the natural leadership of his older brother and the playfulness of his second brother, who was a real tease I tell you, always abounding in joy, but they were pretty close as brothers go. And they were raised in the same home, with the same parents, the same foundation. Truth is, I have wracked my brain trying to understand where the difference lies, what explains it, or even if it's a difference at all. Perhaps instead it's just some kind of manifestation of random divergence in the genetic and cultural heritage in which his destiny was fired. Or a touch of evil somewhere in the wind, maybe that, or maybe something much more mundane, a simple weakness of fear that causes courage not only to collapse at the slightest threat but to transform into violence. When his brothers started to get involved in discussions about labor, about organizing a socialist front in Region IX, he went along and not without passion, mind you. I remember thinking at the time that he was in need of greater confidence and that with time and maturation, he would find his own voice. But he was always the more fearful of the three, worried about getting into trouble. Your grandmother liked that about him, of course, mostly because Manuel, my second son—oof!—he knew how to keep things interesting when they were young, you know, always running into some kind of trouble—innocent trouble for sure—but really all three of them were good, happy boys. Playful, curious, capable of the sweetest joys. That's maybe the hardest of all to remember, you know, that sense of the three of them, together, coming in after working in the fields, throwing dirt balls at the rock wall, playing *fútbol* with an old balled up rag, or exploring the streams and wetlands for frogs. Always dirty, they were, always covered in dust. God, if I could go back and hold them there in that innocence. Only six years between the three of them. Like puppies, they were. It seems like suddenly the oldest two are married, Luís is not yet serious enough with anyone, and there was this overwhelming feeling of opportunity that with Allende elected, there was a real chance to make a difference, to bring about real reform. Our September 11, in 1973, like yours I suppose, divided our nation between what it was before and what it would become. It was an utterly crushing blow to what many of us had worked for so long to achieve. And it was clear that it was done by someone who hated us, who hated our vision for the country, hated it enough to rage with bombs and fire and to rule with instruments of torture. My boys were taken so early, some of the very first in fact, just days after September 11. At that point, surprisingly, all they did was show up at the house. Three policemen came, demanding the arrest of our three sons, none of whom was home. We told them so, and they said that they would have to report to the police station by midnight. It was a dark day, that much I remember, pouring rain with black skies. I can remember Luz wailing in the back of the house from our bedroom, wailing for her boys. She couldn't help it and later she would repent of it, but that night she blamed me, she screamed at me for teaching the boys my ideas about agrarian reform. I didn't try to argue with her, but there was nothing I could do to comfort her, short of getting her sons out of danger. Luís was still living in our house, but his older brothers, you know, were married and living on the property up the lane. Roberto had a son who was four at the time, and a two-year-old daughter. Manuel was just married."

"When they got home, I had to tell them. We discussed our options and even though Roberto briefly thought about going into hiding, we finally agreed that showing up at the police station was the right course. The four of us all drove down together, and as fearful as you would have thought my boys were, I remember the look of confusion on the faces of their jailors. They didn't seem to fully understand what they had been asked to do, even though they did their level best to convince us that they meant business. As I understand it now, they were given the mandate to clean house, to arrest all visibly active supporters of Allende and then to extract from them as many names as they could get of those who were also involved, no matter how marginally. These were men we knew, you know. Men who had lived in the same community, who knew us as friends and neighbors. One of them had grown up with Roberto. They did not yet know what evil they themselves were capable of, but we would all soon know what fear can do. There was a mad search for weapons, even though this was an absurdity. No one knew of any stockpile. We had never talked about any kind of armed conflict. *La maldad tiene mucho miedo, ¿sabes? Es la apoteosis de la paranoia. Se esfuerza, se manifiesta como una forma de anticipar toda eventualidad.* My only minor victory was to convince the police to let the boys come home as long as they would return every morning and evening to sign in. I told them that if they arrested all of the boys like that, *de una vez*, it would ignite a fire of anger in the town. They released them, knocked about a bit but not tortured, not yet anyway. When I returned home with them in the middle of the night, they immediately started to compare stories of how they had been treated. They were each interrogated for several hours and asked to specify the extent of their activism and what they knew about weapons. They were asked to name others, of course, and they all claimed they gave no names to anyone. That turned out not to be true.

Roberto and Manuel were emboldened by the experience, as if it had lit an even brighter fire of conviction in them that their cause was just. Sure, they were afraid, but we believed in democracy, true democracy, something that hadn't really taken hold here in the frontier, and this was such a naked abuse of democracy. It seemed unacceptable to us that we would countenance this. My paternal pride lies in the fact that the one thing evil doesn't anticipate is the way its machinations awake in the human spirit a resolve that, like a seashell that hardens and fossilizes, refuses to be dissolved but instead stands out against the forces of erosion. And Roberto and Manuel were two of the young lives cut down too soon in those days, but they would be followed by hundreds, thousands, and tens of thousands who found their courage. Evil has its day, always does, and every time it is because it can count on acquiescence. It counted on it here. It has counted on it in your country too. There is the acquiescence of the tortured, of the beaten, of the utterly defeated, but that is not what I mean. I mean the quick lending of a hand, the sudden adoption of a new reality and a new vocabulary, such that people accept lies without hesitation. You wouldn't have believed that they could say what they said with straight faces, but, following the *golpe*, the Junta announced on national television that they only meant to bring law and order to a country that had suffered on the border of chaos for too long. They insisted that they did not intend any vengeance against their enemies, nor any ideological purging of the country, that this was a pragmatic necessity that they themselves, as good military men, did not aspire to but would do nevertheless for the good of the country. They fully expected democracy to return, they said, as soon as enough stability was established. *Mientras más desnuda la mentira, la más eficaz, ¿sabes?* No need to dress up lies. Just say them and repeat them enough and suddenly, suddenly, you know, you have enough agreeing, some even celebrating, while in the very same moment thousands are imprisoned, tortured, executed, or forced into exile. That first week a schoolteacher in Temuco was beaten in front of his young students, fourteen-year-old boys and girls watching while their teacher, whose crime had been his legal and public participation in the democratic process as a socialist, was bloodied mercilessly in front of them. To teach the children the lesson of fear. And suddenly what you have is a completely broken country: broken families, a devastating fault line that opens and bifurcates into two realities. We are still seeking to suture that wound. You know, I loved the house I grew up in in Puerto Saavedra. It is gone now. But my love that took that house for granted is nothing compared to the love with which I have reassembled it in my dreams. *¿Entiendes?* We have a great opportunity right now if we can do this right, and I am not just talking about our country. I mean you and I, right here, but it requires facing in all honesty the kind of wrongs that have left things broken. So forgive me if this hurts, my dear. I don't know you, but I love you. I love you. You hear me?" He reached to touch her shoulder and looked her straight in the eye.

"Yes. Thank you. I love you too."

"I have loved you without ever knowing you, isn't that strange? You were with me all this time. Your arrival here was not a surprise." He continued the narrative with a kind of urgency that couldn't afford long pauses of emotion. "But there's more. We didn't realize how forceful things would get, but we did start to hear reports of murders in Santiago. Under such pressures, some fought harder. But most cowered. Your father was shaken by the experience and kept expressing regret that we had gotten involved. He wasn't tortured, but I guess that interrogation was enough to break him. As each day passed and they continued to sign in morning and night, he started to back out. He started arguing with his brothers and with me, telling us that we were too willing to endanger the lives of others around us, that Allende had only brought chaos to the country. Chaos. One night at dinner, he announced that we needed to respect law and order. Law and order. Those were his words.

'*¿Y como es, hijo, que lo que aquí se hace puede llamarse legal?*' I was more stunned than I was angry, but his face flinched. I do remember that.

'*Hay que respetar a la nueva orden.*'

His brothers didn't take this well. Respect for the new order was out of the question. It was power that had been seized illegally. This coup disrupted the very process of democracy that had elected Allende and that was still available to any other citizen of good will. This was the sort of thing we Chileans might have thought could happen in Peru or Brazil, but not Chile. And let me warn you, don't go thinking this sort of thing can't happen in your own country. *Tarde o temprano los estados unidos van a latinoamericanizarse.* Don't kid yourselves. This too is America and this too is part of your history as a nation. The truth is the opposition hadn't waited to let the country find its footing nor had they made an honest effort to participate in the democratic process. They were already disrupting in every way they could the success of the president and then turning around and calling him out for his failures that they had caused.

Luís wanted to make the case that his brothers were not living up to their responsibilities as husbands, that it was selfish of them to put their families at risk. He said this in front of their wives, both of whom were firmly supportive. Sure, we were all afraid, but it was not a question whether we were going to back out or not.

'What are you proposing, Luís?' asked Roberto. 'I don't see what good can come of this conversation. We have been arrested. We are technically still under arrest. There is no way out now in any case.'

'There is one way,' said Roberto, staring firmly at Luís. 'He knows it. We know it.'

'You will stay strong, Luís, right?' Roberto asked. And at that, Luís got up from the table and left the room. I hoped that maybe things would ease up, but we were learning of the hundreds quarantined in the National Stadium in the north, and you knew it was just a matter of time. One evening, they left the house to sign in. I never saw the two boys again. That was it. They walked into the night, never to return. I can still remember their faces, their kisses, their embrace of their mother and father. After an hour, we began to worry. And then your father returned alone. He wouldn't speak, wouldn't tell me what happened. At first, I shouted at him to speak, to tell me where they were, where they had been taken, to explain what had happened. He sat in the chair in our living room and stared at his feet. I calmed down, pulled up a chair next to him, and put my hand on his sloping shoulders, leaned in to him, and said softly, 'If you have done something to hurt your brothers, you must tell me. Just tell me. Let's keep the truth in the open. Here you can trust your father to be honest.' I could see that he was struggling.

'It isn't right,' I continued, 'that any son of mine cannot feel comfortable under his own roof, being who they are, doing what they have done. We are all one. Speak to me, son.' When he remained silent, it occurred to me that maybe he was traumatized by what had happened and that he just needed some time to process things alone. 'When you are ready, I will give you my ear, son. Always.'

I told Luz I was heading down to the police station to ask questions. I got nowhere, of course. They told me they had been transferred but they didn't know where to. I asked them why they had been taken and not Luís. At this they laughed. 'Ask him. I am sure he would be happy to sing,' one of them said. When I came home, Luz was sitting on the couch completely still, not saying a word, not crying, just staring ahead. 'What is it? Where is Luís?' She said nothing. I went to his room, and it was a mess. He had thrown his things together and was gone. He took all the cash we had in the house. Luz had been unable to stop him and to her dying day, she never spoke of what transpired between them. I am not naive, Alba. I know the police say lots of things, they tell so many lies to twist us around against ourselves. Surely they wanted to punish me by making me believe my son was what we called a *sapo*, a traitor, someone who would turn others in to protect himself, but that doesn't mean it can't be true, you see. Luís's behavior added up to a very bad narrative that we began to construct in our minds to make sense of the outcome that night. You see, your uncles were not the only ones taken that day. Others were disappeared, a total of five, all of them never seen again. And the only common denominator among them was that they all knew your father. He never returned. He has never made an effort to make himself known to us again. He knows perfectly well where he can find me. Always has. His mother died without ever seeing her son again."

At this point, their car had arrived at the top of a bluff overlooking Puerto Saavedra. Gardenio parked and turned off the engine. Alba could see the ocean spread out in front of them. The wind was strong. Yellow flags, warning of the risk of tsunamis and indicating the bluff as a safety zone, whipped in the wind. The fog was long gone and it was a stunning day. The ocean roared below, the breakers began far off shore and stirred up white seafoam all the way to the shore. She felt open, permeable, attached to the sky, to the wind, and to the angry sea. It wasn't exactly peace that she felt but there was harmony in the motion of the elements and acceptance, of what exactly? Of flux? She could see driftwood gathered by the sea below and with each wave, they were nudged a little farther, burnished a little more, conformed to the indefatigable rhythm of the sea.

"But you are sure he is still alive," Alba asked. "Why is that? I mean, my mother told me that he was involved in the revolution in Santiago a few years later."

"Your mother told you this?"

"Yes. At least that is what she suspected."

"Knowing and suspecting are two different things. You have to understand that your father turned in his friends. He turned his back on his own blood. And it wasn't just a passive thing, you know. Sure he was frightened, but he gave details about his brother's activities and their close working relationships with others. I know this. I don't suspect it. It took a few months but we later traced their names and the names of the other three Luis had turned in to a detention center in Santiago where they were later taken and dropped into the ocean."

"Villa Grimaldi?"

"The very one. These were friends, you know—they had known each other since elementary school. There were others still who were tortured and some who eventually were let go. I spoke to two of them, and both confirmed that Luís had developed a close relationship with one of the policemen in particular, that they overheard them talking about the involvement of others. It got so bad the imprisoned stop speaking to Luís, for fear of being betrayed even further. And then, they take my sons and kill them and release Luís with barely a scratch. I saw him that night, I know."

"I am in no position to doubt any of this. I don't know anything. But I have lived my whole life believing that my father was disappeared, that he was a victim, and now you are telling me that he was a victimizer and that he might still be alive. I don't even know what to say. What am I supposed to feel? What am I supposed to do with this information you are telling me? I even imagined that he had been guiding me all this time from heaven, you know, pushing me to come here to be able to piece together his story. So who or what is it that has led me here?"

Gardenio was silent for a long time. A stiff breeze blew through the tall grass and Alba watched as the trees swayed. With their windows open, her hair blew around her face. The clouds were high and few. On today of all days, what beauty stood before her.

"Alba. There is a lot I don't know. And a lot more I don't understand. You have to see that this isn't just our problem, yours and mine, right here. This whole country, and every living person in these hills, why they all have their own share in the burden of insanity that is our history. It's not over, nor will it ever be. I can't begin to tell you how much it hurts to disappoint you. Believe me, I wish I could point to my family, and say, 'Here they are . . . here is who they were. And this is how we raised them, as you can see.' But they are gone. Even my two grandchildren. If you can believe it, they live in Spain now with their stepfather. I am alone." He paused. "And here you step into my life, a beautiful, soulful woman, a child wanting to believe her father was a hero. I so wish I could give you that."

"I don't mean to be contrarian, but is it at least possible that he had a change of heart. Maybe he lived long enough with his own shame and guilt that he finally turned against the regime and sought some kind of redemption, however imperfectly. Wouldn't that qualify him for a quick execution? My mom said that he was out often at night and that it was all secretive."

"Listen. We all feared for you, for his one child. It was not the legacy you deserved. Your mother certainly understood that. I think it is why she came down here with you, just to be sure, before she left. From her descriptions of his behavior, I was convinced his weakness wasn't just women, as she believed. He was working for the government and worked by seduction. I told her so."

"Wait, I met you before?"

"Step outside for a minute. This is what I wanted to show you."

They stepped out of the car and he pointed her to the south, where she could see a large opening in the coastline, a similar bluff on the other side, and only several hundred feet of pebbly sand separating a lake to the east from the ocean.

"You were only four, so it is not surprising that you wouldn't remember. This is *Boca Budi. Lago Budi* to the east there runs right up against the ocean here, as you can see."

"But I don't remember Temuco at all."

"That's because your grandmother and I weren't there then. We had nothing to stay in Temuco for, so we returned to the coast where I was born, to Puerto Saavedra. And this is where

I took you. From this spot, you and I walked right across that mouth there and up to the other side where you can make out a trail. See it there?" She looked but couldn't see anything familiar. The wind was strong and the seafoam raged white. "*Me encanta el mar bravo. ¿A ti?*"

Alba caught herself losing balance briefly, maybe it was temporary vertigo overlooking such an expanse, and she grabbed Gardenio's hand. She looked up at him and looked back at his hand.

"It was you."

"It was me?"

"You. You were the one who held my hand that day, after it had rained. I remember the calm after a storm. I remember raindrops on the back of his hand, holding my hand, walking on a beach. I thought it was him. It was you."

"Yes, this is where I took you. A hard place to forget, isn't it?"

"Hard place and a hard person to forget too." She squeezed his hand tightly and leaned against him and watched as the breakers continued their steady pounding of the coast.

"You look at these hills and you think they look innocent and beautiful enough, and they haven't changed much over my lifetime, which is saying something. But if you live here long enough, you learn that its tranquility is deceptive, and so you don't quite give yourself over to its beauty. You savor it but you can't hold it with desperation, you see, because it is a moment and so too are the earth's darker moments. If you are going to love the earth, you have to accept all of it. The sea, you know, those waves, that persistent drumming and throbbing heart of the sea, it insists that you forget it all, that you accept you are destined to become broken shells, tiny scattered fragments of bone on all the beaches of the world. You stand under these skies and you can scarcely believe you are one. And that's when you realize that the pain of life you carry is not yours alone. So I find the sea a welcome reminder that you are really nothing, only temporarily organized into this body and into this particular set of memories. It isn't just the dictatorship we have had to bear and the idea that the bodies of the disappeared might be buried out there at sea somewhere. We had moved to Temuco in 1954 to raise our family, but then the earthquake came. It was 1960. The largest earthquake ever recorded in human history, centered down near Valdivia."

"I never heard about it."

"This is a lonely land. I mean, just look at it. It's as if it wants to be left alone, and when you see the coast, when you feel the fierce wind blow, and watch the violent waves, and imagine the length of this desolate coast, you won't take much convincing that this is true. But you know, there were people here, your people in fact. It was a fishing village. It registered 9.5 on the Richter scale. Just a day after we felt a pretty strong quake from Concepción. Temuco was bad enough, but we made out okay. But we knew we had to worry about the coast, about the chance of a *maremoto*. All communication was lost and I feared the worst. I made it out to Puerto Saavedra as soon as I could. Your great-grandparents had a house down in the village, not far from where I live now. It was buried, the whole town. Some people managed to get to the hills, because, well, there were three successive waves, and the initial sign of the sea retreating quickly from the coast. Rio Imperial was virtually sucked out to sea from its delta, and while many headed for the hills, others stayed behind. The first wave was only four meters or so, but the last one was eight meters and it took everything inland but a few pieces of the church and one city building. Roofs, walls, furniture, everything a family might own, brought to piles at the point of the wave's final exhaustion, spreading across all the flat land, the violent tail of the ocean lashing against the shore, abolishing our illusions of permanence. We found piles and piles of wreckage, just like those waves down there gather the small deaths they cause, the fragmented shells, the driftwood, the torn bodies of sea plants, at the point of the wave's retreat, only on a scale that diminished us all to mere dross. And yes we found bodies, bloated and torn beyond recognition. A neighbor of my parents told me he had run to my parents' house to find them. He went inside the home and no one was there. After frantically calling for them, he ran. As he was climbing the hills, he could see in the distance individuals wandering far out onto the seabed gathering the secret and hidden treasures of the ocean that they had been searching for all their lives, like Odysseus's sailors drawn by the sirens. My father was a fisherman, you see. And my mother an expert at cooking his catches. They loved the ocean. They loved its detritus. They were always gathering a piece of driftwood, shells, objects refined by the crushing blows of the churning waters that had taken on human significance. They adorned their windowsills and bookshelves with these relics, these survivors of nature, so, you know, they were intrigued by a phenomenon they had never before seen." He paused. He rubbed his face with both of his hands. "It was a scene I never want to remember, but I always do. Sometimes just closing my eyes and there it is, this land of green fields, of wetlands, of dark sand and white breakers, and this blue lake all dark, all mud, pieces, clothing, broken walls, *el deshacimiento de toda cosa incorporada, de todo muro, el momento en que el mundo sólido quiere fluir y huir, esparcirse, empezar de nuevo.*" Gardenio put his hand across his brow and rubbed his forehead as if he had a headache. His eyes were closed. "And the smell. The smell."

Alba was silent, trying hard to look for the human pain under the surface of the beauty that lay all around them. For a moment, she felt revolted by the beauty, its utter indifference to the words he spoke and the pain he bore. She wanted to yell at the passing clouds, to stop their silent dance across the horizon, to cease the pounding war of erosion against the solidity of things. In this incessant nonsense of nature was a dagger driven through the heart of human remembering, loving, treasuring, building, and it made a mockery of the mere idea of family, community, belonging.

"Forty-two years ago, it was. Your father came with me to help clean up and do some rebuilding. We were here for two weeks. It was hard on the boy. He was maybe eight. And I have often wondered, you know, given how things turned out, if it was a mistake to bring him here at such an age. It hung over his youth like a gray cloud."

"And you never found them? I mean, the bodies of your parents?"

"What we found, we buried."

* * *

That night Alba lay sleepless on a bed Gardenio made for her. She could hear his deep breathing in the next room. The wind rattled the siding of the house and the oxidized corrugated roof let off a whistling sound whenever the wind hit it at just the right angle. After what seemed an hour of wind, the rain arrived suddenly with a high-pitched drumming against the metal. Streams fell down the window by the bed in the dark. It was so loud, she could scarcely hear herself think anymore, which was a relief, as her thoughts were circling around and around, fruitless, uncertain of everything, and in need of an anchor. The desire to pray she had felt earlier returned again and she slipped out of the bed to her knees and pled for some relief or clarity. It was a short prayer. Sometimes she analyzed her prayers and wondered if she had enough faith, or what it was she might be feeling or thinking that could be inspiration. She had grown tired of such analysis and that was why she had had trouble praying in recent weeks. The impulses in her were too strong, too instinctive, to spend her time examining and maybe doubting. But now she had come to the end of what she could trust herself to know. She was fervent in that moment about her own poverty. She pulled herself back up into bed and curled up on her side.

The day's events had left her split open. She had come seeking her roots, her story, some connection to her father, and while he remained more mysterious than ever, she now knew for certain that he had existed and maybe even existed still, that he had a history, a childhood, sibling relationships, a family, a place, a designated role in the unfolding of a family history that she had inherited without knowing how or even what, exactly, she had received. The links were partially visible now and she wondered if she could ever restore a clear vision of the long chain of cause and effect that had brought her into being, that had given her life, mind, body, and soul its definitive shape. All of this had come from the relentless discourse of Gardenio talking, talking as if no one was listening, talking as if this was all one could do, as if all that one was, was a single mouth. The rain pounded with the same heaviness with which Gardenio's words had been washing over her all day long. He was remarkable. His capacity for maintaining a steady rain of words awed her. His was an inexhaustible inextinguishable voice against the elements that would silence him. And he could feel after so many who were gone, all taken from him without explanation, without sense, and he could still give order and meaning to things, even if that meaning was a mere hint and only bolstered by a depth of feeling. The fact that he could still feel, still remember, and still tell demanded an answer. And from whom? From her, of course. She was the ear, the heart, the imagination into which his words poured, seeking form. As she listened to his breathing in the next room and thought about his windblown white hair, his weatherworn face, these simple walls of a home, she felt overwhelmed by compassion and love for him, for his dead wife, his missing sons, his drowned parents.

Christ, she had believed, suffered the greatest agony of all, but was it sacrilege to wonder how the physical pain of crucifixion could compare to the torture suffered by her uncles, the agony suffered by her grandparents, the insult of so many lives vanished only for her grandfather Gardenio to find himself alone, facing the sea, at the age of eighty-four? Wasn't his suffering Gethsemane enough? She wondered if there was something she had missed in all of her reading, studying, praying, and preaching, something indispensable, some core truth that held everything together, because it didn't seem that the center could hold much longer. As the rain beat down harder and harder, she wondered if they would find themselves washed out to sea by flooding and what she would hold on to and why, what for. Maybe Gardenio would welcome the flood, maybe he would swim with the tide and dive in search of his sons and parents and perhaps she would follow. Or maybe she would need to stay afloat, to stay breathing for just one more day on this wet planet that seemed destined to be swallowed by water, because maybe God would regret his promise to Noah and once again baptize the earth one final time to make it clean of human memory once and for all. Maybe God, she thought, has grown tired of so many words, so many stories. How could he stand to listen to so many souls pleading for him, pleading for mercy, for relief from the storms that it seemed even he knew not how to stop?

She reached for her scriptures and read for a while to calm her mind. She read with the kind of attention that Jesus once called blessed. It was hungry attention, emptied of spirit, lacking in faith, poor in wisdom, and bloodied by memory, knowing all the while its own insufficiency but wanting, hoping for recompense. She read slowly, tasting and savoring every word, and the beauty pierced the sadness and raised it to holy sorrow. The split hemispheres of the planet were being stitched together while Jesus cited Isaiah to those on the American continent, and, as she read, it seemed that time collapsed upon itself at the moment her mouth formed the words penned by the poet-prophet Isaiah more than two millennia ago, translated into English by scholars in England four centuries ago, recited by the resurrected Lord in a forbidden time and place that no history book recognized but that was brought back or maybe brought forward to memory through the decipherings of the young creator and restorer Joseph Smith.

Sing, O barren, thou that didst not bear; break forth into singing, and cry aloud, thou that didst not travail with child: for more are the children of the desolate than the children of the married wife, saith the Lord.

What, she wondered, is this song? A song of jubilation? Because although barren and denied posterity, you now have adoptive children to take care of? More, in fact, than can fit into all the homes of all the families of the earth? She could see the spread of homes in her valley in Utah, the wide and bright streets, and she imagined thousands of other such places on the surface of the planet where cars pulled in and out of separate driveways with children safely buckled in, each child called by name, known by name, loved by name, enclosed within the walls of family bonds. And she saw streams of children and then streams of men and women, old and young, all unattached, unwalled, exposed and cold and wet, as if emerging from the sea walking on the wet sand seeking shelter, without a face to recognize them, all flung into a dark world without homes, without streets, without names. She understood at that moment that the world properly seen is dotted with orphans and childless mothers and fathers and broken families and that surrogacy was the rule, not the exception. A human face, properly seen, is always orphaned, always the desolate in need of renewing bonds of an adopted family. So that is why he commands, without irony, that this desolation be cause for rejoicing, that each sees herself as the barren mother facing the needy motherless children. Opportunity, the counter-intuition of mercy, is the lack that is really an abundance if only seen aright. *Enlarge the place of your tent,* he says. The doors of homes, of churches and schools, the very doors of strong and healthy nations flung wide open, and the streams pouring in, a confluence, a reunion, and all forging a new and expanded family bond, stronger than before, like scar tissue, for the wounds of history and for the foolish time wasted in separation.

Thou shalt forget the shame of thy youth, and shalt not remember the reproach of thy widowhood any more. For thy Maker is thine husband; the LORD of hosts is his name; and thy Redeemer the Holy One of Israel; The God of the whole earth shall he be called. For the LORD hath called thee as a woman forsaken and grieved in spirit, and a wife of youth, when thou wast refused, saith thy God.

Such compassion, she thought, for the childless and widowed, such profound purpose in depravation as a seedbed of opportunity. Without a father, you have sought out and gained surrogates, and as yet without children, you have more children than you ever imagined. You were widowed and now have a holy marriage with your Maker. And this marriage, like your marriage to John, is based on adoption not blood. You make a family, you make new bloodlines by choosing loyalty to a stranger. He calls you in your grief. He called you *to it*. But he shared and bore that grief, not because he caused it, but because deep in the dark foliage of sorrow lay the burgeoning roots of hope and love, and the discovery of a holy human purpose. The fortunate, the happy, anyone who lives in plenty would need to share their security to learn the sorrows of the orphan, because by adopting each other as family, made kin not by blood but by bonds of fidelity, they would know what it means to lose a child and what it means to give birth again to children, parents, siblings; to rearrange and expand the bonds of biology and remake family in the image of true community is to confront the reality of human pain. This would be holy suffering because it is finally willed, wanted, sought for, and accepted. And to what end? To the end of overcoming human tragedy, the falsehoods, the fire sale of the sacred earth, the alienations of abusive power, the forsaking, the abandoning, the denial of accountability, and even the accidents of nature that had sent the streams of people in search of refuge.

For a small moment have I forsaken thee; but with great mercies will I gather thee. In a little wrath I hid my face from thee for a moment; but with everlasting kindness will I have mercy on thee, saith the LORD thy Redeemer. For this is as the waters of Noah unto me: for as I have sworn that the waters of Noah should no more go over the earth; so have I sworn that I would not be wroth with thee, nor rebuke thee. For the mountains shall depart, and the hills be removed; but my kindness shall not depart from thee, neither shall the covenant of my peace be removed, saith the LORD that hath mercy on thee.

A small moment. Would her grandfather agree or any of the elderly, would even the dead someday say that the Lord is just and merciful and quick to answer prayers, that suffering was a brief pause on a journey to deeper happiness? Would the slow tedious sequence of sunrise and sunset, of storm and clear weather, of terror and peace, someday seem like a dream, like a blink? Can we let the world be, let ourselves act and feel, let ourselves love and die, let trees fall, tectonic plates shift, wild winds howl just because that is what they are wont to do? Can we tell the difference between nature's ancient violence and our own willful degradations? Could we forgive God for our desolations because we understood finally the impossible interdependencies of shifting land and morphing bodies of water, of the mutuality of bodies of plant, animal, and human, because it is finally with the eyes of love that we see? Where will we find the strength to forgive ourselves in the face of catastrophes of our own making? How can we even separate cosmic justice from personal accountability, in any case? Can we still love ourselves for having survived a world we ruined and with renewed Eve-like innocence strive again to save ourselves and repair the world?

Maybe her sorrow was not sacrilege but holy, holy because it bound her to her grandfather, a man who held her hand at the age of four, who only hours after meeting her this morning began to pour out his story to her in waves in one day, a story that was now hers and had changed everything, holy because now she felt His compassion for so many others, because her maternal impulse would never be limited to her own flesh, because she now understood that the bonds and sorrows of family are but a type for all human relations. Her father still alive and lost somewhere to her, perhaps forever, but this had given her the gift of other family she could love. The burdens that she had felt increase on her shoulders in Utah now seemed like gifts of opportunity. Her life, her very existence was a blessing. Hers was one story — precious and unique — among so many, each just as valuable. And she had time for listening, for remembering, and retelling the stories around her. That would be gift enough.

The rain had stopped. She rose from the bed. Her steps felt light, her body almost weightless. She approached her grandfather's door, which was ajar, and listened silently to the sound of his deep breathing. She leaned against the doorframe and closed her eyes to the darkness and prayed again. *Lend him breath, Lord, and lend me the breath to speak for him when he is gone. Let me give birth to him again.*

Chapter 10

Dear S.,

I finally got an email from Alba. They were getting kind of sick of me at the library. I include it here. Is it just my imagination, or would you have been like her? Probably my imagination, yes, but that's all I got.

Alba Powell
Sent: January 15, 2002 11:29 am
To: Zacharias Harker

Dear Mr. Harker,

I hope you are well! I hope you are surviving the winter weather well enough. I can imagine that you are still moving through the mountains on your snowshoes and backcountry skis, never to be stopped by the cold. What do you see in the mountains? Is it a bad snow year still? I know you were concerned about how little snowfall we had in December before I left. And I wonder how they will handle the Olympics if there isn't more snow. I know you care for the watershed itself, for all those wonderful flowers, and your beloved mountain companions—the deer, the goats, the sheep, the varmints, as you like to call them, and all the others—but it will be interesting to see what we do when the whole world descends on us in February if we don't have "the greatest snow on earth"!

Mr. Harker, I can't thank you enough for helping me with this trip. I don't even know where to begin, but I feel I should share as much as I can about what I have seen. I am keeping my promise to write! I think about you every day and see things partly through your eyes, since you have taught me so much about the world. It is amazing! I won't do it justice, but I will make a try.

There is too much to say. I have spent the last couple of days with my grandfather, Gardenio, my father's father. What a miracle and what a gift he is! He is a man who has lost everything and yet inside of him is an inner light of fierce strength, hope and love, and a boyishness that I cling to madly. He says it is having found me that has brightened the end of his days, but I have told him that it is mutual. I have a family history, finally! It is not a happy history overall, but it is mine, and that is enough for me. I can bear the sadness of it because I can feel its beauty too. I am not sure anymore what the difference is. I can't explain it. I can cry from sorrow and yet feel so holy doing it that it is self-healing to learn to bear the darkness. It seems better to have a story to bear than to have no story at all, you know? That's strange I know to feel happiness when all that I have been given is a whole bunch of sadness, but there is something joyful in knowing that I can share sorrows. I don't know. It makes me more human, I guess. And I have prayed hard to have the strength to bear this with dignity and the Lord is holding me up. I rely heavily on a verse that teaches that the pure love of Christ is a gift. It doesn't come naturally. What comes naturally is the anger, the despair, the desire for vengeance, the selfish and hurtful retreat. But this is overcome by the gift of Christ's forbearing love, love that we must desire and ask for. I didn't realize before just what his suffering meant, but I think it's more clear to me now. I think I saw sorrow too narrowly, you know, like it was only and always about me, mistakes I made, the burden of my life, and as if I was the only one. Part of what finally heals us from our own sins and the burdens of our own lives is learning to share the pity God feels for his children, if that makes sense. We are too selfish, too impulsive, you see, even if we are justified in our pain. That's how these new sorrows feel anyway. They would be too much for me to bear, too, if not for God's help. I feel love that is not mine, if that makes any sense. (You are just going to have to tolerate my God talk, Mr. Harker! It's who I am! I think you understand. How I miss our conversations!)

I will spare you the details of my family story until I get home and can tell you in person. It is so much more complicated than either of us had imagined and even though I don't have all of the answers yet, I do have enough of a portrait of who my father was that I think I am at peace to return home in a few days. I think one of the main things I have come to understand is that to be Chilean means living with a fragmented image of the past, and while it is unfortunate that it has to be this way, it has given me a greater feeling for my fellow Chileans and for all of you back home. It's hard to explain. The broken shards of the past, you know, we can either carry them around all by ourselves and pity ourselves for our incomplete inheritance, or we can try to share the burdens together of what is lost. That is what the Chileans are trying so hard to do right now, and it is really beautiful. It feels so different in America right now, don't you think? Like it's all coming apart. The Chileans won't get all the answers about their past, but they will hopefully have found themselves in each other's arms as a nation. You are going to be riveted by the story I have to tell. That is a comfort to me, knowing you care. And John too, of course. I know this has been hard for him to understand, but I hope you know that he is a good, good man with a good heart. And he loves me. I think I love him more than ever. Don't be too hard in your judgments of him, for my sake, anyway. Deal? I hope you haven't forgotten what you promised me.

So I met my *abuelo* at the sea, at a place called Puerto Saavedra. After we spent a day talking—well, he did most of the talking and I did all the asking—I lost track of all time and place listening to his sweet voice, like a bassoon sounding melodies I had never before heard but fell in love with as soon as they hit my ears. It was like an out-of-body experience, as if I were a disembodied angel recording the unspoken wishes of his lonely heart. He has been entirely alone for the past year since *abuela* died. Well I guess once I showed up on his doorstep, it was a great unburdening. You would like him. He has often made me think of you. I can't put my finger on it, but one thing you will be pleased to know is that he loves nature like you do. He's no expert, but he certainly knows a lot and he is a pretty vigorous man, even at his age (he's eighty-four). He spent most of his life working as a farmer, mainly growing alfalfa, but he also has some impressive carpenter skills, which is how he has supported himself in his later years doing odd jobs for people.

So we drove around the Budi Lake. An amazing place. This is the land of the Mapuche Indians. You might remember I had hoped to discover that I had some of their blood in me. It doesn't look likely, but that's fine enough. From the little I have been able to observe, they are a strong people deeply tied to the land and with a proud history of resistance to conquest. I can at least admire them from a distance and feel nourished by their history and their presence. I have spoken with only a few of them, some of them who know my grandfather and some I have met on my own. I can't explain what it is that is distinct about them. The complexion around here is more copper or soil than in Santiago, the people somewhat shorter perhaps, and their circumstances are quite simple, but their poverty doesn't seem as sad as that which I have seen on the reservations in Arizona, for example. They are still in their own land, still fighting off the abuses of the government and of big business, and they are struggling to hold on to their ways, their language, and their beliefs. As we drove, we saw their cattle and farms, some of their *rukas* (thatched roof homes), and we stopped and talked to them as we passed them along the high and dusty and primitive dirt roads that go around the lake. Their homes and villages are separated by impressive distances, and many walk or ride horses. The real highlight was the chance to hear a reading by a Mapuche poet while we were passing through Temuco on the way to the mountains. Absolutely mesmerizing. He was reading in one of the plazas and a good crowd had gathered. He read in

Mapuche and then read in Spanish. I bought a copy of his work
to show you when I get home. When he started, his voice rose
and fell in a rhythm that felt more like prayer, or some kind of
ritual, than poetry. They were incredibly sad verses but there
was something comforting in them too. I can't quite explain it.
It was as if I had heard this language all of my life, and I don't
just mean the Mapuche language—I mean the language, I guess,
of the planet. I felt as if the pain he expressed was not unique
to him or even to human beings, that it was maybe part of a
suffering the beauty of nature asks us to share with one another,
with the promise of a kind of healing that I associate with the
suffering of Jesus but which is expressed by the Mapuche as the
suffering of the earth itself. There are spirits among us, that I
have always believed. I used to think it was my father. But they
came before us. It's a crowded earth and we are not alone in our
sorrows. And something holy in our tears. Here's a line I have
translated for you in a poem about the *copihue* and the *chucao*:

"Your tears, you should give them to the flowers"

And I can tell you that the *copihue* (are you proud of me?)
is a stunningly beautiful bell flower, like the bluebells we love,
that exists in the mountains here, but it is larger, deep red, and
it has little white spots on the inside of the flower, sort of like
faintly spilled paint. It's the national flower of Chile. I am sure
you can find photos on the internet. And the *chucao*, we saw lots
of those too in the mountains. A small gray bird with a rust-
colored throat. Its song is vibrant, short—a throaty chirp. There's
a lot of wisdom in those lines. I keep thinking about it. Do we
mourn our separation from nature? Is language a symptom of
that separation? Are tears a truer, more universal language we
share with the earth? The sound of his native tongue was so
enticing. I wish I knew something of this language. He read a
poem about the Cautin river that is near here—a glacial river of
such topaz!—and described the mouths of his ancestors on the
riverbed, speaking in water words. *Abuelo* tells me that Cautin

means "reunion." Isn't that beautiful? My mind can't stop! I thought of your beloved American Fork river and about how rivers are made from springs, runoff, and they in turn contribute elsewhere to other systems of exchange. A watershed, you have taught me, represents a set of relationships that makes it impossible to insist on separation and individuality. I have been thinking that "fork" is a funny word. The Spanish would be *afluente* (a lovely word that rolls off the tongue and means "flowing toward"), which I think I prefer, only because fork, you know, implies a kind of split or division, which is only because we are looking at it in the wrong direction, upstream. Do you see my point? What appears to divide or split or force a choice is really reunion, confluence when seen looking downstream. Anyway, hearing his native language like that was like listening to a great musical performance by a virtuoso. Maybe it was just me being the envious outsider, but it was certainly more like music or the tongue of the earth than human language.

Anyway, the lake borders the ocean and in two places it almost reaches the ocean directly. I am told that in the winter the lake rises to enough of a height that the line that separates the sand from the ocean is overcome and the sea and the lake intermingle for several months. *Abuelo* says that this used to happen naturally without assistance, but since the earthquake of 1960 they have been using bulldozers more frequently to make it happen. Do you know about that quake? Long story, but it brought a massive *maremoto* to the coast and changed the ecology of the entire area. I did learn that it took the lives of both of my great-grandparents. More to say about that, of course. The Mapuche have many stories about floods, like we do, and they represent similarly an end but also a beginning. I have been thinking a lot about Noah lately. I know you find the idea of a literal worldwide flood over the whole earth absurd, but it is easy to miss the point of the story, I think. Think about it. The world falls into despair, into darkness. We are getting it all wrong, and the earth swallows us, it feels as if God's wrath is upon us, and then there is this chance for rebirth, a reemergence from the darkness and into the light, a baptism and renewal of all the earth, a chance to see, even in the wake of all that sorry history, a chance at getting it right, of starting over. It doesn't make the past go away. I mean, it's not a real beginning, just a kind of rebooting of our chances. And God's promise that despite his wrath, despite the inexplicable horrors of this life and no answers to our questions about why they had to happen, he gives us a second chance. That's what I mean.

How strange that I left Salt Lake only to find another one! I kept thinking that it feels like the world has been turned upside down. It does the soul good to see things reversed from what one is accustomed to seeing. It turns out it isn't an opposition like you might have feared, it's more like a cousin reality. It's only because the world is a sphere and there is no way to see it all. All you can do is keep trying a new angle before oppositions finally start looking like angles, refractions. Like you always say about mountains! Curiously, this lake isn't saline for the same reasons as our lake. This isn't water that has no exit and has spent millennia evaporating at the bottom of our Great Basin. Rather the basin (*cuenca* in Spanish) is fed by streams from the surrounding hills and the distant mountains, but it does manage an escape because it has an annual meeting of the waters with the ocean, not to mention the seeping effects of sea water that filters through the sands underground, right? I asked *abuelo* if the earthquake would have changed the salinity of the lake, but he didn't know. It seems inevitable, right? Not to mention the quantity of sedimentation it would have dumped into the waters. He did say that excessive sedimentation is a real problem with the lake—it's not very deep. I can't put my finger on it yet, but there is some meaning in this comparison to Salt Lake that intrigues me. No doubt you will have something to say on this. That's your first assignment, ha!

It is a beautiful country, lots of steep hills and winding roads, and the lake is surrounded by wetlands filled with birds, the most beautiful of which is the black-necked swan. The water's edge is muddy and dark and it has a slight saline smell. The winds blow hard, so the water is always getting whisked and oxygenated (as you taught me about lakes!), and the clouds moved quickly across the sky. You can never be sure it won't cloud over and rain.

At one point we stopped on the south end of the lake and wandered around a little bit. It felt good to get out of his truck since it isn't the smoothest of rides. The wind was blowing against us, the lake's whitecaps headed straight at us, and little bubbles of foam formed in the wind and moved through the air like our favorite cottonwood drift in the wind. Across a small inlet, I could make out where the trees reached the bank, but because the water level was low, their roots were exposed. *Abuelo* caught me staring at the trees and didn't ask any questions when I pulled out my sketchbook. Earlier I had seen the same trees reflected almost perfectly on the surface of some still water in a location to the north of the lake, and as I was drawing it, I kept thinking about reflections, about what is lost or what is gained in the representation of an object when it is mirrored by the work of light against an opaque surface. But here the surface had withdrawn, and the trees, you know, they looked like their "lie" had been exposed, that they were utterly naked and caught in their competition for nutrition in the soils and in the waters, and I wanted to tell them that there was nothing shameful about this truth, that their roots were as beautiful as their branches. Now I can't see branches without imagining the untold story of the roots. One must learn to imagine what things hide. That is what I have decided. I couldn't really explain this epiphany to my grandfather, but he was at least glad that I was happy. You know me. I was almost to the bursting point! These trees, by the way, are called Temú trees. And the city of Temuco, where my father was born, means the "waters of the Temú tree" in Mapuche. I love that. The idea of a tree having its waters. It's a riparian tree, for sure, thirsting for the water of river banks and wetlands, and right now it is in bloom with white flowers. It's not the most striking tree, but it is hardy, *abuelo* tells me, able to sustain itself with its aggressive root system through changing water levels. Isn't that something? Its roots and bark are red and they have a tentacular shape, like muscular arms bending their elbows at different angles, giving it a capacity to work around the obstacles the environment presents to it. The image stunned me and is emblazoned now in my mind. I can't shake it, and I find myself drawing trees, over and over, all kinds, and each time insisting that I capture the shape of the underground tree as much as I render what is visible in its trunk and along its branches. Sometimes I sketch them upside down, sometimes right-side up. Some are tall with shallow but horizontally expansive roots, some disguise a deep tap root or a larger tree underneath the surface. In other words, I have found my project for my MFA! I am calling it: "Arbolario: The Spirit of Adoption," which is really going to confuse you, as it does me still, but for a quick reference, it is a phrase from Romans 8. But also check out Isaiah 54 and Isaiah 56. Just thinking about how trees make their life from an incorporation, a remembering of the fragments of life around them, like all of us! Their roots are not symbols of belonging, of legacy and heritage, so much as symbols of adaptation, accommodation, and adoption. Remember my painting of the tree in water with symmetrical roots that you liked so much? Can you receive a prophecy and have no idea what it means? My only mistake was assuming that I saw things symmetrically, I guess. I am trying to be more of a botanist (because you have stuck in my conscience! Curses, Mr. Harker! Ha!) but in the end, I can't quite control my "whimsies." They demand expression too, just as the world demands to be mirrored and twinned in our eyes, by our words and by our brushes. I am beginning to understand the value of that perpetual struggle.

Later we spent a few days in the mountains. Oh, where to begin?! The Chilean forest is so spectacularly beautiful. It's like nothing I have ever seen. *Abuelo* keeps repeating to me something that he says Pablo Neruda once wrote, that if you don't know the Chilean forest, you don't know this planet. I told him that as overwhelmed as I was, it was overstatement because I knew of at least one person who knows this planet pretty well! And that I refused to choose between one beautiful landscape and another. All are precious unto God, just as we all are individually, despite our strange differences. I can't escape the feeling that every leaf, every tree, every flower manifests the glory of God, that in all this diversity there is the breath and the smile of Providence. Maybe the principle is this: to know the planet and even to love God, one must know—and love!—one's environment. And that includes its ugliness, our damage to it, and its violent indifference. The local ecology is where such knowledge begins—it is intimacy, you know, intimacy from which one gains this connection. You have that. That's what I admire so much about you, and it is a principle that will remain with me for the rest of my life. Thank you! One can learn so much just from a flower, right? That's what you always say. Besides, it's not as if this place operates according to different rules than what we face in Utah, even if the conditions are different, right? It is all changing under our hand, either way. I wish everyone would just open their eyes.

We hiked in a few parks in the area of the volcanoes and mountain lakes at the foot of the Andes. Oh, Mr. Harker. I cried so many times just from the beauty. Have you ever seen an *araucaria* tree? I am sure you have, but look it up just in case. I am in the midst of these giants, along with the *coigue*, the *lenga*, and the *roble*. I don't know their English or Latin names, but they are enormous, towering trees, their bark covered in moss. My favorite, of course, is the *araucaria*. Its bark reminds me a little of the surface of a pineapple: ridges all the way up the trunk.

It seems whenever they grow alone away from all others, their branches behave more like other evergreens, you know, like in a pyramid. But it is still so different because the branches are very, very thick, covered all the way around in large, sharp, pointed needles (which are more like short blades, like you might see on a century plant, only much smaller) that make them dangerous to the touch. In their largest forms and in groups, they only have branches at the top, so they look like giant umbrellas. When you look at the mountainside and see them together, their bright green mossy trunks stick out, shining in the sun under their dark green canopies. Oh, they take the breath away. And the *coigue*. Enormous trees. Huge trunks, with large branches that jut out at a right angle briefly before turning straight up again to the sky. They are majestic, monarchical. They feel like friends, company you want to keep, and I am aching already at the thought of having to leave them behind, my trees, my other country. I tried to sketch to convey the size of their trunks, but it is hard to appreciate without seeing them. I saw a guide to the different kinds of trees in the Chilean forest and they used an image of a man riding a horse next to each one so you could have an idea of their comparative heights. That seems like a good method anyway. *Abuelo* says it is rainforest here, but I always associated that word with the tropics, with thick and hot humidity, so this has been different. I even found mushrooms, which at first I thought were some kind of fruit that had fallen from the trees, since they always seemed to be beneath the *robles*, but a park ranger told me (thank the good Lord for park rangers, right!) they are mushrooms that grow in the branches of the *robles* and then eventually fall to the ground. Round, textured, orange-colored, like large golf balls. Wow. There are strong breezes, lots of rain, of course, but cool air, and this interesting plant everywhere that looks like small bamboo shoots called *chusquea*. They fill the ground spaces between and among the giant hardwoods, much like our ferns do, but they are higher and they stretch upward one plant at a time in a vertical shape. What else? I have learned the names of a few other new flowers. One that I love in particular is the *amancay*, a bright yellow/orange blossom that seems to like the hillsides near small springs and *lagunas*. They remind me of the California poppies, but they are tighter, not as floppy, and not as orange. And the *estrellita*, which means "little star," bright red and drooping star-shaped petals. Must be an aster of some kind, right? Of course, I have seen many of our old friends. I am pretty sure I saw something akin to the monkshood, right by the cool streams of spring water, and daisies, dandelions, I even saw what looked just like our Western wild rose. Does that make sense? I heard so many birds, some that sound like small monkeys and others who sound like a scared child. So haunting. And then there are long silences in the forest when the winds grow still, and I could stand and listen for the sound of the forest breathing. There is an endangered woodpecker here that I could hear drilling against the bodies of the giants deep in the forest, but I never saw one. There aren't mosquitoes here, as far as I can tell, which surprised me, but plenty of what look like flying ants and bees, and very little that gets on your skin or in your face. That was pleasant enough. You know how I hate my deer flies! Ha!

The really remarkable thing about this place are the volcanoes. They are enormous and plentiful. There are at least nine major volcanoes all within several miles of each other in this range, but *abuelo* says there are dozens more everywhere, some smaller. In fact, we visited one volcano, Llaima, by car, and next to it was an eruption from what is now a small crater only ten or fifteen years earlier. Imagine! The entire area was a massive mountain of gray ash, some of it so fine that I could toss it into the wind and it would dance away like a ghost and the fine black dust particles would stick to my skin and my pores. It was exhausting to walk on, but we made it to a small summit above the crater after passing through a field of lava rocks and from there we could see a frozen river of lava below us that had poured down into a neighboring valley, completely torching the landscape and leaving it a monotonous gray, but, you know, right next to such death were green forests that had escaped the wrath of the burning lava. And we could see massive, snow-capped volcanoes in every direction and miles of these beautiful forests.

Mr. Harker, I don't know what it is that is happening to me, but this is such a beautiful world and I feel more committed than ever to using my art, doing whatever I can, to save it. I can't see this beauty now without thinking of the repentance we must do. The climate, the rising seas, the eroded soils, the plants and animals all struggling to adapt to our thoughtless impact. All of it can feel like cause for perpetual self-hatred, but I am not sure that solves the problem. It's my religion speaking, I guess, but the goal isn't shame but holy, godly sorrow that inspires hope for change. I guess precisely because I've passed through so much sorrow, so much anxiety, and so much uncertainty during this trip, this beauty feels like a hard rain on parched ground. I can barely absorb it all before it runs away from me, leaving me in a state of want I never knew I could feel. But unlike the wanting I have felt before for my father, for my Chilean story, this longing doesn't hurt. I mean, it hurts but it heals too, almost in the same moment that it inflicts its pain. It's a sweet pain, one I crave, one I need. Hurting for my father felt like an insatiable desire, an unhealable wound that filled me with a voracious anger, and I started to think, as I learned more and more (and as the information I got raised more and more questions) that I was falling fast into a deep pit and that I would be utterly devoured, enveloped by the fog of the past, buried by the unknown and the unknowable, but you know, maybe a bit like this lava rock, experience bursts forth: it burns the soul, it demands that we reckon with its angry force, it shakes the ground underneath, it clamors like a raging bull or an impetuous child, and then it falls silent again and what it leaves is a scarred but beautiful landscape that continues in the relentless march of life. We are changed but not vanquished, and awakening from the nightmare that is the past, we seem to see ourselves more properly. Sorry. Maybe I am trying too hard here. All I know is that after a few hours walking on what felt like the surface of a scorched moon, when we arrived back to the entrance to the park where we were and the enormous *araucarias* stood still in their enormity and magnificence, I felt such profound peace.

I have been holding *abuelo*'s hand a lot. He seems to like it, as do I. I am so happy to be able to love him, and I think he feels the same way. What a gift this life is, Mr. Harker. It is such a dark passage we must cross but there is so much to be grateful for, so much that is miraculous about our odd chance of being here, in these bodies, on this earth, now. And to have each other. Life must be treasured! And despite your misgivings, I must say that I cannot escape the conviction that we are bathed in God's love, all of us, utterly immersed. Fish discover water last, they say. Maybe we have to lose before we can even begin to contemplate what we have always had. Maybe that is our challenge now with the planet too. I hope it doesn't sound corny, but I am glad I have John and I have you!

Un abrazo fuerte, Alba

* * *

After all these years of living in silence (I am NOT blaming you, of course. Your silence is the order of things, but couldn't you whisper my name in the wind, couldn't you visit me in my dreams?), her sonorous letter broke through the silence with such music, such beauty. I have read it over and over again. I feel this overwhelming urge to nurture and protect her, exposed and vulnerable as she is, like my beloved flowers on the hillsides and stream banks with no gardener to till and take care of the place. Nature does its own caretaking, but we learned anciently the impulse to tend and to direct the course of things, to be gardeners of our own flowers, probably because we simply couldn't tolerate the violent unpredictability of things. Sure, this was first an impulse to feed ourselves, but even that impulse was about the children, about forestalling the threat of starvation for our little ones, about shoring up security against the weather. It was never possible to just live and let live. I can see that, but will I have the courage to learn again to tend, to nurture? Such risk there is in caring. I learned that once already and I long ago decided once was enough for me. I was reconciled to my childlessness and if an angel had declared to me that I would care again, I would have doubted and asked for a sign. And then this young woman came into my life. I can see that she has already suffered enough of the insults of a free and forbearing universe that does not seem to care one whit about whether or not she learns the truth of her father, whether she lives or dies. Human affection must announce itself. It must resist the inevitable flow of things into decay and transformation. It must plow the soil, plant the seeds. That's its bravado. And yet how easily these affections become denial and destruction in the face of the very laws of the universe that made our life possible in the first place. How to love and yet how to accept that the sun rises indifferently each day? Isn't it precisely nature's indifference that I so admire, that I hunt and hunger for every day? But isn't it precisely nature's indifference that steals those we love? I can't resist the opening to the canyon. Somehow you and your mother are nearer to me there, even though it is the beauty of the canyon that announces your absence. Alba insists that God's love is everywhere. I don't know how to understand this, but I don't have the will anymore to argue the point. She draws strength from such an idea. It is what makes her beautiful to me, so who am I to crush its fragile petals? Am I getting soft? Maybe. Maybe this is what you want. Without a word from you, I feel your pushback. Congratulations.

So I wrote her back, of course, after doing a little research about trees and flowers in Chile. I couldn't resist.

Zacharias Harker
Sent: January 15, 2002 9:33 pm
To: Alba Powell

Dear Alba,

I very much look forward to hearing more about your genealogical quest when you return. Your cryptic descriptions have certainly piqued my interest. I must say that I am indeed very jealous of such an experience in the forests there. One of my graduate professors had done a lot of work in Chile and he often described it to us as one of the more remarkable places he had ever seen. I still remember the slides he showed us. Time and circumstances have never allowed me a chance to get there, but I am gratified knowing that you are there and that this trip has been so fruitful.

About John. You will perhaps be surprised, but certainly not unhappy, to learn that we have actually spent some quality time together since you have been gone. It was at his instigation, I must confess. It is not my natural inclination to arrange such things, as I told you, but he called me some time back and requested that we talk. As is my wont, I dodged the invitation to go to lunch or to bring him to the house. Face-to-face conversations just don't work for me. But he was rather insistent, so I told him that I was going snowshoeing almost every day and that he could join me. He murmured something about having never snowshoed before, at which point I suggested that he should have his Utah birthright revoked. Imagine. A native son of Utah, and he has never experienced the mountains in the winter, except on top of some chairlift! I told him his parents had failed him. I meant it.

I am not going to pretend that the idea of spending time with him was easy for me. I prefer the silence and solitude of the mountains to myself. Theo comes with me, and we are society enough. So when he didn't show up at our appointed time, I had a mind to leave without him, but duty (duty? Duty to you, I guess) kept me waiting for fifteen minutes, at which point I prepared my things to go. He came pulling in the driveway just as we were pulling out. He was wearing blue jeans and an old pair of basketball shoes and a sweatshirt. Who raised this boy? You have a work in progress, you do. He at least did manage to rent some snowshoes but had no poles. If he didn't have you, I fear he would die of exposure to the elements, or starvation. I am amazed he managed two years as a missionary in Korea. There was nothing to do but to make the best of it, but I let him know in no uncertain terms that he was going to be cold and wet and that I wasn't going to turn back for his sake. He was unfazed, irritatingly so.

I took him up Tibble Fork trail. We hiked it in the fall, remember? It makes a fine loop in the winter. I think when we hiked it, we headed straight up to the ridge trail that divides American Fork Canyon from Provo Canyon, but the winter trail turns east before the ridge and drops back down Willow Hollow. It's a great walk among the spruce and bald aspens with several open areas and some very cold spots in the shady forest. The snow has been better since you left, much to the relief of those damn corporatists who are selling Utah for the Olympics, but also to the relief of those of us who care about the health of this place. Fortunately, up to this point my canyon has not garnered much interest from the developers and we remain relatively unaffected by the commotion up north. What will it take, I wonder, to keep it this way? The world has been arriving in Utah, as you might imagine, and we are days away now from the opening ceremony. But up in the canyon, one hardly notices that anyone has ever even settled the place. That's still the saving grace of the Wasatch Front, especially down here in the south away from all of those gentiles up in Salt Lake (that's a joke).

It was a good snow day, for sure, and this meant John was

going to get wet. Just below the ridge, we hit a broad opening in the forest with spectacular views of American Fork Twin Peaks to the north and the Pfeifferhorn to the northwest, completely blanketed in white. It was bitterly cold that day and had been for some time, so much so that the surface of the snow had formed into tiny ice crystals, like small shards of glass. No one had been up there after the recent storms, so the snow was plenty deep and powdery. The snowshoes blew the powder and the crystals underneath with each step, making a kind of tinkling sound as we went. Theo ran through the powder giddily, sometimes almost entirely buried by the snow, like a mole burrowing an underground tunnel. Sometimes I wish I could trade places with Theo, just to exist purely for a moment in his joy. I trail-blazed, of course, to spare the poor boy some of the discomfort of the deep powder that he could not protect his ankles from. We were working hard enough that he stayed warm, even though I could see the diminishing returns on our work pretty clearly: his snow-covered jeans were soaking wet before too long. Every time I turned around to look at him, he gave off steam from the perspiration. Boy needs to get out more. He offered his usual excuses about too many papers to write, not enough time. The bare branches of the aspens were covered with crystals, too, giving them a jagged appearance. The overall effect was magical. There must have been a fog at some point, something that caused all the condensation. You could look at entire groves of trees and see what looked like a glass grove everywhere. The sky was clear, the sun reflecting brightly against the surface of the snow. By the end, John was quite burned. I guess my skin is just used to it. And he was plenty wet and cold, but I think he had a good time.

I wasn't much in the mood for conversation, but he seemed rather concerned about you, so I did my level best to reassure him. I didn't mean to speak for you, and I assume you and he have talked at length in any case, but, you know, I told him that from my limited experience it was important to give a woman the space she needed for solitude, for her own journey in life, and that you, in particular, have an exceptional need for such space, given the burdens of your family story. It's a bit hypocritical of me, because I have often regretted that I lived with an excessive trust that people flourish better when they are not over-managed. Control isn't the answer, but neither is laissez-faire. Sort of the paradox of our relationship to this earth too, you know. He desperately wants what is best for you, but I guess he is just not sure what that is. That's not an easy thing. I too want to see you home, safe and sound. I even felt a little compassion for the guy. Especially knowing that he wasn't getting much help from his parents. He dodged some of my inquiries, maybe because he didn't want to give any fodder to my already curmudgeonly attitude about religion, but can I just ask, is it some kind of revelation to your in-laws that you have talent, that you might need to pursue it? And are they really that clueless about Chile's history to imagine that you are overreacting or idealizing who your father was? No doubt you will want to protect them from my judgment, but I find it absurd for them to assume that you should just feel nothing but gratitude for all that America has given you and all that they have offered you as a new member of their family, so much so that you should just turn your back on Chile and on your father's story and embrace a version of American history that ignores our own national sins. I understand that your father was a socialist and that this is worse than dirt to these people, but that's also because they can't even begin to imagine why socialism or any other kind of radical measures to solve endemic poverty and disparity of wealth might be needed. In their philosophy, they are doing right by the world simply by being the world's most wasteful consumers. You don't actually have to know a poor person, let alone feed them, or worse, change society to make poverty less likely. All you have to do is use your credit card more often. Hell, make it a family event and take the kids on a pleasure cruise, and somewhere downwind, downstream someone will be thanking you for the wealth that has magically trickled into their hands. This is charity without love. It doesn't even matter in such a philosophy if I consume with indifference or even with hatred in my heart for the poor. They will still get to count themselves fortunate for being recipients of a form of compassion that is as warm as a cold machine. I mean, I don't buy it, but even if you did, how could you accept such thinking as even remotely Christian? How Christians ever tolerated such crass materialism to marry itself to the teachings of the poor carpenter, I will never understand. The only opinion, as far as my scriptural memory serves, that Jesus ever proffered about what we now call capitalism was something against the idea of usury. And he certainly wasn't lenient with the wealthy. But here we hear all about the virtues of the market, the noble virtues of leaving it as "free" as possible, which generally means allowing the wealthy to spend and invest with the least restrictions possible, without any talk of how to ensure any comparable freedoms for the poor. I have nothing against freedom, but what about responsibility? How is poverty freeing? As far as I can tell, the prevailing philosophy around here is that as long as you are kind to your own kids and you comply with your church duties, the world will take care of itself. People, the earth, everything will benefit. I have to admit, that's an enviably comfortable world to live in. We don't have to see poverty nor can we imagine real injustice from our suburban paradise, even in our own country, let alone elsewhere.

I will say that it's clear that John is a good son and that he loves his folks, but I think most of all, he loves you. That, at least, was reassuring to me to see. And I think that it is good that he is wrestling with how to negotiate this. Offer no apology for wanting to be your own family. Don't be programmed! That's the best thing about you two. For a people who have limitless optimism about human potential, you Mormons sure seem suspicious of new and innovative or idiosyncratic ways of doing things. It's laudable that you want and work so hard for the traditional family life. Heaven knows no one else is doing it. But why does this have to come at the cost of such irascibility and discomfort when someone suddenly finds themselves outside of the pattern?

Sorry. I should know better. If anyone understands this, it's you. And no doubt you are more loving and forgiving of your in-laws than I feel right about now. Maybe I will learn something from you yet.

I did a little research on the Chilean forest, and you will likely have seen many trees that are older than the Conquest. *Araucarias* can live up to 1,000 years and can reach a height of well over 150 feet. So if you have seen some large ones, just imagine the history that they have witnessed! You have seen evidence that *araucarias* grow in ashy soils near volcanoes, so there is, indeed, a kind of co-dependency there between the volcanoes and the forest, even though they seem almost opposed to one another and can cause mutual harm. That contrast between death and life, gray and green, is in fact a co-dependency, even if it means irrevocable loss, because it also means inevitable growth and change. Those magnificent trees are endemic only to Chile and parts of Argentina. Did you know that? So they are, indeed, a rare treasure. And rarer all the time. That's because the Chilean hardwood forest is already 50 percent less than it was in pre-Columbian times. What you are looking at is an endangered ecosystem, but thank goodness that at least portions of it are protected as parks. Oh, and one more fascinating ecological fact. The forests of southern Chile are more biologically akin—that is, there is more genetic commonality among species there—than in the comparable temperate forests in the northwest here in the States. There are also more broad leaf trees and fewer conifers. These are rare forests, you know. Only in Chile, the northwest corridor up into Canada, in Tasmania, in New Zealand, and in parts of Europe. You may have noticed that red flowers and red fruits are predominant in the Chilean forests. I don't understand all of the reasons why, but it is explained in part by evolution, to attract birds and assist in the spreading of seeds.

If I had thought of it, I would have sent you with some containers to bring home some samples. Of course, that might be complicated with customs these days, especially since you aren't a formal researcher, but it would be lovely to study this more together. We will finish our book this summer and then, who knows, maybe we will venture a book on the flowers of that part of the world!

It will be good to see you again. Please, please travel safely.

Best,

Mr. Harker

* * *

Looking over these letters, I feel like I scarcely recognize myself. Such a cheerful chatterbox. I mean, hell, I talk to you 'til I am blue in the face, but that's not really talking, right? It was such a stupid idea when I first started writing you anyway. It happened by accident, literally. I was sitting on my porch one glorious summer afternoon. There was just enough of a breeze that I could sit and rock on my chair without sweating. It was that time of year, early summer, when the dandelions are sprouting all over the lawn. You know me. No pesticides for this place. Give me weeds, give me wild. I don't care. No one ever saw a lawn so beautiful as one carpeted in bright yellow. So anyway, there I was. I was tired after a long hike in the canyon and I had grabbed a few apples and a slab of cheese from the fridge and was cutting them with my pocketknife. I think it had honestly been some time since I had felt that strangling sorrow that had lain heavily on my chest every night since I lost you. You know, time does funny things to you, and I guess it had finally put me into a state of temporary oblivion. I wasn't even thinking of you and your mother at all. I was just, you know, being, just being myself, just existing. I could hear my mouth chewing the apples, I could hear the sounds of flies and bees around me, and the soft murmur of the breeze through the leaves. And I felt such a moment of stillness, it was like I had fallen asleep with my eyes open and all of life was, well, fine. Not ecstasy, not resolution, just existence as a good thing. After a few moments of almost unconscious stillness, I heard tires screech right above the house on Route 92 and then the crunch of metal. And by God, I jumped up and screamed. I mean I lost it. I screamed to bloody hell, "Don't you take them away, don't you take them away, you son of a bitch!!!" I said it over and over at the top of my lungs. I went screaming up the hill in a sprint, right through the scrub oak and brush, bypassing my long driveway. I was damn near pawing my way to the top on all fours, slipping and falling several times, still screaming until I got to the top. I must have looked like quite a sight, crazed eyes, ripped clothes, and dirty hands and knees. When I got there, two cars were in the middle of an intersection, some broken lights and a dented fender, and both drivers talking calmly to one another. There were people getting out of their cars too. They had heard me screaming, so they all looked at me in astonishment, waiting for me to explain myself. Someone asked if I was okay.

"Am I okay? Am I okay? I am not the one who has had an accident!"

"Sure as heck looks like you are," someone said. I looked at everyone, trying to see a face of a friend or neighbor perhaps but I didn't recognize any one of them. What was I looking for, anyway? Well, you and your mother, of course. I suppose it was the first time I had heard the sound of crunching metal, the violence of speed with which we live in modern life, since I lost you. And maybe I had just been imagining in my mind the sound of the crash, the terror of the moment for far too long, but it was as if I had been there, been a witness. I can't tell you how many times I have dreamt I was in the car with you, anticipating what was going to happen, trying over and over again to assimilate it, to get you and your mother to anticipate it, or to find some way to get your mother to take a different turn, to slow down, to speed up, anything to change the trajectory of destiny that would take you from me, leaving me desolate, childless, widower.

I don't remember if I said anything else. I walked back off the side of the road and down into the gully. I was out of my mind, in a state of retroactive shock. I cried for a while, just lying on the slope in the middle of the brush. I think it was the realization that you were stolen from me again, right then, and I would always be losing you forever, never gaining you back. Time heals, they say, but that is just because we are forgetful. All I had done was forget you, briefly, and that provided my respite, but there I was as broken as I had ever been.

I remember my mother telling me a story about my great-grandfather who was a bit of a visionary man, at least as his descendants remembered him, you know, one of those old-time Mormon settlers, someone who had been brought into the church by a dream and stayed because of a lifetime of visions. Uprooted himself from England, he did, despised by his family when he joined. I guess in a way God stole him from his family too. In retrospect, I wonder if he wasn't a bit of a quack, but he gathered his family together at the end of his life down in Spanish Fork amid his peach orchards and announced that his mother had come to him in a vision to tell him she had died long ago, that she was sorry for having kicked him out of the home for being queer (I remember that's how my mother put it), and that she waited for him with loving arms. He commanded his family to commence the temple work for her immediately. And my mother volunteered to do the baptism. She would have been just barely twelve years old. Even though her own life was a bit of a wreck, my mother held on to that memory tight, like it was the only thing left that was real. So you know, I had secretly hoped that maybe if I could just see you both, just passing wordlessly through the trees, just once, even if you didn't look at me, I would be content and I could go on. I closed my eyes tight on that hill and wished and prayed for it, just something to let me know that you were not really dead, that this life is not really all there is. Because that's the thing about death. You can't be theoretical anymore about belief. And sitting there alone that afternoon, I realized my faith was in shatters, that I had no more idea about God than I did about life on other planets, that all I thought I knew was gone and all that was left was what I could see, touch, taste, smell, and hear. I told God that I knew this was not right, that I needed more faith, but if he could just give me that one little boost of a momentary vision, something to kindle again the fires of belief, I would devote myself to him for the rest of my life, that I could be content waiting to be with you again. But the old buzzard, well he just didn't answer and nothing came.

That was when I started to write you. I thought, well hell, if he won't let me see you and if he won't even hear me, then I should at least speak up. No one can stop me from talking if I don't want to, right? And damned if I was going to let myself heal just by forgetting. I would remember everything. I would just never shut the hell up. It was a nutty idea, but as I sat there, I started to talk out loud to you. I don't know why but I guess it was my lingering guilt that made it more comfortable to talk to you than to your mother, and besides, I know your mother agrees with me on this one, we would both gladly trade places to let you have the full life you deserved. I mean, losing your mom, I can't put it into words, but if I know her, she would agree that losing you, well, that's just more than anyone should have to bear. So I talked to you for a good hour there on the hill, telling you all kinds of things about what had happened in the months since I lost you, about the change of the seasons. Hell, I was a sight to see, no doubt, sitting in the brambles talking like a madman, but it felt good, it even got me off of my feet and walking back to the house. You and I talked a lot in those first few days if you remember, but then I thought I was repeating myself and that maybe I should take a little time every so often when the inspiration came and write you a letter, you know, just something for conversation. It was a nice rhythm I fell into, something that grounded me, and helped me to cope. It gave me something to look forward to, even though all of our chats were about the past. As you might remember much of those early letters were attempts to help you to remember some of your favorite experiences and places and people, but eventually I knew I had to come around to telling you the things about my life that would have come out eventually but would have been too much for your nine-year-old heart to absorb.

*　*　*

I ended up ABD. I mean, how was I going to go back to school under those circumstances? I had no desire. Sorenson was none too pleased, mind you. He tried visiting a few times and often called. He was compassionate at first, but then he got pretty exasperated with me and snapped at me on the phone, told me that I was throwing my life and talent away in self-pity. Don't judge him harshly for saying so. He was right, but I didn't care. I had gone back to the campus a few times to make an attempt to start over, but I couldn't bear the sanctimony of the place. I was going to hit the next guy who was going to tell me something they knew but which God had apparently not bothered to tell me about where my wife and daughter were and what you were doing. I was ornery, to be honest. People were good to me, I have to say now in retrospect, but I was in no position to see it. I just wanted everything and everyone to shut up, to go away. I wanted to start all over. So when I saw a posting for job as a researcher for the state forest, I jumped ship and was gone. Old Martin understood that I had to support myself and that it would give me some stability for a while, but he kept hoping I might come back at some point. We stayed in touch for a while but I made it clear I wanted him to stop calling so he did eventually. This life hasn't been half bad in the end. I have managed to keep some pretty flexible hours and nowadays I can do ad hoc work as needed and get by. Keeps me in solitude most of the year, which works well for me. I used to spend weeks, even months at a time in the mountains, and no one would ever notice or care that I was gone. I loved that feeling. I have always loved the solitude. There is nothing quite like it. But it has been nice to have the companionship of words to read and words to write. For a man who didn't use to say much, I have a veritable case of verbal diarrhea. And I can spend all day on the couch with my books. It is amazing what worlds have opened to me and what companionship I feel. Theo helps too.

Chapter 11

It wasn't a theoretical question anymore. As she sat on the plane, she knew that a child was waiting. Not yet waiting to be born but waiting to be conceived, even as she conceived him in her mind. And it would be a son, she was certain. And she knew there were others too, one girl, maybe more, but this first one, it was almost as if she could see him. She already knew his name. She had crossed the Americas for Chile, haunted by the unremembered face of her father and now crossing back, she yearned for the unseen face of a son. The landscapes she had seen were still fresh in the memory of her senses. She couldn't shake the site of the black ash volcanoes, the bright green moss on the trunks of the staggering *araucarias*, the clear flow of the rivers, and the sea salt smell of the coastal wind. The memories hung like dreams before her eyes, threatening to dissipate with the dawning of the day. Her hands held tight to the papers she had in her lap that her grandfather had given her. He had made careful copies of letters he wrote to the government on behalf of his sons and kept correspondences with lawyers, his daughters-in-law, and friends. There were photos of ancestors and extended family with names and faces she studied with a zeal, photos of Puerto Saavedra after the *maremoto* and its reconstruction. The brutality of the world was more clear to her than ever before, the brutality against children, cutting them off from their stories, their ancestry, their chance to understand their belonging in the world. Sometimes it happened in a swift and crashing blow by human hands, sometimes with the sudden strike of nature or simply the steady erosion of time. It took so much work just to transmit a fragment of what was known and experienced from just one generation to the next, no wonder most preferred to just give in to obliviousness. Ancestral stories must be taught and cultivated and written down and passed on again and again, reworded, reimagined and retold. And all because of the violence—the violence of politics, the violence of arrogance and power—decisions made by only a few men at such a remove from the living world of children and mothers and fathers and cousins and uncles and aunts, the wide spread of genealogical seeds that are planted in landscapes of hope that would stretch forth in unbroken lines across the globe if not for the fact that land and people are things to be bought up and exploited and cast about before their lives can take root.

So what then? What is to be done? What kind of work and living is possible in light of this brutality? Alba thought about the thousands of people who had worked for decades to protect and recover lost memories of children and parents and brothers and sisters, those who had honored the dead and made of themselves a broader family bond, a communion that would not be broken by temporary displays of power. Rather than cower in the face of evil and violence, her answer would be creation—naming, knowing, and nurturing human lives and giving them a chance for real happiness. Homemaking, in the most profound sense, she thought, was the sacred work of building and protecting an environment where all life might flourish. This would be work at home, in the world, and with the earth itself, work and worry on behalf of the children of the desolate and its recompense of affiliation and affection, of fellowship, of perennial brotherhood and sisterhood. It was this passion that mattered, the fire she needed to keep burning. She felt a hunger for John that she had never quite experienced before, a hunger that was as intensely about having him as it was about having a human family to love. She would give him no more reasons to worry.

She could see the white-capped mountains below the window and the frigid winter, and she felt like weeping at the sight of it. She would never look on the Wasatch Mountains without seeing in her mind's eye the mountains surrounding Santiago. She would always see in stereo a world forked apart by continental drift, by history, by language, and by politics, but those external and formal markers of difference could only temporarily disguise the profound underground currents of kinship that knitted the hemisphere into a whole. Surely there was something in her that could contain and circumscribe the continents, that could make a home out of her perpetual homelessness. Something that could express what it felt to be straddled between this America and the other, between this world and the next. So many gaps and gulfs in the world and so much traversing to be done to make it whole again.

Alba was disappointed that John wasn't at the gate as she had hoped. She had forgotten the new system of security at the airport meant no more immediate gratification upon deplaning. She had seen two missionaries onboard in the back and noticed that as they departed the plane, they also seemed disappointed to have to wait to get to the baggage area before the big greeting. When they had left just two years earlier, she thought, it had been a different world no doubt, one in which family and friends and physical contact were there until the last possible moment of departure, one in which the body was no longer a source of suspicion, no longer separated, one by one, and scanned. No one could have imagined that common objects could become weapons of destruction, that the world could suddenly turn strange and threatening, that the face of a foreigner would be treated with suspicion or hostility. She knew this had long been the reality of places such as Chile where even kitchen utensils could be transformed into weapons of torture, methods for undoing the individual capacity for speech and for long-suffering and for counter-memory. This was the brutality: how the familiar, the commonly known and trusted, could be converted into the enemy, even brothers and sisters and fathers and mothers weaponized to betray and destroy their own blood. She touched one of the missionaries on the sleeve as they walked down the corridor and said, "Welcome home, Elder."

"Thanks." He blushed awkwardly.

"Where are you coming from?" she asked.

"Spain."

"*Pues, bienvenido.*"

He smiled nervously. "*Gracias.*" She heard his acquired Spanish accent.

"Life is good, Elder. Both the life you just left and the one to come. Don't let them be separate things." He nodded. She remembered that day like it was yesterday as she walked toward the gate, waiting to see the familiar faces of her mother and friends around the corner. She remembered the feeling that she was being born again, starting life over, and it seemed it was happening again to her now.

The airport was more crowded than she ever remembered. And it was more diverse than ever before. She could see people of all nationalities and hear various languages as she walked out of the terminal and down the stairs to the baggage claim. At the bottom were two large groups with banners welcoming home their missionaries and crowds of milling people looking lost in a new city. She scanned the faces for John but couldn't find him anywhere. And then she felt his arms around her waist from behind. She dropped her bags and turned around and kissed him until he backed away and laughed, complaining that she had hurt his lip.

"Hey beautiful," he said. "Go easy on me! I'm fragile."

"I could eat you alive," she said and kissed him again. "Can we go home?"

"Actually I have a big surprise," he said. And he pulled out two tickets.

"Guess what tonight is?"

"Our night?"

"Well, yes, there is that. But it's the opening ceremonies. Dad got us the tickets. This is going to be incredible."

Alba was a little disappointed, only because she just wanted to be with John and she was so absorbed in her family story that the idea of spending her evening with 60,000 people wasn't exactly a draw. But the gift was generous.

"I *am* pretty tired, you know. But I will make a go of it." She smiled reassuringly.

There were a few hours yet before the ceremony began, and she was hungry, so they stopped at a taquería on the outskirts of the city to sit and talk. She hadn't yet said anything about her father, and he was almost afraid to ask. The last she had communicated was what she learned from her grandfather: that he might still be alive, but she had not had the chance to email him again before the flight home. They got their food and found a seat in a corner away from anyone else.

"I'm still trying to assimilate what happened," Alba said without any prompt from John. "No doubt you want to know how things ended."

"I'm all ears," he said. Alba untied her ponytail and ran her hand through her hair and looped the band around it again. She looked out the window at the wintry scene. The twilight caused the distant Wasatch to glow in orange light.

"Not sure how to express it," she finally said. She looked at John directly. "When I got back to Santiago, Marycruz took me in again. She was thrilled with my story about what had happened, about Gardenio. It really was incredible, you know. You would love Gardenio. Such a man. And he's my grandfather!" She teared up.

"He sounded amazing. I wish I could have met him. Maybe someday."

"Yes, I would like that. *He* would like that! So together Marycruz and I looked through the papers he gave me. It's all so fascinating. It's my genealogy, but it still feels like I am adopted, you know, because they aren't part of my memories, at least not yet, but I want them. I want them all. Anyway, we called Tito to see if he could help us. You see, we had been looking for his name among the missing all that time and here before us was the simple possibility that he might be in the phone book, just sitting there, waiting for a phone call. Of course, we looked right away in Marycruz's apartment, in her phone book, you know, but that would have been too easy. He wasn't there. I honestly was prepared to stay as long as it took to locate him, but I felt such urgency, you know, just my usual impatience. To be that close! We called Tito to get his help and he had some ideas. I think once he heard the whole story, it changed what he looked for, who he talked to, that kind of thing, because, well the truth is, we no longer assumed he was on the side, you know, of the Revolution. Gardenio is certain he was working for Pinochet all that time. We had covered so many theories. Was he a louse who screwed up? Was he screwing up because he was running from his own guilt? Was he collaborating, working for the military? All I can tell you, John, is that the whole thing is crazy. People did the strangest things, directed enemies to their friends and neighbors, turned over their own blood—torturers and the tortured might even fall in love with each other. People acted with double faces, living double lives, sliding back and forth in between in the shadows. So we were confused, to say the least. All bets were off. And I was tired, tired, I mean, tired of the mystery, tired of the burden of his lies, tired of chasing his ghost and resentful like I had never been before of what a mess he had left behind."

"Yeah, I get that. I have felt it myself. Did for much of the time you were gone."

She touched his hand. "Well, so Tito calls us back a few hours later with an address in El Quisco, by the coast. It's a few hours away and without a moment of hesitation Marycruz is driving me like a bat out of hell out of the city and toward the coast. She was cursing at the traffic, honking like a mad woman. It was pretty funny, actually, but I was a bundle of nerves of course, barely able to speak. We got there in the late afternoon, which was ideal in any case since it meant he might likely be home from work.

We found ourselves in a neighborhood of cinderblock homes, a newer development, the kind of which I hadn't seen in the city nor in the south. This is where people were moving, I guess, as the economy grew. So we drove around until we drove right past the house, a small place, with a faint eggshell color and a red door. Marycruz parks across the street, you know, and I am sitting there, hardly able to move. I sat for a long while, I mean for like an hour. We just watched. No one came in or out, and I just couldn't move. She was patient with me. She insisted it was my decision, but we tried to cover the pros and cons. You know, I mean, what was it all about anyway? What did I want from the encounter? I wasn't sure, really, but just some recognition maybe, just the basic acknowledgment that he fathered me. I thought maybe that that would be enough. He wouldn't owe me anything. I didn't need him any longer. That much had been made clear to me in the preceding days. I mean, I had what I needed in my grandfather. And I have all I need right here, John. You must believe me on this. I am sorry if you ever doubted me." She reached across and touched his hand again and held it tightly.

"I know. I know." John said. Alba reached across to wipe a tear from his face. "Sorry," he said. "It's just that . . . man. Sorry. I can't tell you." He cried a little harder while Alba held his hand. After a moment of silence, he said, "Go on. I am all ears."

"Well, there was still the question, then, of what to do, you know? It was starting to feel like maybe I should just turn around and go back, but finally, a man steps out of the house and I didn't wait even two seconds. I mean, I jumped out of the car. I still hadn't decided what I was going to say. It was all on instinct. He was walking out to his car in the driveway and I approached and said, 'Are you Luís?'

He looked at me. His hair was graying and balding, just a little, you know, at his forehead. He was thin, like his father. But there was his face, finally, right there in front of me and after all my efforts to imagine it, I couldn't make heads or tails out of it, like it was some kind of puzzle with missing pieces or a broken mirror. I couldn't recognize anything at all in the shape and coloring of his face. I tried. I am not sure I could draw it now. I looked at his brown eyes and it was like they looked right through me with a hundred mile stare. Well, what did I expect? That he would recognize me? I don't know. I guess I had that hope. But his glance was, I don't know, empty, lifeless, cold. I know he only thought I was a stranger but still, you know how sometimes you can see life in a stranger's eyes, love, light, friendliness? Well, there was none of that, I tell you. None. It was lights out.

'Who wants to know?' He says. He was calm, you know, unflustered.

'I do,' I said. 'I want to know if you are Luís Alberto Sepulveda Torreon, son of Gardenio Sepulveda Pérez and Graciela Torreon Díaz, born in 1952 in Temuco. Do you recognize this as your name? Do you recognize Gardenio as your father, Graciela as your mother?'

'Who are you?' I could tell he was trying to play it cool, you know, but I sensed him flinch slightly, a sudden tension in his face. I don't know. I mean, those names alone must have said enough, right?

Well, just then, a young boy comes out of the front door, about, I don't know, twelve or so. And he says, 'Papi.' I am just stunned at this, you know, flat out shocked. I hadn't even thought about that, hadn't even imagined it. I mean, there is my half-brother. Here he has been living and starting over, I guess, making a new family and a new identity. I almost lost my nerve entirely. I thought, what am I doing here? What is he to me or me to him? All the logic of forgetting, of just letting things go swept over me for a second. It reminded me of that first time I did street contacting as a missionary in Ohio. I was yellow with fear, you know, because suddenly I was putting myself on the line, making my private convictions public, and there was this dread that it was all a waste of time, that it might have even been a kind of arrogance, and I wanted to hide, go home, shut the door and shut my mouth. So he turns and looks at his son and gestures for him to go back inside. The son looks confused but starts to obey. And suddenly I hear myself yelling out to the boy, 'Hey, *muchacho*, tell me, your father Luís Alberto, can you tell me where he is?' He turns and looks at me confused and points awkwardly at his father and then he goes back into the house.

At this he says to me, 'Look, I don't know who you are or what you want, but I don't know what you are talking about. I don't know those people. You have me confused with someone else.'

'I think you are the one who is confused,' I said. 'I know you are the son of Gardenio and Graciela, two parents who never stopped forgiving you for denying them, for denying your brothers, Roberto and Manuel, and who knows who else. Parents anyone would consider it an honor to have. A mother who died without a word from you and a father who continues to honor the memory of the two sons he lost and who has never forgotten the son who lost himself.'

He turns his back on me to leave to go back into the house.

'Wait a minute. I am not finished,' I said. I felt desperate, urgent. I followed him and spoke deliberately. 'My name is Alba, Alba Hidalgo Powell, daughter of Isabel Hidalgo Carrasco and Luís Alberto Sepulveda Torreon, your own flesh and blood. That's my brother who just went inside your house. I came all the way from the United States to Chile to find your grave, but here you are.'

He turns to me before opening the door and says, 'I told you I don't know what you are talking about.' At that he closed the door. Just like that. So I raised my voice, not so much out of anger, but you know, so he could still hear me. I said in a loud voice, 'I know you buried your grandparents in 1960. I know about the *maremoto*.'

I waited a moment and nothing. I turn to leave, but the door opens again and he sticks his head out and speaks with a kind of venomous hatred, real slow, the likes of which I have never heard before. '*Quítate . . . de mi . . . pórtico.*' Get off my porch. That's what he said. Like he wanted to kill me. Scared me to death. And then he closed the door again."

Alba stopped talking and things were silent for a moment.

John looked at her as her head bowed toward the table.

"Wow. I don't know what to say," said John finally. "I mean, what does that all mean? What kind of man do you think he is, or was?"

Alba lifted her head and continued.

"Hard to say. I have thought over all the possible scenarios. But darkness like that, denial that hard, well it has to be hiding a lot, you know? I don't really care to know at this point. Serially dishonest with women, dishonest about his own convictions, no remorse for betraying his own. Deception that deep and consistent, well, I don't know what hope there is. But clearly he has at least tried to start over. I wish him well. I do. But I haven't an ounce of respect."

"So that's it, I guess?"

"That's it. That's all I got."

"I am so sorry, Alba. So sorry." He looked carefully at her to see if he could get an idea of how she was holding up. "Do you feel, I don't know, worse off? Do you regret going?"

"No. No. But you know, that took something out of me. I don't know what it was, but for a minute there I felt completely composed, but when I got in the car with Marycruz, I started to cry and I cried so hard that I vomited. No kidding. I vomited right there in the gutter. So yeah, it was the scariest, craziest experience of my life, but when it was over and we were back at the apartment, going through the papers grandpa had given me and I started to pack for my return, well, I felt a kind of inexplicable joy. I felt it all the way home. Makes no sense, I guess, but I think I finally understand that my home will be what I make with you, here. It was all I could do to wait to get to you to make a home and to make, you know, a life. I have what I needed all along. It's a funny thing. Blood doesn't mean much, really, only what you decide you want it to mean, I guess. Without faithfulness, care, sacrifice, all the things that make a family—blood is nothing. Isn't that the funniest thing? And finally, finally, you know, I feel nothing for him, no longing, no nostalgia, and not even any ill will. I mean I guess I feel pity for him. I love Chile and I will always honor my past, but my father, no, I feel nothing at all. You and I, we are going to make a home, make a family. We are going to do it right. I am all in, John, I am all in."

* * *

They spent some time wandering around the streets of downtown. John had brought her coat and hat to keep her warm, but the biting wind was hard to take after the Chilean summer. The streets were lit in bright colors, stores and restaurants were open, and hundreds of people filled the streets almost shoulder to shoulder: couples holding hands, friends arm in arm, people shouting and laughing and greeting each other with bright eyes full of good intentions. They heard many languages, most of which they didn't know, but she recognized the accent of Spain and at one point, she heard an unmistakable Chilean accent as she passed a group of people dressed in the red, white, and blue of the flag. She stopped John in an attempt to go back and greet them, but by the time they turned and looked behind, the sea of pedestrians had swallowed them. This was a Utah and a Salt Lake she didn't recognize but that she liked immensely. For once, she didn't feel like the standout in the crowd with her black hair and brown eyes and olive skin. Here in the very streets founded by Mormon settlers walked the peoples of the earth. She could see the lights of the temple as she passed just south of Temple Square. After much struggle and controversy, the state was playing host to the whole world and all differences and tensions had seemingly disappeared. In the performance of playing hosts, the community had come alive, found and embraced itself, and stood proud and unified for one glorious moment.

There had been considerable anxiety leading up to the event about security and the possibility of a terrorist attack, and the memory of this anxiety caused a brief flash of panic in Alba. After listening to so many testimonials about such violence in Chile and after realizing that even the small clan of Mormons in Chile had gotten caught up in the crossfire, resulting in the bombing of a few Mormon chapels, the freshness of her memories caused the fear of violence to surge quickly through her veins. Utahans had wondered out loud if the world's hatred for America might see Salt Lake City as an especially apt target, a city known for its American-grown version of Christianity sending out missionaries across the world in their white shirts and ties. She felt her heart rate quicken. She scanned the faces of strangers frantically looking for enough familiarity to calm her nerves, but the closer she looked, the more threatening this strange world of so many strangers started to become.

The whole country was anxious since September 11. Chile had taught her how easily fear could cause a nation to revert to its worst tendencies rather than its obligation to allow all within its borders to flourish. She repeated her grandfather's words in her mind: never become the children of fate. Resist passivity, resist fear, resist abusive power with dignity and a clear voice. *No basta con ceder a las cosas. Hay que crearlas*, he had said. The threat of violence, of course, had always been there. Even the bombing in Oklahoma had startled the nation into this awareness, however briefly, but this was different. September 11 certainly was a more spectacular ruin of a symbol of American pride, the death of hundreds more, but it had also been perpetrated by foreigners, strangers, faces who were seen like the alien Canaanites in the midst of Israel. The nation was moving increasingly toward a posture of purging itself from within, cleaning house, making itself "right" again. Mosques, previously ignored within the nation's borders, were suddenly identified and feared. And meanwhile, because of the Olympics the Mormons were in the spotlight too, as if for the first time, under the scrutiny of the nation that had once expelled them. Mormons had been suspect, they had been the Canaanites deemed a national threat on the heels of Joseph Smith's martyrdom, and maybe still were. That was the question. Who were they? They provided an exotic people and history for the nation and the world to gawk at. Were they Christian fundamentalists? Worse? Were they a cult who held crazy beliefs in prophets and revelation? The world had been expending more energy in recent months to get to know this culture and it seemed journalists rarely got it right. She could feel that stigma of being perpetually mistaken. It was so strange to her that her love of country and of her religion left her feeling increasingly at odds with the growing effort to protect the "true" America. As a Mormon and as an immigrant, she felt for those she had read about who after spending their entire lives devoted to this nation had learned that their Arab names and Muslim practices were now seen with suspicion. And she felt for those seeking refuge here. She was likely to be taken for a Muslim, and she decided that in solidarity with them she would gladly confuse others.

Her own fear was irrational, she knew this, but the instinct to protect one's children, one's future was nothing to ignore. As she walked close to John, she disliked how this fear felt. It was uncomfortable to imagine so many enemies, to distrust the appearances of communion, to feel obligated to withdraw from this carnival of connection. Perfect love, she told herself, as she had so many times in recent months, casts out all fear. Perfect love. What nation knew of such a thing? A nation of nations. Is this what it would feel like?

They could hear live music coming from around the corner and as they neared, the music drowned out all the sounds of the crowd. All she could see was the chaotic rhythm of the people, some moving to the beat of the music, and others leaning over to speak in someone's ear, leaving or arriving, or greeting someone they knew. She could hear the crowd singing the chorus in unison:

I'm leaving Las Vegas
leaving for good, for good
I'm leaving for good
I'm leaving for good

As she looked around at the crowd, the children on their father's necks, the women pushing strollers, the grandparents, the happy lovers kissing and holding each other, she could feel the fear dissipate. As with so many impressions, it felt like a choice, as if the world was too malleable, too complex, or too undecided to predict its own meaning, as if you lived by the lights you gave yourself, by the faith you chose, and once chosen, things would order themselves to confirm to how you set out to see the world.

She could feel the jetlag coming on and she leaned into John for respite. He put his arms around her and pulled her close and kissed the top of her head. Alba raised her head to look up at John and they kissed slowly. The smell of his breath and the taste of his lips sent a shiver of desire through her body. She stopped kissing and squeezed her arm around his waist.

"We can start heading for the stadium," John said. "We'll find a place for you to sit down."

*   *   *

Alba awoke from John's lap to a thunderous cheer from the crowd. The lights had dimmed and the ceremonies had begun.

She felt warm with her head in his lap and could easily have willed it all away for another time, for a replay on the television on the comfort of her couch, but the excitement woke her. The air was cold. She could see the steam of John's breath and the breath of everyone nearby as they cheered in the dark while the stage below on the field lit up and fireworks exploded from one end of the stadium. A pageant of vibrant colors streamed across the deep blue of what was an ice rink, the bright whites of figures with upraised arms and angelic wings twirling around in circles around a small boy in red holding a light as he wove in and out of danger. An announcer spoke of the storms of life, the struggle to light an inner fire to overcome obstacles. At different points, the audience was asked to hold up lights that were under the seats of each audience member making the entire stadium a parade of light. The thousands of performers on the stage were impressive enough but when the tens of thousands of observers joined in, it was as if no room was left for distant observation. This was Ritual, Pageant, Festival on a massive scale.

Then began the story of this corner of the world, celebrating the Native populations of Utah with vibrant drumming and traditional clothing, marking the trek of the Mormon pioneers across the plains and into the valley, and connecting again the railroad that had made the nation into a geographical unity. It was the visual dramatization that most impressed her, the vibrating, pulsating, and fluid movement of color and form. The union was enacted by two large caravans of train cars coming down the stairs onto the field below. Dancers filled the stage while Copland's "Hoedown" filled the air. On such a scale, it was hard to feel the particulars of each story but it was a gesture and conveyed a sense of history as made up of strands of human stories, each possessed of unique struggles but each related to and helping to constitute the whole.

The lights dimmed again and a singer with a guitar and a cellist played with the immense and angelic choir singing behind them and the words drifted into the air while soft white skaters floated across the blue ice holding and gently bending kite bird wings in the air above them:

If blood will flow when flesh and steel are one
Drying in the color of the evening sun
Tomorrow's rain will wash the stains away
But something in our minds will always stay
Perhaps this final act was meant
To clinch a lifetime's argument
That nothing comes from violence and nothing ever could
For all those born beneath an angry star
Lest we forget how fragile we are

Alba's eyes filled with tears. The weight of her own story felt absorbed into the collective burden of the events of September, which hung heavily in the air. She could feel collective compassion, however momentary, that went beyond national boundaries, shared across all the human differences that declare themselves in all of their beauty and variety but which were never intended to separate the human family. An announcer introduced the torn flag that once flew at the World Trade Center as it was brought out by police officers under a spotlight. The stadium was absolutely silent. The question was if sorrow would lead to a sustained compassion or to a lashing out, a fear stoked anew.

The aura and magic of illusion hung in the air as the parade of nations began. She didn't have to wait long for Chile's small contingent to come out. John put both of his arms around her and let out a roar of approval. When the final crowd of American athletes made their way to their seats, the Olympic chairman spoke to the crowd, the Mormon man who had rescued the Salt Lake Olympics from scandal. He spoke briefly but powerfully. His words stuck in Alba's mind:

"After September, more than ever before, our generation longs for a world where the dreams of all the children may come true."

John looked at her. "He seems downright presidential, doesn't he?"

She laughed. "You know, right, that Mormons and Muslims were recently identified as the two most distrusted religions in America?"

* * *

When they finally returned home, they fell asleep in each other's arms, too tired for what they both so badly wanted, but when the morning broke, Alba wasted no time waking John and John wasted no time in turn.

He eventually got out of bed and made her breakfast, her favorite cinnamon French toast and bacon, set the table for her and sat himself down. She emerged from the bedroom with disheveled hair in her baggy pajamas and her slippers. She ran her fingers through his hair and kissed the top of his head and sat down to eat. She was starving but quickly filled up, unable to finish.

"I want to be pregnant," she announced.

John looked at her in stunned silence. He wasn't one for lots of words, but she knew his heart well enough to understand what the silence meant and what he meant to say when he put his shaking hand on hers.

"I know I hadn't seemed so sure about things over the last couple of months and I know that my trip scared you, but I want you to know that I am not going anywhere. I am all yours, John, and now there will be three of us. At least." She smiled.

"You are always full of surprises, Alba. All of them good ones." He began to cry. She swung her chair around to his side of the table and cradled him in her arms. When he could manage a few more words, he said, "Sorry. I don't know where all this is coming from. I missed you so much. I wish I were as strong as you, Alba, but without you, I find myself lying around like someone shot a cannonball through my chest." He cried some more, gently quaking as he leaned his head against her shoulder. "I so desperately want you and I so desperately want this child."

"John, I have so much to tell you. I don't even know where to begin. So much to show you." She stroked his back.

"We have lots of time, you know," he said, raising his head and wiping his eyes. "They gave us the entire two weeks off from school. We can talk all day. We can watch the Olympics. We can go play in the snow. Whatever you want. I just don't want to be alone. That sounds stupid, I know, but just be with me, will you?"

"Not stupid. Sounds beautiful to me."

She spent the morning revisiting all the details of her search, about her aunt, her grandfather, the hikes, the sadness, about her new ideas about her final project. They looked over the papers her grandfather had given her. She talked and talked. John asked questions and was more engaged in listening than she ever remembered.

After watching some Olympics for a few hours, she grew tired, stood, and told John she needed a nap.

"Sure, babe. Get your rest." He rose to hug her. "Maybe after the nap, we can talk about some things that have happened to me over the past few weeks."

Alba blushed.

"I haven't even asked you about things, have I?"

"No, you haven't."

"I am really sorry. I just, I don't know."

"It's really okay. I understand. You have a lot going on and I have loved hearing about it all. Get your rest and we can talk."

"No, let's talk now."

"No, no. You take your rest."

"I am fine, John. Let's talk. What's on your mind? What has been going on?" She sat back down on the couch and pulled him down next to her. "What is it?"

"My father. My father is not very happy these days."

"Happy with what?"

"Happy with me. With us."

"With us? What do you mean?"

John adjusted himself on the couch.

"Listen. You have to understand that my father . . . well, you know he doesn't see things like you do. He's a pretty traditional guy. Pretty rational, you know. He doesn't understand emotion, and, look, I get it. I am the first person to admit that I know what that is like. I know I am my father's son, but the difference, I guess, is that I fell in love with you."

"John, what are you saying?"

"Well, you know, he just doesn't understand you and he didn't like the idea of this trip."

"I know that, John. He wasn't exactly trying to disguise his disapproval. I'm okay with that. I don't like it but I can live with his questions. I do love him, you know."

"Well, maybe you are better than I am."

"Did something happen between you two?"

"Yeah, you could say that. Something happened. I kind of snapped." John sat forward with his elbows on his knees and rubbed his face. Alba waited.

"He was really upset with me for letting you go."

"*Letting* me go? You mean he thinks you get to make all my decisions?"

"Something like that. Look, you know how he is. He is a strong-willed man. It's hard to talk back or to push back. I mean, he's loving and all that, but then he just has this way of digging and controlling. He took me out to dinner and it started out real well, like he was all proud of me and, you know, that I was a great son. So he butters me up and feeds me this stupid steak, and then he starts telling me how I need to rein you in, that you are going to leave me if I am not more careful, that your free spirit and your art are a danger to our future children. He said he wants me to close your 'Chile chapter,' that's what he called it. And he wants to know why you have been hesitant to start our family, that my education, not yours, should be our top priority." John looked at Alba and smiled ironically. "I guess he will at least be relieved once we get pregnant."

Alba sat quietly, trying to remain calm. "Rein me in? He really said that? Does he, does he even . . . man!" She tossed her hands up in desperation.

"Look, I know, it was awful. I was mad as a hornet. I mean, he meant well, I think, but I just couldn't take his orders anymore. So I snapped. I said some pretty awful things myself. So no matter how bad he sounds to your ear, just imagine it was twice as bad when I opened my fat mouth. I am the one you should be ashamed of."

"I doubt that. But now I really have to know what you said."

"You need to know something, Alba. You need to know that I had some of those same feelings before you left. I admit it. I think you know that. But I don't know if you realize how much I resented the freedom you had to just up and go, to explore yourself, and how much I have envied your freedom to, you know, just express yourself, find yourself, *be* yourself. I don't even know what I am feeling half the time. And you, you have this rich life inside you, all to yourself. Me? I am nothing without you. That's why I felt, I don't know, so ashamed. I hardly had a life of my own, never have, always just doing what is expected. But I guess I realized that I don't have to be ashamed anymore. I want you to know that. I need you. I treasure every day with you. And I love your freedom. I want some of my own, that's for sure, but it isn't your fault that I don't have it. It's my own fault. Look, I was smart enough to want to marry you. He wasn't thrilled in the first place at the thought of our marriage. I have never really told you how hard he tried to talk me out of it. It wasn't until some friend of his talked to him about how spiritual

Lamanites are supposed to be that he came around to the idea."

"He knows that I don't have any Indian blood in me at all, right? I'm as European as he is."

"One disappointment at a time! It's bad enough that I agreed to slow down my progress toward graduation so you could do your degree. I feel like I have tried to do right by you and at every turn I have resented you at the same time when all along the person I should have been resenting was him, or at least my own willingness to let him control me. I mean, it's like I can always hear his critical voice echoing inside my brain, and sometimes I just want to shut him up. When he went on like that, that's what I told him. I told him to shut up. To shut the hell up. That's what I said. And that I didn't respect his opinion anymore, that he was a controlling father, that I couldn't respect a father who demeaned and controlled his wife like he did. I asked him, why did he think I married someone so different from Mom? I said I meant nothing against Mom but against the kind of man who had killed his wife's spirit."

They sat quietly for a while, looking out the window at the snow-covered trees. It had snowed pretty heavily before Alba came home. The white world of winter was a shock to the system compared to the green and wet world of summer she had just come from, but she liked the contrast. And she liked the feeling of needing to be cozy indoors, of huddling close, wearing extra clothes, and sipping hot chocolate. It was strange that she would feel an almost paternal love for John, as if the love of a lover were not enough to heal the whole person, that she would have to be his father, his mother, and maybe at times his child too, that loving each other would be a family affair, with or without children.

"I have to say that Mr. Harker kind of had a hand in this."

"What do you mean?" she asked.

"I am not a big fan of his bluntness, as you know. He is a bitter man, but you know we spent some time together and in all our talking, it always seemed to come around to you and my need to cherish you. So different from what I was hearing from my father, oddly enough. Isn't that strange? I mean, Mr. Harker is so irreverent, so intentionally provocative but he seems to understand marriage. Mr. Harker has some serious sorrow, you know. He carries it all the time, I realized. I guess I hadn't seen it before. I couldn't get much more out of him about his family situation like you wanted, but he made it clear that if I let my burdens get the best of me, he would slap me upside the head—that's what he said!" John grinned, knowing as they both did that his insults were just backward expressions of affection. "Because from where he sits, he said, I am the luckiest man on earth. I wasn't going to disagree with him."

John leaned back and stared at the ceiling. "I am not proud of what I said. I mean, I am glad I found some courage to speak my mind. I only wish I hadn't done so much damage along the way. A child of an abusive parent who never amounted to anything in his life is no easy burden to bear, and yet my father, all things considered, has made something beautiful of his life after such a rough start and wants nothing more than for his children to make even more of theirs. It's like he can't forget what almost happened to him and fears it's around the corner for any of us. I just don't understand why everything and everyone have to answer to his ideas about what is right all the time. It's all always about him, a reflection of him, an extension of him. No one and no thing is interesting just all on its own merits, just for being. He has to evaluate everything and everyone to see if they measure up, you know. Maybe I have been reading too much philosophy lately, but I decided he is a Christian narcissist. That's what I called him."

John stood up and started wandering around the room picking things up. Alba watched him.

"You called him a Christian narcissist?"

"Yeah, I know. I am not even sure I know what it means but

it felt good." They both smiled. "Now I'm not feeling so good."

"You will make it right, John. I will help. Just tell him you are sorry. We will let him know about our plans, we will show him our unity, and leave it at that. He has to figure out what kind of father he wants to be into the future. At least you have let him know he needs to change, but if he won't, then we will just have to keep at a distance. You don't deserve such criticism."

"Neither do you, Alba. At first I thought my father would be ashamed to know that you have been the stronger person spiritually. Now I realize he doesn't know the first thing about you. You amaze me. And maybe, after all is said and done, he doesn't know much about the spirit either."

Alba signaled for him to join her on the couch. As he sat down, she rubbed his back and hugged him. Later this week, she thought, she would need to see Mr. Harker to thank him.

Chapter 12

Dear S.,

She told me today that she and John want to start a family. We were back in the house after an outing, going over the layout of the book. I had cut paragraphs with my scissors and had laid them out in a sequence, hoping to align them with the right images. The weather has been pretty schizophrenic as it always is at this time of the year. Just last week we had snow, but today it reached 70 for the first time in the season and the trees are starting to bud. I could show her where the cheat grass was cheating too, growing green before the other grasses. We broke a good sweat in the late morning sun.

I had been on a rant about the overdevelopment of the valley, the choking pollution, the increasing signs of global warming — you know, my usual speech. She has heard it many times before, and maybe she thought I was going to disapprove, so she just blurted it out.

"John and I want children and we are starting our family right away."

I didn't respond at first.

"I just thought you should know, you know, in case you don't approve, but I am hoping that you do. I am hoping for, I don't know, your blessing, I guess. Can we have that?"

"My blessing?" I laughed. "I don't give those anymore, you know that."

"Well, I don't mean a priesthood blessing, not exactly anyway. But any time you want to give me one, that's fine by me. I just mean, your opinion means a lot to us and I would like to know you think well of this decision. I know you aren't a big fan of children and the idea of me pregnant probably upsets you."

So what was I going to say? I think it's obvious that the world needs more people like Alba. And it is certainly obvious to me what a child means to a parent, but none of this was clear to her. I am a little more ambivalent about how many Johns the world needs, but he's not so bad, as far as that goes. Helluva lot better than I ever was. And I didn't deserve replication in any case. Look, I don't hate myself, but there was never any doubt whose you were from the very beginning. Someone said to me once you were too good for this world. Sure, it was meant as a compliment but it insults this world, so I don't buy it. This old world does pretty well for itself. Nothing like it, in fact. And there wasn't anything like you. You left me to stammer in the face of the oddness and beauty of this planet, I guess. I am good enough at that, I suppose. That is my sum of my purpose until I am too old to get up the trails. I am slowing down, no question.

"Is John committed to giving you the time and the space that you need to be an artist?" I had to know.

"That's the plan, anyway. I finish my thesis this summer, so the timing is perfect," she said.

"I don't mean this summer. I mean for life," I said, my paternalism kicked into gear. "Look, sure, bring a baby into your home. Be the young mother standing pregnant in the grocery store line, push your stroller in the park. Hell, be the mother calming the crying child in the halls of your church with the rest of them. As long as you keep painting. Just don't kill your creativity. If I see another Mormon woman waste her talent for the sake of a family that would have been much better off with her talent shining and guiding them like a bright star, well, I won't stand for it. Have your cake and eat it too. This isn't no monastery Mormonism asks you to make of this life. Live it up. Live it full."

"John understands. He understands that I need to paint like I need to breathe and that I need to write too. I have been writing, you know."

"Writing what?"

"My experiences. I want to remember all of it while it is fresh in my mind, starting with when I was first hired by you. I am writing down the details but also the feelings. I want it to be something for my posterity. I can't bear the thought that the past was all brought to the surface just so that it could be buried again when I am dead and gone. I need a posterity to whom I can give these stories, you know."

"That I understand. Yes. That's good. You should write. You should write and paint. Write and paint, I say. The world suffers for all the silent women. Have babies too."

I returned to my notes and found a paragraph I had written, but for the life of me I couldn't remember what it was for, what painting I had thought would go with it. It was something about morphology of leaves in the semi-arid climate of the Great Basin, about how it affects all aspects of plant growth and can challenge our capacity to identify plants successfully unless we are aware of both the inner structure and the qualities of the surrounding environment. "Didn't you do a painting that had some of the Gambel oak and the bigtooth maple in the background. I think it was of a wild asparagus. Do you remember the one?"

"Yes. It's right here, I think." She dug beneath a pile of paintings and pulled it out.

"That's the one I meant. Yes. Perfect." Looking at it again more carefully, I was full of admiration again. "That's nicely done." Alba came over from the couch where she had been sitting and looked over my shoulder at it and smiled gently. She seemed pleased that I liked it.

"How do we keep ourselves, our memories, our lives, you know, *alive*?" she asked. She sat down in the chair next to me. "Do you keep a journal? Is there any corner of this house where we could find the official memories of Zacharias Harker?"

"I am not sure what the purpose of that would be." Fact is, I have no one to orphan. I've been orphaned by my child, divorced by reality. And here she is, writing for her posterity. Those stories, they could cure deafness and I am not even family. At first they made me angry for her sake. Made me want to spit. But she had a smile on her face and tears in her eyes while she told me about her grandfather and the experience of tracing the footsteps of her father. Seeking the father, only to find out that he is a ghost or a shell in the end but finding in the meantime some roots and some healing. That's remarkable. Instead of being freshly wounded, she comes home empowered, knowing who she is, how she wants to live, wanting to love John more than ever, wanting to paint with even more passion, and now wanting to start a family. There appears to be enough love between her and her mother that their relationship has survived all that honest talk, thankfully. She might even say it has thrived since her return. I gather it wasn't the sweetest of reunions at first, though. There was just too much for her mother to explain, to apologize for, and too much for her mother to have to listen to about what Alba learned on the visit. But Alba says she finally understood what her mother was protecting her from, what she misunderstood about her father, and she says that now they are not as far apart on things as they were, that her mother has even loosened her defense of that bastard Pinochet. They both seem persuaded that the father was actively working covertly for the government. She says that her mother was relieved that Alba finally knew the truth now, relieved that she no longer had to stage-manage the past like she had. They go to the temple every week to do the work for the dead, and from the sound of it, it's a regular family reunion in those walls. She is pretty passionate about that, I tell you. All that stuff about the dead waiting on us, about them appearing in dreams, visiting the living to ask for favors.

Just so you know, you have my full permission to show up and scare the hell out of me. I would like the hell gone in any case. I don't mean to complain. Probably not worthy in any case, at least as far as my bishop would see it, but hell, I never heard of visions and angels coming to the perfect. Seems, in fact, they have come to some pretty notorious sinners. I would gladly be struck dumb for days just for the chance to be reprimanded directly by you or your mother. I envy Alba's peace. They go to the temple for her ancestors, one by one, and she says it's as if the powers of heaven and the power of ancestral love are bringing about healing across the generations. All those lost fathers and mothers, lost children, lost bonds and ties. Except the irony, of course, that she continues without a father, without a father's story. It doesn't seem to be bothering her anymore though. I envy that, I guess. Somehow knowing something, even if it was a story of deceit and abandonment and cowardice, put a human enough face on the mystery she had lived with, and it gave her a mission, a sense of direction and focus that she had so desperately wanted.

But I digress. The bottom line is that she wasn't going to let me dismiss journal writing so easily. She responds to me: "So that your posterity can remember you, so that you don't just vanish when you are gone. That's not an overstatement. You know I speak from experience. I have inherited a terror of the void, the silence and refusal to share. These are great sins, you know."

"I guess that's not a bad idea. If you have to worry yourself about such matters." I shuffled some papers. I am pretty sure she could tell I was uncomfortable with the question. I mean, I got it. I understood, but I wanted to move on to other topics. "As long as you have both been in school, John has been pretty good. I will grant you that. It's another story when he is in law school or worse, at his first firm, putting in eighty-plus hours a week, when you both start to feel that his work must come first. I have seen it before. I let it happen to my wife, you know."

It just came out.

"You let what happen?" she asked, without hesitation, as if she had been waiting for me to say that. I turned and looked at her. She was leaning forward, with both elbows on her knees, almost daring me to not answer. It was mid-morning and although it had started out promising blue skies, the wind had picked up outside. I could hear the whistle of the wind through the bare branches. My pear tree was starting to blossom, just barely. I could have waited there forever. I did not want to speak and I didn't want her to ask another question, but I could see in her eyes that she wasn't going to let my aside slide by. She wants traction on my story whenever she can get it. And I admit that I don't give her much. I am not proud of my reticence, but you see, somehow after all these years of conversing with you privately, the idea of sharing you with someone else steals the elusive glow I feel whenever I sit down to write, like it would take you away forever. I have almost felt the temptation a few times to stop writing altogether, but that feels like walking away from your grave. I think that's the paradox of it all. I knew better than most dads, I suppose, that you and your mom were gifts, and as gifts I guess that means you were only on loan.

But if I admit you were gifts, that means I have to believe you could suddenly be taken away, that your death would balance the account somehow. Naked we come. Naked we go. But damned if I am going to let God get away with that. Because, you see, you were here, in this house, and I can still hear your bare feet flopping on the wood floors early on a Saturday morning, running down the hallway to fetch something important from your room. I can hear the chirp of your voice talking to your mom over your Cheerios, asking questions about the world. I can remember how you used to come in to our bed when you were maybe three or four, crawling beneath the covers and snuggling right in between us, before the sun had barely risen. You used to stroke my hair and lie on my chest and hold my face between your little hands and demand that I open my eyes. I am still trying to wake up, still trying to understand what it was to have you two beside me, breathing, pulsating, alive and warm to the touch, giving off your little laughs. And what it is to be alive myself. Why am I here? Why was I given any chance at all at life? Just to inhabit this animal of my body, to walk among these mountains with Theo and relish the world? What is it all for? Does your silence mean it is all for nothing? Sometimes I think I am writing just to forestall this conclusion, but then I think that that is just such a stupid cliché and I should close up shop, move on, take up plumbing or auto mechanics or something else useful in this world, instead of expending so much energy in thought. I know a few good folks, all of them good Mormons, whom I envy just for the fact of their fundamental simplicity and decency. Maybe you remember good old Brother Jorgensen. Had a tool for anything. Always ready, on call, to assist with just about anything. Wore himself out just helping and helping some more. He hated talking. He home taught us for a while when you were young. He finally just stopped trying to teach and would just come and do something for us. And sure, there was always something for him to do. At first I felt inadequate, but I could see how happy it made him, and frankly, although I am not so bad around the house, he knew stuff I had never learned. He even solved the mystery leak that was making a ruin of our basement. The Brother Jorgensens of the world just aren't the types long on opinion. They are the ones who have the common sense to keep quiet most of the time and say little. And thank God Mormonism has no shortage of these people. We have our loudmouths, but we have our monks too, except ours wear overalls. They are designed to be doers, and in all their doing they scarcely have any time to spout off on things, and despite what Socrates said about the unexamined life, I am not so sure they shouldn't be envied. I just don't know what it takes. Seems like you either got a simple personality or you are out of luck. Me, I am definitely out of luck. I got so many arguments running through my mind, so many damned questions, and a bunch of ghosts that just haunt the hell out of me. You aren't the only ones I can't forget, mind you. Day doesn't go by when I don't have the image of my mother on the couch, beaten by her own raw stupidity. And I still want to shake her and tell her to get up and get out. I guess what sticks in my craw is the thought that life never really furnishes finish lines for anyone or closing acts. It just ups and cuts you off, like a phone call gone dead. Okay, maybe some people get closure, but the slight chance of that happening is nothing to base your philosophy on. Those are just the lucky ones. And then that life hangs there, like a narrative someone was in the middle of telling, and nothing now can change the outcome and no one can speak the closing chapter. No matter how you go back and try to rearrange the storyline, it always ends up the same. They are dead and neither they nor you could stop it from happening. Sure, you can go back and try to rearrange the sequence of events, just in case there is some chance of loosening the grip of fate, but the fact is, it is all sealed. We like to imagine that we are free, but that's just it: we are only free to imagine. Life will do what it will and each day will unfold as it does, and through your hands every second of every day the free and indeterminate future slips into the locked and unchangeable past. So death gets you thinking that maybe it is merely an illusion to look forward into the future as a source of hope. Feeling that we still have a shot at genuine choice gives us that hope. But I can't stop pitying the living because, you see, we still think we can afford such illusions. The dead know better, if they know at all. Truth is, I should be writing letters to every one of my dead, but if I wrote for everyone, why, the entirety of my life would be spent imagining how the dead look back upon the living. And if I did that, I suppose I would learn that all you would want is for us to live and to live abundantly.

I admit that as I faced these paragraphs all cut and waiting for proper sequencing, I felt a sense of excitement and anticipation. I want to believe that the book has a kind of inevitable destiny and like Michelangelo, I am just looking for the proper form inside of the block of stone, trying to eliminate what isn't the real book, the right book. Writing feels like a way of finding that inner freedom within the constraints of destiny. But it's as if the book has only become more of a mess, really. At times it overwhelms me, frightens me. I don't know if I am up to the task.

So anyway, I paused a little, gathered my thoughts, and said, "Oh, you know, I let my plans get ahead of my wife's. I let my studies overshadow what mattered most." It was the least I could say. I turned back to my desk and shuffled some more papers.

"And what is that? What matters most to you, Mr. Harker? What matters more than your precious mountains?" I flinched a bit at this. I turned and looked to see if she meant this to have a bite, but she looked at me with those wide, brown, earnest eyes. No, she didn't mean to mock me. She only meant to ask an honest question, one to which I had not given an honest moment of thought, at least not to anyone but you.

"My wife. My daughter. They matter. They mattered more." I looked down at my papers as I said this. This caught her off guard.

"Your daughter? You have . . . had . . . a daughter?"

"Something like that," I said.

"Oh, Mr. Harker. I had no idea." She drew her hand up to her mouth as if she might cry. I certainly didn't need any of the drama, of that I was sure. She waited to see if I would say anything more, which of course I didn't. I was frozen. Had she asked, had she probed, who knows what would have happened. I might have broken. The walls might have all come down, the illusions collapsed. But she respected me enough to leave it at that, for now. I could tell that she felt awkward for having caught me off guard. I was deliberately trying to keep it cool, but it only resulted in no one saying anything at all for a few minutes.

I finally broke the silence. "It's all right. You lose your parents or you are lost to them. Those are the only options. That's the deal, see. But, you know that already, so by all means have a daughter. Have a son. Have a busload of them. And love them like mad."

I kept my back to her while I spoke and stayed on task, moving the pictures around and trying to match them up with an appropriate paragraph. She had already accused me of being a troglodyte for refusing to digitize the images and the writing so that we could move things around more easily, but I wanted to physically handle the paintings and to physically cut and paste paragraphs and I wanted to do it with her beside me to advise me. I liked how our minds worked together. It's been strange how our age difference, our different dispositions and training have made it easier, not harder, to communicate freely across those differences. So there is going to be in the end a kind of inner poetry to the collection that no one else will be able to appreciate as much as we will. We will remember the day of the painting, the exact location, the conversation and we will understand the logic behind the juxtapositions of words and images. We don't want it to be a mystery to our readers, of course, but it will be something of a private language shared publicly.

"Are you still regretting we aren't doing this on a computer?" I asked, pointing to the mess all around us.

Obviously I didn't want this conversation to go much further, but why I should have expected her to respect that, I don't know.

"Lost. What do you mean by lost?"

I turned to look at her and tears were welling up in her eyes. Damn it. Damn it. Damn it. What the hell have I done? I thought. I didn't want her pity. Not sure what I wanted, other than the work we were doing on this book together. That's what I wanted. But she wanted something else. I felt downright pissed off at her father, I can tell you, leaving behind such a girl and leaving someone like me with the obligation to put salve on her wounds. Did he have any idea what it's like to worry about her, off on her own, rootless and searching? Even made me mad to think that had he truly known her, he might have tried to claim some genetic responsibility for her remarkable nature. Of course, I could see the story that was forming in her mind and that maybe had crossed mine a time or two, that we two poor sots, cast upon the shores of life amidst the wreckage, could assemble a makeshift fort, could make something of our lives together to bring us shelter, cover, in some sort of surrogate arrangement. She wanted and needed a father. Maybe I needed a daughter. Sure. I had thought it. Many times. But as I looked at her wet eyes, it hit me. This can't be allowed to happen. I had to refuse the story that was forming.

"I don't think it's any of your business," I said as coolly as I could. I didn't look to see the expression on her face. I just kept working. She didn't respond right away. She must have been gathering herself, fighting the urge to scream at me. Who knows. But I wasn't going to budge. I knew that much about myself. This was familiar territory.

* * *

We worked steadily for the next few weeks and made good progress on the book, and she never brought it up again. Well, okay, maybe progress is overstating it. I mean, I am writing furiously and we have consulted for many hours, thinking about the sequence and arrangement of images, but I confess to you (not to Alba, mind you) that I am writing so much, thinking of so many connections, that the thing is metastasizing beyond my control. I am beginning to realize that I was motivated by an ambition to poke a finger in the eye of a God who pretended to be more rational than he is, a way of saying that he couldn't hide anymore behind the mask of benevolent and supreme governance, that we understood and accepted our tragic existence, thank you very much. And a few people's eyes to poke in the process too. But, true to form, it is dispersing before my eyes. I can't stop the experimentations, the digressions. If there is a God, maybe he can't either. Fact is, maybe I am discovering a kind of solidarity with a deity who is never quite sure if he got things right, so he just keeps trying. That's someone I could pray to, believe in. Every time I am outside and I touch the leaves of a squaw bush or run my fingers down the stem of a columbine or see the white petals of the redosier dogwoods in bloom, I understand all over again what a rare and strange privilege it is to enjoy the shapes and colors and smells of this accident of a planet. Time and chance. The chances of it are staggering and the time for such awareness is shortening. And I have to admit that I love it more intensely, more passionately, and more painfully without you. I doubt that I would have ever created something quite like this mountain of prose otherwise. It might not be a book yet, but it is certainly a testament to something. I don't know what yet. But Alba needs something more concrete. She needs reassurance that we are getting somewhere. What to tell her?

I would throw every page away in a heartbeat if it meant I could show you what I have seen. Maybe that's the reason we fill the world with books. So many lost lives. And yet books are so inadequate. If they weren't, why would we write so many? I don't know why it is that we humans are so vulnerable to doubt, so capable of playing small. I try to give Alba every breath of wind she deserves to fill her sails, because for one, she is a helluva painter and it has far more to do with her sensitive soul than it does the craftsmanship of her hands. Sure, she paints a fine line and knows the lineaments of things, but that's the least of her skills. What sets her apart has something to do with the gentleness of her own presence in the world. I mean, you never see her in her paintings, but you always sense that a person of great gentleness and kindness, a presence so respectful is quietly sitting beside the world she seeks to present as if she doesn't want to startle a thing. And then there is the paradox I see in each painting—that the more anonymity she seeks beside the plant world she inhabits, the more present she becomes. A talent that good, that humble is a fragile thing, a soft candlelight, something that can be extinguished at any moment. Besides, I know too something of that feeling of sitting still on the flat water waiting for motion, waiting for a reason to believe you can move. Everyone needs some wind and if it doesn't come from those closest to you, it almost doesn't matter if it is coming from elsewhere. I am not going to blame things on my parents. They were what they were and they did what they did. I doubt they had anyone filling their sails in any case, so why should they turn around and fill mine? My poor mother was a broken vessel and my dad, well, he was an ornery SOB. But good enough, as far as that goes. And they gave me life. And here I still am, outliving the whole lot of you.

I haven't really decided to tell her anything. Possibly by the end of the summer, I'll tell her. She seems willing to leave it in my hands, but her frequent calls and questions about the layout or about the editor's expectations suggest to me that she is beginning to doubt. Well, the editor, that's a longer story, but let's just say that the guy at the university press is not pressing me and I am not getting any closer to the finish line in any case. I didn't get the most enthusiastic response when I first pitched the idea. I am pretty sure they would prefer something more straightforward about the flowers themselves, but I didn't want them to say no before having to look at it. So who knows? She finally insisted that she have access to my prose so that she could better understand my overall philosophy. I had pretty much already given her the essence of the book on all our outings, and she had read paragraphs here and there as we worked together on a few sections, but I knew I had to give her something concrete, so I went through my piles of pages and selected what I thought might represent something of the core. I was nervous when I first loaned it to her since it was my only copy, handwritten, like this, on loose-leaf papers all stacked awkwardly into a couple of manila folders. But she took the folders for a few days some time ago now and read them intensely, she said, over a few days. She read them a second time and called me to talk it over. This was back in the early winter and our visits had become less frequent and she was in the middle of her preparations to go to Chile. I had been growing a bit anxious with any portion of the manuscript out of my hands, fearful of some mishap that might lead to catastrophe. There was no way I was going to start over.

"Mr. Harker?" she said as I picked up the phone.

"Yes, Alba. It's me. Who else lives here?" I asked.

"Sorry, I knew it was you. Just habit I guess. Listen, I wanted to tell you that I have finished reading the manuscript and that I can return it to you tomorrow if you would like."

"I would very much like it. I feel like Joseph Smith, worrying himself over the 116 pages. Only I have no divinely directed backup plan."

"I took care of that for you."

"What do you mean?" I asked.

"I made photocopies of the manuscript. The whole thing. And with your permission, I will keep my copy here at my house. That way if anything should happen to the originals, we will be safe."

For some reason the idea of a copy wandering the world without my surveillance rattled the nerves. "Where will you put it?"

"Well, I had an idea. John and I were talking about it. John says that to keep himself occupied in the evenings while I am gone to Chile, he can transcribe the manuscript onto computer. I mean, we have to do that at some point anyway, right?"

"Right." Of course that was earlier, back when I was a little more suspicious of the character she had married and not so sure I wanted his hands on any of my pages. I dreaded the thought of him reading it and then wanting to debate me on every little nuance he didn't agree with. But how was I going to argue against this offer for free labor?

"You make sure he understands that he is strictly forbidden

to add or subtract anything from the text, you understand?"

"Yes, of course," she replied.

"I mean strictly forbidden. I don't care if there are typos, misspellings, anything. He copies exactly what he reads. Nothing more and nothing less. Woe unto him who shall add or subtract from the Word, for he shall mourn. I mean it. I just might kill him."

"Are you saying you mean it? I mean, how serious are you about this, really? I can't tell." She was trying to tease me, but I didn't soften.

"And if he so much as breathes a word of the text in his sleep, let alone to anyone he knows in his waking hours, I will castrate the boy and then where will you two be? This isn't time for monkey business. I mean it."

"I think I got the point," she said. Her voice sounded as if she were smirking on the other end. "He won't change a thing and I will duck-tape his mouth until I get back."

"That would be a great service to mankind," I said.

"One more thing, Mr. Harker. I want to make sure you know this. This reading. I couldn't put it down. Really. I think I understand things so much better now, even though I know you have been trying to tell me your ideas all along. But seeing it in its raw handwritten form was quite moving. It wasn't too hard to follow, although I admit you move at quite a pace. I had to read it twice, slowly. It is a real testament to the beauty and value of this place. I don't know how to put it. Maybe this will offend you, but it feels like it says so much about you. I didn't expect that. And even though I know you don't consider yourself any longer a religious man, it felt like a good sermon."

"Yeah. I am offended," I said.

"Well, my point is simply I just don't know that it could have been written with more religious passion, you know, for what you often call 'this fragile world.' You make the world feel holy. Did you mean to do that?"

"Well, hell, I don't know. That depends on what you mean by 'holy.' I'm not at all invested in the idea of natural theology. You know, the idea that the world bears the signature of the Creator and that my job as a botanist is to do the translation. I made that clear in the manuscript. I mean if his signature is on everything, it's all hieroglyphics anyway. No one's going to translate that stuff."

"Yeah, I saw that. But isn't that the mystery of it? I mean, I can't help thinking that you are still searching for God. He isn't irrelevant. Just because you can't prove him doesn't mean he isn't there."

She was good. I enjoyed this sort of thing more than I wanted to let on.

"Doesn't mean he is either," I said.

"Well, sure. I am not trying to prove his existence any more than you are trying to prove his inexistence. But what you wrote haunts me and it feels like, I don't know, a presence, I guess. I don't know how else to put it. I just don't see how what you wrote makes sense in a world where God can't exist. God's existence makes me want to paint until the sun comes up or until I starve. And painting to me feels like prayer, a good all-night prayer. It seems art is worth doing precisely because of the possibility that there is a God."

"Tell that to the existentialists."

"I have wondered about that. Maybe they are the exceptions. Maybe even they need the possibility of his existence to make their denial meaningful. Or maybe it's just because God won't be pinned down, because he likes to keep things interesting."

"Ain't that the truth."

"It's an interesting world. There's no denying it."

"Well, if my writing makes you want to paint, I concede: the world is holy. God is real. Go for it. Just paint, damn it, paint."

She laughed. "I knew I could force a confession from you."

"Don't get confused, girl. Concession is not confession."

"Whatever. I just think I came away thinking a lot too about our fragile presence here, you know, on this earth. There is such beauty in that idea. I kept thinking about the irony. Something dies and we mourn its loss and suddenly we see it more profoundly than ever before, even though it is gone. And you know it's almost as if you have to experience death or know death to really see life."

And this was before her trip to Chile, so she didn't yet appreciate the irony of what she said next. "I didn't experience my father's death directly," she says, "but he looms larger precisely because I have lived my life in his shadow. And I feel like I am searching all the time. Makes me see things along the way I would have otherwise missed, I suppose. Reading your prose made me feel that this world—the mountains, the flowers, the water, all of it—is some kind of compensation, somehow. So I just wanted to make sure that I said thanks."

I haven't really ever expected much from people and I certainly would never expect that from most. Your mom and I talked a lot, of course. It was the way she entertained my doubts and my questions with such directness, with such sincerity. I never felt like she was trying to steer me or shape me. She never cut corners in her own thinking, and if I sounded like a fool, why she would let me know right off. You couldn't get away with hyperbole with her. She was utterly reasonable. But faithful too, you know, in the religious sense. She seemed open to God, open enough to allow questions, to admit what she didn't know or understand, but all that space for questions never seemed to shake her trust in God. That was the kind of faith I wanted. Seems like the only kind, really. Otherwise, it's just some kind of stubborn insistence and presumption of knowing far more than we do. Her faith was ultimately what drew me to the church and made me feel like belief was possible. Problem is there are far too few such people in the world. I can't waste my time with those whose certainties about the world are unshakeable. For every Brother Jorgensen there is an equal and opposite force in the church, the member who feels it is his duty to announce repeatedly how others should be measuring up, as if the purpose of life were some exam to test how right we are in our thinking about issues, how right we are in our daily behavior, as if the sum total of our human existence were found in what we think and do. Seems like God said something about how we look at the external man, but he looks upon men's hearts. Seems like Jesus was all about the heart—not the mind, not the words, and not even the actions but our hearts. He wants our hearts, laid on the altar. It's a gory image but it captures the essence of the Christian religion, but for some reason the religion inspires armies of nosy know-it-alls, folks who see nuance and irony and paradox precisely nowhere and precisely never. And not one ounce of recognition that it is because of our nature as beings who often intend well but fail that makes Christ necessary. In their minds what's wrong with the world is simply that men fail. No kidding. That's like saying that what's wrong with the world is that something is wrong with the world and what would make it right is that if everything were, you know, right. For them, it simply boils down to the fact that people aren't trying hard enough. And instead of shining the light of divine compassion and love on the world, they expend their energies coming up with yet another socializing scheme to motivate, cajole, or otherwise herd people into moral conformity. I mean the whole lot of them seem downright proud to be incapable of changing their minds about anything, and yet right there in their own scriptures, God himself makes it clear: your thoughts are not mine, so just knock it off! Mom's trust might have been unshakeable but it never seemed to translate into unshakeable certainty about what she thought she understood about the world or God's working in it. I mean, any honest look at the world has to at least give us pause or teach us the wisdom of silence once in a while. Besides, if God is so almighty, why the hell would he need puny brains like ours to defend him?

I remember one time when I was particularly heated about a comment Sister Mansfield made at church. She wanted everyone to know that she and her family had recently decided to up the ante and stop watching PG-13 movies, avoiding R-rated movies just wasn't enough, and as a result, their son got into college, her daughter's wedding plans had gone much more smoothly, and I don't know what else, maybe it didn't rain on the wedding day or something about the cost of the sprinkler system. Seems like God has an excessive interest in the Mansfields, I said, as we were driving home. Seems like he really feels it is important to make their life as cozy as can be. Seems like he owes the poor Knecht family an apology, I said, considering as how Brother Knecht never failed anyone as far as we know but, well, I guess maybe he watched too many PG-13 movies and had to come down with cancer, suffer untellable pain, and then die, leaving those four kids without a father. Seems like God feels pretty strongly about movie ratings, I said, enough to make an obvious point of it. Mom just listened to my rant. You were in the back and young enough that it was mostly lost on you. I will say that when you got older, Mom would urge me on to other topics with her inimitable savvy so that my cynicism wouldn't infect you, but this time Mom just absorbed the waves of venom that came out of me. Stuff like that made me crazy, made me not want to be party to such lousy theology. I mean, sometimes it seems as if God took quite a gamble, you know, believing he could trust us enough with some basic revelations to guide our lives. What a mess we have made of God. We are such children. Maybe because of our intense desire to do right by God, we invented a veritable playbook of how to live, how to dress, what to read, and all the bad things we need to weed out of our lives, so that we could have guaranteed protection from life's whims. Problem is, it turns out that learning the playbook takes so much time and energy, we seem to have little energy left over for worrying ourselves about the fate of the world's poor or for the planet. No by golly, we have to get poor Jonathan from looking at too many boobs and we need to get Jenny to stop hiking her skirts above the knee because, you see, these are the things that really matter, the things upon which our fate depends.

Well, I gave your mom an earful. She just listened and occasionally she smiled at my witticism while she drove. She thought I was funny when I ranted, which in a way comforted me, made me feel like maybe I could laugh too, but she never joined me in a good rant. How I wanted her to! I was often frustrated that she wouldn't, even though I knew deep down she knew there was at least a kernel of truth to my frustrations. Ultimately, it was just therapy. She would sincerely listen, and even without her saying anything, I would feel better. Rarely, but often enough to keep me honest, she would push back, like she did that day. By the time we got to the house, I was pretty well spent. She turned off the car, pulled the keys out, and stopped and looked at me with kindness, not with judgment.

"Did you know that Sister Mansfield lost her father to suicide?"

Of course, I didn't, so I just sat there.

"Practically had to raise her siblings," your mom continued. "She means well enough. I know why these things bother you. I get it. She just needs to hold tight to a few certainties to get her through. That woman lives life with white knuckles, terrified of what she might lose. But I will say this, she has more discipline and determination than just about anyone I know." And then the zinger. She didn't mean it to hurt but she definitely wanted to teach me a little more humility. "She has always been good to our little family, and she says nothing but nice things about you."

Still hurts to remember it. I did vow to try harder after that, I assure you, and I think I did. That was back in my penitent days, back when, with a little help from your mom from time to time, I could find my way back into the pews on Sunday without suffering too much. But you know, after you died, I couldn't feel any comfort from all the kindness and charity from the ward, least of all when people said things about how I would see you again or that you two had some mission to perform on the other side. And without your mom to talk me back from the edge of cynicism, I couldn't help myself. I started telling people just flat out how utterly ridiculous I thought their faith was, how nonsensical. I guess I wanted to know how far I had to go before that veneer of niceness wore off on everyone. I offended everyone in sight. Even poor Sister Mansfield. I might as well confess it, and you can tell Mom and you can both shake your heads at me, but one night she dropped by with a meal, and I could sense she was nervous. Truth be told, I was sitting in the living room full of piss and vinegar. I mean, I was mad, mad at God. And there she came to my door holding a warm pot of stew, a smile, and her attempt at comforting words. I noticed the tight grip of her hands on the pot handles and maybe I noticed how white her knuckles were. I don't know. She said something about your mother, about how kind she had always been to her, and that she was sure the Lord was making good use of her skills in the spirit world, teaching all those needy souls up there.

"Well, maybe she can teach that stupid-ass father of yours a thing or two about courage."

It just came out. In some weird way, I think it felt like a compassionate thing to say, but it came out distorted, like in a funny mirror. It's been that way for a long time now. I mean to be honest, and I might even mean well, but it always seems I am like the bull in the proverbial china shop, unable to move without destroying things. She went ashen, stared at me in disbelief, and dropped the pot on the step and ran back to the car. She never had the courage to come back for the pot and I never had the courage to return it, so there it sits in the pantry storing my potatoes. I guess if I think I am confessing, it's because I feel that

I was wrong, but it honestly felt good at the time. It was a relief to feel fully and completely separated. Solitude gave me solace somehow. I felt free for the first time in my life, free to haunt the mountains and to be haunted by you and your mother, with no interference. So you can see, can't you, the dilemma that Alba and her questions present to me? You are silent but she on the other hand asks questions and talks back, pushes me, urges me toward reasonableness and kindness and decency. And trust. You probably like that.

It's clear that Alba was stung when I closed the door to her on all this. She has not said a word about it. I know it's cruel, but it's just that the more she advances, the less reason I feel I have to write you, because, without even saying so, she would replace you or try to and then what? Who will remember you, if not I? And what will be left of us all when no one knows our names, no one cares? Who will write the dead? Write their names?

Sophie. Sophie. Sophie. Marianne. Marianne. God send you back to me, Marianne and Sophie. Forgive me, Marianne. Forgive me, Sophie.

I make no sense. I want to finish this book but I don't. I just can't see past it. I haven't the foggiest idea of what to do next. I want to stop writing but I am afraid of what happens when I do.

And damned if I can't find my energy these days. I don't know what is going on with this body of mine, but truth is lately I have lost the almost automatic daily urge to get into the mountains. I go but then I come home tired as hell. The other day I couldn't muster my way past Emerald Lake, if you can believe it. Sort of hung out in the bowl below the saddle while Theo ran through the lupine that had gone to seed. I was glad for it. Sat my sorry ass down and let him run himself ragged. Pissed me off to think that he had so much more energy. Isn't he getting old? Yesterday I slept ten hours straight.

Alba got nosy about this earlier today. It started because she found some bloodstain on an old shirt I was wearing, on the back. Big deal, I said. Just some old scab. But she had noticed I seemed lethargic. I guess I had complained a time or two. She seemed bent out of shape about it, to be honest, but I just told her it was arthritis, but she didn't believe me: kept pressing me about going to the doctor, about when my last checkup was. I acted like I had been recently and had always been given a clean bill of health, but when she asked for details about who knows what tests I should have had, well I guess I was a little vague, and she got angry with me. Since when does an artist know her latest updates on septuagenarian male health codes? Good grief. Truth is, I haven't been to a doctor, well I don't know since when. I turned my ankle a few years back. I just wrapped it. That's all I got.

"Don't tell me what to do," I told her. "I have taken good care of myself for many years. I don't need any help."

This seemed to make her feel bad about her nosiness, as if it were insensitive, so I guess it had its desired effect. I know lots of things would be different if I didn't live alone, but I gave up worrying about those things a long time ago. I eat when I want, what I want, and I clean up when I feel like it. I am not a slob, but I don't dress up for just about anything. Shorts and an old pair of running shoes are all I need to get most things done. And, well, I guess I don't shower with the greatest regularity, so sure, I live the life of a bachelor. I grew accustomed to the life a long time ago and have never looked back. I suppose sexual hunger drives most men either to remarry or at least to a life of dating, and sure I feel lonely and hungry at times, but let's be honest, enough time goes by and the old engine just shuts down or cools to a quiet purr. Besides it wasn't until much later that thoughts or dreams of desire came to me and by then, things were pretty shriveled up. In fact, after the accident, the only dreaming I did were odd replays or reconfigurations of the past. I dreamt of the two of you and always the same theme: happiness suddenly and violently obliterated in the wink of an eye, like life was just one cruel joke and all joys were ephemeral. One time we were walking in a park all together and there were some kids doing donuts in their ATVs and making a mess of the grass. I ran over to them to give them a piece of my mind. What the hell were they doing? I wanted to know. Your mom, in that way of hers, tried to calm me down and pulled on my arm, just when one of the boys lost control of his ATV, went spilling over the side, and his riderless engine smashed into the two of you, ripping your mother right out of my grasp. I awoke in a sweat. There was another one, I remember. We were together on a trail as an illegal motorcyclist came crashing down the trail and ran right over a little child who was in front of us. We looked at the crushed body and watched as the blood dripped down the trail. Yeah, they were awful. It was strange that I never saw you two bloodied in any of the dreams, mostly just violently ripped away. The only time I saw blood was when it was another victim, and it was more than blood. It was the whole gory mess of an accident, as if my mind had displaced the original violence done to your bodies, a violence I never wanted to imagine, and shifted it over to others. I did have to identify you, you know. First time I have written those words, I know, but it was enough for me to be haunted by the specter of the terrible last seconds of fear in which you expired. It's that thought that if something like this could happen to someone, well then it could happen to anyone, and if there is a God, he would let anything happen to anyone. In which case, what's he for? What good is he? That's what I want to know. He could stand to be more reasonable, more kind, more decent.

My dreams stopped when I started to collect those stories in the news of awful and shocking deaths, as if to prove that my imagination was indeed telling the truth, that the world is filled with blind accident and that for every story of providential fortune there is an equal and proportionate story of random stupidity and that the universe doesn't know a head from an ass. I didn't have to dream up scenarios to process what had happened. I just had to read the news. I don't know why such stories were comforting to me but they took away the nightmares and replaced them with a living reality I finally felt courageous enough to face head on.

But when she pressed me to commit to see a doctor, I said, "It's my body. I will worry about it."

"It's not just your body!" She almost yelled this.

"Well, what could you possibly mean by that?" I asked. "Is it yours?"

"It's yours but you are not yours alone. What about those who care about you? You owe them at least some attention to your own health. You can't just pretend that you live in a vacuum!" She was on the point of tears. Damn it all. I could see I wasn't going to get her out of the house without some reassurances. But honestly what the hell did I care if things were slowing down? I guess I could almost feel a little hope swelling up in me that finally it might be my turn and that the world might seem just a tad more just as a result.

"I will call. Promise."

"Promise?"

"Didn't I say 'promise' just now? I promise. Look, I think it's time you got going anyway. I'm tired from the work. I'll go over what we have organized in the morning again. I'll be in touch."

She rose to gather her things and left, but I could see that she was shaken. A desire to reassure her possessed me, but I just couldn't. What could I possibly say?

Chapter 13

The warmth and greenery had arrived earlier than expected and then just as quickly the weather slipped into the dry and hot days of mid-summer and the grasses in the foothills turned toe-head blond. Alba's pregnancy, a few months in, already had the effect of making the days seem longer, but without air-conditioning in the house or the car, they seemed interminable. Her nausea didn't help either. On top of it all, she had become a victim of springtime allergies. It felt as if she had spent the spring and early summer sneezing, wiping her itchy eyes, and throwing up, as if it were not a time of rebirth but rather a time of ritual purging and cleansing. She had little energy to worry about the baby. She was too easily disgusted by sights and smells that she had never noticed before. Only a predictable diet of oatmeal, soda crackers, and soups seemed to help, along with as little movement as possible.

Mr. Harker had hoped they could explore the mountains again so that they would have a point of comparison from last summer to understand synchronization better, but when he saw her condition, he canceled their plans and instead they devoted more time to the preparation of the images. She was surprised that Mr. Harker wasn't more annoyed and more restless. He was much less prone to long speeches, acerbic banter and asides. He even talked at a lower volume, as if he were tired. He stopped referring to outings that he and Theo had been on. Theo seemed restless at first, jumping up whenever Mr. Harker stood for any reason, until finally he sat listless by the door. It was especially disconcerting to her that their deliberations about the book seemed to be going in circles. They must have spent weeks trying to decide on a title alone. Mr. Harker at first insisted on *The Great Gamble*. Something to really put the precarious nature of the problem right up front. Too confrontational, Alba had said. A week later, she had him all but convinced to go with *So Much in a Flower* since that was one of his favorite sayings. But then one day he announced that it was too cute. She suggested *Wildflowers of the Field* as kind of twist on the phrase from Jesus. Something to communicate the moral attention they deserved, she said. Mr. Harker shook his head emphatically. There were others, and then one day, as Harker was complaining to Alba about the warmer temperatures, the seasons being out of balance, and the homes sprouting like weeds, the highways widening, the strip malls tearing down orchards, he explained:

"Maybe if people could just spend more time observing the natural world around them, if just a little, I think it would make a difference, you know. They might be able to see their own handiwork a bit. It's the Heisenberg uncertainty principle on a global scale."

"What does that mean?" asked Alba. They were working at his desk.

"It means that the more we seek to observe the world, the more we see evidence of our observing it. It used to be, you know, that we looked at nature as a book, right, as something to translate the meaning of God for us. We've changed the world and the closer we try to understand the world on its own terms, the more we inescapably see ourselves looking back at ourselves in the mirror. There is no such thing anymore, Alba, as nature. Forget any ideas you ever had about it as that thing out there, separate from humanity, a thing from which we distinguish ourselves. It is a thoroughly humanized world now. You see that air out there, you see the quality of the afternoon light as it hits the foothills? You think that is an entirely natural thing but it isn't. That, my friend, is the world filtered by pollution, and those foothills, as you well know by now, why they don't have half the native plants they used to have and all that tall grass along the foothills that has lost its green coloring, that's our beloved rye. Did you even notice how early spring came this year? You get it?

It's our world now. We just haven't admitted this to ourselves. I don't blame the deniers, really. Understand them in a way, but it still doesn't make it right to pretend we haven't changed the world." She looked at his eyes. The same content was there, but the fire, the earnestness had gone out of them.

"That's it," she said.

"What's it?" he asked.

"*The Mirror of Nature*. That's your title. You know, as in not the Book of Nature anymore, the translation of the manuscript of God."

He looked at her thoughtfully. After a moment, he nodded and said, "Yeah. Yeah, that's it." They both smiled.

* * *

Now that the heat of mid-summer was at its most intense, Alba felt sweaty all day. She could feel sweat between her legs, on the nape of her neck, between her breasts, and it didn't help that her entire body felt swollen and that their little home's several fans hardly did the job. The excitement of the pregnancy had certainly worn off long before and now she was just hoping to hang on until it would be over.

She had worked furiously on her MFA project. As she had explained to John and Mr. Harker, it was a play on the idea of genealogy as blood, as rootedness, and instead suggested something of the importance of imagination and creative play with the past, so as to forge a different future, something more like adoption than inheritance. She painted furiously, image after image of tree roots, tree branches, drawn from the forests of the Wasatch and from *Araucanía* in Chile, displayed like a yearbook. It was only roughly representational. She kept it on the edge of fantasy and of dream, like images only dimly perceived, suggestions of something almost manifest. She also used images of ancestral faces faded by use or amnesia, like the faces of the disappeared she had seen on a memorial wall in Santiago where an assassination of priests had taken place. She painted yellowed and faded faces of young children and the elderly, drawn from the clippings she had found in her grandfather's box and embedded them in the bark of the branches or in the undulations of the roots avoiding obstacles and seeking nourishment. It caught the spirit of what she wanted her life to be, a confluence of that which had been dispersed or divided against itself. She was haunted by the phrase she had read at one of the memorials in Chile, "*si estoy en tu memoria, soy parte de tu historia.*" She wanted to emphasize that although we are broken and fragmented from one another, memory grafts us together. Each face, each voice is like a living organism, a carrier of an inheritance, a complex and deep history of loss and change but evidence too of continuity, of life always emerging from death. Memory is not the most reliable thing, but for that same reason maybe the imagination can make up for at least some of it. The rest we could leave to God. But how to represent that tenuous hope and the work it required to make dreams resemble reality?

So whenever she felt the exhaustion from her visual metaphors, she turned to prose, bringing her memories together into stories of Chile, stories of Utah, stories for the future. She continued to write too of her experiences with Mr. Harker, since it was from him that she had learned so much about her home. She recreated their hikes, their arguments, she described his manner. And then back again to the language of silent symbols painted by the brush, losing herself in relationships of color, texture, and line. She relished the chance to play with the compositions, shift perspectives and tonal relationships, as if she were composing music or an abstract form of poetry. The freedom of creation was as fulfilling as anything she had ever experienced. But there was always that sneaking suspicion that there was a missing piece, like a missing lyric in a ballad or a way of seeing otherwise than how she had seen, that was still needed to complete things.

The freedom, she knew, was real but not total. The baby was a constant reminder that she was indeed attached to her body and to the ground and that the life of the mind was only one part of life, not the whole of it, and while she resented the discomfort, she appreciated the grounding the baby provided. She could feel her breasts swelling, she could feel the new breadth of her hips when she placed her hands at rest, all of which let her know that the future had a definitive form. Such a promise gave her art a form too, something to lean into, a reason to express hope. I will paint and write for the children, she kept telling herself, as a way to assure them that I never lose sight of them, that however inadequate the world they will inherit, it is a world I seek to care for and love for their sake.

* * *

Alba and John were getting dressed for a birthday dinner with the in-laws to celebrate John's mother, Connie. John had apologized to his father, but his father had offered no apology in turn. He had instead remonstrated him further for disrespecting him. To help keep his own frustrations in check, John had tried to turn his focus to finishing his preparations for the LSAT and on helping Alba get through her final project. He was more passionate than he had ever been in their relationship and more invested in building Alba's record of family history, in assisting in the temple work with her mother, and more interested in offering his opinions about things, especially politics. He had been following the developments in Afghanistan closely and the emerging attention given to Iraq. He wasn't sure what to make of it all, since it made sense on one hand to defend America from further attacks, but it also didn't feel right, like it might be a step toward a much more violent and fearful world. It was hard to know whom to trust for information, since it seemed the news was increasingly polarized, but John was no longer content with quick and easy answers; he was determined to keep reading and learning and asking questions.

John's parents pulled up to the house and honked. "You ready?" he called back to the bedroom. "They're here."

"Coming!" A minute later, Alba emerged, wearing one of her maternity dresses Connie had bought for her for church. She didn't much like its dull colors, but she knew it would make Connie happy. "Let's do this," she said as they closed the door behind them.

In the car, John and Alba wished Connie a happy birthday, her forty-ninth. Connie remarked on the cute dress. "Thanks to you, Connie!" she said.

"Oh, I was so glad when I found it. I knew it was just the right thing for all kinds of occasions. That's the thing, you know, having versatility. At your stage of life, you can't afford to have many outfits, so versatility is key, don't you think?" Connie was wearing a purple dress she liked. It hid her round body beneath loose folds. She wore a new necklace of shells. Alba complimented her on it, and Connie smiled as if she had been hoping someone would notice. John's father Jack offered a terse hello and then they drove to the restaurant in silence.

Even though it was her birthday, Connie was quiet, silently eating her meal. As he watched her, John felt a mix of anger and pity. Alba drew her out with questions about the ward, about her visiting teachers, and about the funeral that had taken place last weekend for the young woman who had died of cancer. This warmed her up, and she answered energetically. John and his father, sitting across from each other, listened to the women.

"How are you feeling these days, Alba?" asked Connie.

"Oh, you know, heavy! It's a lot of work just to get up and to get around. I won't miss this when it is over."

"You might miss the chance to carry your baby inside of you when it is born and needs to be held and carried everywhere."

"I guess that's right. I hadn't thought of it that way. But at least I will have John to help at that point, right?" She touched John's shoulder.

"Well, he might have other things to do. You can't count on the men." She said this with a smile, as if it were a universal rule.

"He will help, whether he wants to or not!" Alba said this with a smile. "But I already know John wants to."

John grew nervous and changed the topic to the news, which only proved to make things worse.

"That Osama Bin Laden sure seems to be hard to find. I am starting to wonder if he is even in those mountains."

"They will find him. We have the best military in the world. Besides, we have a praying president for once," offered Jack. Alba noticed John's tightened lips. Jack had unfailing confidence in this country. He worried whenever he sensed his son sounding like he was losing that faith. Faith in God, faith in country, faith in family, these were hallowed principles and no self-respecting American should be found without them.

Alba was pleased to notice that she didn't flinch or feel that familiar rush of adrenalin that his comments sometimes inspired. Ever since she had returned from Chile, she felt more compassion for John's father, admiration even. She felt she could see him more in context than she had before. Jack had never said much about his own father, but she knew that John's grandfather had been broken by the war and, even though he found temporary respite in family life, he just couldn't lay the bottle down. In the end, he lost his self-control and then lost his family. Jack protected his mother and his sister from his father's abuses and had married and raised a good family. She understood that Jack was fiercely determined to be the opposite of his father, even though in his determination he had become domineering, impatient with opinions and wills different from his own, and increasingly irritated, almost frantic, at any sign of social decline. She could hear in his firmness a desire to be strong and that was far more, she well knew, than her own father had ever given her. Jack had made it clear on a number of occasions that he was hoping to have a grandson, that John's sisters hadn't been able to produce the son yet, and Alba understood that it wasn't just male vanity for him. It would be a vindication of the kind of father he had tried to be. She knew too, without resentment, as just a cold naked fact, that if she didn't work to keep this family together, things would never hold. She couldn't rely on the men and she couldn't rely on poor Connie. Jack and John were caught in that ancient struggle of wills, the father needing the submission of the son and the son needing validation and separation. John's older sisters had married strong-willed men, like their father, and moved out of state, and this seems to have suited them well.

John glanced quickly at Alba and felt reassured by her calm reaction. He stated his opinion with a steady voice, even making sure his face was relaxed as he spoke, just in case it made a difference. He knew it wasn't going to go over well, but he had given this issue so much thought recently that it seemed a waste to say nothing. "We might have the best military in the world, but that hasn't stopped us from fighting expensive and inefficient and unsuccessful wars. Just look at Vietnam. Besides, terrorism seems like a whole new ball game, and we haven't figured that out. Seems like we're always fighting our last war, rather than the one in front us." Jack didn't react right away, and then John heard himself add, "And if the president's prayers are working, why hasn't God told him yet where to find the guy?"

His father was sensitive about Vietnam, since he had been turned down for service on account of his poor vision. And he had long been of the opinion that everything that happened in the countercultural movement of the 1960s was a mistake and the result of immature youths wanting increasing levels of permissiveness. Jack's was a Cold War world with clearly drawn lines between good and evil, right and wrong, a world that was struggling to understand the new reality of terrorism. The old alliances were no longer reliable. The new enemies behaved differently. They struck and hid. They seemed to have no nation, no story, no context. Their motives, to his way of thinking, came out of nothing but pure evil and irrationality. When Afghanistan was compared to Vietnam in the press, he grew angry at the insinuation that America had ever lost its moral footing in the world. Afghanistan was John's first armed conflict as an adult, but for Jack it was just another battle in the long war against the enemies of freedom. He noticed a tone of growing confidence in his son's observations, and this irritated him.

"Son, our military and our president need our prayers and confidence right now, not our criticism."

"I wasn't criticizing. I was just commenting on how hard it has been to find Bin Laden. I am starting to worry about the expense, the risk of life, sure, but it's becoming apparent, isn't it, that this isn't going to be easy. Besides, don't you think a country needs to rely on engaged citizens? That's all I am trying to be."

"Well, you need to try a little harder. Folks these days think that with a little armchair criticism, they have fulfilled their democratic duty."

"Didn't I say that I wasn't criticizing?"

"You did, but you're wrong. You were. You always do. All you want to talk about are our mistakes, never our triumphs and successes. Do you have any idea what price is paid every day by the men and women who defend our freedom? And here we sit thinking about how inefficient they are? I am beginning to think you would prefer to live somewhere else."

Alba reached behind John and gently rubbed his back, which helped him to take a few deep breaths before responding.

"I know some other places that aren't so bad," Alba chimed in with a laugh.

"Well, no offense, Alba, but I hope you all aren't thinking of moving down *there*."

"No plans, Jack. We've never really talked about it. But

worse things could happen, you know. Besides Chile is really an exciting place right now."

"I'm sure it is," said Connie out of the blue.

"What do you know?" Jack asked.

"Hey, Dad. Come on."

"Come on, what? She hasn't the foggiest idea of what she's talking about."

"Let her have an opinion. That's all."

"I'm just stating the obvious. She knows nothing about Chilean history. All she knows is what Alba feels for her country. That's not a lot to go on."

"It's not nothing either. At least she trusts her daughter-in-law isn't deluded. Besides, I would rather stay open-minded about things I don't know firsthand than to pass judgments based on secondhand opinions."

Jack looked at his son and then at Alba. Alba's eyes seemed full of pleading. No doubt she wanted him to be gentle with her husband, but he couldn't help resenting her for changing his son's thinking. He imagined that this was due to their late-night conversations as she subtly changed his loyalties, changed his outlook to come around to her free-spirited ways. He could see the attraction she was to John when they first met. She was a beautiful woman with a charming smile who took a genuine delight in people. And there was no doubt she was talented and bright. He had come around to the idea of such a daughter-in-law who seemed hungry for a father figure, but at some point he became aware that she didn't relish his advice as he had hoped she would. Maybe it was the first time they argued about Chile, but somewhere along the line he lost her. It wasn't that she was unkind to him. He well knew she was kinder than John these days. But he had wanted something more than respect. He wanted admiration. Hadn't he offered everything to her? Hadn't he welcomed her into this family? Hadn't he raised a fine son?

"I never said Alba was deluded."

"No, but you have never trusted anything she has ever told you."

"I don't see how that means I think she is deluded. You are putting words in my mouth. Why don't we let Alba speak for herself?" He turned to her for resolution. Surely she would back him up.

"You've never said I was deluded. Of course not. I don't think John meant that. Look, we all know we aren't very much unified as a family when it comes to politics, but maybe that's okay. We don't have to agree on everything. I think all John is trying to say is that we can all listen and learn together, maybe. I think that's possible. Besides, it's Connie's day. We're here to celebrate her."

She smiled as she said this. Her tone was gentle but strong. Jack blushed and wiped his forehead and returned to his meal in silence. During an awkward pause, Connie ran through in her mind something she could bring up, something that would shift the focus.

"What is the latest on your project with the botanist? Is the book almost done?"

"Oh yes, Connie, thanks for asking. Mr. Harker says it should be off to the press within a month or so. Of course he has been saying that for some time. I'm not really sure how it all works. Presumably we will get some suggestions for revision or maybe he is already getting some feedback from an editor. And then at some point we will present the final proofs."

No one else spoke up, so she continued. "Well, that's certainly exciting, isn't it? A book! Imagine that! Are you worried about not being able to work after the baby is born?"

"Well, Mr. Harker thinks that most of the work will be his, since it is likely to have to do with the writing at that point, but he has told me to be on call for possibly reworking a painting or two. I assume I can make that work." She added, "With John's help."

"It will be lovely to have it on our coffee table!"

"It's funny you say that because Mr. Harker is always insisting that this isn't going to be a coffee table book. He has more ambition for it than that. He wants it to change the way people think about the environment, about our place in the universe even."

"Well, that sounds presumptuous," chimed in Jack.

"Yes, it is. I admit it. Mr. Harker, well, you would have to meet him, but he is one of a kind. He is, how can I explain it? Just remarkable. He has opened my eyes on so many levels. I like to argue with him, ask him questions, pick his brain, and chide him too. He doesn't like people much, least of all Mormons. Or religion. But he loves the outdoors so much, it's contagious. I can't explain it, but he has been an unexpected source of, I don't know, inspiration, I guess. He has been very helpful with my project, my trip to Chile, with everything."

Jack sat up straight and wiped his mouth with his napkin. "Sounds like a real charmer. Loves trees more than people or God. I have met those types before. No thanks. He won't be charming me."

"It's funny you say that because I have often thought it would be nothing but fireworks if you two were to meet! Don't you think, John? He and your father are about as different as can be. But similar too. I can't explain it."

"Don't tell me. He believes we should shake hands with Bin Laden, apologize, and get back to what really matters: saving the dolphins and solving global warming and hiking on Sundays."

Alba was taken aback. Connie looked down at her plate and said under her breath, "Please, don't, Jack. Can't we just enjoy this dinner?"

"Don't what?"

"Don't badger them."

"Is that what I am doing? Badgering?" He slid his seat away from the table. "Look, I don't think any of you appreciate just what is at stake here. This nation faces a crossroads. We are at a tipping point. Either we choose to preserve our traditions in the face of significant opposition or we cave in. And I have my doubts about how well we have preserved our traditions in the past, but any more steps in the wrong direction, and we are in big trouble. I wish you two would appreciate the reasons for my concern. I am not alone, not some crazy man who doesn't get it. The writing is on the wall, and a backlash is coming if we don't do our job. Americans will not stand for internal enemies. Just you wait and see. Thank goodness this president had the common sense to pass the Patriot Act. We have to start sifting and winnowing to identify our troublemakers. We can't keep worrying ourselves over things that are secondary to our basic freedoms. We lose them and we lose everything." Everyone at the table remained quiet. John finally spoke up.

"Well, at least we can agree that we can be our own worst enemy. Right, Dad?"

* * *

That night back at the house John was busy trying to fix a leaky faucet in the bathroom, well past their bedtime. Alba was in bed reading but watched as he grunted and then finally slammed his hand down on the sink in frustration.

"Hey, what is eating at you, John? Why are you trying to fix this now? Let's go to bed."

"I'm sick of this thing dripping all night long. It's driving me nuts!" He threw the wrench back into the toolbox. He looked back at Alba in the bed. She had returned to her book. "Why didn't you challenge my dad tonight? Why did you let him make those comments about global warming? And the Patriot Act? After all you have been through, you didn't say anything."

"What would've been the point?"

"The point? The point would've been to correct him. You could've told him about what you have learned about torture, for one, or what you now understand about climate change. I mean, those aren't exactly distant topics for you these days."

"You sound disappointed . . ."

Yeah, I'm disappointed. Heck, yeah. I mean, what kind of a birthday dinner was that anyway? Spouting off his views like that and not one word of praise for my mother. It was supposed to be her night."

". . . and angry . . . with me."

He stopped. He put down the toolbox and slumped down onto the reading chair.

"Maybe just a bit. Sorry. I shouldn't be."

"No, you shouldn't. You didn't challenge him either and he's your father, not mine."

"No, I didn't. But if I do, all he does is get more angry."

"And that wouldn't happen if I spoke up? And I have to take the heat? That's not fair. Don't *you* care about those topics?"

"Well, of course I do. You don't get it."

"What don't I get?"

"He gives me a heart attack. I wanted to yell. I felt like I was fighting myself the whole night."

"Well, that was your choice then. To not fight with him. And it probably wasn't a bad one in any case. He isn't going to change his mind and arguing with him further would have only made it worse for your mom. You said some nice things to your mother at the end. She really appreciated that. I am glad you didn't yell. It hurts, doesn't it, because you expect more from him."

"I get it. I sound all wrong in your mind, don't I?" John looked embarrassed.

"No, not wrong. Just, I don't know. You don't see yourself, I guess. I mean, you *have* a father, here and now in the flesh and in your life and as imperfectly as he loves you, he loves you. Maybe we just need to show more interest in his life and he won't feel so defensive."

He stood up and placed his hands on the footboard of the

bed. "That would be like feeding an already out of control fire with more propane. I mean, everything, absolutely everything is about him. The more attention I give him, the more he takes it and runs with it, the hungrier he gets."

"Are you sure about that? I mean, have you honestly tried?"

"I used to, when I was younger, but I think I started to see how everything revolved around him and I resented it, so I stopped. I grew up, I guess, and stopped thinking of him as a god." He laughed. "This is, like, the oldest saga in history, isn't it?"

"You don't have to change his ego. That's his own battle. You just have to change your relationship to him. And every time I watch him get angry and huffy, I can tell it's because he senses he's losing affection from others. No doubt every time that happens, it's like his father's abandonment all over again. That would be a terrible feeling."

"Your father was no saint. How come you aren't like that?"

"What makes you think I'm not?"

"For one, you don't get huffy and feel hurt all the time."

"I get hurt. I get hurt all the time. You know that." She put the book down on the nightstand and invited him to sit next to her. He sat on the bed.

"You are a helluva lot nicer and more talented and beautiful, so that's gotta help."

She smiled. "If you say so." She leaned over and gave him a kiss.

"Everyone loves you, just not my dad so much."

"He loves me just fine. That's what I tell myself. I just don't need him to love me like he needs me to love him." She paused, suddenly tired. A slight groan escaped her lips.

"You okay?"

"Just another kick in the ribs. Man, this baby wants out."

"I would tell him to take his time. The future will come soon enough, but right now, he's got it pretty good in there. Free meals, no duties. Warmth all around. What's the rush?"

"Well, maybe because Mom is tired of waddling and peeing all day?"

* * *

The summer proceeded along its unrelenting hot course when Mr. Harker called one day in a panic about some of the images. He needed an image of the late summer flowers gone to seed, and any would do. He just wanted some signs of parasitical insect activity, preferably moths because he had written some new passages about the symbiosis between insects and flowers that were part of pollination and the insect life cycle and needed an accompanying image. He sounded downright despondent to Alba, as if he feared the entire project were threatened. Even if she couldn't hike up into the riparian areas of the higher mountains, he thought that at least she could get John to drive to some areas above Tibble Fork he knew of where she might see some from the road or not far onto the trails. Her due date was still almost two months away, but she felt immense. Even a drive over some dirt roads could be miserable, but he was urgent about the matter. If she didn't feel well enough to paint in plein air, she decided without telling Mr. Harker that John would photograph it and she would work on it at home, outside on the porch so that the watercolor could at least set in the dry air.

John and Alba had spent that morning watching news reports of ad hoc memorials in New York and across the country to mark the one-year anniversary of 9/11. International leaders gathered in the city to light a flame and the screen played images of the collapsing towers, homemade videos of scenes in the streets, and interviews with witnesses. The horror of the day came back to Alba in waves. She leaned on John's shoulder as they watched. Her mind drifted to the day's significance to Chile and wondered what was happening there this day. She got up to look on the internet for reports and read reports of a demonstration of unity for the American anniversary in the streets of Santiago, soldiers firing their arms in solidarity. She appreciated the gesture, but she thought of the men and women she had met, the many stories she had heard, and of course of Gardenio and his sons, and she wondered why she wasn't reading reports of commemoration for those whose lives were lost or irrevocably changed for the worse after September 11, 1973. In one year's time, it would be thirty years, and she wondered if Chile would be ready to give the occasion a proper recognition. She thought of those who were still working so hard to keep the names of the disappeared at the forefront of the national imagination. Was their commemoration of the American tragedy a distraction from their own national trauma and need for mutual compassion? She read of the president of Chile visiting the U.S. Embassy in Santiago in a show of solidarity and the ambassador told the Chilean nation that "people who hate the United States must be controlled, arrested, or eliminated." Chills went down her spine. She hated that this made her resent the commemorations for the dead, but it was a question that lingered in the air for her, had ever since last year: how to remember and honor the dead, how to right a wrong, without unleashing more violence on the world?

Most of the drive that afternoon was smooth, until they got to the reservoir and began the three-mile drive up a very bumpy road. It had rained a lot in recent weeks, so the grooves in the road were worse than usual. They could hear the muffler scraping against the protrusions in the road and with every setback, Alba groaned. What was she thinking? She started to panic. John was already driving at a snail's pace, but there was no place to turn around. She would have to endure it and then manage the way back down again. It was obvious by the time she got to the parking lot at the trailhead that she was in no condition for walking, so she sent John ahead with his camera while she waited in the car.

Sitting alone, she began to have small contractions that hurt just enough and came frequently enough that she began to wonder if these were not just the Braxton Hicks but the real thing coming early. Please, hurry, she said under her breath. This was a terrible place to be, easily an hour from a hospital and at least thirty minutes from civilization, and what for? For Mr. Harker's exacting demands. Her mind grew dark and she found herself resenting the man, resenting his constant calls and concerns, his rants about the world. She couldn't find the usual warmth in her heart for him, the familiar pity. All she felt was revulsion. And John too. What was taking him so long? Didn't he realize how stupid they were to have come up here? Would she deliver this child by herself? Would he have to do it? The thought made her sick. He was not competent. She had married a child, a bumbling insecure child, and she thought they were ready to be parents! What of her own preparation? What had led her to believe that she could do this successfully? No sisters to show her the way, no close girlfriends who had taken this plunge before her. She wanted her mother desperately. Yes, her mother would come. She would help. She, in all of her suffering and anxiety, had been the most heroic figure in her life. What could have led to the collapse of a weaker relationship only made them stronger when she came home from Chile. She cried, thinking of her mother, thinking of the joy it would bring to her to hold a grandchild in her arms. Maybe she would be wrong about the gender and it would be a girl, and the three of them could make a life of their own, away from the other half of the species who never seemed to get things right. She reached frantically for her cell phone to call her mother, but there was no service. Suddenly she felt it was hard to breathe. She rolled down the window and began to scream for John. A man getting out of his car across the parking lot came rushing to her window.

"What's the problem, ma'am?"

"What does it look like? Please get my husband. He's up the

trail somewhere."

The man took off at a sprint, and within a few minutes John and the man came running back down the trail.

It was a false alarm. The contractions never picked up their pace and eventually dissipated once they got back onto paved roads. But they had the pictures. Alba was a bit shaken by how panicked she had felt. "Please stay close to me," she asked John. He set up her paints and brushes on the deck and opened the window so that they could talk while she painted and he studied. She had ice-cold lemonade and a fan on her face while she began her work. Once she got going, she found that the work was a welcome distraction. The world fell away and it was nothing but her hand and the thing itself, the thing that asked to come into being through the work of her hands. And the thing, of course, wasn't a discrete object but a relationship. John had caught a late-blooming monkey flower, by the side of a stream where a massive web of cocoons caused the stem of a dead lupine to droop. The monkey flower, she assumed, was named for its bearded appearance like a monkey sticking its tongue out, the splashes of red deep in its throat, two of the petals sticking up like a face and the lower three like the jaws of a whimsical mouth. There was really nothing so extravagant as such a flower, and the thought that this was no tropical flower that relied on unimaginable amounts of rain to publish its exaggerations, let alone the genetic engineering of commercial flowers, that this was a gem on the bank of a wild stream of spring water, that these streams had found their arterial spaces on the sides of mountains and in the canyons and valleys below the snowmelt without anyone ever needing to know of their existence or to give them a name. Maybe the world could do without them: bees could pollinate with other flowers, and no one would be the poorer for it. Except that everyone, everything would, she thought. Unique, superfluous but also for that same reason indispensable. Could Mr. Harker really be right, that in the stories of these little flowers, we had stuff enough for all the great books, all the great poems, all songs of all praise? She had considered the lilies, or at least the monkey flowers, the lupine, the Queen Anne's Lace, and this had changed her, but she couldn't put her finger on what it was exactly. Extravagance as necessity? As grace? She understood the evolutionary story that could explain the reasons for certain colors and forms, but she understood it well enough (Mr. Harker was a good teacher, after all) to see that this too was guesswork since we are caught in a moment in time where things are all in midstream of change. Who knows if what she observed in the shape of these petals was a function that was naturally selected or if it just happened to serve a temporary function before it moved on to something much more useful or perhaps even more extravagant. Mr. Harker, she thought, has so many arguments with God. Why hasn't he argued with the very existence of this flower? Isn't this enough of a conundrum? Why should the difficulty of an explanation be cause for denial?

*　*　*

Another month passed and several more episodes of Braxton Hicks came and went. Alba would be displaying her MFA project at the end of the fall semester. The sooner the baby came, the better chance she had of being ready. Alba and John had gotten used to false contractions, so by the time the contractions came in earnest one night after a double date with friends, three weeks early, they were hesitant to rush to the hospital. They made it in time, but only just barely. By the time they had Alba in her room in her gown and the nurses were checking her cervix, she was already 100 percent effaced. Within minutes, she went into transition. No one but John and the nurses were present as she pushed the child down the birth canal and out into the air. Isabel wouldn't arrive for another ten minutes even though she was speeding through the streets to get there. This was certainly pain like nothing else Alba had experienced, so much so that she thought afterward it almost had its own kind of anesthetic effect. She was so entirely inside the pain, so entirely consumed with the task of giving this pain over to holy purpose that it came with no existential anguish. In Chile she had read reports of torture in Chile, about how the pain was only made worse by the assault on the dignity of the person that was the intended effect of the pain. Inflicted pain of this sort reduces the body to a thing, it intends to obliterate the person's relationship to others and to the world. Alba, by contrast, felt raised up in her pain, dignified by it, she felt more herself in losing herself to it, more aware that she was a body connected to other bodies. Had there been no pain, she was not sure she could have truly appreciated the miracle of having nurtured a new human life inside of her, from her, from her own blood and water. She had given a part of herself that became another human being, a life that was once inside of her but was now free, breathing, needing. John would say repeatedly how courageous she was, but it was the most natural thing in the world to give herself over to it. Besides, it's not like she had any choice, she kept saying. He also couldn't get over the amount of blood and water. He would later comment to friends, "It's the violence and the struggle of birth that impressed me most. We come into the world in blood." Together they stared speechless at the tiny face, tiny hands, the vulnerable life before them with his roaming and wondering eyes.

John's parents crowded into the room shortly afterward. Jack was uncharacteristically emotional. He kissed Alba and left some of his tears on her cheeks, gave Isabel a warm embrace, and he couldn't stop putting his arm around John. He pulled John aside and Alba could see him place both of his hands on John's shoulders, patting him affectionately and then embracing him. John was noticeably shaken. Connie and Isabel both sat by her side and compared their experiences of giving birth and breastfeeding while Alba gave her index finger to the boy's tiny grip. Alba couldn't stop staring at the boy's face.

"We didn't even ask. What's his name?" Connie asked.

All looked at Alba in anticipation of the answer.

"We haven't quite decided yet," she said, looking at John for agreement. "Sorry. We will call him Jeremiah Johnson for now! How would that be?" Jack laughed out loud, since this was his favorite movie.

After the parents left, they made an attempt to call Mr. Harker, but he didn't answer.

"He needs be the first to know about the name," Alba had insisted. "Why don't you drive there and see if you can track him down. I will be okay here for a while. I have all the help I need." John was hesitant to leave Alba, in part out of concern for her well-being but also because he didn't want to stop staring at her radiant and holy smile, but he understood the task and left.

John called later to say that no one was home, that the car and Theo were gone, and that based on the litter on the porch and a few stray bags and extra cups and receipts, it looked like he had taken camping gear with him. Maybe he would be gone a few days. John wondered if he should leave a note. He did, telling Mr. Harker that they had some very exciting and important news, could he call as soon as he arrived? He didn't own a cell, so they would have to patiently wait this one out. Alba felt uneasy.

Chapter 14

Dear Sophie,

I feel more comfortable writing your name now. I am not entirely sure why I couldn't before. What is it about naming? Brings things into relation, I guess, makes us answerable. I guess I feared it would expose this hope that you are really there as pure fiction. Now that I have, I guess I have accepted the fiction as my act of faith. It has nothing to do with knowledge. I know less and less all the time.

Speaking of which, the book really should be done by now. I have written far more than enough and now when I look at my stacks of pages and folders of papers, I get overwhelmed. And the guilt rises up inside. There lie Alba's images, all tidy and ready to go, and I had the idea of slipping in lean, clean sections of prose between and around those images. I wanted to be minimalist but provocative, efficient. But the words wouldn't stop. And now I have little energy lately for the project, little energy for much at all, to be honest. This body of mine has felt like it has aged a decade in the last few months. I struggle to get up in the morning. Everything aches. I have had my share of such old-man pains, I guess, so it isn't all that new. The knees are always rickety in the morning, the feet sore. I have always had some of that after a day hiking, but for some reason it seems that recovery of the bounce in my step is harder to come by. I guess I shouldn't complain. I am seventy-two this month. Alba is so pregnant these days, she isn't much help. Truth is, I don't need much. Wish I did. They have been more focused on the pregnancy, his preparations for law school, and her final project. She promises I will get to see it, that I have had a lot to do with it, which is flattering I guess. She thinks we are close to getting the contract. I don't have the heart to tell her. Maybe I will increase my hours as a free hand for the Forest Service, just to keep me busy and get my mind off things.

It certainly hasn't been for lack of writing time. I guess I shouldn't feel too bad about it, but that is the nature of these things. You are trying to put yourself out there, to risk something, maybe everything, as an act of love, and then you are supposed to wait to see if it pays dividends, if there is some reciprocation. Maybe that is my fear. I don't want to run the risk. Maybe I am supposed to have purer motives, to not care what people think, but it seems to me that if what I write doesn't speak to anyone, I would have been better off keeping my mouth shut. So there is that. And there is that feeling of just not caring anymore, about anything. I have been here before. Thought I had escaped, but it's back.

I feel old, Sophie. Old and tired. My body doesn't feel like it used to. Like it has worn out its usefulness. You never got to experience that, of course. You were just starting to explore your body and the great body of this earth. It was all new to you. So I know that must be some unforgivable sin for those who die young. Forgive me, Sophie, if you can. Maybe I will snap out of it. Sweet Alba, she is so excited to have a baby, and I want to be excited for her, I really do, but I struggle to feel unambiguous joy. She will love intensely, like I never could. Her heart is the size of a mountain. She deserves nothing but long life and lots of progeny. What a legacy she will leave.

I don't think I ever finished telling you about John, but he and I are old friends now. I like him and feel for him. Mainly because his dad is a bit of an ass. He doesn't know how to sort it all out. I think he was expecting me to piss on the old guy, but I felt for him, you know. Can't explain it really. I sure as hell know only too well how the best intentions can go awry. But you know after we went snowshoeing while Alba was gone, he kept coming around for more, even after Alba got back. He was suddenly hungry for advice and eager to talk about all kinds of topics. We didn't always agree on things, but I think he liked that

I ventured opinions and that I more or less respected his. I mean I would tell him when I thought his thinking was stupid, but he knew I meant for him to gain a kind of authenticity. And so we made some progress. I think Alba was happy to see this. She has thanked me more than once. It's not like I am doing it out of charity, but okay. I told her she was welcome.

His old man shares the opinion with apparently every elected official in this state, with the exception of our governor, that climate change is a complete fabrication. He has been reading the scripts sent out by the think tanks, so he can sound knowledgeable, but I keep telling John, he is speaking from a script that isn't his own, that if John could get his father off the script, they would probably find some common ground. His father is a pretty orthodox Mormon, so I told John to talk about Joseph Smith's revelations about stewardship. They always inspired me back then. It's an exceptional earth-friendly theology, as far as that goes, just hijacked by the inexplicable Mormon love of all things capitalist. Focus on principles, I told him, not policies or politics, ask him why he should care about a dying planet, about his grandchildren. Hell, it's not even speculation that in fifty years' time, this globe will be 1-2 degrees warmer on average. He may not understand what that means, but maybe he could think about air, or water, or, hell, the canyons. We'll see. These things are so often wrapped up more in family psychology and political ideology than they are in facts. I don't have much hope in human rationality.

The summer and fall have been really hot, I mean really hot. It has chased me higher and higher into the mountains. I could live up there, to be honest, away from the steaming concrete, the noise and haze of summer. Give me the flowers, give me the open sky. I can't believe the way this valley is exploding. Orchards are disappearing. Everyone is making money. Houses are being built faster than people can buy them, it seems. Hardly seems sustainable. And yet people keep coming, keep reproducing.

And this nation is growing tired of difference. It's as if we whites are in some convulsive drive to oust the very last brown person from our sight. Suddenly realizing that we have lost control but still acting as if we still had the keys to the car. The borders are closing everywhere. Some of the Mexicans I always see down at the Chevron say that even though the work is plentiful, there is little hope now of naturalization. It's a pity. Those are some hard-working people, I tell you.

* * *

One last thing. I promise. Remember how I was telling you about Mom, about our trouble with my wayward heart, about her hurt? You know more than I do at this point, I like to think, but that night when you left, when Mom packed some things and put you in the back of the car and drove off in the night. That night, did she tell you where she was headed? And did she say why? I guess I can imagine she would have said something about Mom and Dad needing some time to be apart, to do some thinking. Or maybe she said nothing at all and just drove with tears in her eyes. But you would have noticed and you would have asked, because nothing was lost on you at that point. You were an observant one. So where were you going? Was Mom mad? Was she sad? Won't your mother speak to me? Dare I speak to her?

What were you thinking and feeling that night, Marianne? What have you two talked about all these years ever since? Can't we just close the chapter, once and for all, can't we just get some answers from each other, Marianne? You see, you drove away that night and the only time I saw your faces again was in the morgue. What kind of cruelty is this, I ask? If timing is the Lord's, then what the hell, I mean what the hell is that all about? No chance to say I'm sorry? No chance to make up for my mistake? No chance to make amends? Knock them off as punishment? If that is the kind of universe this is, I want out. I have had to pay a price so out of proportion to my sins, this is no kind of moral instruction. Or does the Big Man want me to finally admit that my sins were indeed deserving of my losses? I won't do it. I paid that price in spades. I am done with the self-flagellation. Done with the remorse. I just want you back.

We like to think that there will be things that only in death we can truly understand. That's one impulse, and it's religious in nature, but there is too another religious impulse to want to believe the dead can and do speak to us, that you can reach back into this world and shake us from our slumbers and tell us what is real, what is true, what is valuable. That too might be our way of imagining ways to transcend those very same limits. In either case, I guess, it seems that we can't think, we can't exist without the dead. Had you remained with me, both of you, what would I be thinking about now? Would I be happily coasting into old age with my beloved companion, Marianne? Marianne, would you still be loving me now? Would I have finished my degree, become a teacher? Would we have had more children? We were trying, but no luck, but maybe the luck would have changed. Might we have adopted? We had started to talk about it, had started to wonder if that might be the answer or even God's purpose in deprivation, back when I hoped about such things. And where would you be now, Sophie? Married? With children? For that matter, would I still believe in God? Is belief a function of circumstance? It wasn't for Job. That was the point of the story, I guess, but who is like him? God takes everything away and then takes him high into the mountains and asks him what he knows about the breadth and the depth of the earth, what he knows about the treasures of the snow, the wilderness where there is no man, what he knows about the rain, about when the wild goats have sex and have calves. What does he know of the leviathan, the behemoth? I guess if Job had lived here, God might have asked about peregrine falcons, about the limber pine, about the sculpins and the daces in his streams, and, well, the primroses, the wild carrot. And surely the black bear and the mountain lion, the big horn sheep, the mountain goats, the elk, the deer, all of them. And Sophie, I have seen all of them. I mean, he would go on and on and I would have been able to at least nod in recognition of most of it. Fact is, there are a lot of people paying attention to these things these days. So that's not the problem. The problem is that not too many others are paying attention to *them*. God, you see, he searches after every green thing. That's what he tells Job. Those are his words! Botany is his profession, his work. He is the father of the rain. It's all his, you see. Nothing escapes his notice. Didn't Jesus say he notes the sparrow's fall? Hell, he could ignore my hair if he wants, but pay attention to the sparrows, yes, for God's sake—and here I am NOT taking his name in vain—PAY ATTENTION TO THE SPARROWS! I don't claim to have god-like knowledge or anything, but you know if there is one thing I try to do it is to search after every green thing. I want nothing more than to understand how all these plants, insects, animals, ecosystems, how they replicate, copulate, when, why, how they feed themselves, how they defecate, where their bones rest, what happens to their flesh, what in essence is the flesh of the earth and why, why for God's sake, do I get to take it all in?

So I read Job over and over, and one thing I can't get my mind around is why Job doesn't curse God after all. Because even after everything is restored, is it really? A new family? What of the old one? Is he supposed to forget they ever existed? Isn't loving the new going to be perpetually haunted by that loss? What would be so wrong with a curse or two? What would be so wrong about a good old-fashioned rant? Is God so weak he can't handle a little criticism, a little whining from his children? Okay, fine, Job was a perfect man, but the rest of us, life leaves us wanting to spit venom until someone starts listening. Why can't we? Why shouldn't we? I have. No one has struck me dead or dumb yet.

And that's just it. My best guess is that no one is listening. Not God. Not you. And for all I know no one will ever read my book. We are all stone deaf.

Well, Alba isn't deaf, at least. I grant her that. I gave her an earful not too long ago about Job and she listened and she was moved. She could tell I spoke from a place of great pain, and she felt compassion. She didn't offer answers. But of course, I couldn't tell her everything. I barely told her anything at all. Is that wrong of me? She went home that night and called me from her home. It was kind of late, but no one ever calls here, least of all at that hour, so of course I answered.

"Mr. Harker?"

"Yes, Alba. What's going on?"

"Sorry to bother you. I just wanted to ask you something, something about Job. Would that be all right?"

"Of course. Shoot."

"Well, I was reading Job, reading it real careful, and I, well, I don't want to be one of those friends who offers you words of wisdom in your pain and only adds salt to your wounds. The truth is, I don't know what you have been through. I want to know. I want you to know that."

I didn't really know what to say to that, but I felt frozen. I just let her voice hang there in the ether. So she continued.

"Well, so, I was reading what the Lord says to Job in those passages you were telling me about. I have never noticed them before. I have never heard about them. Why is that? Why would such an important speech about the creation, you know, so central to the whole story, go totally unremarked in our Sunday School lessons? I don't know that God ever speaks for so long, uninterrupted, anywhere in all of scripture. And we don't even talk about it."

"Well, don't get me started, but you might consider the fact that those questions God poses make no sense to someone who doesn't even know the wilderness. Presumably, Job knew enough to know what he was up against in life, as would any other citizen of his century anywhere on the planet. I mean, people knew what it took to live, to survive, and they knew that nature could eat them, that it would, given the chance. Fear of God back then, you see, was the same as fear of nature. Still was by the time the Mormons crossed the plains. But we have beat nature back now, or at least we think we have. That's the arrogance of our time, you know. We are offended by the very thought that we are making a mess of the systems of life, and what, after only a few generations of having made our modern advances over nature. We are an incredibly stupid species, I tell you. It's not like we don't have libraries full of the world's wisdom. It's not like we don't have access to the information that can tell us what we are doing to the planet. But we deny the whole lot of it."

"So we just don't relate to what the Lord is trying to say?"

"I guess. Something like that. That's my guess, anyway. Nature has been cut off from Christianity as it has from most religions. It's apathy that Christianity preaches nowadays, apathy toward the suffering of God's creation."

"Can't we recover some of that? I mean, can't we make it right? These verses, they shook me. And it's not like those verses have gone anywhere. They're still there."

"Well, if anyone can pull that off, it would be people like you, Alba. I don't believe in God and I don't believe in religion, but I believe in you."

"You should believe in God. Sorry if that offends you. You understand him better than most. You just haven't gotten over your anger for some reason."

"If there is anyone capable of rekindling my belief, it's you, Alba. But don't work too hard at it! I can sniff out those Mormon stratagems better than anyone."

I meant it. I still do. I think that is what causes me so much fear right now because, it sounds so childish to say this, but if I lose her and John, I have nothing left.

"What do you make of this verse in chapter 40? God is in the middle of his speech. Job says he is vile, that he will, you know, basically shut up from now on, that he knows nothing, and that he accepts God's will. And the Lord tells him, here I will read it: *'Gird up thy loins now like a man; I will demand of thee and declare thou unto me. Wilt thou also disannul my judgment? Wilt thou condemn me, that thou mayest be righteous?'* What do you make of that?"

"I don't really know, Alba. I will need to look at that. Why, what do you think of it?"

"Well, it seems like maybe the Lord is saying something about belief, that if you are going to accept the idea of God, you know, being the Creator of everything, of having all that power, then you can't spend your time trying to justify yourself or to justify experience. And especially if you love nature and can appreciate something of its beauty, you shouldn't expect your own life to make any more sense than, I don't know, the sight of an eagle snatching a trout in its talons. Remember that day we saw the eagle on the Provo do that? I will never forget it. Because, I don't know, maybe making too much sense of things ends up missing the mark and all you end up with is a narrative that blinds you to, you know, the reality and glory of God. You will spend your life making sense of God but will instead end up justifying yourself and knowing nothing about him or for that matter nothing about yourself."

You see, Sophie, I have a treasure in my life, someone who speaks to me so gently of things that I sometimes wonder if you nudged her my way. I know that sounds uncharacteristic of me, but in my softer moments I almost want to believe it. Through the mouths of babes. I couldn't say that to her because it sounds like an offense. She is no child, but still.

"Is this one of your stratagems, right now? Did you call just to get me to read those verses?"

She laughed. "Of course it is, Mr. Harker. What would you

expect? I will never give up on you."

"Thanks, Alba. You have a good night," I said.

"I mean it. Never. Good night, Mr. Harker, and God bless you."

So I have been pondering that verse and pondering what she said to me. I am not ready to concede, not yet. Okay, so say I stop trying to make sense of God and trying to maintain some sense of the injustices of my life. Say I give that up and I open myself to who God is. Will he then admit that, hell, maybe he too has denied the injustices of life, the things that we all have had to suffer that make no sense, just to justify his own righteousness? Or that he expected far too much of us? Is that too much to hope?

* * *

There is a memory I can't quite shake. Well, the truth is I don't want to shake it, but unlike other memories, this one feels more or less involuntary, like it is some embedded chip in my brain and the temperature and humidity get just right and it sends off a signal and up pops your mother's back, leaning over you on the ground, talking quietly to you to calm your tears. You must have been about two. You were such a sweet thing, so full of smiles and laughter. I mean you cried about things, like any toddler does, but you could shake off the tears quickly enough with just a gentle redirection of your attention, which was your mother's gift. She knew how to move on to something else. You were both sitting on the carpet in the front room of our little apartment, and you had been crying about a smashed finger, and after your mother massaged your finger and held you and kissed your head, she turned you around away from the offending toy that had harmed you, and talked to you about this unusual houseplant we had. Well, it wasn't so unusual, but Mom had the gift to make every mundane thing seem magical. For the record, it was an aloe vera, and she talked to you about its spiky leaves, its hard exterior and soft interior, how it survived without much water. She reached your hand out to touch it and you felt its prickly surface. You were still shaking from your crying and your eyes were still full of tears, but you were already moving on, trying to laugh through your tears, showing interest in what your mother explained to you about the plant. And then she did a remarkable thing. She told you about the healing qualities of the plant, broke off a leaf and took the sap and rubbed it on your finger. You were stunned. Maybe it was the sacrifice of the plant's own finger for the sake of healing yours, but you and that plant were bonded ever after. You took care of it from then on like a pet. You watered it, you spoke to it, you even named it Gretel! Well, I am here to tell you that Gretel is still with me. Well, the rebirth of offshoots anyway. I kept her spirit alive with my nursing care. I can see Gretel from where I sit. She has lots of companions, of course, and anyone looking at my living room, would not necessarily know how special Gretel is, but she is my totem, my relic of that memory.

I struggled with my happiness so frequently in those days. Truth is, I am constitutionally unhappy because that is what I learned about how one spent one's life, see, but your mother, her darker moments were definitely the exception. And my depressions caused me such intense shame, you see. Sometimes I think I sought to bring her down, just so that I could feel justified for feeling the way I did. Another memory I can't shake is me lying on the couch while you danced around the room before me. You were inside yourself, enjoying the twirl of your dress, entranced by whatever inner music you could hear. And I was more than tired. Even without the addictions of my mother, I too was a wreck on a couch, and you sensed it. You went over to Gretel, broke off a piece and brought the sap on your finger and rubbed it on my face, because that is what you could see was hurting. I am still pretty much nobody's favorite guest, of course, but in some ways I made a kind of peace with my darkness. It's more like a way of life now, and without anyone around, it doesn't fluctuate so violently. It's more like a steady and quiet stream of melancholy that touches all of life but never floods its banks. But back then I wanted to rise out of it so badly for Marianne's sake, for yours. I was so afraid of being the cause of sorrow rather than a source of healing for you. When you grew tired and cried uncontrollably, everything I would do only seemed to make things worse. Marianne tried to coach me, to tell me to remember that you were so young and tender, so incapable of understanding your own emotions, but see, I guess that was the thing. I still felt like a toddler myself, totally incapable of understanding my emotions. They just seemed to sweep over me, with just the slightest trigger or setback, and Marianne, she had to spend her time taking care of the two of us. I hated that. I hated it when you were hurt and needing someone or when she was. Back then, I wasn't even making money. Marianne wanted me in school, which meant she had to work thirty hours a week, and so you and I, see, we spent a lot of time together, which is why I was reminded so often of my inadequacies. I was so ill equipped to parent a young child, Sophie. I am sorry. I'm glad I'm not guilty of anything serious. I hung in there. I did do that. And I did protect you from my worst. But I wasn't patient.

Brother Garcia. He lived next door and he must have heard me one too many times yelling at you about something or another. One day at church he pulled me aside and almost tearfully told me how much he missed his young children, all of them who were now grown, that this stage of life was a treasure, that I should appreciate every moment while I had you so young and in my arms. That stung. I didn't have the courage to ask the obvious, if he doubted my abilities. I did understand what he meant and I redoubled my efforts, but damn, it just was so hard to change and here you were growing up before my eyes and I was still practicing being a parent, trying to make incremental changes, and the next thing I knew you were gone forever.

And of course, Professor Sorenson. Hell, he was just one. All of them. All of the men I worked with at the university, to a person, they were model fathers, as best as I could tell. I mean sure, maybe they lost their tempers, maybe they manipulated their kids, maybe they weren't as liberated as men today, but from all I could tell they were decent, present, and they were good providers, which is a helluva lot more than I can say for my parents. So I hung in there, chased down my demons, and as I was making progress in my program, I started to gain some self-esteem and started to see myself as potentially the kind of men they were. Potentially. Yeah, I had my doubts, but I would have never even entertained the idea had it not been for your mother. You deserve some credit too, you know. You were resilient. No matter my mistakes, you came to me in the morning hours, your little body, your wild nappy hair, the gentle flub of your feet running up and down the floor to your room. Mornings, they were the grace of life, to feel the newness of each day, to look forward rather than behind, to feel the forgetfulness of sleep, and to awake to free affection.

Do you miss mornings too? Do you look back from your perch and miss the simple things, like I do? Do you find yourself haunted by fragments of memories, wanting to get back to the tangible life you led? I touch this life for you and for your mom, but I touch it as someone already dead, it seems, or at least in anticipation of death. Once your loved ones are dead, a part of you has already departed and caused you to look at life in retrospect, as if always saying good-bye to it, always departing. I don't know why I just can't *be*. There are moments, but they are brief and they are always in solitude in the mountains, moments when I am only what the senses tell me is real, when my conscious mind is finally at rest and as good old Wordsworth says, I can finally see into the life of things. But then it is gone, gone into memory, gone because I am already trying to share it with you and with your mother.

* * *

I was born in what is now Torrey in 1930. It was a brief existence there, but it was nice enough. I don't remember a whole lot about it from my childhood, but as a park ranger, I would get to know every corner of the area. My mother had grown up in neighboring Loa, a tiny blink of a town on the way to nowhere She didn't meet Dad until after she had been doing secretarial work in Salt Lake for many years and traveled around the world with a close girlfriend. Somewhere in there she must have developed her habit, but they briefly settled in Torrey because my father had an offer to help run a ranch there. They got pregnant twice and then left the town and their one buried child behind five years later with their only remaining progeny, me. Dad was trying to get away from mining, which is all he had ever known in Vernal. I can remember mother's laughter and I can remember her bouncing me on her knee, taking me on walks, talking to me about everything under the sun. Dad went to school at Carbon College when it opened in 1937 to study soil science. That's when Mom died. Don't ask me how she got her drugs. No doubt she had enablers. I never asked my father if he was one of them. I didn't have time to sort things out before my dad was gone too, just months after he had graduated and taken a job in Price. I told you that story already, but I guess what I am sorting through here is a sense of what my legacy is, what I can say that I have learned from my past. I moved around a lot after that and never really felt at home inside the walls of a house. I could feel utterly alone outside and utterly at home at the same time. And while I hungered for human contact, whenever I got it, it only reminded me of what had been taken from me, so I wasn't much for holding on. So, I guess, being a hermit has become my way of being in the world, because I was only too aware of the high costs of caring for and attaching yourself to others.

But there was no getting around it either, as one discovers

soon enough especially in Mormon life. Always someone reaching out and every so often someone you decide you care to have around. Fact is, few people are better for that than the Mormons. Who could I name? Sister Jensen in Price. She was my first caretaker after my dad died. No blood relation but a middle-aged single woman, with beehive hair, floral dresses, and permanently in an apron, it seemed. She did laundry for the neighbors, so I remember her ironing all the time. She was kind. If I was good, which I usually was, she made caramels for me. They were goopy and delicious. She always had to wipe my face and hands after I was done. We prayed together. She always prayed for my parents by name and asked the good Lord to be merciful to me, to let me know that I was loved. It wasn't long before my cousins had arranged for me to come to Manti for the summer. They were good people from my mother's aunt, Ethel. Her husband was a nut. I remember that much. Always yelling "God is good!" at the top of his lungs when he would come home from work, whatever it was he did all day. He gave his kids and me big bear hugs. Those hugs frightened me. I would go as limp as I could so that he wouldn't crack my ribs. And he liked to give charismatic prayers at dinner, while we all held hands. Ethel was stressed out all the time, which is not surprising given the passel of children who ran in and out of the house at all hours. I don't even remember how many kids there were, but I do know there was never enough money and never enough food. They didn't need another kid in that house, and so it wasn't long before they found a place for me in Salt Lake with a foster family named Harrington in Draper. Steady income, good school, a room to myself, and foothills to explore. I was raised more by the church at that point than I was by the Harringtons. They were kind enough, but they needed the money and had the room in their house since two of their children had already left home. Brother Harrington was an electrician, so he had steady work, even if low-paying, and Sister Harrington quilted and sold blankets.

Sometimes I helped. And their last daughter, Maggie, an obese girl with low self-esteem, was a few years older than I. It was Brother Darling whom I remember the most from those years. We kept in touch for some time after that. He did make it to the wedding. He was my scout leader and taught me everything he knew about the outdoors and probably first gave me the idea of working for the Forest Service. I never knew if he had children. He never talked about them. I have often wondered if he had broken relationships he didn't like to talk about. He lived alone, but I was pretty sure he had been married.

So I guess you could say that I was raised by the church, in essence, and there were some good surrogates, but I was so transient, there was scarcely a chance for anything to last. By the time I married, my guest list consisted of a few friends from the park service and Brother Darling. My cousins from Manti had not kept in touch much, and I didn't really know them anyway, and the Harringtons moved to California after I graduated from high school. I generally had the impression that the rest of the world had rooms and things and pets and street corners that were theirs. To me the whole world was a foreign place, always worth exploring, but never quite deserving of my permanent residence.

I suppose that by now I could consider myself a native of American Fork. I mean, I have been here for the better part of thirty years. This was the first and only home I ever owned, and we had no intention of going anywhere, but clearly circumstances have left me stranded whether I wanted it or not. And I have liked this place just fine. More than fine. Thankfully it wasn't stolen from me. My paths to the trails are well worn. I know every tree, every plant on the property. I know which trees lose their leaves first (always the maples) and which last (always the mulberry, unless you count the sycamores which start earlier but basically never finish dropping their leaves until the spring buds finally force out the remaining die-hards). I know the moods of the stream that runs past the house, its sources in the mountains. I have worn down every object in the house. Just look at my hairbrush, and you will know what I mean. I think I have owned it since 1945. My books, they are mine through and through. No one else has been arguing in the margins with the authors. My appliances, my clothes, my furniture. I haven't had much interest in upgrades.

I haven't traveled in ages. Except for journeys into the mountains and up the canyons and an occasional trip down to Provo for meetings related to the book, I haven't been anywhere really for a long time. But I dare say I have the largest sense of community of anyone, given my natural neighborhood. Which is why it is strange to find myself on this fine summer afternoon, feeling anxious, like I need to get out of here, wanting to see the old grounds. Maybe a drive? Of course, knowing me, if I take the drive, I will drive to the mountains and then when I see the fire roads leading up to the trailheads, well it will all be over at that point. I want to see Price, but the idea of fishing and wandering and losing myself on the south side of Boulder Mountain where I first met your mother appeals to me the most. This tired old body has something left in it yet, I'll bet. I wouldn't mind seeing that very spot where she squatted down and blew on the fire as she held her hair back with her left hand. I would just lay my back down against the same tree, sit down with my back leaning against the same rock, and wait and look and listen and maybe my Marianne would come to me. She would take my hand and ask me where I have been and tell me that she had forgiven me a long, long time ago and that it was time for me to get on with the business of living and loving and she would tell me that she had read my book, that she was proud of it and that you were well, that you had enjoyed my letters, that you had so much to tell me, and that our reunion would be sweet, that it was only a matter of time, that I shouldn't worry myself about things anymore, that I should look back over the whole of my life without remorse or hurt and that maybe if I looked carefully enough I could see the graceful arc of mercy over the whole of it running in and through and around everyone I knew, in all the places I had seen, and present at every moment of surprise I had experienced in the mountains, every time a cottontail darts across my path, or the mule deer stop and stare as they do before lifting their haunches up the side of the mountain to wherever they are going, or whenever the light catches the grasses in the foothills and lights them on fire, all of it, every moment of beauty was a moment of mercy, was mercy itself. Marianne would know and she would understand and she would show me what path awaits me. She would even forgive me for being such a fool for holding on to her as I have. It wouldn't seem strange to her at all because she alone would understand how she had given shape and meaning to things for me and why without her I had had to hold myself still and steady right here in this little house in this corner of the valley among these hills so as not to fall off the edge of the world and lose myself forever. Because my memories were a mercy too, anchors that held me more than I held them. And as memories, they were my story, my very being. She would tell me that the living and the dead are one, that we are not separated but that we inhabit each other's dreams and speak so softly into each other's ears that we can no longer tell the difference between our own words and thoughts and those of our loved ones who are gone, because language is our prayer, our reunion, our resurrection. It is our incarnation because, you see, we don't believe in our own flesh unless we can translate it into the ether. This word is my flesh and my blood and Marianne and Sophie and Mom and Dad and all the rest are no more absent than I am from this page. I am always already gone, here where my elbow rests on this table and my hands press against this paper and make visible the tables of my heart, gone.

I will arise and go now. Wait for me. I come quickly.

Chapter 15

The days had been shortening for some time; the warm late summer evenings gave way to cooler, darker nights. The first cold storm had blown in and touched the tops of the mountains with snow but most of it had melted already, but it was enough to break and collapse many of the dead plants and matte them to the ground where they would await their final conclusion in the earth. Some still stood resolute and rustled their dry leaves in the wind, crackling when a cottontail or squirrel made its way through the brush. The trees held few leaves. Most lay on the ground. The yellow aspen leaves had turned pewter and lay strewn about the forest floor. Some hung on to their branches and spun awkwardly in the wind. The maples, in their typical rush to beat their neighbors, were already long spent, naked in the cold night air. The gambel oaks had followed with their ochre yellows creating a patchwork of browns and yellows along the foothills of the Wasatch. Several spots of bright yellow could still be glimpsed at the highest elevations where aspens hung on to their late summer glory. Families and lovers had spent the previous weeks driving the canyons on late Sunday afternoons, their awe of the colors tinged by the bittersweet moods of autumnal mountains.

For Alba the excitement of motherhood was clouded by worry about Mr. Harker. She was desperate to share her news and tried calling daily for several days, but his phone rang endlessly whenever she called. If he disappeared, who else would have noticed? Who else would be responsible for him if not she and John? The thought that something had happened to him and that he had no means of getting help was more than she could bear. She had made her mind up and John agreed. Isabel came to watch the baby. Once they were assured the baby was asleep, they left and took the thirty-minute drive to his house to see if they could break in and find anything inside that would provide a clue to his whereabouts.

Out front they could still see empty Tupperware containers on the porch seat, an empty box of Clif bars, and some unused water bottles. The same evidence John had seen from before. Nothing appeared to have changed. The door was not locked.

"Mr. Harker? Are you here?" Alba called into the house as they stepped inside and flipped on a light. "Mr. Harker?"

They could see assorted camping gear strewn about on the carpet and the couch held some maps, ropes, and fishing gear, as if he had brought out and sorted through everything he owned. A cold cup of coffee sat on the carpet where he had apparently been preparing his things. "I'll check his bedroom and office," said Alba.

"Wait. Are you sure we should be doing this?"

"I've straightened this house a time or two. I know my way around." John still looked hesitant. "Look, John. He would understand. I'll ask for forgiveness if I have to. I can't bear it any longer. He'll have to deal with it." Alba left for the back of the house. John looked around at the objects in the front room, looking for clues about where he might have gone.

In the bedroom, his closet and dresser drawers were open and some clothing was on the floor but otherwise it was surprisingly neat. On the dresser, she found pictures of a young girl and a woman, smiling for the camera on different hikes and once at the zoo. There was a beautiful photo of Mr. Harker holding the girl. She couldn't get over how young he looked—brown hair, shaven face, less weatherworn, bright eyes. She picked up one framed photo, wiped off the dust, and looked at it closely. She had Mr. Harker's distinct nose and bushy brow. The woman in the other photo was beautiful: sandy blonde, very earthy with a stunning, vibrant smile. The discoloration of the photo and the clothes they were wearing evidenced the passage of time. A wave of sorrow came over her. She looked at the nightstand and then at the bed, which was still unmade, and noticed dark and somewhat faded spots of red dotting the sheet by the pillows. She remembered the stain from his shirt and the scab. On the nightstand, she found a small black worn notebook. Hoping that she might find a clue, she opened it with reverence. There were fragments of sentences, phrases, questions posed. They seemed mainly to be about plants and ecology, alongside some sketches of leaves, petioles, or stems. Sometimes a bit about elevation and climate. She sat on the bed and thumbed further. She found what looked like a note from one of their conversations. *As long as we remember the dead*, he wrote, *they are part of our history and remain.* Next to this, he put *Alba in Chile.* On another page, he wrote a list of what he called *Christian fundamentals* and underneath the words, *compassion, humility, concern for the poor and the widows, equity, and mercy* and then *deregulation!? I don't think so!* Locations were named with dates throughout: Box Elder, Ridge Trail, Battle Creek, Dry Canyon. And sometimes paragraphs beneath them, either about plants or animals he had identified or brief insights. One caught her attention: *love of a mountain's shape is really the love of one's place, since its shape changes with every movement in and around the mountains. Recreation — expansion of the familiar and acquaintance with the strangeness of home.* There were more mundane things too — to-do lists, book titles, and occasional expenses.

She opened the door to the nightstand and found a stack of files and a handful of similarly worn black notebooks. She opened one, dated 1981. Its first entry was a longer passage that looked like a speech he would have given were he a preacher or an academic philosopher, dated December 17:

It seems an undue risk to ever fail to properly register and embrace all good things. We would be fools to deride science or art that believers, in their limited understanding, deem contrary to God's will or to his providence, when we might be contemplating his very handiwork unwittingly. The risks of deception are real but so too are the risks of underestimating God. Atonement surely includes the redemption of souls and ideas, by bringing them back into proper context and by perceiving them in the light of love, whereby they rejoin themselves to the Great Body of Truth, no longer deriving their force from the illusion of opposition but are instead nourished by their relation in loving context to the lives of those who perceive and express them. There is opposition in all things. Otherwise, we are told, God would cease to be God. Does that mean he contains or encompasses all contradiction? Take, for example, the idea that there is no God. A falsehood, cry the believers! A lie that stands diametrically opposed to his existence. But if we were to abolish this idea, if we could wipe it out of the mind of man and thereby win a victory for Truth, God would cease to exist. The very existence of God redeems rather than abolishes this falsehood. It is only meaningful to say that God exists if we were to imagine it possible that he doesn't. Pray as if everything depends on the Lord, says Brother Brigham, and then act as if everything depends on you. Split your mind into two possibilities and this will energize your faith that must act as a meta-cosmology that somehow encompasses both "as ifs." That way, our mind is raised to a consciousness of the uncertainties and complexities that surround even the simplest of principles. This is not to say we should fail to live or act or think simply or directly. Such capacity is essential to the promotion of the good; it is the fruit of faith. But this capacity is most meaningful and the most heroic when it is sustained by an awareness of infinite possibility, lest we fail to appreciate the breadth, fullness, and magnitude of God's suffering, which includes even his suffering for his inexistence.

She marveled at the voice she hardly recognized. 1981. Slipped among the notebooks was a manila folder, bulging from newspaper clippings. She opened it and saw pictures of a gruesome car accident on Highway 24. A head-on collision in the late evening of October 16, 1982. Two cars, both totaled, pictures of a car door where the jaws of life were used to extract the passengers. One driver who was suspected of having fallen asleep at the wheel, in intensive care, a Philip Lee, age 79 of

Bicknell, driving a silver 1980 Ford F-150 truck. And two dead on impact, a Marianne Harker, age 42, and a daughter, age 9, a Sophie Harker, driving a black 1970 Datsun 510.

She broke down in tears.

John heard her crying, and when he entered the room, she pushed the folder toward him on the bed and pointed. "See for yourself, John. That's his wife and daughter."

John was speechless as he read and then he put it down on the bed. "1982. Wow. I don't know what to say."

"John, I can barely breathe. We have to find him. But where is he? We need to find him."

"There are maps in the front room. I think there is a clue there." John returned to the front room.

Wiping her face, Alba looked further in the nightstand and pulled out the other files. They were newspaper clippings of events in the town, ward bulletins, Girl Scout badges, anything that involved his daughter, her school, their ward. It was an unfinished scrapbook. The other files had much more information about his wife and her life, her diploma, an award she had won at work, thank-you notes from ward members whom she had served, photos of old friends, of what looked like her family, photos of her as a child, and letters written between the two of them, wrapped in old yarn. She felt reverence for all of it, like they were holy relics, and placed each item back in its place delicately as she wiped away tears.

"Alba. Come here." She went into the front room again. "Here. Look here." John was at the work area where Alba and Mr. Harker had often worked on the book. It was an old door propped up by bricks that served as a very large desk under the south facing window. She had always seen the papers and books strewn about, along with his usual pile of pages for the manuscript. She could see them there, but it seems the number of folders and papers had multiplied or maybe he had pulled out more from storage, as if the book had never stopped growing.

Neatly stacked in a black portfolio case were her paintings. She pulled out a few folders and read through them. They were different than what she had read, more wide-ranging, less coherent but marked by his characteristic exuberance.

"He has never sent it off to the publisher. It's all right here. And it's enormous."

John had found a yellow loose-leaf page that lay next to a stack of over one hundred similar pages inside an open unlabeled manila folder. These were handwritten pages, like the manuscript, but their content was different.

"Read this."

The lone and unfinished page had just a strange paragraph about a woman telling him *the living and the dead are one* and ended with his words, *I will arise and go now. Wait for me. I come quickly*. "What does he mean, *I am always already gone*?" she asked. They looked at each other in confusion. Alba leafed through the preceding pages and read quickly, mumbling words as she read, seeking for a clue. At last, she found mention of his desire to go to Price and Torrey.

"I think this is it, John. He has gone to Price and Torrey, for whatever reason. I think he told me he was born in Torrey, didn't he? I am not sure! Why wasn't I paying more attention? What was it he told me about that place?" She leaned both of her arms against the table and stared down at the stack of paper. "But what *is* all this?"

She picked up more pages and read further. She found breaks in the writing where sometimes he appeared to have changed pens or when he took up a new topic, but there were no dates, no addressee identified by name as far as she could tell, even though he frequently addressed a "you." Then she saw a "Dear S." The writing arrested her, as if she were reading the inner thoughts of his soul, even more intimate than the bedside notebooks because they contained a dialogue with an unknown person. They read like prayers, prayers of the most innermost feelings of the heart.

She read about herself, about their trips into the mountains, about his impressions of John. Her eyes caught the phrase *your mother*.

"He has written these to his daughter! Sophie was his daughter's name. But she has been dead for twenty years! I don't get this. And look at all these pages! How far back do you think they go?" She reached for one of the folders off to the side and opened it up. It was more of the same.

"Hey, are you sure we should be reading these things, Alba? I mean, for all we know he's going to walk through his own door any minute in perfect health and ask what the heck we're doing with his stuff."

"You're right, but I had to know." She closed it and pushed it back to where it was. "What do we do now? Call the police? Check for missing person's reports? Is there even such a thing in this country? I can't . . . I can't . . . I can't do this again, John." She sat down on the chair limply. "This is just too much. Where is Mr. Harker? Dear God, find him, help us find him, please! Please bring him back to us, let us tell him our news and fill his heart with some joy."

"Let's get back home and we'll figure something out."

They returned to a crying baby. Alba's breasts had begun to leak, and she quickly satisfied the baby who gasped and gulped in desperation, while Isabel gathered her things and said good-bye. John immediately got on the phone. He started with Price and called the hospital, the Forest Service—nothing. She thought of the miles and miles of roads, as she looked at the baby's sucking mouth. He was feeding desperately. He would need burping for sure after this session. Those letters bespoke an intimacy with this daughter she could never approximate and made her feel foolish for the thought of a kind of surrogacy. And an intimacy of longing and hurt that she couldn't expect to step in and wash away. He would always be haunted by that loss, but maybe, she hoped, maybe she and John and the baby could offer something in his old age, after untold waiting, some measure of peace made all the sweeter precisely because of what he had lost. Not a substitute but recompense, maybe.

They tried Price. No word in the hospital there and the Forest Service was closed. No sense in driving down there, was there? What would they even be looking for? Alba was a wreck. This was nothing like searching for her father in Chile. This felt worse somehow, like a reality being torn away from her, rather than trying to make the imagined real.

"What about his car? Can't we call like the police stations or something to see if they have seen the car, or at least report it as potentially missing? We should've looked for his registration or something in the house! I don't know his license plate number, do you?"

"Oh, I doubt he ever registered that thing anyway."

"What was it, an old Toyota truck, white, right?"

"Okay, let me see who I can get through to."

Alba was so exhausted by her emotions, she closed her eyes while he conversed. The baby was awake but perfectly still and content in her arms. She felt herself drifting off to sleep but the thought of the baby slipping out of her arms made her nervous, so she sat up and spoke to him. "Hey, hey," she said softly. "How is my baby? Yes!" She smiled at him. He stared back at her with that look of quiet amazement. A rush of such affection seized her that she had to hold her breath in case it fled just as suddenly. His little head was scrunched by her arm, and the folds of his soft skin came down on his forehead. He had a thin lair of tiny black hairs and penetrating dark eyes. Such perfection, such beauty in one child. She was glad she had had an October baby. She loved the fall. It was her favorite time of year. And the irony that he was a Columbus Day baby no less. She would be sure to give him a speech at some point about how dates and history don't predetermine our fate.

October. "John!" she yelled suddenly. "John, it's October!"

"Yeah, so what?"

"What is today? The 20th?"

"Right."

"Well, why didn't we notice it? It's been twenty years since his wife and daughter died! The 16th, in 1982. That's what he was doing. He was marking the anniversary somehow. He wouldn't . . . you don't think he was, I mean, that would be so awful!" She startled the baby with her loud voice and he started to cry. "Shhh. Shhh. It's okay. John, he went to Torrey because they died near there. Highway 24, that's down there. Boulder Mountain, too. He's mentioned that before. That guy who killed them was from Bicknell."

"What was Price all about, then?"

"I have no idea, but you need to look up where the nearest hospital is to Torrey and see if they've seen him. I mean, just to be sure. We can only hope he is still hiking somewhere down there, but it's been too long now. I can't bear it!"

John searched and found two hospitals within an hour of Torrey. He called them. At the second, in Sevier, they had the name.

"He was admitted when? . . . The 16th. Okay. . . . Uh, huh. Yes, that's correct. We know he went backpacking somewhere near Torrey but we just didn't know where exactly. Wait. What? Cancer center? Are you sure?" asked John. "Oh. Okay. . . . That long, huh? Wow. . . . I see. Okay. . . . Yes, we will go see him there. Thanks so much." He hung up.

"What did they say? He is in a cancer center?" asked Alba in desperation.

"Yeah, look." He approached her gently and sat down and spoke deliberately. "It appears he was found by a lake on Boulder Mountain semi-conscious. Some hikers found him there, got him out of there and brought him to the hospital. Somehow they figured out he had other problems. She wasn't allowed to tell me, but she said they life-flighted him up to Salt Lake to the cancer center." John looked at Alba's face and could see her fear. "Look, it's getting late. Let me go," he said. "You need to stay with the baby and get your sleep. I will find out what is going on and call you."

"I am not going to sleep, are you kidding me? Not now."

"You don't have to sleep, but you need to stay with the baby. We aren't supposed to take him out yet and we don't know how long it will take to see him or what kind of condition he will be in. Please. You need to stay."

"It's okay, John. I'm coming. We're all going. It's a hospital, for crying out loud. They're clean." She started to gather the baby's car seat, the diaper bag.

"It's are also where sick people go, Alba," he started, but he could see there was no stopping her.

* * *

At the hospital, they spoke to the nurse at the front desk. Yes, he had been checked in three days earlier. He was down the hall, but she wasn't sure if he would be coherent.

"You are the first people to visit him, by the way," she said as they walked down the hall.

Inside the room, Mr. Harker was sleeping. He looked shockingly thinner than usual and his breathing was heavy. Alba fought back tears as she placed the baby in the car seat down on the floor next to the bed. She reached out and touched Mr. Harker's hand.

"Mr. Harker. Mr. Harker. It's Alba and John. We have a surprise for you."

His eyes opened, revealing a vacant look. He didn't seem to recognize her at first.

"It's Alba. Alba and John. We came to visit. Oh, Mr. Harker, we have so many questions. Are you awake?"

He nodded and managed a breathy "Yeah."

"We are so sorry. You had us so scared. We didn't know where you were, but we found you, you see? We found you and we are here and everything is going to be okay. We are here."

His lifted his hand and patted hers. She squeezed his hand and held on, stroking his hand repeatedly.

"Maybe you're too tired to talk, Mr. Harker, but you see they won't tell us anything about what has happened to you, because technically we aren't family."

"Technically?" he asked faintly.

"Yeah, because we *are* family, right Mr. Harker? We are. So what has happened to you?"

He looked up at John.

"Your dad." He said faintly.

"What's that, Mr. Harker?"

"Your dad. Still . . . an ass?"

Alba and John laughed, and Mr. Harker managed a smile.

"No, Mr. Harker. He and I are doing much better now," answered John. "Something very special happened recently and, well, it softened the old man's heart and I guess it did mine. He managed an apology and so did I, so it's almost like we are two grown-ups now. You tell him, sweetie."

"What?" he asked. "What are you going to tell me?" He looked at Alba.

She nodded to John, who bent down to pick up the baby.

"We want you to meet our son, Mr. Harker. Born October 12."

He looked at the child and reached out a trembling hand. Alba lifted the baby so that his head would touch Harker's hand. Mr. Harker was silent for a moment and then mumbled with a faint smile, "Poor child."

"Very funny, Mr. Harker. And he has a name. We have been waiting to tell you. My mom and everyone in John's family know him simply as 'dude' until we name him, but you see, we already did, but we wanted you to be the first to know. His name is Zacharias."

"Ah. Poor, *poor* child."

Alba lifted the baby and brought him up close so he could get a good look. He groaned a few times as he stared at the tiny hands and feet. The baby started to squirm, so John stepped in and picked him up and began bouncing on his feet to calm him. He reached for Alba's hand again and squeezed it slightly and closed his eyes. A tear spilled down his cheek. His breathing grew more labored for a moment.

"Mr. Harker. Maybe this embarrasses you, but, and I meant to tell you this under far different circumstances, but you need to know. I, we, love you. We want our son to have your name, you know, because, look, you are our teacher, our friend, and we want our relationship to continue past the book, you know. We were afraid you would have no more need for us once it was done, so now you have no choice. You will have to see this namesake at least from time to time, right?"

"No words. No words," Mr. Harker managed. Alba stroked his hand.

"Can you tell us what is wrong? Why are you here?"

After a moment, he opened his eyes and made a concerted effort to speak clearly and strongly.

"It seems . . . I have melanoma. Skin cancer. And it has stages. Stage IV is not good. On my back. Lungs now. Brain too. Well, hell. Ain't that something? Done in by the sun, it seems. I felt, not so strong. Been feeling tired and sleeping a lot, yeah, and I thought: I'm out of shape . . . or something, catching my breath, too much work on that damn book." He tried a laugh. "No end, really. Listen, I need your help to find Theo. They say he is at some humane society. I want you to take him." He looked at them earnestly.

"I didn't even think to ask about Theo," said John, glancing at Alba. "Of course, we will take care of him." Alba nodded.

"Thank you. He, you know, my only companion, for a long time. Until you two showed up." He attempted a smile. "Lots I want to give you. So, I don't know, I went . . . I don't know. I was hiking on Boulder. That's where they found me. By that lake."

"What lake?"

"Divide. Divide Lake. That's where I met her."

"Met who, Mr. Harker?"

"Marianne. My wife. Saw her there. First time . . . was 1964."

Alba looked at John. They hadn't discussed how much they were going to admit that they knew, but she was tired of the pretenses.

"We know, Mr. Harker. We know that your wife and daughter were killed in a crash on Highway 24 in 1982. We know why you went down there. October 16 was the anniversary. I don't want to wear you out, you need your rest. So I'll spare you having to tell us all about that. I just wanted you to know."

"How? How do you know?"

"You'll have to forgive us, but we went to your house because we hadn't heard from you, and we were worried sick about you. I mean, just imagine, Mr. Harker, how I felt under these circumstances. I am not about to have another father disappear from my life without explanation."

Mr. Harker looked intently at her, unable to speak.

"So we poked around and found some papers, some photos, and things that helped us to piece things together. Forgive me."

Mr. Harker made a weak motion of the cross.

"Absolved." They all smiled.

"Well, we're glad you're not mad," said John. The baby began to fuss a little, so John volunteered to walk him up and down the hallway, leaving Alba alone with Mr. Harker.

"You need to know, Alba. This thing. I waited way too long. It's not good. I was going to call. Sorry. Didn't want to scare you. Didn't want that."

"Okay. It's okay." She began to cry quietly.

"Mr. Harker. I found some letters."

"Letters?"

"Yeah, at your house. A big stack. I only read what was on your table."

"You can read them. Read them all. There's a lot more. I want you to have them, to have it all. It's already done."

"What? I don't know what you mean. What are they, anyway?"

"How should I know? Silly thing, really."

"No, not silly. Not at all. I felt like I was reading the words of a prayer."

"You won't quit, you." He smiled. "Down to the wire. Still want . . . to make me a man of God!"

"I wanted to ask. I read something about your wanting to come quickly to your wife and daughter. That was scary. You weren't wanting to, you know, die, or something, were you? You sounded, I don't know, so different."

"It's okay, Alba. It's all okay now. Don't worry. No, God no. I didn't want to die. I mean, I think I knew, but I just had this crazy idea . . . visit my childhood. And yeah, stop on the highway, you know, where . . . it happened. And then just go to where it all started. I hoped, you know. And I saw her there."

"At Divide Lake?"

"Yeah, Divide Lake. Beautiful spot. Go there. Promise me."

"Of course. 1964. That was a long time ago. How sweet that you remember that first time so clearly."

"I saw her there."

"I know."

"No, I mean I saw her. That day."

"What do you mean? You mean?"

"Hiking. I felt awful, you know. Just weak. But happy, you know? So beautiful. I was crying. . . . Imagine that. Me. And Theo and I get to the lake. I'm staggering, like. Weak. I lean against a tree, right there, you know, where the fire pit had been. . . . And I slide down on my ass and just sit there, looking at the erratics across the water, covered in lichen, you know. Running my hands in the soil. Rich, dark, you know, under the firs. Such peace came to me, there, the water lapping on the shore. And then there she is, leaning against an aspen, radiant, beaming. Like she had been waiting for me. Spoke to me for, I don't know, a few minutes. I didn't open my mouth. Not sure I even breathed or blinked. And I just kept smiling." He paused. "That's where they found me. Surprised I'm still here, to be honest. Thought maybe that was it." He paused. Alba didn't move. "Such beautiful words. Never knew words . . . could be so beautiful."

His speech started to slur, and then he began to be nonsensical. She went to find the nurse to see if he needed something. By the time she came back, he was unresponsive but still breathing. The breathing was raspy and intermittent, and it frightened her. She called for John who came back and put his arm around her as they watched his chest move up and down irregularly. As the nurses attended to him, Alba asked, "Is there someone we can talk to about his condition? About what they're going to do with him?"

"If you are family, there is."

"We are the only family he has."

"Well, then, I will get the doctor."

When the doctor arrived, he asked for clarification of their relation to Mr. Harker.

"He has no family, Doctor. We are his only close contacts. We have no legal proof, but this is our newborn son and he bears his name. Isn't that enough, please?"

"I'm afraid not."

Alba grew desperate. "If I could make him my father, I would. Heaven knows my father . . . look! He did everything he could to deny his biology, you know! Time, history, whatever it was, left me without a father. So I've had to improvise. In the end, what matters is love, not blood, anyway. Why can't anyone see this? Brothers and sisters! Don't you see?" She was angry and the doctor looked more disconcerted and confused. "If he could get away with that, and I could let it go, why shouldn't it count that I choose Mr. Harker for my father? God brought us together. And God brought us here now. I just need to know what's happening!"

"Please, Doctor," John interjected. "We've been through a lot. She has. All we want is some peace. We want to understand what is happening. This is harder on my wife than you might imagine, this not knowing."

The doctor looked at the two of them earnestly. "Look, I can tell you that it is a matter of days. His case is so advanced, there is no chance of recovery. We're just trying to help him be comfortable. And you need to know that because it is in his brain, he is not quite himself. He might hallucinate and see people you don't see or he might come in and out of consciousness. That's perfectly normal, but it can be very disturbing if you aren't expecting it."

"Was there anything that could have been done to prevent this?" Alba asked.

"It's understandable that you would want to know that. It's impossible to say. Certainly had we caught things much earlier, there would have been a chance. But I understand he spent a good part of his life outside. It's hard when a man like this lives alone. It's easy for these things to go unnoticed or for him to ignore the signs. I suspect it was a little of both. Skin cancer is very common here at our elevation, and as he tells it, he never once wore sunblock."

"Or even a hat," said John. "I am not even sure he owns one."

"One thing to keep in mind," the doctor added, "even when he loses consciousness, he can't speak, of course, but he might still be able to hear you. Hearing is the last sense to go, so by all means talk to him even if he can't respond to you."

After the doctor left, Alba turned to John. "Now you need to give him a blessing, John. I want him to stand up and get out of that bed, of course, but more than anything the miracle I want is for Mr. Harker to be enveloped in the love of God and to feel his wife and daughter near him. And I want what I am going to say to him to be heard. That's all. Can you do that for me, for him?" John gave the baby to Alba, reached into his pocket to pull out his anointing oil on his key chain, and entered the room. He took the vial and poured out a drop of olive oil onto his fingers and rubbed it into Mr. Harker's hair, and then he placed his hands on his head and anointed him and gave him a blessing. As always, he had the impression when he closed his eyes that he could see shadows of beings surrounding the top of his own head. It helped him to focus, to forget himself, and to find language to say what he felt God wanted him to say, to speak for another as if he were someone else.

Alba then requested some time alone with Mr. Harker. John paced back and forth in the hallway holding the baby. He could see her leaning in close to his ear, with her right hand on his shoulder, almost as if she were blessing him too. He could hear her soft voice but couldn't make out any words. After a few minutes, she was done and came out of the room with tears in her eyes.

"Give me that beautiful boy, you beautiful man," she said with a smile.

Mr. Harker died three days later. He came to a few times but never again when they visited, but the day of his death, the nurse gave Alba a note he had written for her that morning, during a moment of silent but brief lucidity.

It said, "Alba, his name is John."

* * *

Mr. Harker, I was told you might still be able to hear me. I have faith that you can. John blessed you that you will. John's words are my words, his blessing my blessing. And, we believe, the Lord's blessing. My words too are John's. Maybe too they could be the Lord's. I can't tell anymore when my words are my own or when they are someone else's, especially when I try to speak from the depths of my heart. That's when words start to lose their personal properties to me, like they were never mine to begin with, that they belonged to everyone, to all time, as if I have been speaking them for years. That's when they feel more like music or color. Anyway, that's what I try to paint and what I have wanted to write. I don't know if you hallucinated your wife or if God granted you a vision. I know what I want to believe, but I am not sure it really matters because it's still a tender mercy either way. You had those beautiful words already deep in your own soul and the vision finally allowed you to hear them even if they were also spoken by your angel wife. Isn't that the way it should work? Why would words speak to your soul if they were inconceivable to you? You had to have imagined them, felt after them, longed for them, wanted them to be true, so that when they were spoken, you had the ears to hear and comprehend them. They were spoken a long time before you heard them by that lake, they were the music of your entire life, thrumming from the deep heart's core. You just had to come to the end to finally hear them so you could start over.

If I were to imagine what she said, and I have many times since you left us, I would imagine that she told you that you were a beautiful man with a rare understanding that he lived in a beautiful world, a man who loved so intensely that he never let go of those of his own flesh, that you could only end where your path had begun together. She told you that she loved you in all your earthiness, in all your outrage for the damages we do to ourselves and to the world, that your anger and your arguments with God were a measure of how much more you wanted God to be, more than what our puny imaginations typically comprehend, because you, yes you, understood how often we took his name in vain, how we trampled on all that is holy every day with our shortsighted ambitions, as if you were already living life with the retrospective wisdom of the dead and could see just how much love we squandered because we couldn't see, let alone care for, the great immensity and grandeur of this world. But you, you knew how to live because you already knew how to die, she said, and now that your dying was complete, it came as no shock or surprise but as a gift of breath, an accomplice to life. She told you too that you were a fool. A fool to have failed to let people love you again, that you took the entirety of the weight of your losses on your own proud shoulders, and denied yourself the chance to let human love manifest divine vigilance over your fragile soul. But she told you that you can let that burden down now, that you can finally let angels attend you both here and in the world that awaits you.

These words, Mr. Harker, are yours too because your words are mine now, you see, because you gave them to me. Although gone, you are not lost to us. Once silent, you are speaking, again and always, because I have your words, I treasure them, and write them. As was your wish, we tend the house and care for Theo too. We have his animal joy and every day he reminds us of yours. And I have your photographs. They are in my trees now, you know. That's because you can see now that I have worked to make your story and mine one. These pages here are our meeting place, the confluence, the grafting. Can you hear now how hopeful your words are, Zacharias Harker? Can you hear them weave in and out of my own thoughts and words? Can you hear yourself speak again finally? The book you wanted, the great reconciliation, will have to wait. But it's no matter, you see. Because it's what we can recollect that matters in any case, and this recollection is the best I could do. And that's how your words have become my son's daily bread. I understood your message. I told you we were naming him Zacharias because love matters more than blood. I understand now that you wanted the name to be John to remind me that kinship is a privilege to be honored, but perhaps you understand now that adoption also redeems the weakness of blood. Because our birth is first blood, water, and then spirit. And so it is: John Zacharias Powell.

Poor child. Poor, poor child indeed! Like every single one of us.

Roundfire

FICTION

Put simply, we publish great stories. Whether it's literary or popular, a gentle tale or a pulsating thriller, the connecting theme in all Roundfire fiction titles is that once you pick them up you won't want to put them down.

If you have enjoyed this book, why not tell other readers by posting a review on your preferred book site. Recent bestsellers from Roundfire are:

The Bookseller's Sonnets
Andi Rosenthal
The Bookseller's Sonnets intertwines three love stories with a tale of religious identity and mystery spanning five hundred years and three countries.
Paperback: 978-1-84694-342-3 ebook: 978-184694-626-4

Birds of the Nile
An Egyptian Adventure
N.E. David
Ex-diplomat Michael Blake wanted a quiet birding trip up the Nile – he wasn't expecting a revolution.
Paperback: 978-1-78279-158-4 ebook: 978-1-78279-157-7

Blood Profit$
The Lithium Conspiracy
J. Victor Tomaszek, James N. Patrick, Sr.
The blood of the many for the profits of the few... *Blood Profit$* will take you into the cigar-smoke-filled room where American policy and laws are really made.
Paperback: 978-1-78279-483-7 ebook: 978-1-78279-277-2

The Burden
A Family Saga
N.E. David
Frank will do anything to keep his mother and father apart. But he's carrying baggage – and it might just weigh him down ...
Paperback: 978-1-78279-936-8 ebook: 978-1-78279-937-5

The Cause
Roderick Vincent
The second American Revolution will be a fire lit from an internal spark.
Paperback: 978-1-78279-763-0 ebook: 978-1-78279-762-3

Readers of ebooks can buy or view any of these bestsellers by clicking on the live link in the title. Most titles are published in paperback and as an ebook. Paperbacks are available in traditional bookshops. Both print and ebook formats are available online.

Find more titles and sign up to our readers' newsletter at http://www.johnhuntpublishing.com/fiction

Follow us on Facebook at https://www.facebook.com/JHPfiction and Twitter at https://twitter.com/JHPFiction